新概念英语（新版）自学辅导丛书

新概念英语 2

同步读写练习册

● 易学通英语创作团队 编著

中国水利水电出版社
www.waterpub.com.cn

内 容 提 要

　　英语阅读能力的提高离不开大量的泛读。为帮助《新概念英语2》的学习者进行阅读拓展训练，本书精选了各式文章，内容编排完全与原教材的结构设计同步，每篇文章的最后还给出了难点词汇、习语的解释，同时配有大量的阅读理解练习题以及练习题的答案与解析，用来供学习者检测阅读效果，也可帮助学习者熟悉并适应各种英语试卷的模式。除此之外，书中的部分精美文章还配有美籍专家的配乐朗读录音，学习者可以登录中国水利水电出版社网站 http://www.waterpub.com.cn/softdown/ 免费下载。

图书在版编目（ＣＩＰ）数据

新概念英语（2）同步读写练习册 / 易学通英语创作
团队编著. -- 北京 ： 中国水利水电出版社，2012.2
（新概念英语（新版）自学辅导丛书）
ISBN 978-7-5084-9452-4

Ⅰ．①新… Ⅱ．①易… Ⅲ．①英语－阅读教学－习题
集②英语－写作－习题集 Ⅳ．①H319.6

中国版本图书馆CIP数据核字(2012)第018191号

书　　名	新概念英语（新版）自学辅导丛书 **新概念英语 2 同步读写练习册**
作　　者	易学通英语创作团队　编著
出版发行	中国水利水电出版社 （北京市海淀区玉渊潭南路 1 号 D 座　100038） 网址：www.waterpub.com.cn E-mail：sales@waterpub.com.cn 电话：(010) 68367658（发行部）
经　　售	北京科水图书销售中心（零售） 电话：(010) 88383994、63202643、68545874 全国各地新华书店和相关出版物销售网点
排　　版	中国水利水电出版社微机排版中心
印　　刷	北京嘉恒彩色印刷有限责任公司
规　　格	184mm×260mm　16 开本　18.5 印张　504 千字
版　　次	2012 年 2 月第 1 版　2012 年 2 月第 1 次印刷
印　　数	0001—5000 册
定　　价	**35.00 元**

我们一贯的追求：简单、易学、高效

易学通英语创作团队

编 写 委 员 会

顾　　问：顾玉梅

主　　编：宋德伟

编　　委：刘　静　　靳　萌　　张庆仙　　谢　利

　　　　　高向云　　李可义　　祁　娜　　鲍　倩

　　　　　陈海庆　　陈丽辉　　郭　梅　　韩秀丽

　　　　　李慧祯　　王　娣　　王海涛　　王　悦

　　　　　徐　静　　姚微微　　殷晓芳　　詹莉芳

　　　　　张艳敏　　张治中　　张　静　　胡秀梅

致 学 习 者

英语阅读能力训练向来是中国学生学习的重点，同时也是各种英语考试的测试重点，分数比重最高达45％。学习《新概念英语》的读者一方面为教材中短小精悍、丰富幽默的短文赞叹不已，另一方面也感觉到靠有限的几篇课文是无法满足广泛的阅读需求的。教材中的各种文章结构比较严谨，语法点丰富，非常适合学生做精读训练，掌握各种句法结构。英语阅读能力的提高离不开大量的泛读。适量和适度的泛读不但可以帮助学习者巩固精读过程中学习到的各种知识点，同时还可以拓展学习者的知识和视野，提高英语语感，为提高英语考试成绩奠定良好的基础。

本书的编写正是基于以上思路完成的。编者在从事《新概念英语》的教学过程中，除了指导学生进行正常的课文学习外，还给学生提供了大量课外阅读的素材，收到了非常好的教学效果。书中大部分文章是编者在执教过程中不断收集和整理的。本书的具体特点如下：

一、英语阅读、翻译和写作同属英语书面语言的学习与运用范畴，读、写、译能力又同属文字思维能力，三者之间是既相对独立而又相互依赖、相互作用的关系，能够互相促进、共同提高。本书编者充分考虑了这三项语言技能的兼顾训练，对提升学习者的书面语言运用能力作用很大。

二、本书与《新概念英语2》教材同步编写，学习者可以根据教材的学习进度灵活安排读写练习，一课一练。

三、书中的阅读练习既考虑到了学习者的适应能力（难度水平），又兼顾到了练习形式的多样化（与各种英语考试接轨）——问答题、改错题、判断题和选择题都有。

四、书中的翻译练习以巩固课文句型和知识点为主，能帮助学习者更好地吸收教材课文中的语言精华。

五、好句好段环节从部分英文名著当中精选了个别段落，这些段落用词简洁，句型简单，但表达的意境却非常丰富。通过模仿和背诵这些好句好段，对学习者积累词汇句型、提高写作能力，大有裨益。

六、书中部分精美阅读篇章还配有美国专家的朗读录音，录音加入了罗扎诺夫推荐的有助于记忆的古典音乐。这种把音乐与学习有机结合的音乐暗示法，是当今世界影响最大的学习方法之一。在淡淡的记忆音乐背景中，欣赏精美的英文录音，对于英语学习者来说，一定是一件非常快乐的事情。

七、本书所有练习题均配有参考答案（含阅读理解练习题解析及译文），请登录中国水利水电出版社网站 http://www.waterpub.com.cn/softdown/（下载中心）免费下载。各类培训机构（学校）可以在课堂上或课后组织学员集中使用本练习册，这样可以有效避免部分学员边做练习边看答案的不良学习习惯。

▶ 学习英语为什么要选择《新概念英语》

英国著名英语教育专家路易·乔治·亚历山大（L. G. Alexander）先生与北京外国语大学何其莘教授联合编写的《新概念英语》是完全针对中国学生英语学习特点而编写的一套英语教材，侧重于听、说、读、写四种语言技能的综合训练，注重实际运用能力；语言活泼，趣味性强。自出版以来，《新概念英语》以其严密的体系性、严谨的科学性、精湛的实用性、浓郁的趣味性深受广大英语学习者的青睐。

这套教材语言最大的特点就是往往看似平淡无奇的常用词准确而传神地表达了丰富的意象。亚历山大先生在课文的甄选和编排上表现出了深湛的功力和慧眼卓识。这些课文文思兼优、雅俗共赏，难度由浅入深，篇幅由短到长，层层递进，有条不紊。

教材中所选文章一般以幽默故事为主，适应了不同专业、爱好的学习者的阅读口味。这些课文的题材是相当广泛的，涉及社会、政治、人物、艺术、考古、科技和自然等方方面面。各篇课文的语言风格大体一致，即便是科技类文章行文也是活泼生动的，没有多少刻板的学究气。课文不仅适宜阅读，而且还可以作为学习写作的良好范本。

▶ 《新概念英语 2》的学习重点

第二册是过渡，同时也是转变。它使学习者从一个会说日常英语的人，提高成为一个敢动笔进行基本写作的人。第二册以 96 篇小故事为素材，培养学生听、说、读、写的基本能力，其优势在于扩充词汇、统揽语法、结合实践、听说兼修。在掌握第一册基本语法的基础上，由浅入深逐步讲解语法要点，使学习者轻松掌握枯燥的语法。通过对句型结构的分析及对短语基本用法的讲解，使学习者能真正在听说读写中运用地道的句型，从而系统地掌握从词汇、时态开始的语法知识和各种句型，同时加强了写作能力。

▶ 《新概念英语 2》的读者对象

初中级英语学习者——
- ⇨ 已经学完了《新概念英语》第一册或任何一种初级英语教程的英语学习者
- ⇨ 学习英语不久，已经具备了基本词汇量（1000 词）的学习者
- ⇨ 语法基础薄弱者
- ⇨ 已经放下英语多年，但有一定基础，希望重拾英语的学习者
- ⇨ 欲在高考英语中取得高分的学生
- ⇨ 想为自己的英语打牢根基，学习正统英文的学习者
- ⇨ 对大学英语学习感到吃力者
- ⇨ 具有一定英语基础的成人英语自学者
- ⇨ 对必须面临的英语考试（四级、六级考试、职称考试和专升本考试等）一筹莫展

的考生

➪ 参加 PETS 二级和三级考试的考生

➪ 想通过英语学习改变在工作单位的处境，使自己更具有市场价值者

▶《新概念英语2》的学习目标

学完第二册后能够达到的水平——

➪ 能用英语毫无障碍地与人进行普通的交流

➪ 能用英语写出流畅的、时而还闪着幽默的记叙文

➪ 可以达到每分钟 50 个英语单词的阅读速度，能阅读中等难度的英语文章

➪ 可以掌握英语中常用的前缀、后缀及词根，为继续扩充词汇量铺平道路

➪ 练就浑厚的内力，轻松准备各种英语考试

➪ 具备一定的英语自学能力，知道如何去解决学习中的难题

➪ 掌握高频词汇 1500～4000 个

编者

2011 年 11 月

目　　录

Lesson 1

语言基本功
阅读理解◈ | **Reading Comprehension**

✦✦ （1） ✦✦

We Are Going to Iceland

Ann's father, Mr. Black, works in a hospital. He's friendly to the patients and so he's busy all the time. The girl is seven and begins to be at school. She often watches TV at home. Some of her friends often go traveling abroad, but her father doesn't have time. He and his wife can only take their daughter to some cities in England.

This summer Mr. Black has some time. He's going to take his family to Iceland. Ann is very happy and tells her friends about it.

"Why are you going to travel in Iceland, Ann?" asks a girl.

The little girl does not know what to answer. She thinks for a few minutes and says, "We're going to see it before it melts."

---

1. Iceland   *n.* 冰岛
2. patient   *n.* 患者
3. abroad   *adv.* 国外
4. melt   *v.* 融化

▶阅读上面的短文，从每题所给的四个选项中，选出一个最佳答案。

1. Mr. Black is a _____.

   A. worker
   B. teacher
   C. doctor
   D. policeman

2. Mr. Black cannot take his family to travel abroad because _____.

   A. he has no time
   B. he doesn't like them
   C. he has not any money
   D. he forgets it

3. _____, so they can only travel in some cities in England.

   A. Mr. Black loves his country
   B. Mr. Black doesn't have much time
   C. Ann is often at school
   D. Ann is too young

4. The opposite word of "happy" is _____.

   A. glad
   B. smile
   C. unhappy
   D. like

1

5. Ann thinks _____.

    A. Iceland is an English city   B. Iceland can soon melt

    C. they are going to see a building   D. they're going to live there

✦✦ （2）✦✦

Ghost

I went on a camping trip in the mountains with my classmates. After hiking all day, we found a place to camp for the night. We made a campfire so that we could cook our dinner. We roasted some hot dogs and potatoes and drank lemonade. Then, when it got dark, we told ghost stories around the campfire.

Later when we lied down to go to sleep, we listened to the sounds of crickets and small animals moving around in the grass. We thought there were some ghosts nearby. "What's that?" my friend Kathy asked. "What?" we asked. "I think I hear someone walking in the woods." Kathy said. Soon we all heard footsteps and we were all so scared that we could't get to sleep.

Of course, there was no one there, but we had very active imagination.

---

1. ghost   *n.* 鬼

2. camping   *n.* 营地

3. roast   *v.* 烤

4. lemonade   *n.* 柠檬汽水

5. cricket   *n.* 蟋蟀

▶ 阅读上面的短文，根据其内容，回答所提的问题。

1. What does "scared" mean in Chinese?

2. Which word in the passage means "sound of some one walking"?

3. What do the students in the story do on their camping trip?

4. Why do they make a campfire?

5. Why are they scared?

语言基本功
英汉翻译◈ | Translation Exercises

▶ 翻译下列句子

1. 你的英文越来越好了。

    _____

2. 半个小时后，校长会来检查我们的学习。

    _____

3. 她总是乐于助人。

    _____

4. 他们没告诉我她是否已经走了。

5. 海南岛是中国的第二大岛。

_____

6. 我想预订一些歌剧的座位。

_____

7. 比赛是在三点钟结束。

_____

8. 你是如何打开门的？

_____

语言基本功
好句好段◈ | **Writing Samples**

✔ Conradin's parents were dead and he lived with his aunt. The aunt did not like Conradin and was often unkind to him. Conradin hated her with all his heart, but he obeyed her quietly and took his medicine without arguing. Mostly he kept out of her way. She had no place in his world. His real, everyday life in his aunt's colourless, comfortless house was narrow and uninteresting. But inside his small, dark head exciting and violent thoughts ran wild. In the bright world of his imagination Conradin was strong and brave. It was a wonderful world, and the aunt was locked out of it.

　　康拉丁的父母已亡故，他和姑妈住在一起。姑妈不喜欢康拉丁，经常对他不好。康拉丁从心底里恨她，但是平静地服从她，而且毫无怨言地服药。多数时间他远离她。她在他的世界里没有一席之地。在姑妈单调、不舒服的家里，他真正的日常生活狭窄无趣。但是在他又小又黑的脑袋里，活跃的思想在狂奔。在想象中的明快世界里，康拉丁健壮而勇敢。这是一个美好的世界，姑妈被锁在了这个世界之外。

Lesson 2

阅读理解◇ Reading Comprehension

✦✦ （1）✦✦

Our classroom faces our school garden. After class we like to look out of the windows to enjoy the lovely view. Our school garden is the most beautiful place in the school. There is a small pool in the middle. Some goldfish are swimming in it. Around the pool there are all kinds of flowers. We can always see flowers, even in winter. Between the school building and the flower-beds there is a lovely lawn. Boys and girls like to take a walk in the garden after school.

But some years ago, there was nothing here but broken bricks, and wild weeds. We, teachers and students, built the garden with our hands. Since then, we have planted trees and flowers every year. Everyone of us wants to do his best to make our school more and more beautiful.

1. face   *v.* 面对
2. lovely   *adj.* 秀丽的；好看的
3. view   *n.* 景致；景色
4. pool   *n.* 池塘；水塘
5. goldfish   *n.* 金鱼
6. lawn   *n.* 草坪
7. brick   *n.* 砖
8. wild   *adj.* 野生的
9. weed   *n.* 野草

▶阅读上面的短文，从每题所给的四个选项中，选出一个最佳答案。

1. Where is the school garden?

   A. It faces the pool.

   B. It faces the writer's classroom.

   C. It is beside the pool.

   D. It is beside the writer's classroom.

2. Which of the following is not right?

   A. There are all kinds of flowers around the pool.

   B. There are goldfish in the pool.

   C. There is a small pool in the middle of the garden.

   D. The students can't see flowers in winter.

3. Between the school building and the flower-beds there is _____.

    A. a garden   B. an office building

    C. a lawn   D. nothing

4. Who built the school garden?

    A. Students.   B. Teachers.

    C. Teachers and students.   D. Workers.

5. Which of the following is not right?

    A. Everyone likes the school very much.

    B. Every student wants to make the school more and more beautiful.

    C. The school garden was built fifty years ago.

    D. The students plant trees in the school every year.

✦✦ （2）✦✦

Who Are They?

It had been snowing very hard for days. Jigs and Reads had nothing to eat for a day. They know that things weren't right at home. So yesterday morning they wanted to go out. Bob helped them get out through a window, because the snow was so deep outside that he couldn't open the door. Last night, they didn't come back. Bob said to himself, "They are only five months old. This weather will kill them." But just then Bob heard them calling him. He looked out and could not believe — they were drawing a big hare through the snow. They dropped it through the window into Bob's hands. A hare for dinner!

▶ 阅读上面的短文，从每题所给的四个选项中，选出一个最佳答案。

1. Jigs and Reads in the story were _____.

    A. Bob's children   B. dogs

    C. hares   D. neighbours

2. "They knew that things weren't right at home." It means that "they knew _____."

    A. Bob had no food to give them   B. Bob could open the door

    C. it wasn't very cold outside   D. they were too young to eat anything

3. Finally Jigs and Reads returned with a big _____.

    A. fox   B. dog

    C. hare   D. pig

4. The story says that Jigs and Reads _____.

    A. wanted to go out to play with rain   B. asked to look for money outside

    C. ate much more than Bob did   D. were a great help to Bob

5. Choose the right order according to the story.

    1）They caught a hare in the snow.

    2）They went out and stayed outside for the night.

    3）They brought the hare home.

4）They felt hungry and wanted to find food.

A. 1） 2） 3） 4）　　　　　　B. 1） 4） 3） 2）

C. 4） 2） 1） 3）　　　　　　D. 4） 3） 2） 1）

语言基本功
英汉翻译◇ | Translation Exercises

▶翻译下列句子

1. 她长着一双黑黑的漂亮的大眼睛。

_____

2. 冬天黑得很早。

_____

3. 他们把计划隐藏起来秘而不宣。

_____

4. 他们将乘车来，镇上的大部分青年人将到车站迎接他们。

_____

5. 他一上车，我就用法语向他问早上好，他也同样用法语回答我。

_____

6. 秘书告诉我说哈姆斯先生要见我。

_____

7. 今年新学生将增加一倍多。

_____

8. 蔬菜价格上涨了百分之三十。

_____

语言基本功
好句好段◇ | Writing Samples

☑ That happened in my fourth year on the island. In my sixth year I did make myself a smaller canoe, but I did not try to escape in it. The boat was too small for a long journey, and I did not want to die at sea. The island was my home now, not my prison, and I was just happy to be alive. A year or two later, I made myself a second canoe on the other side of the island. I also built myself a second house there, and so I had two homes.

造船发生在我到岛上之后的第四个年头。在第六年里我又造了一只更小的船，但我没有试图用它来逃跑。要想长途航行，这船太小了。我可不想死在海上。现在这岛便是我的家而非我的监狱，我相当快乐地生活着。一两年后，我在岛的另一侧又造了一只独木舟。我还在那儿建了第二座房子，于是我有了两个家。

本书所有练习题的参考答案（含阅读理解练习题解析及译文），请登录中国水利水电出版社网站 http://www.waterpub.com.cn/softdown/（下载中心）免费下载。

Lesson 3

Reading Comprehension

✦✦ （1）✦✦

There is a story about an English sailor who went to countries in the east, the west and the south. He had been to India and China. One day he came home and brought some tea as a present for his mother. She told her friends about the present and asked them to a "tea party". When her friends came to the "tea party", the old woman offered them brown tea leaves. The old woman's friends began to eat them. Of course, nobody liked the tea leaves.

At that time sailor came in. He looked at the table and said, "Mother, what have you done with the tea?" "I boiled it, as you said."

"And what did you do with the water?"

"I threw it away, of course," answered the old woman.

"Now you may throw the leaves, too," said her son.

▶ 阅读上面的短文，从每题所给的四个选项中，选出一个最佳答案。

1. The sailor was _____.
   A. a Chinese   B. a Japanese
   C. an Englishman   D. an Indian

2. The sailor brought _____.
   A. some delicious food for his friends
   B. some delicious food for his mother
   C. some tea for his friends
   D. some tea for his mother

3. Which of the following is right?
   A. All of the old woman's friends didn't like tea.
   B. All of the old woman's friends liked tea very much.
   C. Only a few for the old woman's friends didn't like tea.
   D. Only a few of the old woman's friends liked tea.

4. How did the old woman and her friends have tea?
   A. They had tea leaves.
   B. They had water.
   C. They had water and tea leaves.
   D. They neither had water nor had tea leaves.

5. The sailor _____.

    A. didn't tell his mother how to have tea

    B. told his mother how to have tea, but he didn't say clearly

    C. told his mother to have tea leaves, but not to have water

    D. told his mother to have water, but not to have tea leaves

✦✦ （2） ✦✦

Mr. Black liked to read a lot and could answer all the questions his students asked. One Sunday morning he was dressing his little son, Jimmy, when suddenly the boy said, "May I ask you a question, Dad?"

"Of course, you may," answered Mr. Black.

"Are you sure you answer it?"

"Don't you believe me? I'm sure that I can."

"Well," said Jimmy. "Are there any holes in your socks?"

"Holes?" Mr. Black said in surprise. "It is impossible."

"Look at them carefully. Or you'll be wrong."

It made Mr. Black pay attention to Jimmy's question. He took off his socks and looked at them carefully. Then he said, "No, there is no hole in them."

"How can you put your feet into them, then?" little Jimmy said with a smile.

For a moment Mr. Black did not know how to answer. Then he began to laugh. He understood that his son had played a joke on him.

▶阅读上面的短文，从每题所给的四个选项中，选出一个最佳答案。

1. Mr. Black was _____.

    A. a worker   B. a driver

    C. a teacher   D. a doctor

2. Mr. Black dressed Jimmy because _____.

    A. he wanted to answer the boy's question

    B. the boy was too young to do it

    C. the boy wanted to go to school at once

    D. Mrs. Black wasn't at home

3. Jimmy asked his father to look at his socks carefully because _____.

    A. he wanted to play a joke on him

    B. there were really some holes in them

    C. he didn't think his father was careful enough

    D. there was something wrong with his socks

4. Mr. Black took off his socks because _____.

    A. they were not new

    B. there were some holes in them

C. he hadn't worn them for a long time

D. he wanted to find his answer

语言基本功
英汉翻译◇ | Translation Exercises

▶ 翻译下列句子

1. "我还是买下的好"，我垂头丧气地说。

2. 据说他已经结婚了。

3. 把你的想法用文字清楚地表达出来。

4. 话比剑更伤人。

5. 希望你平安归来。

6. 自然界是一个统一的整体。

7. 整个星期都是在海边度过。

8. 新的大礼堂能容纳 4,000 人。

语言基本功
好句好段◇ | Writing Samples

☑ The Red Death had been in the country for many, many years. No disease had ever been so deadly. People called it the Red Death because it left blood, red horrible blood, on the body and face of each person it visited. And no one, if visited, was ever left alive. Once a person was touched by the Red Death, he immediately felt pains, and soon afterwards started to bleed from every part of his body. In thirty minutes he was dead. After that no one, not even his family, went near the blood-covered body.

红死魔已经在国内肆虐很多年了，还不曾有过哪种疾病是如此致命的。人们称之为红死魔，是因为它每降临到一个人头上，那人的面部和身体就会出血，就会流出恐怖的、殷红的鲜血；还有，罹病之人无一得以幸存人世。一旦某个人遭到了红死魔的触摸，他就会立即感到疼痛，此后不久身体各处开始出血，三十分钟之内准会丧命。然后，所有人，哪怕是他的家人，都不敢靠近那鲜血淋漓的尸体。

本书所有练习题的参考答案（含阅读理解练习题解析及译文），请登录中国水利水电出版社网站 http://www.waterpub.com.cn/softdown/（下载中心）免费下载。

Lesson 4

阅读理解◇ | Reading Comprehension

✦✦ （1）✦✦

Mother's Day is a holiday for mothers. And on this day, mothers don't work. It is on the second Sunday in May. It is celebrated in the United States, England, Sweden, India, Mexico and some other countries. Little by little, it becomes widely celebrated. On that day, many people send presents of love to their mothers. Those whose mothers are still living often wear a pink or red rose or carnation, while those whose mothers are dead wear a white one.

The idea of a day for mothers was first given by Miss Anna Jarvis of Philadelphia. The celebration of the first American Mother's Day was held in Philadelphia on May 10, 1908. Soon the holiday became popular around the country and the world.

---

1. Sweden   *n.* 瑞典
2. Mexico   *n.* 墨西哥
3. widely   *adv.* 广泛地
4. carnation   *n.* 康乃馨

▶阅读上面的短文，从每题所给的四个选项中，选出一个最佳答案。

1. Mother's Day is on _____.
    A. the second Saturday in May   B. the second Sunday in May
    C. May 2   D. May 12
2. When one's mother is still living, she often wears a _____ rose or carnation.
    A. white   B. pink
    C. yellow   D. blue
3. The idea of _____ for mothers was first given by Miss Anna.
    A. a present   B. a week
    C. a day   D. a flower
4. The first American Mother's Day was _____.
    A. on May 10, 1908   B. on May 2, 1908
    C. on May 10, 1809   D. on May 2, 1980
5. The celebration of the first Mother's Day was held _____.
    A. in New York   B. in Philadelphia
    C. in Washington, D.C.   D. in Australia

✦✦ （2）✦✦
Meals in a Hurry in America

Americans eat breakfast and lunch quickly unless it is a social, business or family occasion. The evening meal is usually longer and a time for families to get together. Rushing through daytime meals is part of the fast pace in America. Another reason for rushing through daytime is that many people eat in restaurants that are usually crowded with people waiting for a place so that they can be served and return to work at the proper time. So each one hurries to make room for the next person. As with busy people everywhere there is real difference between meals that are eaten in a hurry and those that can be enjoyed slowly with friends.

---

1. occasion　*n.* 场合，机会
2. pace　*n.* 节奏

▶阅读上面的短文，从每题所给的四个选项中，选出一个最佳答案。

1. What is not mentioned in the passage?

   A. What time Americans eat dinner.

   B. Where Americans eat.

   C. Why Americans eat in a hurry.

   D. Which meal Americans eat more slowly.

2. Which of the following is true?

   A. Americans hurry at meals because they want to eat dinner slowly.

   B. Americans hurry at meals because they don't like eating in restaurants.

   C. Americans hurry at meals because they are very busy.

   D. Americans hurry at meals because they don't like to eat.

3. According to the passage the least busy time in a restaurant would probably be _____.

   A. during busy time

   B. at lunch

   C. at dinner

   D. at either breakfast or lunch

4. The passage suggests that Americans _____.

   A. like eating with friends

   B. do not nap in the afternoon

   C. don't eat much on weekends

   D. eat dinner more slowly than lunch

5. According to the passage Americans _____.

   A. often hurry in the evening

   B. are always late returning to work

   C. eat slower for social and business reasons

D. never eat in restaurants in the evening

英汉翻译 ◈ | Translation Exercises

▶ 翻译下列句子

1. 恶劣气候使小麦减产了两成。

2. 一些计算机的工作速度比人快五十万倍。

3. 在南极站，有一晚上温度下降了三分之二，从零下十二摄氏度降至零下二十摄氏度。

4. 春天快到了，所以服装市场上的冬衣价格下降至少百分之三十五。

5. 我总是在河上呆上整整一上午，然后空着袋子回家。

6. 他们曾向我提供一大笔钱让我走，但我决定留在这儿。

7. 去年，当我们横渡英吉利海峡时，简把写有她姓名和住址的一张纸条装进一只瓶子。

8. 经理开始抱怨起这个邪恶的世道来，却被一阵敲门声打断了。

好句好段 ◈ | Writing Samples

☑ Basil turned away. After a while he said slowly, 'I see that you too have noticed something strange about the picture. Dorian, you changed my life as an artist from the moment when I met you. You became very important to me－I could not stop thinking about you. And when I painted this portrait, I felt that I'd put too much of myself into it. I could not let other people see it.' He was silent for a moment, then turned back to Dorian. 'Perhaps you're right. I cannot exhibit this picture. But will you let me look at it again? '

巴兹尔转身走开。过了一会儿他缓慢地说："我看得出你也注意到了画像有点奇怪。多里安，从我见到你开始，你改变了我作为画家的生活。你变得对我很重要——我无法不想着你。画这幅画像时，我感觉我画进了我自己太多的东西，我不能让其他人看它。"他沉默片刻，然后转向多里安："可能你是对的，我不能展出这幅画。但你能让我再看一眼吗？"

本书所有练习题的参考答案（含阅读理解练习题解析及译文），请登录中国水利水电出版社网站 http://www.waterpub.com.cn/softdown/（下载中心）免费下载。

Lesson 5

阅读理解◇ | Reading Comprehension

✦✦ (1) ✦✦

Absalom's Hair

Absalom was the son of King Dave. He was very handsome. He was tall and strong, his hair was most beautiful of all. It was yellow and long, its length touched the ground. Everybody talked about his hair. Absalom liked it very much.

One day, Absalom fought with his enemies. He ran before the enemies. Absalom ran fast, the enemies couldn't catch him. But when Absalom ran by a tree, his hair was caught by it, and he fell down. He tried to get his hair off the tree. He tried again and again to stand up but failed. At this time, the enemies came up and killed him.

People said Absalom's hair was beautiful, but he was killed by his beautiful hair.

1. handsome   *adj.* 英俊的
2. length   *n.* 长度
3. fought （fight 的过去式）*v.* 打仗
4. enemy   *n.* 敌人

▶阅读上面的短文，根据其内容，回答所提的问题。

1. Who was Absalom?
2. How about his hair?
3. What did people say about his hair?
4. Why could the enemies kill Absalom?
5. What did people think of his hair at last?

✦✦ (2) ✦✦

You can see them in every airport in the world: businessmen and businesswomen. They have to travel for their work. Maybe when they first applied for the jobs, they thought of good food, modern hotels and beautiful cities, and a lot of money. Now they have to sit in the waiting room, tired and uncomfortable in their nice clothes, listening to the loudspeaker announcing: "The flight to Tokyo, or Berlin, or New York is delayed for another two hours." People often say to me, "How lucky you are to be able to travel abroad in your work." They think that my job is like a continuous holiday. But when I get back on the plane, I'm very tired.

There are advantages, of course, and I do think I am lucky. I can go to different places.

1. modern hotel 现代化旅馆
2. waiting room 候车/机室
3. be delayed for 被推迟
4. How lucky you are! 你多么幸运呀！

▶ 阅读上面的短文，从每题所给的四个选项中，选出一个最佳答案。

1. We can see from the passage that the writer may _____.
   A. be a traveler   B. be a driver
   C. work in an airport   D. be a businessman/businesswoman
2. The writer quoted the announcement over the airport loudspeaker to tell us that _____.
   A. flight to Tokyo, or Berlin, or New York is often early
   B. travelers to big cities often have to wait at the airport
   C. travel by air is interesting
   D. flight to those cities is often delayed for two hours
3. From the passage we can know the word "advantage" maybe mean something _____.
   A. useful and helpful   B. trouble
   C. bad   D. tiresome
4. The writer wrote the passage mainly to _____.
   A. tell that he / she made a good choice of the job
   B. tell us both the good side and the bad side of his / her job
   C. tell us he / she was very happy about the job
   D. tell us he / she doesn't like this job
5. What seems to attract the writer to the job?
   A. He / She can go anywhere.
   B. He / She can be free to travel abroad.
   C. He / She can travel to many places like a traveler.
   D. He / She is interested in traveling.

语言基本功
英汉翻译 ◈ | Translation Exercises

▶ 翻译下列句子

1. 手扶拖拉机非常被需要。

_____

2. 我们应你的请求而来。

_____

3. 你会得到你所需要的东西。

_____

4. 去年出口增加了两倍半。

_____

5. 这间起居室比卧室大一倍。

_____

6. 我们班打算下周末去看足球赛，你和我们一起去吗？

_____

7. 当然，买到票了吗？

_____

8. 还没有，因为不知道多少人要去。

_____

语言基本功
好句好段 ◈ | Writing Samples

☑ I do not want to remember the time that I spent on Earraid. I had nothing with me except my uncle's gold and Alan's silver button, and as I had never lived near the sea, I did not know what to eat or how to fish. In fact, I found some shellfish among the rocks on the coast, and ate them, but I was very sick afterwards. That was the only food that I could find, so I was always hungry on Earraid. All day and all night it rained heavily, but there was no roof or tree on the island, and my clothes were cold and wet on my body.

我不想再记起我在伊锐德岛的日子。除了我叔叔的金子和艾伦的银扣子，我一无所有；而且因为以前我从来没有在海边生活过，我不知道该吃什么或怎样捕鱼。事实上，在海岸的礁石中间我找到一些贝来吃，但过后我感到非常恶心。那是我所能找到的唯一食品，因此在伊锐德岛我总是处于饥饿状态。整天整夜雨都下得很大，但岛上没有树，也没有屋檐，我的衣服裹着身体，又冷又潮。

Lesson 6

阅读理解◇ | Reading Comprehension

✦✦（1）✦✦

Peter has been worried all the week. He heard from the police station four days ago. The policemen told him to go to the police station as soon as he got the letter. Peter wondered why the police wanted him to go. He went to the police station yesterday, and now he is not worried any more. At the station a policeman smiled at him and told him that they had found his bike. The policeman said. "We found your bike in a small village five hundred miles away five days ago. Now we are sending it to your home by train."

Peter was very surprised when he heard the news. He never expected he should find the stolen bike. He lost it twenty years ago when he was a boy of sixteen.

---

1. ago 为一般过去时的标志词。
2. as soon as 一……就
3. smile at sb. 对某人笑

▶ 阅读上面的短文，从每题所给的四个选项中，选出一个最佳答案。

1. What has been worrying Peter?
    A. His lost bike.   B. His old mother.
    C. Nothing.   D. The policemen's letter.
2. How did the policemen tell Peter to go to the police station?
    A. They asked somebody to take a message to him.
    B. They phoned him again and again.
    C. They sent him a letter.
    D. They sent him a telegram.
3. At the station a policeman _____.
    A. asked him where he had lost his bike
    B. asked him why he stole bikes
    C. told him his bike had been found
    D. told him one of his friends wanted to borrow his bike
4. The policemen found Peter's bike _____.
    A. at the station   B. in a city
    C. in a town   D. in a village

5. Which of the following is not right?

   A. Peter didn't expect he would find his bike again.

   B. Peter lost his bike twenty years ago.

   C. Peter lost his bike when he was sixteen years old.

   D. Peter had been an old man when he got his bike back.

✦✦ (2) ✦✦

We call the Chinese New Year the Spring Festival. There is a name for each Chinese year. We may call it the year of the sheep, the year of the monkey or the year of the pig. And this year is the year of the dog.

Before New Year's Day, people are busy shopping and cleaning their houses. On New Year's Eve, there is a big family dinner. After dinner, all the families stay up late to welcome the New Year. On the first day of the New Year, people put on their new clothes and go to visit their friends. They say "Good luck" and some other greetings to each other. People usually have a very good time during the Festival.

---

1. the Spring Festival 春节
2. the year of the sheep 羊年
3. be busy doing 忙于某事
4. a big family dinner 团圆饭

▶ 阅读上面的短文，从每题所给的四个选项中，选出一个最佳答案。

1. How many Chinese festivals are talked about in this passage?

   A. One.   B. Two.

   C. Three.   D. Four.

2. We can find every Chinese year is given _____ name.

   A. an animal   B. a plant

   C. a family   D. a full

3. How do Chinese people usually spend New Year's Eve?

   A. They put on new clothes and go to the park.

   B. They visit their friends and talk about the New Year.

   C. They are busy shopping and cleaning their houses.

   D. They have a big dinner and stay up late to welcome the New Year.

4. On New Year's Day, people say "_____" to each other when they meet.

   A. Merry Christmas   B. Good luck

   C. Happy New Year   D. Both B and C

5. The best title for this passage is _____.

   A. Good Time   B. The Spring Festival

   C. Big Dinner   D. The Year of the Dog

17

英汉翻译◈ | Translation Exercises

▶ 翻译下列句子

1. 我突然听到有人喊救命。

_____

2. 请给我叫辆出租车。

_____

3. 这列火车每站都停靠。

_____

4. 球重重地打在他身上，使他差点儿落入水中。

_____

5. 几年之后，小铺子已经发展成了一家雇有 728 人的大工厂。

_____

6. 丹听到这个消息后惊奇万分。

_____

7. 当他正开车在凯特福德街上行驶时，看到一个提着一只装满钞票提包的贼。

_____

8. 上午我买了一本书。书不是很贵。

_____

好句好段◈ | Writing Samples

☑ With his one candle he went slowly up the stairs. It was impossible to see into all the dark corners. Darkness was cheap, and Scrooge liked it. But he remembered the face, so he walked through all his rooms, checking that everything was all right. Nobody under the table or the bed, nobody behind the door! On the small fire in the bedroom there was a pot of soup, and Scrooge's bowl was ready on the table. Nobody in any of the rooms! Sure that he was safe now, Scrooge shut and locked his bedroom door behind him. He sat down by the fire to eat his soup.

他手举起唯一的一根蜡烛慢慢地上了楼，他无法看见所有黑暗的角落。黑暗便宜得很，所以斯克罗吉喜欢它。但他记起了那张脸，所以他到所有的房间都走了一遍，看看是否一切都安然无恙。桌子底下和床底下都没人，门后也没人！卧室微弱的炉火上炖着一锅汤，斯克罗吉的碗已经摆在了桌子上。所有房间里都没有人！确信此刻安全无误之后，斯克罗吉随手关上并锁上了卧室的门。他坐在火旁开始喝汤。

本书所有练习题的参考答案（含阅读理解练习题解析及译文），请登录中国水利水电出版社网站 http://www.waterpub.com.cn/softdown/（下载中心）免费下载。

Lesson 7

Reading Comprehension

✦✦（1）✦✦

I will tell you the story of the ant and the grasshopper. It is a cold winter's day and an ant is bringing out some grains of corn. He gathered them in the summer. He wants to dry them. The grasshopper is very hungry. He sees the ant and says, "Give me a few grains of corn. I am dying of hunger."

"But," says the ant, "What did you do in the summer? Didn't you store up some corn?"

"No," says the grasshopper, "I was too busy."

"What did you do?" asks the ant.

"I sang all day," answers the grasshopper.

"If you sang all summer," says the ant, "you can dance all winter."

---

1. a cold winter's day 冬天寒冷的一天
2. gather sth. 收集某物
3. want to dry 想晒干

▶ 阅读上面的短文，从每题所给的四个选项中，选出一个最佳答案。

1. The ant dries the grains of corn _____.
   A. in the summer
   C. on weekdays
   B. in the winter
   D. when he is hungry

2. The grasshopper is very hungry because he only _____ in the summer.
   A. danced
   C. stored up corn
   B. dried the grains
   D. sang

3. The ant gave the grasshopper _____.
   A. nothing
   B. some grains of corn
   C. some rice
   D. something to eat

4. The title of the story may be _____.
   A. The Ant and the Grasshopper
   B. The Ant Sings and Dances
   C. The Busy Ant and the Happy Grasshopper

D. Store up Some Corn or you'll Be Hungry

5. From the story we can know _____.

A. the ant is our good friend

B. we must think before we do anything

C. people must help others

D. we must work hard for a good life

✦✦ （2） ✦✦

Geoffrey Chaucer was an English poet in the 14th century. He was the greatest poet of his age. In his early years, he wrote in Latin and French like all the other important writers of that age. But later on, Chaucer became one of the first poets to write in English. The language was quite different from the English we know today. Chaucer's most popular and important work was the *Canterbury Tales*. In the *Tales*, he wrote all kinds of people and also gave a picture of the society of his time. Today, the importance of his poetry still makes him popular with his readers and he stands second only to Shakespeare.

1. in…century 在……世纪
2. the greatest poet 最伟大的诗人
3. in his early years 在他的早年
4. later on 后来
5. quite different from 相当不同
6. stand second 排名第二

▶阅读上面的短文，从每题所给的四个选项中，选出一个最佳答案。

1. Geoffrey Chaucer was from _____.

   A. Italy   B. France

   C. England   D. the United States

2. Geoffrey Chaucer lived _____.

   A. in the 15th century   B. in the 4th century

   C. in the 14th century   D. in the 15th century

3. How was the English language at Geoffrey Chaucer's time?

   A. It was different from today's.   B. It was easy.

   C. I don't know.   D. It was difficult.

4. "Gave a picture" here means _____.

   A. 照相   B. 绘画

   C. 描绘   D. 给照相

5. Today, the _____ of Chaucer's poetry still makes his readers like him.

   A. importance   B. language

   C. story   D. characters

20

英汉翻译◈ | Translation Exercises

▶翻译下列句子

1. 我把问话重复了很多遍，他终于听懂了。

   _____

2. 他们总是告诉你一幅画的"意思"是什么。

   _____

3. 雨下得很大，他们发现地里已经形成了一条小溪。

   _____

4. 为此，他甚至一次也没能把自己的车开进车库。

   _____

5. 警察到达时，发现房门开着，房间空的。

   _____

6. 那块美丽的玻璃十分珍贵。

   _____

7. 他们失去了宝贵的工作时间。

   _____

8. 正当他上楼的时候，电话铃响了。

   _____

好句好段◈ | Writing Samples

☑ After some months I decided to go down to Lisbon in Portugal. I had friends there who could help me to sell my land in Brazil, and I needed the money. Friday came with me. He was always a good and true friend to me. In Lisbon I found the Portuguese captain, who took me in his ship to Brazil, all those years ago. It was good to see him again, and he helped me with my business. Soon I was ready to go home again—by land. No more adventures and dangers by sea for me!

过了几个月，我决定去葡萄牙的里斯本。我有些朋友在那儿，可以帮我卖掉在巴西的土地，我需要钱。星期五和我一起去。他一直是我的一位忠实的好朋友。在里斯本我找到了多年前带我去巴西的葡萄牙船长。再次见到他真是太好了，他帮助我做生意。不久我又准备回家——是经陆路。对我来说在海上航行已没有更多的冒险和危险。

本书所有练习题的参考答案（含阅读理解练习题解析及译文），请登录中国水利水电出版社网站 http://www.waterpub.com.cn/softdown/（下载中心）免费下载。

Lesson 8

✦✦（1）✦✦

Play Jacks

Jack is the name of a game. It is quite popular with children. To play jacks, you will need a small ball and ten small metal objects called jacks.

The rules for this game are quite easy. To begin with, you put the ten jacks on the floor or ground in front of you. Toss the ball high (but not too high), pick up one jack and then catch the ball. Keep the jack in your hand and go on to pick up the other jacks one at a time. You lose your turn if you do not catch the ball, or if you do not pick up a jack, or if you drop off the jacks from your hand.

When you finish all the ten jacks, you now try to do the same thing again but with two jacks at one time. This is more difficult, of course, you lose your turn if you make any of the above three mistakes or if you do not pick up two jacks each time.

---

1. object   *n.* 物体
2. rule   *n.* 规则

▶阅读上面的短文，从每题所给的四个选项中，选出一个最佳答案。

1. To play jacks is _____.
   A. difficult for boys   B. interesting for children
   C. difficult for girls   D. interesting for old people
2. The word "toss" here means _____.
   A. drop   B. catch   C. throw   D. pick
3. If you want to finish the first and second parts of the game, you have to pick up jacks _____.
   A. ten times   B. fifteen times
   C. twenty times   D. thirty times
4. The jacks are made of _____.
   A. paper   B. glass   C. metal   D. water
5. After you pick up the first ten jacks, the game becomes more difficult because you may make one of the _____.
   A. two mistakes   B. four mistakes
   C. three mistakes   D. fifteen mistakes

✦✦ （2）✦✦
Mark Twain's First Money

One day, Mark Twain told a story about his first money.

Schoolboys in those days didn't respect their teachers. They didn't take good care of school things, either. The school had a rule: If a student damaged his desk, the teacher would beat him in front of the whole school, or the student had to pay five dollars.

Mark Twain once found his desk was damaged in some way. He had to tell his father about the school's rule. His father thought it would be too bad if the teacher beat his son in public, so he agreed to give him five dollars. But before giving him the money, the father gave his son a good beating. The next day, Mark Twain decided he would take another beating at school, so he could keep the five dollars. In this way, he got his first money.

---

1. respect   *v.* 尊敬
2. damage   *v.* 损坏
3. beat   *v.* 打

▶阅读上面的短文，从每题所给的四个选项中，选出一个最佳答案。

1. In those days, if somebody damaged his desk, he would _____.
   A. leave school   B. pay money
   C. be beaten by his father   D. earn five dollars

2. When Mark Twain was _____, he earned his first money.
   A. ten years old   B. at school
   C. beaten for the first time   D. working

3. Mark Twain was beaten twice because he _____.
   A. damaged two desks   B. damaged his desk twice
   C. wanted to keep the money   D. didn't respect his teacher

4. Mark Twain's father gave him five dollars. He wanted his son to _____.
   A. keep the money   B. hand the money to the teacher
   C. disgrace his family   D. take a beating

5. The phrase "in public" in this story means _____.
   A. 当众   B. 在家
   C. 在学校   D. 在教室

语言基本功
英汉翻译◈ | Translation Exercises

▶翻译下列句子

1. 他们得各人付自己的罚款。

23

2. 给他们每人两个。

_____

3. 她两只手上各拿了一个苹果。

_____

4. 然而，最令人惊奇的是它能够在任何地方降落：雪地上、水面上甚至刚耕过的田里。

_____

5. 这个人想要飞往大西洋上的一个孤岛——罗卡尔岛，弗西特机长之所以不送他去是因为那段飞行太危险了。

_____

6. 你在等谁？

_____

7. 这是谁的伞？

_____

8. 这顶帽子是谁的？

_____

语言基本功
好句好段◈ | Writing Samples

☑ Three days later, in the big, new cemetery two miles from their house, the two old people said goodbye to their dead son. Then they went back to their dark, old house. They did not want to live without Herbert, but they waited for something good to happen, something to help them. The days went by very slowly. Sometimes they did not talk because there was nothing to say without Herbert. And so the days felt very long.

三天后，在离他们家两英里远的一个大而新的墓地，两位老人和他们死去的儿子道别了。然后，他们回到了又黑又旧的房子。没有了赫伯特，他们什么也不想做，他们等待着奇迹发生。时间过得很慢，有时他们连话也不想说，因为没有了赫伯特，就无话可说了。所以他们觉得白天很长。

Lesson 9

Reading Comprehension

❖❖（1）❖❖

Last Saturday, the New Kowloon Primary School football team played against the Ming Tak Primary School football team. Sam was the captain of the New Kowloon team. He was a good player.

The match started at three o'clock. Both teams played very well. It was very exciting, but there was no score in the first half of the match. After resting for ten minutes, the two teams continued the game, but there was no score, either. When it was almost the end of the match, Peter got the ball and passed it to Sam. Sam ran very fast and passed several players of the Ming Tak team. Then he kicked the ball to the top right corner of the goal. The goal keeper could not catch the ball, and it got into the goal. The crowd cheered and waved. They were very excited.

The result of the match was 1 to 0. The New Kowloon Primary School football team won. The headmaster was very happy. He invited all the players to a big dinner.

---

1. play against 打比赛，对抗赛
2. play v. 玩；player n. 运动员
3. the first half of the match 上半场比赛
4. no score 没得分
5. the end of the match 比赛接近尾声
6. pass sth. to 传递
7. the result of the match 比赛结果

▶阅读上面的短文，从每题所给的四个选项中，选出一个最佳答案。

1. Who was a good player?
   A. Peter.   B. Sam.
   C. The headmaster.   D. The goal keeper.
2. When did the match start?
   A. At three.   B. At four.
   C. At seven.   D. At ten.
3. What was the result in the first half of the match?
   A. 1 to 0.   B. 0 to 0.
   C. 2 to 0.   D. 0 to 1.

4. When did Sam kicked the ball to the top right corner of the goal?

    A. In the first half of the match.

    B. At the beginning of the match.

    C. When it was almost the end of the match.

    D. At the end of the first half of the match.

5. What was the result of the match?

    A. 0 to 0.   B. 0 to 2.

    C. 3 to 0.   D. 1 to 0.

✦✦（2）✦✦

Kangaroos（袋鼠）

There are 47 different kinds of kangaroos. The smallest are about a quarter of a metre long; the biggest are taller than a man.

Kangaroos have very long strong back legs. These are used for jumping. They also have long strong tails used for resting on. Kangaroos' front legs are much shorter, and are almost like arms. Kangaroos' heads are quite small, but their ears are quite large.

Mother kangaroos have a pocket at the front. They have one baby each year. When it is born, the baby kangaroo goes straight into its mother's pocket. The baby kangaroo stays there for six months.

The biggest kangaroos stand more than 2 metres tall, and their back legs are so strong that they can jump more than 9 metres. They are very fast, and can travel at more than 50 kilometres an hour. They are very strong, but only eat fruit, leaves and grass.

---

1. different kinds of 不同种类

2. long strong back legs 又长又有力的后腿

3. use for 用来

4. each year 每年

5. back legs 后腿；front legs 前腿

▶阅读上面的短文，从每题所给的四个选项中，选出一个最佳答案。

1. How many different kinds of kangaroos are there?

    A. Seven.   B. Seventy-four.

    C. Forty-seven.   D. Fourty-seven.

2. How large is a big kangaroo?

    A. Smaller than a man.   B. Bigger than a man.

    C. The same size as a man.   D. A quarter of a metre long.

3. Does each kangaroo have a pocket?

    A. Yes, it does.   B. No, it does.

    C. No, it doesn't   D. It does't tell us.

4. How long does a baby kangaroo stay in its mother's pocket?

A. One month.   B. Three months.

C. Six months.   D. Five months.

5. Are kangaroos' front legs stronger than their back legs?

A. Yes, they are.   B. No, they aren't.

C. They are stronger.   D. We have no idea.

语言基本功
英汉翻译 ◈ | Translation Exercises

▶ 翻译下列句子

1. 不要随波逐流。

_____

2. 他满脑子全是问号。

_____

3. 多少往事涌上心头。

_____

4. 你们中哪位得奖了？

_____

5. 我在找那本书，但没有找到。

_____

6. 还有谁跟你去那里？

_____

7. 你究竟在干什么？

_____

8. 你的小刀很漂亮，能借给我吗？

_____

语言基本功
好句好段 ◈ | Writing Samples

Good wine needs no cries.

好酒无需叫卖。

If money be not thy servant, it will be thy master.

不做金钱的主人，就会做金钱的奴隶。

Life is but a span.

人生如朝露。

本书所有练习题的参考答案（含阅读理解练习题解析及译文），请登录中国水利水电出版社网站 http://www.waterpub.com.cn/softdown/（下载中心）免费下载。

Lesson 10

阅读理解◈ Reading Comprehension

✦✦（1）✦✦

A foolish man went to butcher's shop to buy a piece of meat. As he did not know how to cook meat, he asked the butcher to tell him the way of cooking it. The butcher told him how to cook it. "But I cannot remember your words," the foolish man said, "Would you please write them down for me?" The butcher was kind enough to write them down for him. The man went home happily with a piece of meat in his hand and the note in his pocket. A dog followed him on the way. It jumped at him, took the meat away from him and ran off. The foolish man stood there not knowing what to do. Then he laughed and said, "Never mind, you don't know how to cook it. The note is still in my pocket."

---

1. ask sb. to do sth. 要求某人做某事
2. a piece of meat 中 meat 为不可数名词，当表达数量时，要加上量词。类似的还有：
   a cup of tea
   a bottle of milk
   a glass of water
3. write sth. down 写下
4. jump at 跳
5. run off 跑走了
6. what to do 如何做
7. never mind 没关系

▶阅读上面的短文，从每题所给的四个选项中，选出一个最佳答案。

1. A foolish man went to a butcher's shop _____.
   A. to buy a meat   B. for a piece of meat
   C. to cook a piece of meat   D. to send a piece of meat
2. The butcher told the foolish man how to _____.
   A. buy meat   B. eat meat
   C. cook meat   D. get meat
3. A dog took _____ away from the foolish man.
   A. the meat   B. the note
   C. the pocket   D. the hand

4. The dog really didn't know how to eat meat, did it? _____.

    A. Yes, it doesn't   B. No, it did

    C. No, it doesn't   D. Yes, it did

5. At last the note was still _____.

    A. in his pocket   B. in his hand

    C. in his room   D. in the butcher's shop

✦✦ **（2）** ✦✦

Do you know there are two kinds of football game? One is American football, the other is soccer. In China many young men like playing soccer. It is very popular. But the Chinese don't call it soccer. We call it football. There are eleven players in a team. And the ball is round. Only the goal-keeper plays the ball with hands. The other players can't play the ball with hands. In the USA soccer is not very popular. They like playing American football more than playing soccer. There are also eleven players in a team. The ball is not round. All the players can play the ball with hands and feet. And the goal is bigger than the goal of soccer games. American football is quite different from soccer.

---

1. two kinds of 两种；all kinds of 各种各样

2. one... the other... 一个，另外一个，只适用于二者

3. in a team 在队里

4. more than 多于……

5. with hands and feet 用手或脚

6. be different from 不同于

▶阅读上面的短文，从每题所给的四个选项中，选出一个最佳答案。

1. The football in China really called _____.

    A. football

    B. American football

    C. soccer

    D. Chinese football

2. There are _____ players in an American football team.

    A. 10   B. 11

    C. 12   D. We don't know.

3. How many players in a team can play soccer with feet?

    A. 11.   B. 10.

    C. 12.   D. We don't know.

4. How many players can play American football with hands?

    A. Only 1.   B. 11.

    C. 10.   D. 12.

英汉翻译◈ | Translation Exercises

▶ 翻译下列句子

1. 物理学就是历史上被称为自然哲学的科学。

   _____

2. 一旦考试制度生效，全新的局面就会出现。

   _____

3. 该国的免费医疗除了包括普通疾病外还包括精神方面的疾病。

   _____

4. 他滴酒不沾。

   _____

5. 我感觉臂上被人碰了一下。

   _____

6. 那个故事使我们所有的人为之感动。

   _____

7. 去年夏天这里雨水不多。

   _____

8. 还剩多少时间？

   _____

好句好段◈ | Writing Samples

☑ Kiah and Rilla sat down on the expensive green and black chairs and looked at the expensive flowers on the tables. There were no windows in this room. Suddenly, the door opened and a tall, fat woman came in. Her name was Bel, and she was Gog's wife. She had a lot of long red hair and she wore an expensive blue dress. Bel liked expensive things. She carried a cat. The cat was black and white: half of its face was black and the other half was white; half of its body was black and the other half was white.

凯和瑞拉在昂贵的绿黑相间的椅子上坐了下来，观赏着桌子上那些名贵的鲜花。这个房间没有窗子。突然，门开了，一个身高体胖的女人走了进来。她叫贝尔，是高格的妻子。她有一头浓密的红色长发，穿着一件昂贵的蓝色裙子。贝尔喜欢昂贵的东西。她抱着一只猫。那是只黑白相间的猫：猫脸一半黑一半白；猫身也是一半黑一半白。

Lesson 11

阅读理解◇ | Reading Comprehension

✦✦（1）✦✦

Jim was a farmer. He lived in a village far away from the town. One day he was very ill, and everyone thought he would die. They sent for a doctor in town. The doctor reached the village two days later and looked over the man. The doctor wanted a pen and some paper. But there was no pen or paper in the village, because no one could read or write.

The doctor picked up a piece of burnt wood. Using the wood, he wrote the name of the medicine on the door of the house. "Get this medicine for him right away," he said, "and he will soon get well." Jim's family and friends did not know what to do. They could not read the writing. Then the village baker had an idea. He took off the door of the house and took the door to the nearest town. He bought the medicine, and Jim was saved. He would not let anyone wash the magic words off the door.

---

1. far away from 远离
2. die *v.* → dead *adj.* 死
3. look over 检查
4. some paper （注：paper 为不可数名词）

▶ 阅读上面的短文，从每题所给的四个选项中，选出一个最佳答案。

1. People in the village thought Jim would die because _____.
    A. he was very ill   B. the doctor could do nothing for him
    C. the doctor didn't come   D. they couldn't find any doctors

2. The doctor got to the village two days later because _____.
    A. he walked to the village
    B. the village was far from the town
    C. there was something wrong with his car
    D. it was snowing hard

3. When the doctor got to the village, he _____.
    A. found another doctor there   B. gave some medicine to Jim
    C. looked over Jim carefully   D. had no idea and could do nothing for Jim

4. The doctor wrote down the name of the medicine with _____ on _____.
    A. a pen, a piece of paper

B. a piece of burnt wood, some paper

C. a piece of burnt wood, the door of the house

D. a pen, a piece of wood

5. What do you think of the people in the village?

    A. They were rich and clever.   B. They were lazy.

    C. They could read and write well.   D. They were poor and fell behind the times.

 （2）

In Britain, winter is not very cold and summer is not very hot. There is a great difference between summer and winter. Why is this?

Britain has a mild winter and a cool summer because it is an island country. In winter, the sea is warmer than the land. The winds from the sea bring cool air to Britain.

The winds from the west blow over Britain all the year. They blow from the southwest. They are wet winds. They bring rain to Britain all year. The west of Britain is wetter than the east. The moist blow over the highland in the west. They drop more rain there. The east of Britain is drier than the west.

The four seasons are all three months long. Winter is in December, January and February. Spring is in March, April and May. Summer is in June, July and August. Autumn is in September, October and November.

---

1. between *prep.* 在二者之间
2. an island country 岛国
3. blow over 吹过
4. all the year 终年

▶ 阅读上面的短文，从每题所给的四个选项中，选出一个最佳答案。

1. In Britain, summer and winter are _____.

    A. just the same   B. different

    C. very cold   D. very hot

2. In winter the winds from the sea bring _____ air to Britain.

    A. cool   B. cold

    C. warm   D. dry

3. The weather is _____ in winter in Britain.

    A. warm   B. cold

    C. sunny   D. snowy

4. Britain has a lot of rain all the year because _____.

    A. there are lots of trees there

    B. there are many rivers there

    C. winter is not very cold and summer is not very hot there

D. wet winds blow over Britain all the year

5. Which of the following is right?

A. The east of Britain is wetter than the west.

B. In summer the sea is as hot as the land.

C. In Britain any of the four seasons is three months long.

D. There is the same rain here and there in Britain.

英汉翻译◈ | Translation Exercises

▶ 翻译下列句子

1. 闪电是电流从一块云到地面或一块云到另一块云之间的急速传导。

   _____

2. 虽然牛顿很伟大，但他的许多见解今天受到挑战，并且为现代科学家的工作所修正。

   _____

3. 重要的是募集足够的钱，为这个项目提供资金。

   _____

4. 你父亲每天喝多少啤酒？

   _____

5. 她没有多少行李。

   _____

6. 他说他没有很多困难。

   _____

7. 老师没有给我们很多书面作业。

   _____

8. 干得好的工作应得到好的报酬。

   _____

好句好段◈ | Writing Samples

No joy without annoy.

喜中有忧。

Reading is to the mind what exercise is to the body.

读书养神，锻炼健身。

The greatest pleasure of life is love.

爱是人生最大的乐趣。

Lesson 12

✦✦ （1）✦✦

The story about Miss Evans is a true story. On the way to England from the U.S. in April 1912, a new ship hit an iceberg and water began to come over it.

Everyone came out and went up to the higher part of the ship. The man put down some lifeboats into the water and helped the women and children to get on them. Suddenly a woman shouted and wanted to stay with her children in the boat, but there was no more room for her. At that moment Miss Evans let that woman take her place. Soon after that the ship went down. Miss Evans lost her life.

If you speak about Miss Evans in Boston today, nobody knows more about her than that. But she is one of the greatest women in America.

---

1. the story about... 关于……的故事
2. on the way to 在去……的路上
3. come out 出来
4. go up 上升；go down 下沉
5. put down 放下
6. stay with 呆在……

▶阅读上面的短文，从每题所给的四个选项中，选出一个最佳答案。

1. Miss Evans is from _____.
   A. the USA   B. England
   C. We don't know.   D. Japan
2. What's the title of the passage?
   A. A woman with her children.   B. A new ship.
   C. The story of Miss Evans.   D. A nice ship.
3. What happened to a woman?
   A. She lost her children.
   B. She lost her life.
   C. Her children were in the boat but she wasn't in it.
   D. The woman asked Miss Evans to give her a place.
4. Who gave the woman a place?

A. The woman in the ship.   B. Miss Evans.

C. The man in the ship.   D. The woman's sister.

5. Does anybody know more about Miss Evans than that?

A. Yes, they do.   B. Yes, he does.

C. No, they don't.   D. Nobody knows today.

✦✦ （2）✦✦

Air is always around us. It is around us when we walk and play. From the time we are born, air is around us. When we sit down, it is around us. When we go to bed, air is also around us. We live in air.

All living things need air. Living things can't live without air. We can live without food or water for a few days, but we cannot live for more than a few minutes without air. We take in air. When we are working or running, we need more air. When we are asleep, we need less air.

We live in air, but we can't see it. We can only feel it. We can feel it when it is moving. Moving air is called wind. How can we make air move? Here is one way. Hold and open book in your hand in front of your face. Close it quickly. What you feel is the air.

---

1. around us 在我们周围

2. from the time we are born 从我们一出生时起

3. we live in air 我们生活在空气当中

4. living things 生物

5. without air 没有空气

6. more 更多些；less 更少些

▶ 阅读上面的短文，从每题所给的四个选项中，选出一个最佳答案。

1. _____ need air.

A. Some of the animals   B. All the things

C. Some of the plants   D. All the animals and plants

2. We can live for a few days _____.

A. without air   B. without water or food

C. without food or air   D. without air or water

3. We need _____ air when we are asleep.

A. less   B. no

C. most   D. a lot of

4. Which of the following sentences is right?

A. Sometimes we don't live in air.

B. Air isn't around us when we go to bed.

C. We can live happily without air.

D. We need more air when we are working or running.

5. We live in air, but we can't _____ it.
   A. look   B. see
   C. get   D. feel

英汉翻译◈ | Translation Exercises

▶ 翻译下列句子

1. 只有在特殊情况下，才允许新生补考。

2. 在其他条件相同的情况下，一个善于表达自己的人要比一个不善于言谈的人较快地获得成功。

3. 我从未驾船驶过地中海。

4. 云飘过天空。

5. 我们正在学航海。

6. 到 1990 年工业世界自动化市场可望扩大一倍多，达到一千亿美元。

7. 从 1980 年以来，在飞机制造厂工作的人数从二万七千人降到一万三千人。

8. 我们每年将成本降低四亿五千万英镑。

好句好段◈ | Writing Samples

☑ When you are blind, you listen to things very carefully. I used to sit alone in my room and listen to the sounds of the wind outside the house. The wind talks and whispers and sings—it has many voices. I listened to the sounds of the clock on the stairs, and the wood in the fire, and the footsteps and voices of the girls walking round the house. They talked a lot to each other, and sometimes I could hear what they said, even when they were in another room.

当人眼睛失明后，听东西就会格外仔细。我常常一个人坐在自己的房间里，听着屋外风的声音。风儿说着、低语着、唱着——它有很多种声调。我也听着楼梯上大钟嘀哒嘀哒的响声，炉火中木柴的噼叭声以及女儿们在房子里的踱步声。她们经常谈论许多事，有时我还能听见她们谈话的内容，即使她们是在另一个房间。

Lesson 13

阅读理解◎ | Reading Comprehension

◆◆（1）◆◆

Skin-diving

Skin-diving is a new sport today. This sport takes you into a wonderful new world. It is like a visit to the moon. When you are under water, it is easy for you to climb big rocks, because you are no longer heavy.

Here, under water, everything is blue and green. During the day, there is lots of light. When fish swim nearby, you can catch them with your hands.

When you have tanks of air on your back, you can stay in deep water for a long time. But you must be careful when you dive in deep water.

To catch fish is one of the most interesting parts of this sport. Besides, there are more uses for skin-diving. You can clean ships without taking them out of water. You can get many things from the deep sea.

Now you see that skin-diving is both useful and interesting.

---

1. skin-diving   潜水
2. tank   *n.* 罐

▶阅读上面的短文，从每题所给的四个选项中，选出一个最佳答案。

1. Skin-diving is a new sport. It can take you to _____.
   A. the moon   B. a new world of land
   C. the mountain   D. the deep water

2. In deep water _____.
   A. there is plenty of light   B. there is no light at all
   C. you can find lots of blue fish   D. everything looks blue and green

3. You can climb big rocks under water easily because _____.
   A. you are very heavy   B. you are as heavy as on the land
   C. you are not as heavy as on the land   D. you have no weight at all

4. With a tank of air on your back, you can _____.
   A. catch fish very easily   B. stay under water for a long time
   C. climb big rocks   D. have more fun

5. Which of the following is not true?

A. Skin-diving is a new sport.

B. To skin-diving is like visiting the moon.

C. The only use of skin-diving is to have more fun.

D. Skin-diving is not only interesting but useful.

✦✦ (2) ✦✦

Auntie Mame

"Mame" is a play, with music, about a very good woman. Her friends call her "Auntie Mame". Auntie Mame is a special kind of woman. She thinks for herself and doesn't follow others. Mame's idea about life is that everyone should learn something new every day. You shouldn't bury yourself in the same routine. One of the songs in the play is "Open a New Window".

Auntie Mame's only relative is a red-headed young boy. His name is Patrick Dennis. He comes to live with Auntie Mame in New York. With Auntie Mame's help, Patrick has learned a lot of things. He meets all kinds of people. These people have adventures and dress in strange ways.

Mame takes him out of school for a long trip around the world when he is old enough. He also visits India and Africa.

Patrick grows up to be a nice young man. He is not afraid to do new, different and difficult things. He never forgets his love for Auntie Mame.

---

1. bury   *v.* 埋葬
2. routine   *n.* 日常事务
3. adventure   *n.* 冒险

▶阅读上面的短文，从每题所给的四个选项中，选出一个最佳答案。

1. "Mame" is the name of a _____.

   A. piece of music   B. young boy

   C. young man   D. woman

2. Auntie Mame _____.

   A. has many relatives   B. is actually a traveler

   C. is a clever scientist   D. is not a common woman

3. When Patrick goes to live with Auntie Mama, he _____.

   A. is old enough   B. is very young

   C. lives alone in New York   D. is very old

4. Patrick _____.

   A. will not remember his relative Auntie Mame

   B. never forgets his relative of Auntie Mame

   C. say goodbye to his relative of Auntie Mame next year

   D. becomes a very good worker soon

5. Auntie Mame is _____.

    A. very angry with Patrick   B. very kind to Patrick

    C. a woman with a good husband   D. a mother of one child

语言基本功
英汉翻译◈ | Translation Exercises

▶ 翻译下列句子

1. 他用棍子打我。

_____

2. 几个小时之前，有人向警方报告，说有人企图偷走这些钻石。

_____

3. 比尔比乔更为勤奋，种植了更多的花卉和蔬菜，但乔的花园更富情趣。

_____

4. 他没有必要买车。

_____

5. 他很少有机会说法语。

_____

6. 我好几次遇见他。

_____

7. 前两个星期，在比利时家庭日常燃料费用上涨百分之十二。

_____

8. 我们的出口额每年增加一倍。

_____

语言基本功
好句好段◈ | Writing Samples

✓ The next day it was very rainy, so Mary did not go out. Instead she decided to wander round the house, looking into some of the hundred rooms that Mrs. Medlock had told her about. She spent all morning going in and out of dark, silent rooms, which were full of heavy furniture and old pictures. She saw no servants at all, and was on her way back to her room for lunch, when she heard a cry. "It's a bit like the cry that I heard last night!" she thought. Just then the housekeeper, Mrs. Medlock, appeared, with her keys in her hand.

第二天雨下得很大，玛丽没有出去，而是打定主意在房子里转转，看看梅洛太太讲过的那上百个房间。她整个上午都在出入那些阴暗寂静的房间，房间里满是笨重的家具和古旧的油画。她没看到一个佣人，当她转身回房间吃午饭时，听到有人哭泣的声音。"听起来很像昨天晚上的哭声。"她想。就在这时管家梅洛太太出现了，手里拎着大串钥匙。

Lesson 14

阅读理解◇ | Reading Comprehension
✦✦ （1） ✦✦

Bats are the only flying mammal in the world. They can't see very well. It is in many places that all bats are blind. "Blind as a bat" is often heard. Yet they have no trouble flying in the darkest nights and finding their way around very well. How can bats fly and see at night? They fly by radar.

The bat's radar system works the same way as the one that ships and planes use. As a bat flies through the air, he makes a sound that is too high for our ears to hear. If the sounds hit things they come back. The bat's ears receive the messages. In this way they are able to tell the bat where the things are.

Bats go out to look for food at night. In the daytime they hang in some dark place. Some people have the bats as bad animals. In fact, they are useful animals.

1.　the only flying mammal in the world
　　世上仅有的会飞的哺乳动物
2.　too high for our ears to hear
　　太高了以致我们用耳朵听不见
3.　in this way　用这种方式
4.　be able to　能
5.　in the daytime　在白天
6.　in fact　事实上

▶阅读上面的短文，从每题所给的四个选项中，选出一个最佳答案。

1.　This story tells us something about _____.
　　A. the bats are like a mouse with wings
　　B. the radar
　　C. a blind man
　　D. the bat used for playing games
2.　The bat is _____.
　　A. an animal　　　　B. a bird　　　　C. fish　　　　D. a beast
3.　"Blind as a bat," means a person who is _____.
　　A. blind in both eyes
　　B. blind in neither of the eyes

C. not able to see well   D. able to see anything well

4. Bats go out to look for food _____.

    A. at noon

    B. in the afternoon

    C. during the daytime

    D. after the sun sets and before the sun rises

5. Bats are _____.

    A. useful for people   B. bad animals

    C. friends of beasts   D. friends of birds

✦✦（2）✦✦
That Man Knows the Future

Mr. Hunt was cutting a branch off a tree in his garden. While he was sawing, a man passed in the street. Seeing Mr. Hunt, he stopped and said, "Excuse me, but if you keep on sawing that branch like that, you will fall down with it." He said this because Mr. Hunt was sitting on the branch and cutting it at a place between himself and the trunk of the tree.

Mr. Hunt said nothing. He thought, "This is some foolish man who has no work to do and goes about telling other people what to do and what not to do."

The man went on his way. Of course, after a few minutes, the branch fell and Mr. Hunt fell down with it.

"My God!" he cried, "That man knows the future!" And he ran after the man and he wanted to ask him how long he was going to live. But the man had gone.

---

1. branch   *n.* 树枝
2. saw   *v.* 锯
3. trunk   *n.* 树干
4. foolish   *adj.* 愚蠢的

▶ 根据短文内容回答下列问题，每空一词。

1. Why did the man stopped when he saw Mr. Hunt?

    Because he wanted to _____ Mr. Hunt it was _____ to saw the branch like that.

2. Where was Mr. Hunt sitting?

    On the _____ of a _____.

3. What did Mr. Hunt think of the man?

    He thought he was a _____ _____.

4. What happened after the man left?

    Mr. Hunt _____ _____ the tree.

5. The man could tell Mr. Hunt how long he was going to live, couldn't he?

    _____, he _____.

英汉翻译◇ | Translation Exercises

▶ 翻译下列句子

1. 上星期政府宣布三月份工业生产率在前一个月下降千分之二以后，上升了千分之三。

   _____

2. 今年贸易赤字可能达到一千四百亿美元，几乎超过去年二百亿（美元）。

   _____

3. 日本对美国的汽车出口将增加百分之二十五。

   _____

4. 我半年多没有看电影了。

   _____

5. 他于 1993 年 10 月入伍，参军已五年了。

   _____

6. 这是我第一次用电脑写文章。

   _____

7. 美国人每天摄入的蛋白质是他们实际需要量的两倍。

   _____

8. 有些老年人不喜欢流行音乐，因为受不了这么多噪音。

   _____

好句好段◇ | Writing Samples

☑ Then I remembered the piece of wood, which had already saved my life once. It would help me get across the sea to Mull! So I walked all the way back to the beach where I had arrived. The piece of wood was in the sea, so I waded into the water to get it. But as I came closer, it moved away from me. And when the water was too deep for me to stand, the piece of wood was still several metres away. I had to leave it, and went back to the beach. It was a terrible moment for me. I was feeling very tired, hungry and thirsty, with no hope of getting away from this lonely island. For the first time since leaving Essendean, I lay down and cried.

接着我想起了那块木板，曾救过我性命的那块。它将能帮着我渡过大海到达马尔！于是我返回到我到达时的那片海滩。那块木头在海里，我蹚水去取它。可是我一靠近些时，木头就从我身边漂走了。当蹚到水深得连我都站不住时，那片木头离我还有几米远。我不得不任它漂走，回到岸上。这对我来说是很难受的一刻。我感到非常累，又饥又渴，觉得没有希望从这个孤岛上逃身。离开埃森丁后我第一次躺下来哭了起来。

Lesson 15

阅读理解◇ | Reading Comprehension

◆◆ （1）◆◆

A Proud Mother

Mr. and Mrs. King live outside a small town. They have a big farm and they are always busy working on it. Their son, Tom, studied in a middle school. The young man studied hard and did well in his lesson. It made them happy.

Last month, Tom finished middle school and passed entrance exam. Mrs. King was very happy and told many farmers about it.

Yesterday afternoon Mrs. King went to the town to buy something for her son. On the bus she told one of her friends how clever her son was. She said very loudly. All the people on the bus began to listen to it.

"Which university will your son study in?" a man next to her asked.

"In the most famous university in our country!" Mrs. King said happily.

"The most famous university?"

"Oxford University."

Most of the passengers looked at her carefully. Some of them said to her, "Congratulations!"

A woman said, "I'm sure he'll know Jack Black."

"Who's Jack Black?" asked Mrs. King.

"He's my son."

"Does he study in the university, too?"

"No," said the woman, "he's one of the professors!"

▶ 阅读上面的短文，从每题所给的四个选项中，选出一个最佳答案。

1. The story happened in _____.

    A. England   B. France   C. Germany   D. America

2. The word "passenger" in the story means _____.

    A. 行李   B. 乘客   C. 经理   D. 陌生人

3. Mrs. King wanted everyone to know_____.

    A. her son was friendly to others

    B. her son finished middle school

    C. her son

    D. her son was going to study in Oxford University

4. Mrs. King spoke very loudly on the bus, so _____.

    A. her husband could hear her

    B. all the passengers could hear her

    C. she hoped to make all the people happy

    D. all the passengers asked her to stop talking

5. Which of the following is true?

    A. The woman next to Mrs. King wanted to show off（炫耀）her son, too.

    B. Mr. and Mrs. King knew nothing about Oxford University.

    C. The woman wanted to stop Mrs. King from showing off.

    D. The woman liked Mrs. King very much.

He Didn't Think It's Free

An English traveler spent a few weeks in Sweden. When he was about to return home, he found that he had only enough money left to get a ticket to England. Thinking the matter over, he decided that as it was only a two days' trip he could get home without eating anything. So he bought a ticket with that little money he had and boarded the ship.

He closed his ears to the sound of the lunch bell, and when dinner time came, he refused to go down to the place where people had their dinner, saying that he didn't feel well.

The following day he did not get up until breakfast was over, pretending that he overslept himself. At lunch time, too, he kept out of the way. By the time of dinner, however, he became so hungry that he could even have eaten paper.

"I can't stand this any longer," he said to himself. "I must have something to eat." At the dinner table he ate everything that put in front of him. When he was quite full, he felt stronger and at once went to see the waiter. "The bill?" asked the waiter in surprise. "Yes," answered the traveler. "There isn't any bill here," said the waiter. "On this ship meals are already included in the ticket."

▶ 阅读上面的短文，从每题所给的四个选项中，选出一个最佳答案。

1. How many meals did the English traveler eat during his two-day trip?

    A. One.　　　　　B. Not any one.　　　　C. Six.　　　　　D. Three.

2. After buying the ticket, he had _____.

    A. only enough money for one meal　　　B. no money left

    C. very little money left　　　D. some money for breakfast only

3. The first day he did not have his lunch because he did not _____.

    A. feel well　　　B. know the time for lunch

    C. hear the lunch bell　　　D. have the money

4. The following day he got up _____.

    A. much later than breakfast bell　　　B. when he heard the breakfast bell

C. early for his breakfast   D. in time to have his breakfast

5. In the end, the English traveler _____.

    A. had to borrow money to pay for the meal

    B. was thrown into the water by the waiter

    C. learned that the meals on the ship were free

    D. he had to go hungry again

语言基本功
英汉翻译◈ | Translation Exercises

▶ 翻译下列句子

1. 希望你别打断（我的话）。
    _____

2. 交通被暴风雪所阻断。
    _____

3. 出车祸后，皮特（Pitt）先生一直在医院里。
    _____

4. 我已醒了很长时间。
    _____

5. 我希望等我们明年夏天回来时，他们已经修好这条路。
    _____

6. 他把业余时间都花在种树上。他说到明年底，他将种完两千棵。
    _____

7. 红旗迎风飘扬。
    _____

8. 你多久回去看望你的外祖母呢？
    _____

语言基本功
好句好段◈ | Writing Samples

To make enemies, talk; to make friends, listen.
要成仇敌，多讲；要成朋友，多听。
A bad padlock invites a picklock.
开门揖盗。
A ready way to lose friend is to lend him money.
失友都因借钱起。

Lesson 16

Reading Comprehension

✦✦ （1） ✦✦

American schools begin in September after a long summer holiday. There are two terms in a school year. The first term is from September to January, and the second is from February to June. Most American children begin to go to school when they are five years old. Most students are seventeen or eighteen years old when they finish high school.

High school students take only four or five subjects each term. They usually go to the same classes every day, and they have homework for every class. After class they do many interesting things.

After high school, many students go to college. They can go to a small one or a large one. They usually have to give a lot of money. So many college students work after class to get the money for their studies.

▶阅读上面的短文，从每题所给的四个选项中，选出一个最佳答案。

1. How many terms are there in a school year in America?
   A. Four.　　　　　　B. One.　　　　　　C. Three.　　　　　　D. Two.

2. The first term is _____.
   A. from February to June　　　　　　B. from January to September
   C. from June to February　　　　　　D. from September to January

3. When a child is _____ years old he or she can go to school.
   A. five　　　　　　B. four　　　　　　C. seven　　　　　　D. six

4. How many subjects do the high school students take each term?
   A. As many as they like.　　　　　　B. Five.
   C. Four.　　　　　　D. Four or five.

5. Why do many college students have to work after class?
   A. Because some work is helpful to their studies.
   B. Because the teachers ask them to do so.
   C. Because they like to work very much.
   D. Because they need to get money for their studies.

✦✦ （2） ✦✦

Have you ever seen snow? A lot of people in the world have not. A lot of countries never have snow. In the north of England, there is quite a lot of snow every winter, but in the south of

England, there is usually little snow.

When a student from a warm country comes to England in the autumn for the first time, he feels cold at first. There are often dark clouds, grey skies and cold rain in England in autumn, and most students from warm countries do not like this kind of weather.

But snow is different. It is very cold, but it is very beautiful. After a few dark mornings, the student wakes up one day and there is a lot of light in his room. He thinks, "It must be late," and gets up quickly, but no, it is not late at all. He looks out of the window and there is snow everywhere. The light in the room comes from that clean, beautiful white snow.

---

1. have...ever 曾经……
2. never *adv.* 从不，决不，表示否定语气最强
3. in the south 在南方
4. little snow 小雪，snow 为不可数名词，只能用 little 或 a little 修饰
5. the first time 第一次
6. dark clouds 乌云
7. grey skies 阴天
8. wake up 醒来
9. not... at all 一点都不……

▶阅读上面的短文，从每题所给的四个选项中，选出一个最佳答案。

1. Many people _____.
   A. have ever seen snow
   B. have never seen snow
   C. often see snow
   D. see snow once a year
2. There is usually _____ snow in the south of England.
   A. a little
   B. few
   C. a few
   D. little
3. When a student from a _____ country comes to England in the autumn, he feels _____ at first.
   A. hot, cold
   B. warm, cold
   C. warm, hot
   D. hot, warm
4. Most students from warm countries _____.
   A. like the weather in England
   B. don't like the weather in England
   C. don't like snow
   D. often see snow in their countries
5. There is a lot of light in the room because _____.
   A. there is a lamp
   B. it is daytime
   C. it is fine
   D. there is snow outside

英汉翻译◈ | Translation Exercises

▶ 翻译下列句子

1. 道路上交通流量很大。

_____

2. 他们在搞走私交易。

_____

3. 和预料的一样，对这个问题的反应杂乱不一。

_____

4. 这对老夫妇虽然生养了三个儿女，但还是决定收养一儿一女。

_____

5. 经理高度赞扬了员工们所表现出的诸如诚实、勇敢、守信等美德。

_____

6. 洪水每年都造成几十亿美元的财产损失。

_____

7. 这位委员反对变动计划。

_____

8. 该农作物与先前的那种很相似，都适合同一种土壤并具有抗风的特性。

_____

好句好段◈ | Writing Samples

✔ About a week later, we were sailing round the rocky coast of northern Scotland in very bad weather. It was difficult to see anything because of the thick fog. One evening there was a great crash, and the officers ran out to see what had happened. I thought we had hit a rock, but in fact it was a small boat. As we watched, the boat broke in two, and went to the bottom with all its men, except the one passenger. At the moment of the crash, this man managed to jump up and catch the side of the ship and pull himself up.

　　大约一周以后，在非常恶劣的天气条件下，我们沿苏格兰北部的礁岩海岸行驶着。由于大雾弥漫，很难看见什么东西。一天晚上，有一记猛烈的撞击声，高级船员们都跑出去看发生了什么。我以为我们是撞上了一块岩石，但实际上是一条小船。我们观看时，小船碎成了两半，除了这一位乘客外其余的人连船一起沉入海底了。在撞船的那一刻，这个人用力跳起来，抓住了我们这条船的船舷，挣扎着上了船。

$\mathcal{L}esson$ *17*

Reading Comprehension

✦✦（1）✦✦

Long long ago, there was a king. He liked to draw pictures. He thought his pictures were good, so he liked to show them to people. People were afraid to say that the king's pictures were bad, so they all said that his pictures were very good.

One day, the king showed some of his best pictures to an artist. He wanted the artist to speak well of these pictures. But the artist said his pictures were so bad that he should put them into the fire. The king got angry with him and put him to prison.

After some time, the king's guard brought the artist back to the palace. The king said to the artist, "I will set you free if you tell me which one of my pictures is good." Again he showed him some of his new pictures and asked what he thought of them.

After having a look at them, the artist at once turned to the guard and said, "Take me back to prison, please."

---

1. long long ago 很早，很早以前
2. show sb. sth., show sth. to sb. 把某物展示给某人
3. well 在文中为副词，修饰动词 speak
4. so + *adj.* + that 如此的……以致
5. put...into 把……放入
6. bring...back 带回
7. set...free 释放

▶阅读上面的短文，从每题所给的四个选项中，选出一个最佳答案。

1. What did the king like to do?
    A. To buy pictures.   B. To draw pictures.
    C. To keep pictures.   D. To watch pictures.
2. The pictures the king drew were _____.
    A. as good as the artist's   B. better than the artist's
    C. very bad   D. very good
3. Which of the following is right?
    A. The artist said the king's pictures were excellent.
    B. The king thought his pictures were not good.

C. The people said the king's pictures were bad.

D. The people said the king's pictures were good.

4. What did the king do when he heard what the artist said?

A. He learnt to draw pictures from the artist.

B. He put the artist into prison.

C. He stopped drawing.

D. He threw his pictures on fire.

5. What's the meaning of the sentence "Take me back to prison"?

A. The artist liked to be in prison.

B. The artist thought the king's pictures were better.

C. The artist thought the king's pictures were still bad.

D. The artist was still angry with the king.

✦✦ （2） ✦✦

The computer is a useful machine. It is the most important invention in many years. The old kind of computer is the abacus, used in China centuries ago, but the first large, modern computer was built in 1946. A computer then could do maths problems quite fast.

Today computers are used in many ways and can do many kinds of work. In a few years the computer may touch the lives of everyone, even people in faraway villages.

In the last few years, there have been great changes in computers. They are getting smaller and smaller, and computing faster and faster. Many scientists agree that computers can now do many things, but they cannot do everything. Who knows what the computers of tomorrow will be like? Will computers bring good things or bad things to people? The scientists of today will have to decide how to use the computers of tomorrow.

▶阅读上面的短文，从每题所给的三个选项中，选出一个最佳答案。

1. What kind of machine is the computer?

A. The computer is a large machine.

B. The computer is a helpful machine.

C. The computer is a dangerous machine.

2. When was the first large, modern computer built?

A. More than sixty years ago.

B. More than fifty years ago.

C. One hundred years ago.

3. What can computers do?

A. Everything.　　　　　　　B. Nothing.　　　　　　　C. Lots of things.

4. Where was the oldest kind of computer made?

A. In China.　　　　　　　B. In America.　　　　　　　C. In Canada.

5. What can be inferred from the text?

A. Computers can take the place of human beings in the future.

B. Computers will bring good things and bad things to people.

C. Farmers might use computers to plant crops in a few years.

英汉翻译◈ | Translation Exercises

▶ 翻译下列句子

1. 他六点钟才来。

_____

2. 他的文章登在昨天的报上。

_____

3. 我觉得你是对的。

_____

4. 许多旧房正被拆除，以便给新建筑腾出地方。

_____

5. 不能把这些书带出室外。

_____

6. 没有人在昨天的事故中受伤。

_____

7. 你的计划遭老板拒绝了吗？

_____

8. 该机构没有违规，但也没有很负责任地操作。

_____

好句好段◈ | Writing Samples

☑ Buck threw himself against his harness, and pulled. He held his body low to the ground, his head down and forward, and his feet dug into the hard snow. Harder and harder he pulled. Suddenly, the sledge moved a centimeter … two … three… and, little by little, it started to go forward across the snow. With each second it went a little faster, and Thornton ran behind, calling to Buck as he pulled the sledge towards the end of the hundred metres. The watching men were shouting and throwing their hats in the air; Buck had won.

巴克用力抵住挽具，拉着。他的身子低低地向地面弯着，头向前埋着，脚用劲蹬住坚硬的雪地，越来越使劲地拉着。突然，雪撬移动了一厘米，……两厘米……三厘米……渐渐地，雪撬开始沿着雪地移动了。每一秒钟都移得快一点，桑顿跟在后面跑，当巴克拉至100米的终点时喊住他。围观的人们欢呼起来，把帽子扔到空中，巴克赢了。

本书所有练习题的参考答案（含阅读理解练习题解析及译文），请登录中国水利水电出版社网站 http://www.waterpub.com.cn/softdown/（下载中心）免费下载。

Lesson **18**

✦✦ （1）✦✦

When I was lost in London, it had one of the thickest fogs in years. You could hardly see your hand in front of your face. Cars and buses ran very slowly with their lights on, and their horns made big noises. When evening fell, it got even worse. All traffic came to a stop. Since I had an important meeting on the other side of the city, I wanted to walk.

Minutes later I was lost. Then I heard a young woman's voice coming out of the fog. "I think you are lost. Can I help you?" I could hardly see her, but I was very glad to find another person out in the fog. I told her where I wanted to go and she said she knew very well how to get there.

As I followed her through the dark streets, I wondered how she found her way so easily. "I know this part of London quite well," she answered.

"But in such a fog it's difficult to see anything," I said.

"With the fog or without the fog, it makes no difference to me. You see, I am blind," she answered.

▶ 阅读上面的短文，从每题所给的四个选项中，选出一个最佳答案。

1. The story happened in _____.

    A. America   B. China   C. England   D. Japan

2. Why did cars run slowly?

    A. Because drivers could see nothing.

    B. Because it rained very hard.

    C. Because the fog was too thick.

    D. Because there were many cars in the streets.

3. The writer decided to walk to the other side of the city because _____.

    A. he had an important meeting there

    B. he had something important to do

    C. his home was there

    D. his office was there

4. How did the writer get to the other side of the city?

    A. By bus.   B. He asked a policeman to help him.

    C. He followed a young woman.   D. He took a taxi.

5. Why did the young woman find her way so easily in the thickest fog?

A. Because she had good eyes.

B. Because she lived there for many years.

C. Because she was a blind woman.

D. Because the weather changed.

✦✦ （2） ✦✦

Six people were traveling in a compartment on a train. Five of them were quiet and well behaved, but the sixth was a rude young man who was causing a lot of trouble to the other passengers.

At last this young man got out at a station with his two heavy bags. None of the other passengers helped him, but one of them waited until the rude young man was very far away, and then opened the window and shouted to him, "You left something behind in the compartment!" Then he closed the window again.

The young man turned around and hurried back with his two bags. He was very tired when he arrived, but he shouted through the window, "What did I leave behind?"

As the train began to move again, the passenger who had called him back opened the window and said, "A very bad impression!"

1.　　on a train 在火车上

2.　　well behaved 举止文明

▶阅读上面的短文，从每题所给的四个选项中，选出一个最佳答案。

1.　Of the six passengers in the compartment _____.

A. five of them were rude and badly behaved

B. one of them was rude and badly behaved

C. five were always causing trouble on the train

D. only one was quiet and well behaved

2.　When the rude young man got off the train _____.

A. he left his two heavy bags behind

B. he was thrown out through the window

C. the other five passengers didn't help him

D. one of the other passengers opened the door for him

3.　The young man hurried back because _____.

A. he found he had left something on the train

B. he found he had left his bags on the train

C. he heard a passenger calling him by his name

D. he heard a passenger shouting to him that he had left something behind

4.　The passenger who had called him back wanted _____.

A. to punish him for his bad behaviour

B. to have a word with him about his behaviour

C. to help him with his behaviour

D. to return him the things he had left on the train

5. The writer is trying to tell us in the story that _____.

A. a bad impression is easily left on the train

B. young people should behave well in the train

C. people with bad manners are not welcomed

D. don't leave things behind when traveling by train

英汉翻译◈ | Translation Exercises

▶ 翻译下列句子

1. 海报说她今晚演讲。

_____

2. 到今年年底，除两人外的其他所有人都将离去。

_____

3. 每个人手里都有一张申请表，但没有人知道该送到哪个办公室。

_____

4. 语言就像是一座城市，对它的建筑每个人都曾添砖加瓦。

_____

5. 他们是教师，因而不懂得创建、经营一家公司都需要些什么。

_____

6. 杰克，有你的电话。

_____

7. 在贺卡上印有"新年快乐"的字样上面，有一条附言。

_____

8. 她没想到会让她在一大群听众前讲话。

_____

好句好段◈ | Writing Samples

If nobody loves you, be sure it is your own fault.

如果没有人爱你，肯定是你自己有问题。

Life is compared to voyage.

人生好比是航海。

本书所有练习题的参考答案（含阅读理解练习题解析及译文），请登录中国水利水电出版社网站 http://www.waterpub.com.cn/softdown/（下载中心）免费下载。

Lesson 19

阅读理解◈ | Reading Comprehension

✦✦（1）✦✦

"Which meal do we all need most, breakfast, lunch, or dinner?" Miss Baker asks. Boys and girls wave their hands in the air.

They know the answer!

"What do you think, Jim?" Miss Baker asks.

"Dinner!" he answers.

"Dinner is the big meal of the day." Says Miss Baker. "But I don't think it is the meal we need most."

Tom puts up his hand, "Is lunch the meal we need most?"

"No," says Miss Baker. "Breakfast is the meal we need most."

"Why is this so?"

"From night until morning is a long time to go without food." Says Ann.

"That's right," says Miss Baker. "We need food every morning". "What may happen to us if we have no breakfast?" The class have many answers to give.

"We may feel hungry."

"We may not feel like working."

"We may feel sick."

"Yes, you are right," says Miss Baker. "Now let's talk about what makes a good breakfast. Give me your answers. I will write them on the blackboard."

Now it's your turn!

The first word Miss Baker puts on the list is milk. What else do you think she puts on the list? Write your answers below.

▶ 阅读上面的短文，从每题所给的四个选项中，选出一个最佳答案。

1.　—We don't need _____ most, do we?

　　—Yes, we do.

　　A. dinner　　　　B. breakfast　　　C. lunch　　　·　D. supper

2.　_____ are discussing eating.

　　A. The mother and her children　　　B. Some of the boys and girls

　　C. The teacher and her pupils　　　　D. A group of friends

3.　Miss Baker thinks milk is _____ to make a good breakfast.

A. the first thing   B. all

C. no good   D. the only nice thing

4. Why is breakfast the most important meal?

     A. Because it is the first meal.

     B. Because there are usually a lot of nice things to eat at breakfast.

     C. Because people like to enjoy food before going to work.

     D. Because from night until morning is a long time to go without food, people need food most at this time.

5. We may not feel like working. This means that _____.

     A. we may not do the work well

     B. we may not feel strong enough to work

     C. we may not want to work

     D. we may not be able to work

The Fox and the Tiger

One day a tiger caught a fox in the forest. Before the tiger could eat him up, the fox cried out, "You cannot make a meal of me. Don't you know that I am king of the forest? If you eat me up, all the other animals of the forest will be very angry with you."

The tiger did not believe him. "How can such a small animal be king of the forest?" he asked himself.

"If you don't believe me," the fox said, "then take a walk with me in the forest. You can see whether or not the other animals are afraid of me."

The tiger agreed to do so and they set off together. The fox walked in front and the tiger followed behind. When the other animals saw the tiger coming, they ran off as fast as they could. This was what the fox expected.

"See for yourself, Mr. Tiger," the fox called out quickly. "All the other animals are afraid of me."

"Yes, yes," the tiger said, "You are quite right. You are really king of the forest." He then let the fox go.

▶ 阅读上面的短文，从每题所给的四个选项中，选出一个最佳答案。

1. Where did the tiger catch the fox?

     A. In the field.   B. In the forest.

     C. On a tree.   D. On the mountain.

2. What did the fox say when the tiger caught him?

     A. A small animal was the king of the forest.

     B. He was the king of the forest.

     C. The elephant was the king of the forest.

D. The tiger was the king of the forest.

3. Which of the following is right?

   A. The tiger ate the fox up.

   B. The tiger believed what the fox said.

   C. The tiger didn't believe what the fox said.

   D. The tiger was afraid of the fox when he heard what the fox said.

4. Which of the following is right?

   A. The fox walked first in front and then followed behind.

   B. The fox walked in front and the tiger followed behind.

   C. The tiger and the fox walked side by side.

   D. The tiger walked in front and the fox followed behind.

5. Why did all the other animals run away when they saw the tiger and the fox?

   A. Because they didn't want to play with them.

   B. Because they were afraid of the fox.

   C. Because they were afraid of the tiger.

   D. Because they were afraid of the tiger and the fox.

语言基本功
英汉翻译◈ | Translation Exercises

▶ 翻译下列句子

1. 带有人工智能的第五代计算机现在正在被开发和完善。

2. 物体受热时膨胀。

3. 他在回家路上让雨淋了，得了重感冒。

4. 匆忙间他忘了留下地址。

5. 想催她快点是没用的。

6. 人们匆匆忙忙地回家了。

7. 司机们声称此次罢工将一直持续到工资和工作条件问题达成全面协议的时候为止。

8. 昨天我从图书馆借了一本关于历史方面的书。

Lesson 20

阅读理解◈ | Reading Comprehension

✦✦ （1）✦✦
"Thank you" and "Excuse me"

American people like to say "Thank you" whenever others help them or say something kind to them. People of many other countries do so, too. It is a very good habit.

You should say "Thank you" when someone passes you the salt on the table, when someone walking ahead of you, keeps the door open to you, when someone says you have done your work well, or you have bought a nice thing, or your city is very beautiful.

"Thank you" is used not only between friends but also between parents and children and sisters, husbands and wives.

"Excuse me" is another short sentence they use. When you hear someone say so behind you, you know that somebody wants to walk past you without touching you.

It's not polite to break others while they are talking. If you want to speak to one of them, say "Excuse me" first, and then begin talking. You should also do so when you want to cough or make any unpleasant noise before others.

Let's all learn to say "Thank you" and "Excuse me".

▶ 根据短文内容，判断下列句子正（T）误（F）。

1. The American people like to say "Thank you" when they want to help others. ＿＿＿＿

2. When they hear others say that their city is very beautiful, they often say "No, not good." ＿＿＿＿

3. "Thank you" is said only between friends. ＿＿＿＿

4. When you want to cough before others, you should say "Excuse me" first. ＿＿＿＿

5. It is polite to say "Thank you" and "Excuse me" on proper occasions. ＿＿＿＿

✦✦ （2）✦✦
Meteorites

A meteorite is rock-like matter that has fallen to Earth from space. Most meteorites look just like Earth rock, but a meteorite the size of an orange weighs much more than an Earth rock of the same size. Meteorites can be as small as a peanut or as large as a truck.

Most meteorites are dark brown on the outside, and since most of them contain metal, they are silver or gray inside. Meteorites found on Earth are almost all metal inside and are known as iron meteorites, other meteorites are made of stone or a mixture of stone and metal. Iron meteorites are found more often because they are the least likely to break apart while falling through space or when hitting Earth.

Most stony Earth rocks do not contain metal. So if you think you have a meteorite, check it with a magnet. If the magnet sticks to the rock, you may have found a space rock that has fallen to Earth!

1. meteorite   *n.* 陨石
2. peanut   *n.* 花生
3. contain   *v.* 包含
4. magnet   *n.* 磁铁

▶阅读上面的短文，从每题所给的四个选项中，选出一个最佳答案。

1. Rock-like matter that has fallen to Earth from space is called a _____.
   A. rock   B. magnet
   C. metal   D. meteorite

2. A meteorite the size of an orange weighs _____ an Earth rock of the same size.
   A. much less than
   B. much more than
   C. almost the same as
   D. a little more than

3. The colour of a meteorite found on Earth is probably _____.
   A. brown
   B. black
   C. orange
   D. gray

4. We can use _____ to check if we have found a meteorite.
   A. an Earth rock
   B. a magnet
   C. a metal
   D. a special machine

5. Which of the following is wrong?
   A. Meteorites are not all of the same size.
   B. Most meteorites are dark on the outside.
   C. Most meteorites found are iron ones.
   D. The magnet don't stick to a meteorite.

英汉翻译◈ | Translation Exercises

▶ 翻译下列句子

1. 他离开了餐厅没有付账。
   _____

2. 它是有史以来最高大的建筑物之一，因此，人们从各个国家纷纷前来参观。
   _____

3. 现在囚犯们身穿蓝军装，肩扛步枪，在军营前大胆地来回走着。
   _____

4. 罢工定于星期二开始。
   _____

5. 有那么一个小男孩，他在逃学期间旅行了 1600 英里，从而使上述所有逃学的孩子们都相形见绌了。
   _____

6. 他们戴着墨镜，穿着旧衣裳，特别小心地怕别人认出他们。
   _____

7. 天黑下来的时候，她把手提箱当做小床，把两个孩子放了进去，又把所有能找到的衣服都盖在了孩子们身上。
   _____

8. 手术持续了 4 个多小时，非常难做，因为皮肤上覆盖着一层硬硬的树脂。
   _____

好句好段◈ | Writing Samples

✔ It was cold and dark out in the road and the rain did not stop for a minute. But in the little living-room of number 12 Castle Road it was nice and warm. Old Mr. White and his son, Herbert, played chess and Mrs. White sat and watched them. The old woman was happy because her husband and her son were good friends and they liked to be together. "Herbert's a good son," she thought. "We waited a long time for him and I was nearly forty when he was born, but we are a happy family." And old Mrs. White smiled.

外面的马路上又冷又黑，雨一直下个不停。但城堡路 12 号的一间小客厅里却很暖和。老怀特先生和他的儿子赫伯特在下象棋，怀特太太坐在一旁看着他们。老妇人因她的丈夫和儿子是好朋友并乐于在一起而高兴。"赫伯特是一个好孩子，我们等了很长时间才要到的孩子，他出生的时候我都快四十岁了，但我们的家庭很幸福。"老怀特太太想着想着，脸上露出了笑容。

Lesson 21

Reading Comprehension

✦✦ （1）✦✦

We Don't Need So Much Fancy Food

Steve and Wilda said goodbye to the last of their dinner guests. It had been a long evening, the host and hostess were tired.

"Did you notice what poor manners some of our guests had?" asked Steve.

"Yes." Replied Wilda. "They left a lot of food on their plates, why?"

"They all said they were on diets, but I think we were too fancy for them." Said Steve. "This was the first time, some have eaten with us. They don't realize that we serve full-course dinners when we entertain. Their meals are usually much simpler than ours. Well, they'll just have to get used to our way of doing things, everybody's different."

Steve started to clean dishes from the table. He wrapped up leftovers and put them into the refrigerator.

After a while, Wilda said, "Maybe, we will have to change. We don't want people to be uncomfortable when they come to visit. Maybe we don't need so much fancy food."

▶ 阅读上面的短文，从每题所给的四个选项中，选出一个最佳答案。

1. What does "on diets" mean in this passage? It means _____.
   A. eating limited food　　　　　　B. being not so hungry
   C. showing good manners　　　　　D. having different ways of eating

2. Why was so much food left that evening? Because _____.
   A. some of the guests were invited to their home for the first time
   B. the food was not the guests' favourite
   C. all the guests were on diets
   D. too much food was served

3. According to this passage too much food served to the guests will _____.
   A. show everybody is different
   B. show the host and hostess were tired
   C. make the guests feel uncomfortable
   D. make the guests get used to the host's way of doing thing

4. What did Steve and Wilda think of their guests?
   A. Their guests didn't understand their hospitality.

B. Their guests left too late.

C. Their guests had bad manners.

D. Their guests were quite satisfied.

5.　What can we conclude from this passage?

A. Much food served to the guests can show the host and the hostess are fancy.

B. Since you can afford, you should serve your guests as much food as possible.

C. It's good manners to leave nothing on the plate when invited to a dinner.

D. Everyone should change his way of doing things to a dinner.

✦✦（2）✦✦

How to Study

A good way to pass an exam is to work hard every day in the year. You may fail in an exam if you are lazy and don't study for most of the year and then only work hard for a few days before the exam.

If you are studying to take an English exam, do not only learn the rules of grammar, but try to read stories in English and speak in English whenever you can. Then you will learn and know more English words.

A few days before the exam you should start going to bed early. Do not stay up late at night studying and learning things at the last moment. Before you start the exam, read over the question paper carefully. Try to understand the exact meaning of each question before you pick up your pen to write. When you have finished your exam, read over your answers, correct the mistakes if there are any and make sure that you have not missed out on anything.

▶阅读上面的短文，从每题所给的四个选项中，选出一个最佳答案。

1.　Learning the rules of grammar _____ to pass an English exam.

A. is enough　　　　　　　　　B. is not enough

C. is not necessary　　　　　　D. is of no use

2.　It is helpful _____.

(1) to read stories in English

(2) to learn the rules of grammar

(3) to speak as much English as possible

A. Only (1) is not true.　　　　B. Only (2) is not true.

C. Only (3) is not true.　　　　D. All of the three are true.

3.　The underlined phrase "missed out on" at the end of the passage means _____.

A. forgot　　　　　　　　　　B. thought hard

C. given the wrong answer　　　D. hadn't had enough time to do

4.　The underlined word "whenever" in the second paragraph means _____.

A. at any time　　　　　　　　B. what time

C. for ever　　　　　　　　　　D. unless

5. How can you do well in an exam?

    (1) To work hard every day in the year.

    (2) To start going to bed early a few days before the exam.

    (3) To be careful in doing the questions.

    (4) To read over your answers before you hand in your paper.

    A. You should do (1) and (2).   B. You should do (2) and (3).

    C. You should do (3) and (4).   D. You should do all the things.

语言基本功
英汉翻译◈ | Translation Exercises

▶ 翻译下列句子

1. 日夜都可以听见从头顶飞过的飞机声。

2. 那可怕的噪音是什么？

3. 我告诉你这件事会干好的。

4. 飞机正在逐渐把我逼疯。

5. 机场是许多年前建的，但由于某种原因当时未能启用。

6. 有时我觉得这房子就要被一架飞过的飞机撞倒。

7. 大家都说我肯定是疯了，也许他们说的是对的。

8. 我找不到自己的包。有人偷走了。

语言基本功
好句好段◈ | Writing Samples

The greatest talkers are always the least doers.

言语的巨人往往是行动的侏儒。

To marry a woman for her beauty is like buying a house for its paint.

由于面貌美丽而娶妻，犹如由于油漆漂亮而买屋。

A road of a thousand miles begins with one step.

千里之行始于足下。

本书所有练习题的参考答案（含阅读理解练习题解析及译文），请登录中国水利水电出版社网站
http://www.waterpub.com.cn/softdown/（下载中心）免费下载。

Lesson 22

Reading Comprehension

✦✦ （1） ✦✦

It was on a foggy day in the autumn of 1938, when I arrived in London with Aunt Huang and her husband who had brought me to England all the way from my hometown Nanjing.

They left their luggage at their flat, and they took me together with my small suitcase to my parents' flat. But the neighbours told us that my parents had moved away long ago, and no one knew their address.

Good Heavens! What should we do? The only thing to be done was to inquire of the Chinese Embassy. When we got there, we were told that my parents must still be somewhere in London as my father had held an exhibition of traditional Chinese painting in the West End not very long ago.

1.　on a foggy day　在一个大雾天
2.　arrive in　到达（后边接一个大地点）
　　arrive at　到达（后边接一个小地点）
3.　bring sb. to someplace　带某人到某地
4.　move away　搬迁，移走
5.　Good Heavens! 天哪！上帝呀！

▶阅读上面的短文，从每题所给的四个选项中，选出一个最佳答案。

1.　The story happened _____.
　　A. in autumn in NanJing
　　C. in 1938 in NanJing
　　B. in autumn in London
　　D. in 1938 in China
2.　Aunt Huang helped the writer to _____.
　　A. leave his hometown
　　C. look for his parents
　　B. study
　　D. go to England
3.　The neighbours told the writer _____.
　　A. his parents in London
　　B. his parents moved away
　　C. his parents in the West End
　　D. his parents in Chinese Embassy
4.　_____ knew the writer's parents' new address.

A. Everyone   B. Aunt Huang

C. The neighbours   D. No one

5.   From the story we know _____.

A. the writer liked painting

B. Aunt Huang was kind-hearted

C. his parents liked London

D. Aunt Huang's husband left London

✦✦ （2）✦✦
The Grasshopper

A grasshopper spent the summer hopping about in the sun and singing to his heart's content. One day, an ant went hurrying by, looking very hot and weary. "Why are you working on such a lovely day?" said the grasshopper. "I'm collecting food for the winter," said the ant, "and I suggest you do the same." And off she went, helping the other ants to carry food to their store. The grasshopper carried on hopping and singing. When winter came, the ground was covered with snow. The grasshopper had no food and was hungry. So he went to the ants and asked for food. "What did you do all summer when we were working to collect our food?" said one of the ants. "I was busy hopping and singing," said the grasshopper. "Well," said the ant, "if you hop and sing all summer, and do no work, then you must starve in the winter."

_____

1.   grasshopper   *n.* 蚱蜢

2.   hop   *v.* 单脚跳

3.   content   *n.* 满意

4.   weary   *adj.* 疲倦

5.   suggest   *v.* 建议

6.   store   *n.* 储藏室

7.   starve   *v.* 挨饿

▶ 阅读上面的短文，根据其内容，在每个空白处填写一个适当的词，完成句子，要求必须使用本文中的词汇。

1.   While playing football, Tom's left foot was hurt and had to _____ home.

2.   —Why do you look so _____?

     —I stayed up late yesterday evening.

3.   Because of the drought, many people _____ to death here and there.

4.   The boy studied very hard so that his parents would show their _____ to him.

5.   After the heavy rain, we found it was hard to _____ the fruit on the hills in a short time.

英汉翻译 ◈ | Translation Exercises

▶ 翻译下列句子

1. 社会存在决定社会意识。

_____

2. 那使我决意干这件事。

_____

3. 此消息使他决定不再拖延。

_____

4. 我以为你回家了。

_____

5. 上周我听了一场音乐会，这是我听过的最好的音乐会。

_____

6. 昨天下午等所有的学生交了卷我才离开。

_____

7. 我们还没有找到座位电影就开始了。

_____

8. 今天一早他来学校的时候，一辆小汽车撞了一位老大爷。他送老人去医院了。

_____

好句好段 ◈ | Writing Samples

☑ She stopped and looked at me. I wanted to run away but Mr. Nowell's servant stood in front of the door. Then my mother laughed. 'Jennet Device, witch's daughter! You hate us, I know that. Well, it doesn't matter because you're right: you are different. You're my daughter, but you're not the daughter of my husband. Your father was a rich man, but he never gave me money. A witch's child, he called you. And when you were born he never came near me again. Jack Robinson learnt the truth about your father. He told the villagers of Barley and they called me a bad woman, but they didn't call your father a bad man! Nobody in Barley gave me food again, because of Jack Robinson. I hated him, and so I killed him!'

她停下来看着我。我想跑开，可是诺埃尔先生的佣人正站在门前。妈妈哈哈大笑着说："詹妮特·迪瓦斯，巫师的女儿！我知道，你恨我们。嗯，这没什么，因为你是对的：你是不一样。你是我女儿，但你不是我丈夫的女儿。你的父亲是个有钱人，可他从来不给我钱。他管你叫巫师的孩子。从你一出生，他就再也没靠近过我。杰克·鲁滨逊得知你亲生父亲的真相后，便告诉了巴利村的居民们。他们说我是坏女人，却不说你父亲是一个坏男人！从那以后，在巴利村，再也没有人给我吃的了，这都是杰克·鲁滨逊造成的。我恨他，所以我杀了他！"

Lesson 23

Reading Comprehension

✦✦ (1) ✦✦

Trick with Numbers

It is possible to do many simple tricks with numbers. Here is one trick. It has several separate steps.

First, write down your house number. For example, if your address is 73 Lemon Street, you would write down 73. After you write down your house address, next double it. Then add five to this doubled number. For example, if your address is 73 and you double it, you would get 146. Then, if you add five, you'd get 151.

Then multiply this number by 50. In our example here, you'll get 7,550. The next step is to add your age to this total. For example, if you're 26 years old, you should add 26 to this total. In our example here, the result would be 7,576.

After that you have to add the number of days in a year, which is 365. In our example here, 365 added to 7,576 is 7,941.

The final step is this: Subtract 615 from the number that you have. Take away 615 from the total. In our example, 7,941 minus 615 is 7,326.

The result here-7,326-is the trick. The first part of the number is the address and the last part of the number is the age of the person. That is , 73 is the address that we started with, and 26 is the age that we used.

---

1. separate   *adj.* 个别的，单独的
2. total   *n.* 总数，合计
3. subtract   *v.* 减去，减

▶阅读上面的短文，从每题所给的四个选项中，选出一个最佳答案。

1. Which is right?

   A. Every one does tricks.

   B. There're several steps about the number trick.

   C. This text is about an interesting problem.

   D. The final step isn't subtracting.

2. There are _____ steps in the trick?

   A. 5   B. 6

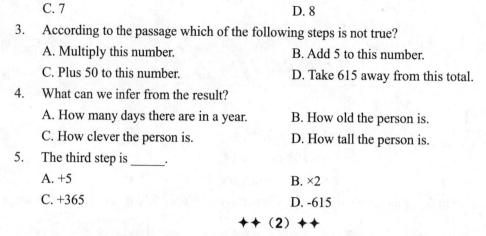

C. 7   D. 8

3. According to the passage which of the following steps is not true?

    A. Multiply this number.   B. Add 5 to this number.

    C. Plus 50 to this number.   D. Take 615 away from this total.

4. What can we infer from the result?

    A. How many days there are in a year.   B. How old the person is.

    C. How clever the person is.   D. How tall the person is.

5. The third step is _____.

    A. +5   B. ×2

    C. +365   D. -615

◆◆ （2）◆◆

It was raining heavily as I was walking up the hill towards the station at six o'clock on a Saturday morning. At this early hour there wasn't much traffic and there weren't many people. Just as I was crossing the road near the top of the hill, a car came round the corner. It was traveling very fast and the driver was having difficulty in controlling it. It hit a lamp post and turned over.

I ran to the car to help the driver at once. He was badly hurt and there was a lot of blood on his face. A young woman hurried into the station and phoned for an ambulance while I took care of the driver. Many people came to see what happened, and there was nothing we could do. A policeman arrived a few minutes later and asked me a lot of questions about the accident. After a while the ambulance arrived and took the young man away to the hospital.

On Monday morning I went to the hospital to see the man. The doctor told me that he was better now. And he would leave hospital after a few days' rest.

▶ 阅读上面的短文，从每题所给的四个选项中，选出一个最佳答案。

1. Where did the accident happen?

    A. Near the school.   B. Near the top of the hill.

    C. In the school.   D. Near the hospital.

2. What happened to the driver?

    A. He couldn't control the car.   B. His car hit a lamp post.

    C. His car turned over.   D. A, B and C.

3. Who hurried to the station to ask for an ambulance?

    A. The writer.   B. A policeman.

    C. Some people.   D. A young woman.

4. What did the policeman do?

    A. He took the driver away.

    B. He sent the driver to the hospital.

    C. He asked the writer a lot of questions.

D. He phoned for an ambulance.

5. The driver wasn't dead, was he?
    A. Yes, he wasn't   B. No, he was.
    C. Yes, he was.   D. No, he wasn't.

Translation Exercises

▶ 翻译下列句子

1. 这栋房子里有许多大房间，还有一个漂亮的花园。

    _____

2. 我们现在住在乡间的一栋漂亮的新住宅里。

    _____

3. 她说她明年要来英格兰。

    _____

4. 所有凑钱买此礼物的人都把自己的名字签在一本大签名簿上，签名簿被送到校长的家里。

    _____

5. 他们俩全都没来得及意识到究竟发生了什么事情，就被猛地抛入了海里。

    _____

6. 在凶杀发生的时候，我正坐在 8 点钟开往伦敦的火车上。

    _____

7. 如果不是因为土壤下面有一层坚硬的岩石，他们的营救工作仅用几个小时就可以完成了。

    _____

8. 虽然他们的食物和饮料都快消耗尽了，但这些人的心情很好，坚信他们很快就会出去。

    _____

Writing Samples

If one desires to succeed in anything, he must pay the price.
如果想做成点事，就得付出代价。
Life is half spent before we know what it is.
等到认识人生，已经一半过去了。
No longer pipe, no longer dance.
运不逢时，事不得意。

本书所有练习题的参考答案（含阅读理解练习题解析及译文），请登录中国水利水电出版社网站 http://www.waterpub.com.cn/softdown/（下载中心）免费下载。

Lesson 24

✦✦（1）✦✦

General Pershing was a great American officer. He was in the American army, and fought in Europe in the first World War.

After he died, some people in his hometown wanted to remember him, so they put up a big statue of him on a horse.

There was a school near the statue, and some of the boys went there every day on their way to school and again on their way home. After a few months, some of them began to say "Good morning, Pershing" whenever they reached the statue, and soon all the boys at the school were doing this.

One Saturday, one of the smallest of these boys was walking to the shops with his parents when he went to the statue. He said, "Good morning, Pershing" to it, but then he stopped and said to his parents, "I like Pershing very much, Mum and Dad, but who's that strange man on his back?"

---

1. in the Army 在军队里
2. the first World War 第一次世界大战
3. put up 建立

▶阅读上面的短文，从每题所给的四个选项中，选出一个最佳答案。

1. General Pershing fought in Europe, but he was from _____.
    A. Europe   B. England
    C. America   D. Japan

2. Some people put up a statue of _____.
    A. him   B. General Washington
    C. horse   D. General Pershing

3. The statue was _____ the school.
    A. not far from   B. behind
    C. in   D. very far from

4. The boys went there every day _____.
    A. on their way to school   B. on their way home
    C. both A and B   D. after class

5. The boy thought that _____ was Pershing.

    A. the shop   B. the stone

    C. the house   D. the horse

✦✦ (2) ✦✦

Mark Twain, the famous American writer, liked to play jokes on others. But once a joke was played on him. One day Mark Twain was invited to give a talk in the evening. At lunch he met a young man, one of his friends. The young man said that he had an uncle with him. He told Mark Twain that his uncle never laughed or smiled, and that nobody was able to make his uncle smile or laugh. "You bring your uncle to my talk tonight," said Mark Twain. "I'm sure I make him laugh."

That evening the young man and his uncle sat in the front. Mark Twain began to speak. He told several funny stories. This made the people in the room laugh. But the young man's uncle never even smiled. Mark Twain told more stories, but the old man still kept quiet. Finally he stopped. He was tired and disappointed.

Some days later, Mark Twain told another friend of his about what had happened "Oh," said his friend, "I know that old man. He has been deaf for years."

---

1. deaf   *adj.* 聋的

2. joke   *n.* 玩笑；笑话

3. disappoint   *v.* 使失望

4. a joke was played on him 他被开了个玩笑

5. never 从不；ever 曾经

▶ 阅读上面的短文，从每题所给的四个选项中，选出一个最佳答案。

1. Mark Twain _____.

    A. didn't like to play jokes on others   B. liked people to play jokes on him

    C. liked to play jokes on himself   D. liked to play jokes on others

2. One day Mark Twain would _____.

    A. give a talk in the evening   B. listen to a talk in the evening

    C. play a joke in the afternoon   D. play a joke in the evening

3. Mark Twain's funny stories made _____.

    A. all the people in the room laugh   B. nearly all the people in the room laugh

    C. no people in the room laugh   D. the young man's uncle laugh

4. Why didn't the young man's uncle laugh?

    A. Because he didn't hear what Mark Twain said.

    B. Because he was a blind man.

    C. Because he was a fool.

    D. Because he was too old to laugh.

5. Who played a joke on Mark Twain?

A. His another friend.　　　　　　B. His young friend.

C. The people in the room.　　　　D. The young man's uncle.

英汉翻译◈ Translation Exercises

▶ 翻译下列句子

1. 中国人民为他们在经济上取得的成就而自豪，这是符合情理的。

   _____

2. 经济增长速度受到市场混乱的影响，这是显而易见的。

   _____

3. 政府试图控制全国范围内的通货膨胀，但没有成功。

   _____

4. 据报道，警察已经在最近三天逮捕了几名嫌疑犯。

   _____

5. 他扔掉旧的报纸了吗？

   _____

6. 我走进饭店经理的办公室，坐了下来。

   _____

7. 我刚刚丢了 50 英镑，感到非常烦恼。

   _____

8. 这是我在这位先生的房门外捡到的。

   _____

好句好段◈ Writing Samples

☑ When I heard that, I nearly fell through the floor, but it was a big piece of luck. It was easy for me to be Tom Sawyer because Tom was my best friend. He and his brother Sid lived with their Aunt Polly up in St. Petersburg, and I knew all about them. Now I learnt that Aunt Polly had a sister, who was Mrs Phelps. She and her husband were Tom's Aunt Sally and Uncle Silas. And Tom was coming down south by boat to stay with them for a bit.

　　当我听到这话时，我差点儿没掉进地板缝里去，不过，这可是太幸运了。冒充汤姆·索亚对我来说是件容易事，因为汤姆是我最好的朋友。他和他的弟弟锡德和他们的波莉姨妈一起住在圣彼得斯堡，他们的事我都知道。现在，我知道了波莉姨妈有一个妹妹，她是斐尔普斯太太。她和她的丈夫是汤姆的萨莉姨妈和赛拉斯姨夫。汤姆要乘船南下和他们小住一阵。

Lesson 25

阅读理解◇ Reading Comprehension

✦✦（1）✦✦

If you do not use your arms or your legs for some time, they become weak, when you start using them again, they slowly become strong again. Everybody knows that. Yet many people do not seem to know that memory works in the same way.

When someone says that he has a good memory, he really means that he keeps his memory in practice by using it. When someone else says that his memory is poor, he really means that he does not give it enough chance to become strong.

If a friend says that his arms and legs are weak, we know that it is his own fault. But if he tells us that he has a poor memory, many of us think that his parents are to blame, and few of us know that it is just his own fault.

Have you ever found that some people can't read or write but usually they have better memories? This is because they cannot read or write and they have to remember things; they cannot write them down in a little notebook. They have to remember days, names, songs and stories. So their memory is the whole time being exercised.

So if you want to have a good memory, learn from the people: practise remembering.

▶ 阅读上面的短文，从每题所给的四个选项中，选出一个最佳答案。

1. The main reason for one's poor memory is that _____.

   A. his father or mother may have a poor memory

   B. he does not use his arms or legs for some time

   C. his memory is not often used

   D. he can't read or write

2. Which of the following is NOT true?

   A. Your memory works in the same way as your arms or legs.

   B. Your memory will become weak if you don't give it enough chance for practice.

   C. Don't learn how to read and write if you want to have a better memory.

   D. A good memory comes from more practice.

3. Which is the best title for this passage?

   A. Don't Stop Using Your Arms or Legs.

   B. How to Have a Good Memory.

   C. Strong Arms and Good Memory.

D. Learn from the People.

How to Learn a Foreign Language?

Today we want to tell you something about learning a language, and English is particular. Students used to learn languages by memorizing grammar rules and words lists. Some unlucky ones still try to learn this way. It is almost impossible to become skillful in speaking a language unless you use it and all modern methods are based on this theory. The course you are going to study is audiovisual: this means it tries to teach you by matching sounds and pictures. The pictures help you to understand, remember and use the language you are learning. These methods can be used in the classroom or in a language laboratory where students practise something that has been recorded on the tape.

English is the official language used in Australia, Canada, the British Isles, New Zealand, South Africa and United States of America. But it is also becoming international and is the principal second language throughout the world. Perhaps through English we will be able to understand each other better. We'll be able to communicate, whatever part of the world we come from.

---

1. particular   *adj.* 特别的
2. audiovisual   *adj.* 视听的
3. principal   *adj.* 主要的

▶阅读上面的短文，从每题所给的四个选项中，选出一个最佳答案。

1. In the past the students usually learned a language by _____.

   A. keeping grammar rules and words in mind

   B. reading and reciting

   C. trying a new method—audiovisual

   D. memorizing the modern methods

2. You can't learn to speak a language well unless you _____.

   A. still try to learn this way   B. memorize the grammar rules

   C. learn it in the audiovisual way   D. use it all the time

3. You can use the audiovisual method by _____.

   A. seeing and speaking   B. matching sounds with pictures

   C. using a language laboratory   D. seeing the pictures and remembering drills

4. The English Language is _____.

   A. mainly spoken in six countries

   B. the official international language

   C. the main second language in the world

   D. the official principal language only in the USA

5. The writer wants to tell us _____.

    A. how to learn a foreign language   B. the importance of learning English

    C. English is widely used in the world   D. something about English

语言基本功
英汉翻译◈ | Translation Exercises

▶ 翻译下列句子

1. 这只箱子装有肥皂。

_____

2. 一加仑等于 8 品脱。

_____

3. 因为吃得太多，他的体重增加了许多。

_____

4. 作为一个深受尊敬的市长，他把自己的一生都献给了改善市民福利的事业。

_____

5. 那家钢铁厂今年生产了四百万吨钢材，创历史最高记录。

_____

6. 那家贸易公司有意招聘他，而他对那家公司却没有兴趣。

_____

7. 他梦见他在海上。

_____

8. 他不该梦想做这样的事。

_____

语言基本功
好句好段◈ | Writing Samples

☑ De Gautet, the Frenchman, was with the other two, and the three men were standing there with their revolvers ready. With a shout, I ran at them as hard as I could. They tried to shoot me, but the bullets hit the table. The next second the table knocked them to the ground and we all fell on top of each other. Quickly, I picked myself up and ran for my life through the trees. I could hear them coming after me. Was Antoinette right? Was there really a ladder by the wall? I reached the end of the garden. The ladder was there! In a minute I was up it and over the wall.

德·高蒂特，那个法国人和另外两个人在一起。他们三个端着上了膛的左轮手枪站在那儿。我大叫一声，用尽全力向他们冲去。他们向我开枪，但是子弹打在了桌子上。紧接着桌子砸倒了他们。我们都倒下了，你压着我，我压着你。很快我爬了起来，穿过树林飞快逃走。我听见他们追了起来。安冬纳特没说错吧？墙上真有一个梯子吗？我跑到了花园的尽头，梯子真的在那里！一刹那间我就登上了梯子越过了围墙。

Lesson 26

阅读理解◈ | Reading Comprehension

✦✦（1）✦✦

Compound Words

Homesick is a compound word made up of HOME and SICK. You know what each word means on its own, of course. But think about what the words mean when they are used together. Homesick means SICK FOR HOME.

Now think for a minute about SEASICK. If you change the word home in the definition to the word sea, would the definition fit SEASICK? Does seasick mean SICK FOR SEA? It means something quite different. Seasick means SICK BY THE MOVEMENT ON THE SEA. When you are homesick, the only place you want to be is at home. When you are seasick, the last place you want to be is at sea.

Have you ever heard of a person being heartsick? Heartsick doesn't mean that something is wrong with a person's heart. People are heartsick when they are hurt deep inside and when they feel as if their hearts are broken.

But, on the other hand, we have such compound words as handshake and handbag. Perhaps you may write definitions for them and knowing something like this must be helpful in your English study.

▶阅读上面的短文，从每题所给的四个选项中，选出一个最佳答案。

1. The word SEASICK means "_____".

   A. to want very much to go to the sea   B. what has nothing to do with the sea

   C. to be sick because of the sea   D. that the sea is terrible

2. When we say a person is heartsick, we mean that _____.

   A. his heart is broken   B. his heart needs testing

   C. he's sorry at heart   D. he's terribly disappointed and sad

3. "The last place you want to be" is _____.

   A. where you want to be most   B. where you want to be least

   C. where you go the last   D. the last place you go to

4. The definitions of handbag and handshake are _____.

   A. easy to know   B. difficult to know

   C. impossible to learn   D. unnecessary to learn

5. The writer wanted to tell us that _____.

A. there are many compound words in English

B. the building of compound words is interesting

C. the definitions of some compound words are hard to guess

D. not all the compound words are what they seem to be

✦✦ （2） ✦✦

Once, when Dick was a boy, his mother went out to work in the back garden. Before she went, she said to him, "Dick, while I'm away, you stay near the door, and watch it all the time." She said this because there were a lot of thieves in their town.

Dick sat down beside the door. After an hour, one of his uncles came, He said to Dick, "Where's your mother, Dick?"

"In the back garden," answered Dick. "Well," said the uncle, "We'll visit your new house this evening. Go and tell her."

His uncle then went away, and Dick began to worry. "Mother told me to watch the door all the time and the uncle asked me to go and tell mother."

He thought and thought, then at last he had an idea. He shook the door hard and tried every way, used all the things he could get to move it, and at last he pulled the door down. He put it on his back and went to his mother with it.

▶阅读上面的短文，从每题所给的四个选项中，选出一个最佳答案。

1. Dick's mother _____ in the garden while one of Dick's uncles came.

   A. worked   B. taught Dick

   C. went out   D. just went out

2. Dick's mother asked Dick _____ because there were _____ thieves in their town.

   A. to stay at home, few   B. to stay near the door, many

   C. to watch the door, much   D. to keep the door safe, much

3. His uncle asked Dick _____.

   A. to go with him together

   B. to go with the door

   C. to give him a cup of tea

   D. to go and tell his mother they were going to visit his house

4. He used all the things to _____.

   A. break the door   B. move the door

   C. move the house   D. break the house

5. From this passage we know Dick _____.

   A. did a good thing   B. was very clever

   C. his uncle was a fool   D. wasn't bright

▶ **翻译下列句子**

1. 我曾碰到过的问题是：不是氧气设备出故障，就是引擎出故障。

   _____

2. 我们来修订安全规则和卫生规则吧。

   _____

3. 人们利用科学知识去了解自然，改造自然。

   _____

4. 她击琴键用力过猛，结果两根琴弦断了。

   _____

5. 孩子们真希望每天都去动物园。

   _____

6. 即使在这个时候他还在写作业。

   _____

7. 有很多人装成很懂艺术的样子。

   _____

8. 我妹妹只有 7 岁，但她总能说出我的画是好还是坏。

   _____

语言基本功
好句好段◈ | Writing Samples

✓ The food, the room, the fire all disappeared, and they were standing outside in the cold, snowy streets on Christmas morning. Although the sky was grey and the streets were dirty, the people looked surprisingly cheerful, as they hurried to the bakers' shops with their Christmas dinners, all ready for cooking. The spirit seemed specially interested in poor people. He stood with Scrooge in a baker's doorway and held his torch over the dinners as they were carried past him. Sometimes, when he saw people pushing each other or getting angry, he lifted his torch over their heads, and immediately they became kinder, or stopped arguing, "Because it's Christmas," they told each other.

圣诞节一早，食品、房间、炉火都消失了。他们正站在冰天雪地的户外。虽然天空灰蒙蒙的，街上也很脏，但当人们拿着他们的圣诞晚餐匆匆赶往面包房准备烤制的时候，他们看上去都出奇的欢喜。幽灵似乎对穷人特别感兴趣。他和斯克罗吉一同站在面包房的门口，当晚餐从他面前经过时，他把火把照在上面。有时当他看见人们相互拥挤或发脾气时，他把火把举在他们的头上，他们立刻就会变得温顺或停止争吵，"因为今天是圣诞节，"他们彼此告诫着。

Lesson 27

阅读理解◇ | Reading Comprehension

◆◆ (1) ◆◆
Peanut Butter

The first peanut butter was made in 1880. It was given as a medicine to a sick man. This man lived in America. He could not eat food, because his stomach would not let him. He was becoming very weak and his doctor was afraid that he would die unless he could eat something.

At last the doctor took some roasted peanuts and asked a nurse to grind peanuts made a thick, dry sort of paste. The doctor added some peanut oil to make it even softer. The sick man was pleased and enjoyed the "medicine". He called it "peanut butter".

Some years later, workers in a factory were experimenting with peanut products. Someone remembered that a doctor had used crushed peanuts to cure a sick man. The workers tried making a paste that could be spread to bread. It was sold in food stores and gradually became popular.

---

1. be made 被制成
2. as 作为
3. unless 除非
4. some years later 一些年后
5. cure a sick man 治愈了一个人
6. spread to bread 抹到面包上

▶ 阅读上面的短文，从每题所给的三个选项中，选出一个最佳答案。

1. Peanut butter was first made less than a hundred years ago.
    A. Right   B. Wrong   C. Doesn't say
2. Peanut butter was first made for the sick doctor.
    A. Right   B. Wrong   C. Doesn't say
3. The person liked the "medicine" very much.
    A. Right   B. Wrong   C. Doesn't say
4. The first country in which peanut butter was sold was America.
    A. Right   B. Wrong   C. Doesn't say
5. People like peanut butter because it tastes good and can be spread on bread.
    A. Right   B. Wrong   C. Doesn't say

2

There are thousands of different languages in the world. Everyone seems to think that his native language is the most important one, as it is their first language. For many people it is even their only language all their lives. But English is the world's most widely used language.

As a native language, English is spoken by nearly three hundred million people: in U.S.A., England, Australia and some other countries. For people in India and many other countries, English is often necessary for business, education, information and other activities. So English is the second language there.

As a foreign language, no other language is more widely studied or used than English. We use it to listen to the radio, to read books or to travel. It is also one of the working languages in the United Nations and is more used than the others.

---

1.   thousands of 成千的，用法类似 hundred
2.   the most important 最重要的
3.   序数词，前面加 the。如：
     the first 第一；the second 第二
4.   more...than... ……多于……

▶阅读上面的短文，从每题所给的四个选项中，选出一个最佳答案。

1.   The native language is a person's _____ language.
     A. first   B. only   C. one   D. foreign
2.   People in _____ use English as their second language.
     A. U.S.   B. India   C. China   D. Australia
3.   People in China use English as a _____ language.
     A. first   B. second   C. foreign   D. native
4.   English is _____ useful working language in the United Nations.
     A. much   B. more   C. the more   D. the most
5.   English is used in _____ ways by people all over the world.
     A. one   B. two   C. three   D. four

语言基本功
英汉翻译◈ | Translation Exercises

▶翻译下列句子
1.   我认为我们这个周末应该去露营。

     _____

2.   傍晚时分，孩子们在田野中搭起了帐篷。

     _____

3. 他们全都饿了，饭菜散发出阵阵香味。

_____

4. 外面一定在下雨。

_____

5. 她说迪克不会那样说的。

_____

6. 我宁愿妈妈不坐飞机去。

_____

7. 她可能明天动身。

_____

8. 这只瓶能装多少？

_____

Writing Samples

☑ It was the strangest game of croquet in Alice's life! The balls were hedgehogs, and the mallets were flamingoes. And the hoops were made by soldiers, who turned over and stood on their hands and feet. Alice held her flamingo's body under her arm, but the flamingo turned its long neck first this way and then that way. At last, Alice was ready to hit the ball with the flamingo's head. But by then, the hedgehog was tired of waiting and was walking away across the croquet-ground. And when both the flamingo and the hedgehog were ready, there was no hoop! The soldiers too were always getting up and walking away. It really was a very difficult game, Alice thought.

这是爱丽丝见过的最奇怪的槌球游戏！球是刺猬，木槌是红鹤。弓形小球门由士兵组成，他们转过身去，红鹤腿着地站着。爱丽丝用胳膊抱着红鹤的身体，但红鹤把脖子一会儿转到这边，一会儿转到那边。最后，爱丽丝准备好用红鹤的头去击球。可正在这时，刺猬等烦了，穿过槌球场走开了。当红鹤和刺猬都准备好时，却没有球门！士兵们也总是站起来走开。这场球可是太难打了，爱丽丝想。

Lesson 28

语言基本功
阅读理解◈ Reading Comprehension

✦✦ （1） ✦✦

Mr. Howe worked in an office. He studied the old things and sometimes bought some for himself. Eight years ago, when he was sixty-five, he retired. He needn't worry about food or clothes. He was busy before, but now he has enough time to rest. He loves playing ping-pong and spends most of his time on the game. He was seldom ill before. But one day he felt something wrong with him. And he went to a hospital. The doctors looked him over carefully and did their best to save him but he felt worse and worse. So he made his son send for a witch.

"Do the people in heaven play ping-pong, Madam?" asked Mr. Howe.

"I'm sorry I don't know, Sir," answered the witch, "Let me go and ask about it for you."

That evening the witch came and said, "I've just been to heaven, Mr. Howe, I brought two pieces of news to you. One is good and the other is bad."

"Tell me the good news first, please."

"Most of the people in heaven play ping-pong," said the witch. "And you'll have a game there the day after tomorrow!"

1.　in an office 冠词 a、an 都代表数量上的

　　a＋辅音：a book, a pen；an＋元音：an apple, an egg

2.　spend...on 在某方面花费钱/时间。如：

　　spend money on books；spend time on the game

3.　look over 检查

4.　do one's best to do sth. 尽某人最大努力去做某事

5.　send for 派某人去请某人

6.　have just been to 去过某地已回来，现在完成时

　　have gone to 去了某地还没回来

▶根据短文内容，判断下列句子正（T）误（F）。

1.　Mr. Howe is seventy-three now.　　　　————

2.　Mr. Howe has little money, so he is poor.　　　　————

3.　As he rested very well all the time, Mr. Howe had a good body.　　　　————

4.　The doctors didn't do their best to save Mr. Howe, so he felt worse and worse.　　　　————

5.　The bad news meant Mr. Howe would die in two days.　　　　————

✦✦ (2) ✦✦

If you are in a town in a western country, you'll often see people walking with their dogs. It is still true that a dog is the most useful animal in the world, but the reason why one keeps a dog has changed. Once a man met a dog and wanted it to help him in the fight against other animals, and he found that the dog listened to him. Later people used dogs for the hunting of other animals, and the dogs didn't eat what they got until their master agreed. So dogs were used for driving sheep and guarding chickens. But now people in the towns and cities do not need dogs to fight other animals. Of course they keep them to frighten thieves, but the most important reason is that people feel lonely in the city. For a child, a dog is the best friend when he has no friends to play with. For a young wife, a dog is her child when she doesn't have her own. For old people, a dog is also a child when their real children have grown up and left. Now people do not have to use a dog, but they keep it as a friend, just like a member of the family.

---

1. a western country 西方国家
2. walk with sb. 和某人散步
3. in the fight 在战事中
4. be used for 被用来
5. for a child 对孩子来说
6. no friends to play 没朋友一起玩
7. as a friend 作为一个朋友
8. just like a member of the family 就像家庭中的一员

▶ 阅读上面的短文，从每题所给的四个选项中，选出一个最佳答案。

1. _____ are more useful than a dog in the world.
    A. Many animals   B. A few animals
    C. Some animals   D. No other animals
2. Now people in cities keep dogs because dogs _____.
    A. fight other animals   B. are like their friends
    C. can hunt animals   D. are afraid of thieves
3. A dog can be _____.
    A. a child's friend only   B. a young woman's son
    C. all people's real children   D. everybody's friend
4. So a dog will _____ in a family in the future.
    A. always be used   B. not be useful
    C. still fight   D. be a good friend

英汉翻译 ◈ Translation Exercises

▶ 翻译下列句子

1. 参加那些讲座使他受益匪浅。

_____

2. 琳达劝我重新考虑自己的决定。

_____

3. 我猜想她不在城里。

_____

4. 我想不出送他什么做礼物好。

_____

5. 请告诉我怎么续护照。

_____

6. 水面上波涛起伏。

_____

7. 你不必费事对此作出回答。

_____

8. 什么事使你苦恼?

_____

好句好段 ◈ Writing Samples

☑ Buck lived in Mr. Miller's big house in the sunny Santa Clara valley. There were large gardens and fields of fruit trees around the house, and a river nearby. In a big place like this, of course, there were many dogs. There were house dogs and farm dogs, but they were not important. Buck was chief dog; he was born here, and this was his place. He was four years old and weighed sixty kilos. He went swimming with Mr Miller's sons, and walking with his daughters. He carried the grandchildren on his back, and he sat at Mr. Miller's feet in front of the fire in winter.

在阳光明媚的桑塔·克拉拉山谷中,巴克就住在米勒先生的大房子里。房子的周围是开阔的庄园和种满了果树的田野。一条小河从附近流过。这样一个辽阔的地方,是狗的乐园。这里有看门狗和牧羊犬,但他们是无足轻重的。巴克是真正的狗王,他生于斯长于斯,这儿简直就是他的天下。他4岁,体重60公斤。他同米勒先生的儿子一起游泳,也陪着他的女儿们一起去散步,有时他还会给米勒先生的孙儿们当马骑。冬天到了,他就偎着炉火蹲坐在米勒先生的脚边。

本书所有练习题的参考答案(含阅读理解练习题解析及译文),请登录中国水利水电出版社网站 http://www.waterpub.com.cn/softdown/(下载中心)免费下载。

Lesson 29

Reading Comprehension

✦✦ (1) ✦✦

The Cat and the Bell

Once there were a lot of mice in an old house. They ate up a lot of food. So the owner of the house got a cat. The cat killed many of the mice.

One day the oldest mouse said, "All the mice must come to my hold tonight, and we'll decide what we can do about the cat."

All the mice came. They thought hard and tried to find a way to save their lives. Many of them spoke, but no one knew what to do. At last a young mouse stood up and said, "Why not tie a bell around the cat's neck? Then, when the cat comes near, we'll hear the bell and run away and hide. Then the cat won't catch any one of us."

The oldest mouse said, "that's a good idea, If we can tie a bell around the cat, it will save many of our lives." After a moment he asked, "But who's going to do it?"

None of the mice answered.

He waited but still no one said anything.

At last he said, "It's easy to say things, but not so easy to do them."

---

1. once 曾经
2. a lot of 大量许多，既可修饰可数名词，也可修饰不可数名词。
3. What we can do about the cat. 我们该如何对付这只猫。
4. think hard 努力思考，苦想
5. run away 跑开

▶阅读上面的短文，从每题所给的四个选项中，选出一个最佳答案。

1. The mice ate up _____ food.
   A. little   B. a little   C. some   D. much
2. The owner of the house _____ the mice.
   A. loved   B. liked   C. hated   D. enjoyed
3. The idea to tie a bell around the cat's neck _____ good.
   A. sounded   B. looks   C. sounds   D. looked
4. _____ went to tie a bell around the cat's neck.
   A. The young mouse   B. The oldest mouse

C. All the mice   D. No mouse

5.   The mice didn't tie a bell around the cat's neck because _____.

A. they had no bell   B. the bell was too heavy

C. they dare not to near the cat   D. the cat was not asleep

6.   To say things is _____ to do things.

A. easier than   B. more difficult than

C. as easy as   D. not so easy as

✦✦ （2）✦✦

Vehicles and Pedestrians

People are often killed while crossing the road. Most of these people are old people and children. Old people are often killed because they usually cannot see or hear very well. Children are often killed because they are not careful. They forgot to look and listen before they cross the road.

A car, truck or bus cannot stop very quickly. If the vehicle is going very fast it will travel many metres before it stops. Pedestrians do not always understand this. They think a car can stop within a few metres. When a car is travelling very fast, it will take a long time to stop. It is very difficult for a pedestrian to know how fast a car is travelling.

The only safe way to cross the road is to look both ways, right and left. Then if the road is clear, it is safe to cross. The best way to cross the road is to walk quickly. It is not safe to run. If people run across the road, they may fall down.

---

1.   while 在……期间

2.   travel many metres 滑行很远

3.   do not always understand 总是不明白

4.   within 在……之内，一般后边接时间

     during 在……期间

5.   look both ways 看两边

▶阅读上面的短文，从每题所给的四个选项中，选出一个最佳答案。

1.   Children are often killed by vehicles because _____.

A. they are very small   B. they always run across the road

C. they are not careful enough   D. they walk very slowly

2.   Old people are often killed by vehicles because _____.

A. they usually cannot see very well and they also have a poor hearing

B. they are not careful enough

C. they are usually interested in the vehicles

D. they usually forget to look carefully before they cross the road

3.   Some pedestrians think _____.

A. it's not safe to cross the road

B. a car can stop very quickly when it's travelling very fast

C. children and old people should not cross the road because they are usually killed by vehicles

D. the vehicles should always go slowly

语言基本功
英汉翻译 ◈ Translation Exercises

▶ 翻译下列句子

1. 我们都非常激动，盼望着奥运会的到来，因为在这个国家还从未举办过奥运会。
_____

2. 他还没等安顿下来就卖掉了房子，离开了这个国家。
_____

3. 当我们穿过旧德里的市场时走了很长一段路，我们在一个广场上停下来休息。
_____

4. 虽然开始时伯德和他的助手们拍下了飞机下面连绵群山的大量照片，但他们很快就陷入了困境。
_____

5. 在湖中薄冰上走是很危险的。
_____

6. 这架奇妙的飞机可以载 7 名乘客。
_____

7. 弗西特机长的第一名乘客是位医生，他从伯明翰飞往威尔士山区一个偏僻的村庄。
_____

8. 我一月份时见过他，但从那以后就再也没见过。
_____

语言基本功
好句好段 ◈ Writing Samples

A bad thing never dies.

坏事传千年。

A rolling stone gathers no moss.

滚石不生苔，转业不聚财。

Diseases come on horseback, but go away on foot.

病来如山倒，病去如抽丝。

Gossiping and lying go hand in hand.

搬弄是非者，必是撒谎人。

本书所有练习题的参考答案（含阅读理解练习题解析及译文），请登录中国水利水电出版社网站 http://www.waterpub.com.cn/softdown/（下载中心）免费下载。

Lesson 30

阅读理解◆ | Reading Comprehension

✦✦（1）✦✦

The United States has many different kinds of climates. On the northwest coast, the temperature changes very little between summer and winter, but the north central states have a very different kind of climate. In those states, people wear light clothes in summer, and they need heavy woollen clothes in winter.

In the northeast of the United States, summer temperatures are very different from winter temperatures. Summer is usually hot, and winter is usually cold. The cold parts of the United States didn't often get frog. Spring temperatures are warm, and fall temperatures are cool.

---

1. different kinds of 不同种类的
2. on…coast 在海岸上
3. in the northwest 在西北部
4. light clothes 薄衣服，单衣服
5. heavy woolen clothes 厚毛线衣

▶阅读上面的短文，从每题所给的四个选项中，选出一个最佳答案。

1. The summer and winter temperatures are almost the same _____.

   A. in the northeastern states

   B. on the north central states

   C. in the western states

   D. on the northwest coast

2. The word "fall" in this passage means _____.

   A. drop

   B. down

   C. autumn

   D. spring

3. From this passage we know that the climate of the United States _____.

   A. is always very cold

   B. is warm in winter

   C. is widely different

   D. changes very little between summer and winter

Tom and John were brothers. They lived in the same room, and were in the same class. One day they had a fight, so they were very angry with each other.

For a few days they didn't speak to each other. One evening Tom was very tired when he came back from school. So he went to bed soon after dinner, of course. He didn't say anything to John before he went to their room. John washed the dinner things and then did some homework. When he went to bed much later than Tom, he found a piece of paper on the small table near his bed. On it were the words:

"John, wake me up at 7:00 in the morning. Tom."

When Tom woke up the next morning. It was nearly 8:00, and on the small table near his bed he also saw a piece of paper. He took it and read these words "Tom, wake up. It's 7:00 in the morning. John".

Tom hurried to school, but it was very late. His teacher was not happy when he saw Tom. But John's face was red. He stood up and told his teacher, "I didn't wake Tom up. It's my fault." When the teacher heard this, he told them to speak to each other and not to fight any more.

▶ 根据短文内容，判断下列句子正（**T**）误（**F**）。

1. They didn't speak to each other for a few days. ____

2. John washed the dinner things and Tom did some homework. ____

3. Tom wrote something that evening and wanted John to wake him up the next morning. ____

4. John woke Tom up in time and Tom went to school in time too. ____

5. Their teacher asked them to speak to each other and not to fight any more. ____

语言基本功
英汉翻译 ◈ Translation Exercises

▶ 翻译下列句子

1. 我一眼就认出她了。

_____

2. 那给他招来了很多麻烦。

_____

3. 他们游览了伦敦的名胜古迹。

_____

4. 这个人由于被人发现而感到非常吃惊，甚至都没有企图逃跑。

_____

5. 伊恩·汤普森先生最近才买的一个小酒店现在又要卖出去。

_____

6. 作为对这些问题的回答，我不是点头，就是发出奇怪的声音。

_____

7. 接着他又问我的兄弟近来如何，问我是否喜欢伦敦的新工作。

_____

8. 将有多少人参加考试？

_____

语言基本功
好句好段 ◈ | Writing Samples

☑ As we made our way to the palace, I began to feel that I really was the King of Ruritania, with Marshal Strakencz, the head of the army, on my right and old Sapt on my left. I could see that Strelsau was really two towns – the Old Town and the New Town. The people of the Old Town, who were poor, wanted Duke Michael to be their King, but the people of the New Town wanted King Rudolf. We went through the New Town first and it was bright and colourful, with the ladies' dresses and the red roses of the Elphberges. The people shouted loudly for their King as we passed through the streets. But when we came to the Old Town, the Marshal and Sapt moved nearer to my horse, and I could see that they were afraid for me.

在去王宫的路上，军队的首领斯特肯茨元帅站在我的右边，老萨普特站在我的左边，我开始感到自己真的是卢里塔尼亚的国王了。我看到斯特莱索实际上是两个城——老城和新城。老城的居民是穷人，他们想要迈克尔公爵当国王。新城的居民却希望鲁道夫当国王。我们先经过新城，城里女人们的衣饰和艾尔弗伯格红玫瑰使得城市明亮艳丽。我们经过大街时，人们高声为国王欢呼。但当我们来到老城时，元帅和老萨普特靠近我的马，我能看出他们为我担心。

Lesson 31

阅读理解◇ | Reading Comprehension

◆◆ （1）◆◆

Most cities and towns in China have night markets. They take place on the same streets every day. During the day, these streets are quiet. At night, they become crowded and lively. Usually, people get there at three or four in the afternoon. By 6:00, the streets are like rivers of people.

Night markets are fun places to shop. Sellers open small booths, or they place their things on mats on the street. You can buy clothes, shoes, and many other things. If you think the price is too high, you can bargain with the seller.

You can also buy lots of delicious food. When you are just a little hungry, you can buy a snack. When you're really hungry, you can sit down for a meal. Smelly tofu is popular, but it really smells bad!

There are also games to play. In one game, you throw plastic rings around the top of a bottle. In another game, you shoot balloons with a toy gun. If you are lucky, you can win a prize. Do you like to play these games? Do you ever win anything?

The best thing is, everything at night markets is cheap! You don't need a lot of money to have a great time.

▶阅读上面的短文，从每题所给的四个选项中，选出一个最佳答案。

1. When you go to the night markets, _____.

   A. you can see a lot of people by six o'clock

   B. you can buy a lot of things at six o'clock

   C. you must get there at three or four p.m.

   D. you may eat all kinds of food during a day

2. If you think the price is too high at night market, you _____.

   A. can call the police   B. can't do anything

   C. can bargain with the seller   D. can shout at the seller

3. You can _____ at the night markets when you are just a little hungry.

   A. buy some food   B. eat only smelly tofu

   C. put your things on the street   D. eat everything

4. The text tells us _____.

   A. about cities and towns

   B. you can buy everything at the markets

C. about night markets in most cities and towns in China

D. people can eat something at the night markets

✦✦ (2) ✦✦

By the Seaside

A store clerk in a large city was suffering from aching feet. His doctor told him it was because he had spent many years standing all day long. He needed a rest, and the doctor advised him to go to the seaside and soak his feet in the ocean.

The clerk had never been to the seaside before. When he arrived he went into a hardware store and bought two buckets. Then he went down to the beach. A lifeguard was on duty. "How much is a bucket of that sea water?" he asked. The lifeguard decided to play a trick on the foolish store clerk. "It costs one dollar a bucket," he said.

The clerk gave the lifeguard two dollars, filled his buckets with sea water and went back to the hotel, where he soaked his feet. After a while his feet began to feel much better.

He decided to return to the beach that afternoon and repeat the treatment. The store clerk looked around in surprise. The tide was now out and the sea was far away.

"Wow!" he cried, looking at the lifeguard with admiration, "you must make a lot of money at this business!"

▶ 阅读上面的短文，从每题所给的四个选项中，选出一个最佳答案。

1. What was the store clerk's problem?

   A. He lost his job.

   B. He had to work as a lifeguard by the seaside.

   C. He had to be a doctor in a beach.

   D. His feet hurt very much.

2. The store clerk suffered from aching feet because _____.

   A. he had put his feet into the ocean

   B. he had spent many years standing all day long

   C. he had worked too hard

   D. he had to carry buckets of water to the hotel

3. The store clerk found _____ on duty on the beach.

   A. a doctor   B. a waiter

   C. a lifeguard   D. a businessman

4. The lifeguard charged the store clerk two dollars because _____.

   A. the sea water was his

   B. he decided to play a joke on him

   C. he loved money too much

   D. the sea water was especially useful

5. Why did the store clerk said to the lifeguard, "you must make a lot of money."

92

A. Because the lifeguard was still there.

B. Because he thought the lifeguard had sold all the sea water.

C. Because the lifeguard charged him too much.

D. Because the sea water was very useful.

语言基本功
英汉翻译◈ Translation Exercises

▶翻译下列句子

1. 请让我在下一个红绿灯处下车。
   _____

2. 不要去旅馆，我可以在我的公寓里给你安排个床位。
   _____

3. 你猜几天前我碰到谁了？
   _____

4. 史蒂夫的嗓音和风度酷似他父亲。
   _____

5. 你这么懒，真不知道你会变成什么样。
   _____

6. 别相信他，不然你会上当的。
   _____

7. 计算机不仅能汇集资料，而且会像高速汇集资料那样储存资料。
   _____

8. 在讨论我们的分歧时，我们中任何一方都不会在原则上让步。
   _____

语言基本功
好句好段◈ Writing Samples

☑ Cyril got in through the window and gave the food to the others, who were outside. There was some cold meat, half a cold chicken, some bread and a bottle of soda-water. Then they all flew back up onto the church roof to eat it. They were very hungry, so they really enjoyed it. But when you are very hungry, and then you eat a big meal and sit in the hot sun on a roof, it is very easy to fall asleep. And so they did—while the sun slowly went down in the west.

西里尔从窗子进去，把食物拿给在外边的其他孩子。有些冷肉、半只冷鸡、一些面包和一瓶汽水。然后他们全飞回到教堂房顶上吃起来。他们很饿，所以吃得很香。可是当你很饿的时候大吃了一顿、又在屋顶上晒着太阳时，那是很容易睡着的。他们就睡着了——这时太阳慢慢地从西边落下去。

Lesson 32

Reading Comprehension

♦♦ （1）♦♦

How Do the Child Actors Get an Education?

Many children act in TV shows. They work several hours every day, so they cannot go to regular school. How do they get an education?

In Hollywood many TV shows are made. About forty teachers give lessons for the children in the shows. They teach wherever their pupils are working. The teachers' job is very important. They are responsible for making sure that the children work only the permitted hours each week. They are also responsible for making sure that children learn the required subjects. They make sure, too, that the children get enough rest and play, along with their education.

Child actors are required to attend classes twenty hours each week. California law says they must be taught from September to June. If they do not make much progress in school, they are not permitted to continue working in TV shows. TV children are usually good pupils, and most of their teachers like this special kind of work. Their classes are held in some wonderful places. Sometimes the "Classroom" is a Mississippi river boat. Sometimes it is the inside of a spaceship. Often the pupils will become famous stars.

▶阅读上面的短文，从每题所给的四个选项中，选出一个最佳答案。

1. The child actors do not go to regular school because _____.

   A. they do not get good marks

   B. there is no school nearby

   C. they have to act several hours a day

   D. they have to work all day long

2. The teachers usually hold classes in _____.

   A. a classroom building　　　　　　　B. some interesting places

   C. a Mississippi river boat　　　　　　D. a spaceship

3. The teachers' duty is to make sure that the child actors _____.

   A. do not overwork　　　　　　　　　B. learn what they must learn

   C. have enough sleep and play　　　　　D. all the above

4. The pupils are not allowed to continue working if they _____.

   A. do not act well　　　　　　　　　　B. go to regular school

   C. do not get good marks　　　　　　　D. cannot become famous stars

5. Which of the following statements is not true?

    A. California law does not allow children to act in TV shows.

    B. Many of the child actors must become famous stars.

    C. The lessons are given by forty teachers.

    D. The teachers must teach them from September to June.

✦✦ （2）✦✦

Long long ago, there was a little clever boy called Sima Guang.

One day Sima Guang and his friends were playing hide-and-seek near a tall big jar. One of the boys wanted to hide himself in the jar so that none of his friends could find him easily. But he didn't know that the jar was full of water. When he climbed up to the top of the jar, he slipped and fell into the jar. The jar was full of water and the little child was too short to keep his head above the water. He cried out, "Help! Help!" The children were so frightened that they could do nothing.

But Sima Guang wanted to save the drowning child in the big jar. But he was very small, too. How could he save the child in the jar? Then his mind worked quickly in danger. Suddenly a good idea came to his mind. He got a stone and knocked the jar with it on the side. Soon he made a big hole in the big jar. Immediately, the water rushed out from the jar and the child was saved.

---

1. hide-and-seek   *n.* 捉迷藏

2. jar   *n.* 瓮；坛子；罐子

3. slip   *v.* 滑；滑落

4. frightened   *adj.* 受惊吓的；害怕的

5. drown   *v.* 淹死；淹没

▶ 阅读上面的短文，从每题所给的四个选项中，选出一个最佳答案。

1. Sima Guang was _____.

    A. a careful boy   B. a clever boy

    C. a foolish boy   D. an interesting boy

2. One day Sima Guang was _____ near a big jar.

    A. playing balls   B. playing games

    C. talking to friends   D. thinking about something

3. There was _____ in the jar.

    A. money   B. much water

    C. nothing   D. some food

4. Which of the following is not right?

    A. When a boy was in danger, Sima Guang didn't go away.

    B. When a boy was in danger, Sima Guang ran away, too.

    C. When a boy was in danger, Sima Guang wanted to save him.

    D. The children ran away except Sima Guang.

5. How did Sima Guang save the boy?
   A. He asked some men to help him.   B. He broke the jar with a stone.
   C. He had no idea.   D. He pulled the boy out of the jar.

英汉翻译◈ | Translation Exercises

▶ 翻译下列句子

1. 他知道自己的责任所在，却退缩不前。

   _____

2. 应该废除许多过时的法律。

   _____

3. 几年前他是个酒鬼，但现在他已经戒了酒。

   _____

4. 我祖母到晚年迷上了歌剧。

   _____

5. 我头痛，今晚出不去了。

   _____

6. 家长有责任教育孩子懂礼貌，懂规矩。

   _____

7. 如果你取消合同，就得付款给那家公司。

   _____

8. 很长时间你一直在虚度年华，现在你该安下心来认真工作了。

   _____

好句好段◈ | Writing Samples

If the beard were all, the goat might preach.
如果有了胡子就什么都行，那么山羊也可以说教了。
Life is long if you know how to use it.
如果懂得好好利用，生命就长了。
No love is foul, nor prison fair.
没有肮脏的爱情，也没有美丽的监狱。

本书所有练习题的参考答案（含阅读理解练习题解析及译文），请登录中国水利水电出版社网站 http://www.waterpub.com.cn/softdown/（下载中心）免费下载。

Lesson 33

阅读理解◈ | Reading Comprehension

◆◆（1）◆◆

In the big cities in the United States, most people only have half an hour to one hour to have lunch. This time is too short for them to go home for lunch because the cities are too big. So most people take lunch with them, or have it in cafeterias.

The children in school take sandwiches, fruit and cookies with them or have lunch in school cafeterias. When you come to a cafeteria, you must stand in the line, pick up a tray, then put a knife, fork, spoon and paper napkin on it. When you come to the counter, you can see all kinds of food on it. You just say what you would like. The man behind the counter will give you what you ask for. If you want to drink something, you just pick up a glass and get the drink from a machine. Then you can find a table and eat and drink.

1.　一日三餐用 have 来表达"吃"，
　　即 have breakfast/lunch/supper/dinner
2.　take lunch with　带午饭
3.　stand in the line　排队
4.　pick up　拾起、捡起
5.　all kinds of　各种各样
6.　drink　*v.* 喝；*n.* 饮料

▶阅读上面的短文，从每题所给的四个选项中，选出一个最佳答案。

1.　Which is right?

　　A. Children must take lunch with them.

　　B. Children must have lunch in the cafeterias.

　　C. Children mustn't go home for lunch.

　　D. Children must have lunch quickly.

2.　In the big cities in the United States students can rest _____ at noon.

　　A. about an hour　　　　　　　　B. two hours

　　C. one or two hours　　　　　　D. one hour and a half

3.　Which is wrong?

　　A. Many people are in the cafeterias at noon.

　　B. You bring a knife, fork, spoon and paper napkin to the cafeteria.

C. You mustn't pick up the food yourself.

D. You can get the drink yourself.

4. You can get the drink _____.

   A. from a man behind the counter

   B. before you pay the money

   C. after you pay the money

   D. after eating

5. Lunch in the cafeterias is _____.

   A. cheap

   B. dear

   C. free

   D. late

✦✦ (2) ✦✦

A farmer who lived in a small village had a bad pain in the chest. This never seemed to get any better. The farmer decided that he would go to see a doctor in the nearest town. But as he was a miserly person, he thought he would find out what he would have to pay the doctor. He was told that a sick person had to pay three pounds for the first visit and one pound for the second visit. The farmer thought about this for a long time, and then he decided to go to the doctor in the town.

As he came into the doctor's room, he said, "Good morning, doctor. Here I am again." The doctor was a little surprised. He asked him a few questions, checked his chest and then took the pound which the farmer insisted on giving him. Then the doctor said with a smile, "Well, sir, there's nothing new. Please go on taking the same medicine I gave you the first time you came to see me."

▶ 阅读上面的短文，从每题所给的四个选项中，选出一个最佳答案。

1. Why did the farmer decide to go to see a doctor in the town?

   A. Because the doctor in the village had been unable to save him.

   B. Because he had a fever.

   C. Because he suffered from a pain in the head.

   D. Because the pain didn't seem to get better.

2. How many pounds did a sick person have to pay the doctor in the town for two visits?

   A. Four.

   B. Three.

   C. One.

   D. Two.

3. Where did the doctor check the farmer?

   A. In the village.

   B. On the farm.

   C. At the doctor's.

   D. In the city.

4. What did the farmer give the doctor?

   A. Some medicine.

   B. Nothing.

   C. Smile.

   D. A pound.

5. The doctor asked the farmer _____.

   A. something new about his illness

   B. to go on taking the same medicine

   C. to come again

   D. to give him some more pounds

英汉翻译 ◈ Translation Exercises

▶ **翻译下列句子**

1. 有三种主要的电流效应，即磁效应、热效应和化学效应。

   _____

2. 因为他没有遵守安全规则，机器出了故障。

   _____

3. 多年来该城市一直有严重的失业现象。

   _____

4. 因为膨胀力的缘故，桥梁必须分段制造。

   _____

5. 他对我一连咆哮了 5 分钟。

   _____

6. 那天一整天都风雨大作。

   _____

7. 我们遇上了暴风雨。

   _____

8. 有我妹妹寄来的明信片，说她下星期一回家。

   _____

好句好段 ◈ Writing Samples

☑ What a battle it was! How the four friends roared as they ran through the hall! What screams of fear came from the surprised weasels and ferrets! Tables and chairs were knocked over, plates and glasses went crashing to the floor. Up and down went the four friends, shouting and roaring, and their sticks whistled through the air. There were only four of them, but they seemed enormous to the weasels and the ferrets. The Wild Wooders ran in terror, escaping through the doors and windows, and even up the chimneys – anywhere to get away from hose terrible sticks.

那是一场怎样的战斗啊！这四个朋友是怎样地怒吼着冲进了大厅！吃惊的黄鼠狼和雪貂发出了怎样的尖叫声！桌子和椅子给撞倒了，杯子和盘子摔碎在地板上。这四个朋友横冲直闯，怒吼狂叫着，他们的棍棒在空中发出嘶嘶挥舞声。他们仅有四位，但在黄鼠狼，雪貂眼里他们似乎非常强大。这些野生丛林动物吓得到处跑，从门那儿，从窗户那儿，有的甚至从烟囱那儿——任何能躲开那些可怕的棍子的地方。

Lesson 34

阅读理解◇ Reading Comprehension

✦✦ (1) ✦✦

Of all the students of Grade Four, Bill is the tallest. He's thirteen, and of course, he's the oldest, too. But he's the worst student. He can't answer the easiest questions in class. And he never passes the exams.

But the boy is the strongest in his school. Even the boys in higher grades are afraid of him. So everyday he leaves home with an empty bag. When he gets to school, his bag will be full of fruit and cakes. Sometimes he brings some home. His mother, Mrs. King, is always happy when she sees them. She praises her son, for she can save some money.

This morning, Mrs. King went shopping in the market. She saw an old man selling eggs there. She chose twenty-four but paid only for twenty. The old man was too busy to count them. She went home quickly and told her husband as soon as he came back for lunch.

"How clever you are!" Mr. King said happily. And Bill was busy eating the eggs, so he didn't say a word.

"What's your favourite food, dear?" asked Mr. King.

"Eggs, of course."

"Well, then," said the man, "can you tell us what can lay eggs?"

The boy thought for a while and said, "Hens, ducks geese ...and ...and mum!"

"Oh? But why?"

"I often hear our classmates call me 'BAD EGG'."

▶ 阅读上面的短文，从每题所给的四个选项中，选出一个最佳答案。

1. Bill never passes the exams because _____.

   A. he's the tallest of the children

   B. he's thirteen

   C. he doesn't work hard at his lessons

   D. he is not the worst in the school

2. Why will Bill's bag be full of fruit and cakes, when he goes to school?

   A. He buys them on his way to school.

   B. He makes his classmates give them to him.

   C. He finds them in the shops.

   D. His parents buy them for him.

3. _____, so Mrs. King is happy.

   A. Bill often comes home early

   B. The children are afraid of Bill

   C. Bill is stronger and older than any other child

   D. Bill often brings some food home without paying any money

4. Bill didn't say a word at table because _____.

   A. he was thinking of a problem   B. he had to go to school time

   C. he was afraid of his father   D. he wanted to eat more eggs

5. Which of the following is true?

   A. Mrs. King can lay eggs.

   B. Bill's classmates think Bill is very bad.

   C. Bill wished his mother could lay eggs.

   D. Bill likes his nickname very much.

✦✦ (2) ✦✦

December 25 is Christmas Day. In most countries it is the most important day in the year. All the people come back to their homes to have the day with their parents or their children.

On Christmas Day bells ring everywhere. The ringing bells tell people that Christmas is coming. New Year is coming. People sing and dance day and night. They have a good time.

Most families buy a Christmas tree for their children. And there are presents hanging from the tree here and there. People also put presents in children's socks. In many places Santa Claus himself brings presents to them. Santa Claus is a kind old man. He is in red clothes. A big bag is on his back. In the bag there are a lot of presents.

Christmas is also a day when people enjoy all kinds of food. But some poor people have no homes to go back and have no food to eat. They even die of cold and hunger on Christmas Day. Have you read the story "A Little Match Girl?" She died on the morning of Christmas Day.

---

1. the most important 最重要的

2. come back to 回到

3. or 连接选择句时表示"或者"

4. day and night 日日夜夜

5. here and there 到处

6. no homes 没有家；no food 没食物

7. on 用于具体的某一天。如：

   on January 1st 1 月 1 日

▶ 根据短文内容，判断下列句子正（**T**）误（**F**）。

1. Christmas Day is a children's day.   ____

2. People usually plant Christmas trees in their gardens.   ____

3. Children like Santa Claus because he brings them wonderful things. ____

4. "A Little Match Girl" was born in China. ____

5. She died because she ate and drank too much on Christmas Day. ____

语言基本功
英汉翻译◈ | Translation Exercises

▶ 翻译下列句子

1. 上星期二他收到当地警察局的一封信。

_____

2. 我们的首次合作是成功的。

_____

3. 目录、样品和价格已在上表中列出。

_____

4. 电视机与收音机的区别在于电视机能接收图像。

_____

5. 糖的价格将会下降。

_____

6. 下了几滴雨。

_____

7. 你必须改掉那个习惯。

_____

8. 这是 20 年前丹还是一个 15 岁的孩子时被人偷走的！

_____

语言基本功
好句好段◈ | Writing Samples

✔ First of all, I wanted to make my cave bigger. I carried out stone from the cave, and after many days' hard work I had a large cave in the side of the hill. Then I needed a table and a chair, and that was my next job. I had to work on them for a long time. I also wanted to make places to put all my food, and all my tools and guns. But every time I wanted a piece of wood, I had to cut down a tree. It was long, slow, difficult work, and during the next months I learnt to be very clever with my tools. There was no hurry. I had all the time in the world.

首先，我把我的山洞扩大。我从洞里运出石头，经过许多天的艰苦劳动，我在小山的一侧有了个大的山洞。然后，我需要一张桌子和一把椅子，这便是我接下来的工作。为此，我不得不长时间地干。我还想找些地方存放我的食物，以及我全部的工具和枪支。每一次我需要一块木板时都不得不砍倒一棵树。这是一项漫长艰难的工作，在随后的几个月里我学会熟练地使用工具了。无需焦急。我拥有世界上的全部时间。

Lesson 35

Reading Comprehension

✦✦ （1） ✦✦

When you send a letter or a postcard, you have to put stamps on the envelope or on the card. When did people first begin to use stamps? Who was the first to think of this idea? In the early nineteenth century, people did not use stamps. They had to pay postage when they received letters. Sometimes they didn't want to receive a letter at all, but they had to pay money for it. They were unhappy about this. The postage was high at that time, because the post offices had to send many people to get the postage.

Rowland Hill was a school teacher in England. He was the first to think of using stamps in the 1850s. He thought it would be much easier for people to use stamps. They could go to the post office to buy stamps and put them on envelopes before they sent the letters. The post office could just put seals on the stamps so that people could not use the stamps again. In this way, the post office did not need to send postmen to get postage. It only needed fewer postmen to send letters.

▶阅读上面的短文，从每题所给的四个选项中，选出一个最佳答案。

1.　People began to use stamps _____.

　　A. at the beginning of the nineteenth century

　　B. in the middle of the nineteenth century

　　C. more than two hundred years ago

　　D. when people first sent letters and postcards

2.　Before stamps are used, postage _____.

　　A. was paid by the letter-writers

　　B. was paid by the letter-receivers

　　C. was got by postmen

　　D. both B and C

3.　Rowland Hill _____.

　　A. invented the first stamp

　　B. was a post man in England

　　C. gave the idea to use stamps

　　D. was the first man to use stamps

4.　After stamps were used, _____.

　　A. post men needn't get postage

B. people needn't pay postage

C. the post office could get more postage

D. people should pay more postage

5. What is the main idea of the passage?

A. How did stamps begin to be used?

B. Why were postmen sent to get postage?

C. When did people first begin to use stamps?

D. Who was the first to think of using stamps?

What must you do when you receive a present for your birthday? You have to sit down and write a thank-you note. The words "Thank you" are very important. We have to use them on so many occasions. We say them when someone gives us a drink, helps us to pick up things, hands us a letter, lends us a book or gives us a bit.

Another important word is "please". Many people forget to use it. It is rude to ask someone to do something without saying "please". We have to use it when we ask for something, too. It may be a book or a pencil, more rice or more sauce, help or advice. It may be in the classroom, at home, at the bus stop or over the counter. We have to use "please" to make request pleasant.

We have to learn to say "sorry", too. When we have hurt someone's feelings, we'll have to go up and say we're sorry. When we have told a lie and feel sorry, we will have to use the same word. When we have forgotten something or broken a promise, we will have to explain with that word, too. "Sorry" is a healing word. We can make people forget wrongs by using it sincerely.

These three words are simple but important. Man had to use them long ago. We have to use them now. Our children will have to use them again. They are pleasing words to use in any language.

▶阅读上面的短文，从每题所给的四个选项中，选出一个最佳答案。

1. When we receive a birthday present, we have to _____.

A. return it   B. give it to one of our friends

C. do nothing   D. write a thank-you note

2. When someone helps us to do something, we should _____.

A. thank him   B. say sorry to him

C. use the word "please"   D. not say anything

3. One of the important words in any language is _____.

A. "hello"   B. "yes"   C. "no"   D. "please"

4. We have to use the word "please" when we _____.

A. hurt someone's feeling   B. ask for something

C. receive a present   D. have told a lie

5. When we have broken a promise. we will have to explain with the word _____.

A. "thanks"   B. "please"   C. "sorry"   D. "hello"

英汉翻译◈ Translation Exercises

▶ 翻译下列句子

1. 他发觉自己的新工作令人兴奋得多。

   _____

2. 罗伊行动迅速，开车直冲窃贼而去。

   _____

3. 没过多久，警察就截住了那辆车，两个小偷都被抓住了。

   _____

4. 新交通规则三月份生效。

   _____

5. 他们差点没赶上飞机。

   _____

6. 电视信号的传输距离很短。

   _____

7. 直视前方。

   _____

8. 请以真诚待我。

   _____

好句好段◈ Writing Samples

✓ In the next few days Mary spent almost all her time in the gardens. The fresh air from the moor made her hungry, and she was becoming stronger and healthier. One day she noticed the robin again. He was on top of a wall, singing to her. "Good morning! Isn't this fun! Come this way!" he seemed to say, as he hopped along the wall. Mary began to laugh as she danced along beside him. "I know the secret garden's on the other side of this wall!" she thought excitedly. "And the robin lives there! But where's the door?"

以后的几天，玛丽几乎所有的时间都呆在花园里。荒原上吹来的新鲜空气让她感到饥饿，而她也变得强壮，变得健康了。一天，她又看见了知更鸟。他好像是在说，"早上好！多好玩啊！上这儿来！"一边沿着围墙跳着。玛丽一边跟在他旁边跳着，一边放声笑起来。"我知道秘密花园在这堵墙的那一边！"她兴奋地想着。"知更鸟就住在那儿！可是门在哪儿呢？"

本书所有练习题的参考答案（含阅读理解练习题解析及译文），请登录中国水利水电出版社网站 http://www.waterpub.com.cn/softdown/（下载中心）免费下载。

Lesson 36

| Reading Comprehension

◆◆（1）◆◆

Something about Tree Rings

Do you know something about tree rings? Do you know they can tell us what the weather was like, sometimes even hundreds of years ago?

A tree will grow well in a climate with lots of sunshine and rainfall. And little sunshine or rainfall will limit the growth of a tree. We can see the change of climate by studying the tree rings. For example, to find out the weather of ten years ago, count the rings of a tree from the outside to the inside. If the tenth ring is far from the eleventh ring, then we're sure that it was sunny and rainy most of that year. If it is near to the eleventh ring, then the climate that year was bad.

Tree rings are important not only for studying the history of weather but also for studying the history of man. Many centuries ago there lived a lot of people at a place in New Mexico. But now you can find only sand there—no trees and no people. What happened?

A scientist studied the rings of dead trees there. He found that the people had to leave because they had cut down all the trees to make fires and buildings. As all the trees had gone, the people there had to move.

▶阅读上面的短文，从每题所给的四个选项中，选出一个最佳答案。

1. _____ in good climate.

   A. Tree rings grow far from each other

   B. Tree rings become thinner

   C. Trees don't need sunshine or rainfall

   D. People can cut down most of the trees

2. The scientists are interested in studying tree rings because tree rings can tell _____.

   A. whether a tree was strong or not

   B. whether people took good care of the trees or not

   C. whether the climate was good or not

   D. how old the trees were

3. If you want to find out the weather of twenty years ago, you should study _____ of a tree from the outside to the inside.

   A. the twentieth ring   B. the tenth ring

   C. the nineteenth ring   D. the twenty-first ring

4. Why did people usually live in places with lots of trees?

    A. Trees could tell the change of the weather.

    B. Trees brought lots of sunshine and rain.

    C. Trees could make weather not too hot or too cold.

    D. Trees could be used for burning and for building houses.

5. The people had to leave the place in New Mexico _____.

    A. because bad weather stopped the growth of trees

    B. because they no longer had water and the land became sand

    C. because they didn't have enough trees for burning

    D. because there was too much rain there

✦✦ （2）✦✦

Peter is a good student. He studies hard and does his homework carefully. He never hands in his exercise books late or goes to school late. All the teachers like him very much.

One evening, Fred asked him and some other friends to dinner. It was Fred's birthday. They had a very good time. They turned on the radio, sang and danced happily to the music. Then they sat down to watch TV. The plays on TV were nice. They watched one play after another, talking and laughing. All of them were very happy.

When Peter came back, it was three the next morning. He was very tired and fell asleep quickly. It was 9:30 when he woke up. He was surprised and hurried to school without breakfast. He was afraid to be late for class. But when he got near his classroom, he saw nobody around. He felt quite strange and stood there for a few minutes. Suddenly he cried, "Oh, today is Sunday!"

▶ 阅读上面的短文，从每题所给的四个选项中，选出一个最佳答案。

1. Which one is right?

    A. Peter often goes to school late.

    B. Peter often hands in his homework late but never goes to school late.

    C. Peter sometimes does his homework carefully.

    D. Peter never goes to school late and never hands in his homework late.

2. Fred asked Peter and some other friends to _____.

    A. play   B. have supper   C. watch TV   D. have lunch

3. The plays on TV _____.

    A. were well   B. were nice

    C. were bad   D. were short

4. Peter _____ the next day.

    A. was late for school   B. didn't go to school

    C. went to school early   D. wasn't late for school

5. Fred's birthdays was _____.

    A. Thursday   B. Friday   C. Saturday   D. Sunday

英汉翻译◈ | Translation Exercises

▶ 翻译下列句子

1. 我想早一点回去。

_____

2. 我的意思是把那件礼物送给你。

_____

3. 你其实不必自己过来，给我打个电话就行了。

_____

4. 晚上通常有许多学生在图书馆看书。

_____

5. 不采用新技术，就不能大幅度提高劳动生产率。

_____

6. 两个问题哪个也没有解决。

_____

7. 没有人能够打开这个保险柜。

_____

8. 我认为他不会操作这种计算机。

_____

好句好段◈ | Writing Samples

Read not books alone, but men.
不要光是读书，还要识人。

The heart of the giver makes the gift dear and precious.
赠予者的心意可使馈赠的东西增加价值而显得珍贵。

Tomorrow comes never.
切莫依赖明天。

A bad workman quarrels with his tools.
拙匠常怨工具差（人笨怨刀钝）。

Lesson 37

Reading Comprehension

✦✦ （1） ✦✦

A Baby's First Haircut

The natives of Peru and Bolivia have a special custom for a baby. They celebrate the baby's first haircut with a fiesta（宗教节日）. At the fiesta there is lots of food, music, and dancing.

The parents do not cut the baby's hair for a few years. They invite relatives and friends to the fiesta.

On this special day the baby sits on a high chair like a king or queen. Then the godmother separates the baby's hair into locks. The number of locks is the same as the number of guests at the fiesta. The godmother then ties each lock with a pretty ribbon.

The godfather cuts the first lock. He also says what gift he is giving. The gifts may be an animal, a piece of land, or a lot of money. After him, each guest cuts off a lock and makes a gift of money. The money can pay for the fiesta, or the parents can save the money for the baby's future.

▶ 阅读上面的短文，从每题所给的四个选项中，选出一个最佳答案。

1. What do the natives of Peru and Bolivia do on the day of a baby's first haircut?
   - A. Have a picnic.
   - B. Go to a concert.
   - C. Have a party.
   - D. Go to a dance.

2. Who separates the baby's hair into locks at the fiesta?
   - A. The godmother.
   - B. The godfather.
   - C. Either the godmother or the godfather.
   - D. Both the godmother and the godfather.

3. Who cut the baby's hair at the fiesta?
   - A. Parents.
   - B. The godfather.
   - C. Relatives and friends.
   - D. Both B and C.

4. Which of the following is the same as the number of guests at the fiesta?
   - A. The number of chairs.
   - B. The number of gifts.
   - C. The number of candles.
   - D. The number of small pieces of hair.

5. Which of the following can't be chosen as a present to the baby?
   - A. Money.
   - B. An animal.
   - C. Clothes.
   - D. Land.

✦✦ （2） ✦✦

Dogs are very popular pets all over the world. Some people keep dogs because the dogs help them. These dogs may protect someone's house. They can also help a blind person by leading the person to places where he or she needs to go. Other people keep dogs as pets just because they like dogs.

Some of the most popular kinds of dogs which people have as pets are German shepherds, Poodles, and Dalmatians. Almost 33 percent of the homes in the United States and England have dogs, and these dogs come in a wide variety of shapes and sizes.

By all accounts, the largest dog in the world is a dog named Zorba. This dog is a mastiff that lives in London, England. When Zorba was seven years old in 1989, he was 92.5 centimetres tall. In other words, Zorba was more than half as tall as an adult man. Some Great Danes can grow taller than 98 centimetres, but they do not grow as large as Zorba. At his largest, Zorba weighed more than a heavy weight boxer at 156 kilograms.

In comparison, the smallest dog was a Yorkshire terrier from England. This dog was only the size of a matchbox measuring 5 centimetres tall and at most, 8 centimetres from nose to tail. It was certainly possible for even a child to pick up this dog with one hand. The dog weighed less than a small bag of potato chips. It died in 1945 when it was only two yeas old.

---

1. pet   *n.* 宠物
2. shepherd   *n.* 牧羊狗
3. poodle   *n.* 狮子狗
4. centimetre   *n.* 厘米
5. mastiff   *n.* 猛犬

▶阅读上面的短文，从每题所给的四个选项中，选出一个最佳答案。

1. Why do people keep pets?
   A. Pets help them.   B. Pets protect their houses.
   C. They like pets.   D. All of the above.
2. How was Zorba different from other dogs?
   A. He was big.   B. He was old.
   C. He was strong.   D. He was small.
3. What kind of dog was Zorba?
   A. A Dalmatian.   B. A Great Dane.
   C. A mastiff.   D. A Yorkshire terrier.
4. The smallest dog in the world is about the same size as _____.
   A. A bag of potato chips   B. A matchbox
   C. A poodle   D. A nose
5. When did the smallest dog in the world die?
   A. In 1943.   B. In 1954.   C. In 1945.   D. In 1989.

英汉翻译◈ | Translation Exercises

▶ 翻译下列句子

1. 生活中有很多令人惊奇的地方。

_____

2. 母亲抱着婴儿。

_____

3. 这绳子经不住大风。

_____

4. 他对新闻界的看法是，记者们不是支持他，就是反对他。

_____

5. 他不跟工人们在一起生活，虽然他依靠他们的熟练技能。

_____

6. 他过于自尊了，不肯让内心里的温情流露出来。

_____

7. 如果病人感觉不好，马上通知值班医生。

_____

8. 就在这时，外面传来车轮的声音。

_____

好句好段◈ | Writing Samples

☑ Two new men took Buck and his team back north on the long journey to Dawson, traveling with several other dogteams. It was heavy work; the sledge was loaded with letters for the gold miners of Dawson. Buck did not like it, but he worked hard, and made the other dogs work hard, too. Each day was the same. They started early, before it was light, and at night they stopped and camped and the dogs ate. For the dogs this was the best part of the day, first eating, then resting by the fire.

另外两个人接手了巴克和他的队伍。同别的狗队一起再度奔赴北去道桑的漫长旅途。任重而道远，雪撬上载满了给道桑寻找金矿的人的信件。巴克很不喜欢，但他非常努力地工作，带着别的狗一起费力地拉着车。日复一日，他们披星戴月，起早贪黑。对于狗来说，晚上停下来安营填饱肚子是一天中最美好的时光，先吃一顿饭，再靠到火边休息。

本书所有练习题的参考答案（含阅读理解练习题解析及译文），请登录中国水利水电出版社网站 http://www.waterpub.com.cn/softdown/（下载中心）免费下载。

Lesson 38

Reading Comprehension

◆◆ (2) ◆◆

Hollywood

When we think of Hollywood, we think of movies and famous movie stars. They are part of Hollywood's history. Today people make movies in other places too. Not all famous movie stars live in Hollywood. But Hollywood is still a very special city in Los Angeles, California.

You can easily see where Hollywood is in Los Angeles. There is a big sign on the hills. It says "HOLLYWOOD". The white letters are fifty feet tall. You can see the sign from far away. The Hollywood sign is a famous landmark in Los Angeles. Many postcards show this famous Hollywood landmark.

In the hills of Hollywood, there is also the Hollywood Bowl. This is an open-air theater. It is one of the largest open-air theaters in the world. It has seventeen thousand seats and a very special stage. The design of the stage was by the great American architect Frank Lloyd Wright. You can listen to all kinds of concerts at the Hollywood Bowl.

▶阅读上面的短文，从每题所给的四个选项中，选出一个最佳答案。

1. Today Hollywood is _____.
   A. a special city in Los Angeles   B. where all the movie stars live
   C. where they make all the movies   D. the biggest city in California
2. You can see where Hollywood is in Los Angeles because _____.
   A. it is a hill   B. postcards show you
   C. there is a big sign on the hills   D. local people will tell you
3. The Hollywood Bowl is _____.
   A. a place where you see movies
   B. one of the largest open-air theaters in the world
   C. a hill in Hollywood
   D. a landmark in Los Angeles
4. Which is not mentioned about the Hollywood Bowl?
   A. Seats.   B. Size.
   C. Stage.   D. Designer.
5. What special things can we see in Hollywood?

A. The Hollywood hills.　　　　　　B. The hollywood landmark.

C. The Hollywood Bowl.　　　　　　D. both B and C.

✦✦（2）✦✦

From Poor to Rich

One day in early March of 1993, Pauline and Tome Nichter and their 11-year-old son Jason, were shopping for a toy in Buena Park, CA. Suddenly, Pauline saw a wallet lying on the floor. When she looked inside, she found $200. The family, homeless and without work, knew that could change their lives. But they took the wallet to the nearby police station and turned it in. The wallet was found to have some other pockets, and more money in-over $2000! The police called the man who lost the wallet to pick it up. The man thanked the Nichters and shook their hands, but did not reward them. Luckily for the family, a TV news reporter filmed the story. People from all over the world heard the story and sent them letters, money, and even jobs. A businessman even let them live in his house for free for six months. So far, the family has received over $100,000. Now the Nichters' future is bright.

1.　homeless　*adj.* 无家可归的

2.　film　*v.* 拍成电影

▶阅读上面的短文，从每题所给的四个选项中，选出一个最佳答案。

1.　From the reading, we can know Pauline is Tom's _____.

　　A. daughter　　　　　　　　　B. mother

　　C. wife　　　　　　　　　　　D. grandmother

2.　Who found out the secret of the wallet?

　　A. The police.　　　　　　　　B. Jason.

　　C. Someone else in the shop.　　D. The man who lost the wallet.

3.　From the reading, we know many people _____.

　　A. work hard to change their lives

　　B. are friendly to the loser

　　C. are ready to help others

　　D. often have good luck

4.　The words "reward them" in the reading mean _____.

　　A. speak to the Nichters　　　　B. give something to the Nichters

　　C. pay the police　　　　　　　D. meet the news reporters

5.　Which of the following is true about the Nichters?

　　A. They got lots of money from a reporter.

　　B. They made friends with the loser of the money.

　　C. They posted letters to the people all over the world.

　　D. They became known to many people.

英汉翻译◈ Translation Exercises

▶ 翻译下列句子

1. 过去他常幻想退休后到英国，并计划在乡间安顿下来。

   _____

2. 他刚一回到英国便买下了一幢房子住了进去。

   _____

3. 他的举动就好像他从未在英国生活过一样。

   _____

4. 碰巧汽车上有位医生。

   _____

5. 这两种文化之间存在着很大差异。

   _____

6. 这次，塔捷耶夫设法爬进了基图火山口，以便能拍摄照片和测试温度。

   _____

7. 在接到把车开出城的指示后，我开始有了信心。

   _____

8. 公牛一直同情地看着醉汉，直到他的背影消逝，才重新将注意力转向斗牛士。

   _____

好句好段◈ Writing Samples

✔ He learnt to eat any food—anything that he could get his teeth into. He learnt to break the ice on water holes with his feet when he wanted to drink. He was stronger, harder, and could see and smell better than ever before. In a way, he was remembering back to the days when wild dogs traveled in packs through the forest, killing for meat as they went. It was easy for him to learn to fight like a wolf, because it was in his blood. In the evenings, when he pointed his nose at the moon and howled long and loud, he was remembering the dogs and wolves that had come before him.

他学会了吃各种食物——吃他咬得动的任何一种东西。他学会了用脚破冰取水来解渴。他变得更加强壮、威猛，嗅觉和视觉也比以前更发达了。从某种意义上说，他逐渐地恢复野性，像以前的野狗一样穿梭在丛林中捕食。对他来说，学会像狼一样厮杀易如反掌，因为这是与他血脉相通的本性。晚上，当他仰首望月，凄厉地长嗥时，他记起了他的祖先。

Lesson 39

Reading Comprehension

✦✦（1）✦✦

Baseball is one of the favourite sports in the USA. Children play baseball in sports fields or parks.

At summer picnic, there is often an informal baseball game. Boys and Girls, young and old take turns to bat. Each team has nine players.

The baseball season goes from April to September. During this time, baseball matches are shown on TV and members of the important baseball teams become America's heroes. At the end of the season the two top teams play against each other. Many baseball fans go along to watch the game. Millions of others listen to the radio and watch television. People seem to talk only about the game. Even long after it is over, they still talk about the result and the players.

American football is perhaps the most popular sport in the USA. The football season begins when the baseball season ends. More people are interested in football than baseball. When there is an important game, thousands of people sit beside the radio or in front of the television set to hear the result.

▶阅读上面的短文，从每题所给的四个选项中，选出一个最佳答案。

1. According to the short passage, which is wrong?

   A. Boys and girls like baseballs.

   B. Baseballs are played in the open air.

   C. A baseball match has nine players.

   D. Children sometimes play baseballs in parks.

2. American people play baseball in April, _____ and September.

   A. May, June, July, August   B. March, May, July, August

   C. January, June, October, November D. February, May, July, December

3. What happened at the end of the baseball season?

   A. People talk only about football games.

   B. Many baseball fans become members of top teams.

   C. A lot of people join the games.

   D. Two top teams play a wonderful baseball game.

4. _____ follows the baseball season in the USA.

   A. The baseball season   B. The football season

C. A baseball match   D. A football match

5. This passage mainly tells us something about _____.

    A. the football season in the USA

    B. football is more interesting than baseball in the USA

    C. the difference between baseball and football

    D. the baseball season in the USA

✦✦ （2）✦✦

A Good Way

Mr. Green lives in a village. He has a few farms and is the richest there. And he has pigs, chicks, cows and sheep. He works in the fields with some workers, and his wife has to do all housework at home. So she's very busy and asks her husband to employ a girl to help her, but he doesn't agree.

"There're so many chicks, dear," said the woman one day. "I can't look after them at all."

"That's easy," said Mr. Green. "There's Mr. Black's farm outside our enclosure wall and the chicks. We'd better make a few holes in the walls and chicks will go to his farm through them and eat his vegetables."

"That's a good idea!" the woman said happily.

And soon Mr. Black found it. Mr. Black told Mr. Green and his wife about it. They promised they would stop their chicks doing it but they didn't keep their promises at all. The man thought for a while and found a way. Mr. Black put nearly twenty eggs near the holes one afternoon. And that evening, when Mrs. Green was counting her chicks, she called out, "Oh, I'm lucky today! I've found twenty eggs in my farm."

Of course, the woman saw it herself. And the next morning, Mr. Black found all the holes had been stopped up.

▶阅读上面的短文，从每题所给的四个选项中，选出一个最佳答案。

1. The Green and the Black lived _____.

    A. in the different villages   B. in the same town

    C. far from each other   D. next to each other

2. Mrs. Green is busy because _____.

    A. she has a few farms   B. she has to do much housework

    C. she has to help her husband   D. she isn't strong enough to do all

3. Mr. Green doesn't agree with his wife because _____.

    A. he has little money to employ a helper for his wife

    B. he thinks his wife is very lazy

    C. he tries his best to save money

    D. he has enough time to help her to do some housework

4. Mr. Green made some holes in the walls to _____.

A. let his chicks go to Mr. Black's farm   B. lay some eggs in Mr. Black's fields

C. make Mr. Black angry   D. watch his chicks

5. The Greens thought _____, so they stopped up the holes that night.

A. Mr. Black would kill their chicks

B. their hens laid the eggs in Mr. Green's fields

C. Mr. Black's chicks would go to their farms

D. Mr. Black's would tell the police about it

语言基本功
英汉翻译◈ | Translation Exercises

▶ 翻译下列句子

1. 他大概还没有到。

_____

2. 他稍微年老了一点。

_____

3. 几乎没有煤了。

_____

4. 有很多伟人出身于贫民窟。

_____

5. 他们相信沉在海底的船里一定有大量财宝。

_____

6. 等到你读到这篇文章时，敏锐的哈勃望远镜已经为我们送来了成千上万张精彩的照片。

_____

7. 大雨不会冲走土壤，而会引起严重的水灾。

_____

8. 人人都钦佩他那绝妙的幽默感。

_____

语言基本功
好句好段◈ | Writing Samples

Life is made up of little things.

生活是由琐事构成的。

No man can be a good ruler unless he has first been ruled.

没受过他人的统治，就不能很好地统治他人。

Ready money is a ready medicine.

现钱等于成药。

Lesson 40

Reading Comprehension

✦✦ (1) ✦✦

She Was Safe!

Just before Christmas in 1971, a German girl called Juliana was flying over a big forest of America. The plane was flying high in the sky.

Suddenly, there was a loud noise. Juliana found herself falling through the air. She closed her eyes. She was sure that she was going to die.

She fell 3,000 metres. When she opened her eyes again, she found that she had landed in a tree in the middle of a forest. She was not dead! To her surprise, she was alive. She wasn't even badly hurt. She was still sitting in her seat. She was holding a bag of sweets. She got out of the seat and climbed down the tree. But she could see nobody else. She was alone except for a few dead bodies here and there.

She began to walk. At first she had nothing to eat except the sweets. Later, she found a little fruit. She had never seen this kind of fruit before. She found that the fruit was safe after she saw some monkeys eating it.

After four days, she came to a deep river, She walked by the side of the river for six more days and at last arrived at an Indian village. She was safe!

▶阅读上面的短文，从每题所给的四个选项中，选出一个最佳答案。

1. The air accident happened in _____.
   A. spring   B. summer
   C. autumn   D. winter

2. The plane was flying about _____ high in the sky.
   A. three hundred metres   B. three hundred kilometers
   C. three kilometers   D. three thousand kilometers

3. Juliana was from _____.
   A. America   B. Germany
   C. England   D. India

4. The girl wasn't badly hurt because _____.
   A. there were a lot of trees
   B. she was young and not heavy
   C. she was lucky

118

D. she had landed in a tree and was still in her seat

5. Which of the following is true?

A. Some monkeys saw her eating the fruit.

B. She could not see anybody else alive around her in the forest.

C. At last she came to a village in India.

D. It took the girl 6 days to walk to the village from the middle of the forest.

◆◆ （2）◆◆

Have you ever been ill? When you are ill, you must be unhappy because your body becomes hot, and there are pains all over your body. You don't want to work. You stay in bed, feeling very sad.

What makes us ill? It is germs.

Germs are everywhere. They are very small and you can't find them with your eyes but you can see them with a microscope. They are very, very small and there could be hundreds of them on a very small thing.

Germs are always found in dirty water. When we look at dirty water under the microscope, we shall see them in it. So your father and mother will not let you drink dirty water.

Germs aren't found only in water. They are found in air and dust. If your finger have a cut and some of the dust from the floor goes into the cut, some of the germs would go into your finger. Your finger would become big and red, and you will have much pain in it. Sometimes the germs would go into all of your body, and you would have pain everywhere.

▶ 阅读上面的短文，从每题所给的四个选项中，选出一个最佳答案。

1. Which of the following is true?

A. If things are very, very small, they are germs.

B. If things can't be seen, they must be germs.

C. Germs are in dirty water.

D. Germs are everywhere around us.

2. What is a microscope used for?

A. Making very very small things look much bigger.

B. Making very big things look much smaller.

C. Helping you read some newspaper.

D. Helping you if you can't see things clearly.

3. Why don't your parents let you drink dirty water?

A. You haven't looked at it carefully.　　B. Water can't be drunk in this way.

C. There must be lots of germs in it.　　D. Water will make you ill.

4. Which of the following is wrong?

A. Germs can be found both in water and in the air.

B. Germs can go into your finger if your finger is cut.

C. If your temperature is not OK, there must be germs in your body.

D. If your finger isn't cut, there aren't germs on it.

5. What's the main idea of the text?

A. Germs may make us ill.   B. Germs are in dirty water.

C. Don't drink dirty water.   D. Take care of your finger.

语言基本功
英汉翻译◈ Translation Exercises

▶ 翻译下列句子

1. 当我在她身旁坐下来的时候，她甚至连头都没有抬一下。

_____

2. 这些袋子装得满满的。

_____

3. 瓶盖是密封的。

_____

4. 一支用这种新机器装备起来的探险队进入了这个岩洞，希望找到埋藏的财宝。

_____

5. 车在接近终点时冲下了山坡，驾驶员费了好大劲才把车停下来。

_____

6. 第二天上午，她又来到这家商店，穿了一件裘皮大衣，一只手拎着一只手提包，另一只手拿着一把长柄伞。

_____

7. 然而到目前为止，还没有一个人暴死呢！

_____

8. 昨天，我丈夫把大门卸了下来，雷克斯很生气，此后我们便再也没有见到他。

_____

语言基本功
好句好段◈ Writing Samples

The heart sees further than the head.
心之所见远胜于目。

Tomorrow is another day.
明天有明天的事。

A bargain is a bargain.
达成的协议不可撕毁。

As a man lives so shall he die.
有生必有死。

本书所有练习题的参考答案（含阅读理解练习题解析及译文），请登录中国水利水电出版社网站http://www.waterpub.com.cn/softdown/（下载中心）免费下载。

Lesson 41

阅读理解◇ | Reading Comprehension

✦✦（1）✦✦

"I would almost rather see you dead," Robert S. Cassatt, a leading banker of Philadelphia, shouted when his twenty-year-old elder daughter announced that she wanted to become an artist. In the 19th century, playing at drawing or painting on dishes was all right for a young lady, but serious work in art was not. And when the young lady's family ranked among the best of Philadelphia's social families, such an idea could not even be considered.

That was how Mary Cassatt, born in 1844, began her struggle as an artist. She did not tremble before her father's anger. Instead, she opposed him with courage and at last made him change his mind. Mary Cassatt gave up her social position and all thought of a husband and a family, which in those times was unthinkable for a young lady. In the end, after long years of hard work and perseverance, she became America's most important woman artist and the internationally recognized leading woman painter of the time.

▶ 阅读上面的短文，从每题所给的四个选项中，选出一个最佳答案。

1. When he knew what his elder daughter wanted to be, Mr. Cassatt _____.
   A. did not love her any longer B. was going to have her killed
   C. burst with great anger D. changed his mind immediately

2. The reason why Mr. Cassatt was strongly against his elder daughter's idea of becoming an artist was mainly that he _____.
   A. was afraid she would live a hard life
   B. was afraid the family might lose the high social position
   C. felt ladies could not succeed in art
   D. felt ladies of good families simply did not become artists.

3. Mary Cassatt never married because she _____.
   A. did not want to be just a good wife and mother
   B. did not think of her marriage
   C. was too busy to form a family
   D. was in such low social position

4. Which of the following is NOT true?
   A. Mary Cassatt began her struggle as an artist in 1864.
   B. Mary Cassatt persuaded her father to support her.

C. Mary Cassatt kept on working hard at art all her life.

D. The social position made Mary Cassatt's "struggle" to become a recognized artist especially hard.

5. Which of the following sentences is the main idea of this passage?

A. Mary Cassatt succeeded in art only by giving up her social position and all thought of a family.

B. Mary Cassatt succeeded as an artist only through perseverance.

C. Mary Cassat was brave in going against her father's will.

D. Mary Cassatt was brave in going against old ideas.

✦✦ （2）✦✦

The Teacher Who Cared

"Mrs. Barrow, Room 501, Room 501," I repeated to myself as I scanned the hallways looking for the room number. It was my first day of fifth grade and I was really scared.

I came to the end of the hall and found an open door. Stepping into the room, I suddenly felt out of place. I tried to act normal, but Mrs. Barrow saw right through me.

"Good morning, Courtni. You may pick your seat."

I looked about the room and took an empty seat near a girl named Wendy Barber. As the year slowly progressed, Wendy and I became good friends. I felt no closeness to Mrs. Barrow, though. I saw her as "just another teacher."

Mrs. Barrow had us write a paper on what we wanted to be when we grew up. Some kids asked why. She explained that when her former students left school, she liked them to come back and shared their fifth-grade dreams together. I decided right then and there that I liked Mrs. Barrow.

Then, my grandmother, who lived with us, suffered from cancer. About a month later, grandma died. I missed some school because I was so sad.

At the funeral, I was sitting there feeling sorry for myself when I looked up and saw Mrs. Barrow standing there. She sat down next to me and held my hand. She comforted me and gave me a beautiful ivy plant in a pink pot and a card which read:

> *Courtni,*
>
> *I'm sorry about your grandmother. Never forget, I love you. You are like one of my children.*
>
> > *With love*
> >
> > *Mrs. Barrow*

I wanted to cry. I took the plant home, watered it and put it in my grandma's old room. I am in eighth grade now and I still have that plant. I never thought a teacher could care that much about her students. Now I know.

> *To Mrs. Barrow*
>
> *I love you very much. You're much more than a teacher—You're like a mother to me.*
>
> *Courtni Calhoun, thirteen*

▶ 阅读上面的短文，从每题所给的四个选项中，选出一个最佳答案。

1. When Courtni walked into Room 501, she felt _____.
   A. happy   B. frightened   C. interested   D. excited

2. Courtni decided that she liked Mrs. Barrow _____.
   A. the first time she met her
   B. when she asked the students to write a paper
   C. when Mrs. Barrow came to see her at her grandma's funeral
   D. when Mrs. Barrow gave her an ivy plant

3. Courtni didn't go to school because _____.
   A. she didn't like Mrs. Barrow   B. she got on badly with her classmates
   C. she was too sad to go to school   D. she didn't like school

4. Courtni is now in _____.
   A. Grade 2   B. Grade 8   C. Grade 5   D. Grade 6

5. Which of the following is wrong?
   A. At first Courtni didn't like Mrs. Barrow, but later she loved her very much.
   B. Mrs. Barrow sent Courtni a card and an ivy plant.
   C. Mrs. Barrow took good care of her students.
   D. Courtni would remember Mrs. Barrow forever.

语言基本功
英汉翻译◈ | Translation Exercises

▶ 翻译下列句子

1. 我们在这家帽店已经呆了半个小时了，而我的妻子仍在镜子面前。

   _____

2. 我的妻子戴着一顶像灯塔一样的帽子！

   _____

3. 我坐在一个新式的满是网眼儿的椅子上，等待着。

   _____

4. 我也不必提醒你昨天买的那条糟糕透了的领带。

   _____

5. 10 分钟以后，我们一道走出了商店。

   _____

Lesson 42

阅读理解◇ Reading Comprehension

✦✦ (1) ✦✦

People first heard about Laika in 1957. On November 3 of that year, Russia sent a satellite into space. It was called Sputnik 2. The world first space traveler was on board. She was a dog named Laika which means "barker".

Until Sputnik 2 went up, no one knew what would happen to living things in space. Could animals live there? Could people travel safely in spaceships? What dangers would there be in space? Laika's trip answered many of these questions.

For seven days the dog circled the earth. She lived in a special cabin that was kept cool for her. Laika barked and moved about. She got food the same way she had been trained to get it on earth. The dog was well and happy.

People on earth were learning that animals could live in space. Maybe men and women could be space travelers, too.

The Russians did not know how to bring Laika back to the earth. She died in space. She gave her life so that people could learn about safe space travel. And people have not forgotten her. Laika's spaceship is sometimes called Muttnik 2.

▶ 根据短文内容，判断下列句子正（**T**）误（**F**）。

1. People didn't know what would happen to living things until Sputnik 2 went into space. ＿＿＿＿
2. Laika had been trained before she went up. ＿＿＿＿
3. Laika was tied down and could not move. ＿＿＿＿
4. Laika died in space. ＿＿＿＿
5. Sputnik 2 is sometimes called Muttnik 2. ＿＿＿＿

✦✦ (2) ✦✦

Icebergs

Did you see the famous film "Titanic"? Titanic was the largest and finest ship in 1912. It hit an iceberg on its first sailing from England to America and sank very soon, leaving a love story to the people. Do you know what an iceberg is?

The earth is round, like a ball. The top of the earth is the north. The bottom of the earth is the south. At the top and the bottom of the earth, there is a lot of ice. It is very cold there. Sometimes there is no sun for many months. There is ice everywhere all the time. Large pieces of ice fall into the sea. They do not go to the bottom of the sea. They float near the top of the water. We call these large pieces of ice "icebergs". Some icebergs are bigger than a tall building. Icebergs are dangerous to ships. Sometimes a ship hits an iceberg, then it sinks.

You can make a small iceberg. Put a piece of ice in a glass of water. Look at it. The ice does not sink.

---

1. sailing *n.* 航行
2. bottom *n.* 底部
3. float *v.* 漂浮

▶ 阅读上面的短文，从每题所给的四个选项中，选出一个最佳答案。

1. "Titanic" was the name of _____.
   A. a ship   B. a man   C. a film   D. A and C
2. There is snow everywhere _____ all the time.
   A. in the west   B. in the northeast
   C. at the top and the bottom of the earth   D. on the earth
3. Which is the correct order of icebergs coming into being?
   a. Large pieces of ice float near the top of water.
   b. There is much snow everywhere.
   c. Large pieces of ice fall into the sea.
   d. Snow becomes into ice because it is cold.
   A. a, b, c, d   B. b, d, c, a   C. b, a, d, c   D. d, b, c, a
4. If a ship hits a large iceberg in the sea, it will _____.
   A. break the iceberg down   B. go down
   C. not leave until the iceberg melts   D. keep moving on
5. Which of the following is NOT true?
   A. The ship "Titanic" would leave for England on its first trip.
   B. The earth looks like a ball.
   C. Icebergs don't go to the bottom of the sea.
   D. Everyone can make a small iceberg.

语言基本功
英汉翻译 ◈ | Translation Exercises

▶ 翻译下列句子

1. 过了一会儿，我们注意到广场的那一边有一个带着两个大筐的耍蛇人，于是就走过去看看。

_____

2. 他一见我们，就拿起了一个长长的上面镶有硬币的管乐器，并掀开了一个筐的盖子。

_____

125

3. 当他开始吹奏一支曲子时，我们才第一次看到那条蛇。

    _____

4. 当耍蛇人突然又吹奏起爵士乐和现代流行乐曲时，我们感到非常惊奇。

    _____

5. 显然，它分辨不出印度音乐和爵士乐！

    _____

6. 电话会越来越多。

    _____

7. 现在没有什么事可做。

    _____

8. 昨天报上有一条关于不明飞行物体（UFO）的报道。

    _____

语言基本功
好句好段 ◈ | **Writing Samples**

☑ Hal, Charles, and Mercedes had started the journey happily; but now they were tired, cross and miserable. Charles and Hal argued about everything, because each thought that he was working harder than the other. And Mercedes was unhappy because she thought that she shouldn't have to work. She was tired, so she rode on the sledge, making the work even harder for the dogs. She rode for days, until the dogs could not move the sledge. The men asked her to walk, but she would not leave the sledge. One day they lifted her off. She sat in the snow and did not move. They went off with the sledge and traveled five kilometers. Then they turned, went back, and lifted her on again.

哈尔、查尔斯和玛尔赛蒂开始旅行时高高兴兴，但现在他们疲惫、暴躁又沮丧。查尔斯和哈尔为每件事争吵不休，每个人都自觉比别人干的活儿更多。玛尔赛蒂也不高兴，因为她觉得她不应该工作。她很累，所以就坐到雪撬上，这使狗的工作更加艰难。她一直坐着直到狗拉不动雪撬了。男人们请求她走路。但她不肯离开雪撬，一天他们把她抬了下来，她坐在雪地上不肯起来，他们扔下她走了 5 公里，然后又返回来捎上了她。

Lesson 43

✦✦（1）✦✦

The Pollution in Our Society

Our surroundings are being polluted faster than the nature and man's present efforts cannot prevent it. Time is bringing us more people, and more people will bring us more industries, more cars, larger cities, and growing use of man-made materials.

What can explain and solve this problem? The fact is the pollution is caused by man—by his desire for a modern way of life. We make "increasing industrialization" our chief aim. So we are often ready to offer everything: clean air, pure water, good food, our health and the future of our children. There is a constant flow of people from the countryside into the cities, eager for the benefits of our modern society. But as our technological achievements have grown in the last twenty years, pollution has become a serious problem.

Isn't it time we stopped to ask ourselves where we are going and why? It makes one think of the story about the airline pilot who told us his passengers over the loud-speaker. "I've some good news and some bad news. The good news is that we're making rapid progress at 530 miles per hour. The bad news is that we're lost and don't know where we're going." The sad fact is that this becomes a true story when we speak of our modern society.

▶阅读上面的短文，从每题所给的四个选项中，选出一个最佳答案。

1. Man cannot prevent the world from being polluted because _____.

    A. the pollution of the world is increasing fast

    B. people use too many man-made materials

    C. we have more industries

    D. we are producing more cars, trucks and buses

2. People crowd into the cities for _____.

    A. they want very much to find well-paid jobs

    B. they are anxious to enjoy the achievements of our society

    C. they have become tired of their homeland

    D. they have a strong wish to become industrial workers

3. According to the passage, what does man value most among the following?

    A. Industry.   B. Health.

    C. Clean air.   D. The future of the children.

4. The story about the airline pilot tells us that _____.

A. man knows where the society is going

B. people do not welcome the rapid development of modern society

C. man can do little about the problem of pollution

D. the writer is worried about the future of our society

✦✦ （2）✦✦

Hundreds of years ago, life was much harder than it is today. People didn't have modern machines. There was no modern medicine, either.

Life today has brought new problems. One of the biggest is pollution. Water pollution has made our rivers and lakes dirty. It kills our fish and polluted our drinking water. Noise pollution makes us talk louder and become angry more easily. Air pollution is the most serious kind of pollution. It's bad to all living things in the world.

Cars, planes and factories all pollute our air every day. Sometimes the polluted air is so thick that it is like a quilt over a city. This kind of quilt is called smog.

Many countries are making rules to fight pollution. Factories must now clean their water before it is thrown away, they mustn't blow dirty smoke into the air.

We need to do many other things. We can put waste things in the dustbin and not throw it on the ground. We can go to work by bus or with our friends in the same car. If there are fewer people driving, there will be less pollution.

Rules are not enough. Every person must help to fight pollution.

▶ 阅读上面的短文，从每题所给的四个选项中，选出一个最佳答案。

1. Hundreds of years ago, life was much harder than it is today because _____.

A. there were not any modern machines

B. there was no modern medicine

C. both A and B

D. there were not many people

2. What is the biggest problem in today's life?

A. Water pollution.　　　　　　　　B. Air pollution.

C. Noise.　　　　　　　　　　　　　D. Pollution.

3. The most serious kind of pollution is _____.

A. noise pollution　　　　　　　　　B. air pollution

C. water pollution　　　　　　　　　D. A, B and C

4. Factories must clean their water _____.

A. before they are thrown away　　　B. when they are thrown away

C. after it is thrown away　　　　　　D. before it is thrown away

5. From the passage we know that _____.

A. a few years ago, there was no smog at all

B. today people don't have to talk to each other in a loud voice

C. we can drink water from the polluted rivers and lakes

D. people are making rules in order to fight pollution

▶ 翻译下列句子

1. 但他们很快就陷入了困境。

_____

2. 伯德马上命令他的助手们把两个沉重的食物袋扔掉。

_____

3. 于是飞机可以上升了，它在离山头 400 英尺的高度飞越了过去。

_____

4. 伯德这时知道他能够顺利飞抵 300 英里以外的南极了。

_____

5. 飞机可以毫无困难地飞过这片茫茫无际的白色原野！

_____

6. 国际形势看上去相当危急。

_____

7. 没有比冰雪更糟的事了。

_____

8. 他们没有别的办法只好自己制造这些商品。

_____

Govern your thoughts when alone, and your tongue when in company.

一人独处慎于思，与人相处慎于言。

If the counsel be good no matter who gave it.

只要忠告中肯，谁提都行。

Life is measured by thought and action, not by time.

生命的价值是用思想和行为来衡量的，而不是寿命的长短。

Lesson 44

语言基本功

阅读理解◇ | Reading Comprehension

✦✦（1）✦✦

Tooth Cavity

James' favourite food is chocolate. His parents and teachers often say that it's bad for his teeth to eat much chocolate, but he doesn't believe it. He often puts some in the milk for breakfast, the juice for lunch, even the soup for supper. His mother has to put some chocolate in his bag before he goes to school. Sometimes when she goes shopping with him, he doesn't leave the shop until she buys some chocolate for him.

The little boy came back from school with a painful look yesterday afternoon. A tooth hurt and he had nothing for supper. His mother made some soup for him. He wanted to put some chocolate in it, or he refused to drink it. His mother had to agree. His father bought some medicine for him, but it was no use. And this morning his mother took him to the dentist. The dentist found that there was a cavity in his bad tooth. So he had to fill it with something.

"Now, young man," said the dentist, "what kind of filling would you like for that tooth?"

"Chocolate, please," answered James.

1.　cavity　*n.* 洞
2.　painful　*adj.* 疼痛的
3.　dentist　*n.* 牙医
4.　filling　*n.* 填充物

▶ 阅读上面的短文，根据其内容，在每个空白处填写一个适当的词（词首字母已给出），完成句子。

1.　James likes chocolate b _____.
2.　James always puts some chocolate in his d _____.
3.　His parents and teachers tell him not to do that, but he doesn't l _____ to them.
4.　In the shops, James always a _____ his mother to buy some chocolate for him.
5.　James' tooth began to hurt when he was at s _____.
6.　James had nothing for supper e _____ some soup with chocolate in it.
7.　This morning his mother took him to a h _____.
8.　The dentist thought the b _____ tooth made James painful.
9.　James can't stop e _____ chocolate though one of his teeth is bad.

✦✦（2）✦✦
Do You Want a Bit More Grass?

One afternoon, a wealthy lawyer is riding in the back of his limousine when he sees two men eating grass by the roadside.

He orders the driver to stop and gets out to see.

"Why are you eating grass?" he asks one man.

"We don't have any money for food," the poor man replies.

"Ok, come along with me, then."

"But sir, I have a wife with two children," comes the reply.

"Bring them along! And you, come with us too!" he says to the other man.

"But sir, I have a wife with six children!" the second man answers.

"Bring them as well!"

They all squeeze into the car, which is not easy task, even for a car as large as the limo.

While they're on their way, one of the poor men says, "Sir, you are too kind. Thank you for taking all us with you."

The lawyer replies, "No problem, the grass around my house is about one metre deep!"

---

1. grass   *n.* 草
2. wealthy   *adj.* 富有的
3. lawyer   *n.* 律师
4. limousine   *n.* 豪华轿车
5. reply   *v. & n.* 回答
6. squeeze   *v.* 挤

▶阅读上面的短文，根据其内容，回答所提的问题。

1. Why does the wealthy lawyer stop his car?
2. What does the poor man eat grass for?
3. Is the lawyer very kind to take them home for food?
4. How many people squeeze into the car except the driver?
5. What does the lawyer take all these people to do?

语言基本功
英汉翻译◈ | Translation Exercises
▶翻译下列句子

1. 安·斯特林夫人在穿过森林追赶两个男人时，并没有考虑到所冒的风险。

_____

2. 刚才，当她和孩子们正在森林边上野餐的时候，他们冲到她跟前，企图抢走她的手提包。

_____

3. 斯特林夫人非常气愤，向着他们追了过去。

_____

4. 只追了一会儿便上气不接下气了，但她还是继续追赶。

_____

5. 这两个人吓了一跳，扔下提包逃跑了。

_____

6. 我只是不喜欢纽约。

_____

7. 我上下张望，但没有看见什么东西。

_____

8. 八月份不可能有雾。

_____

语言基本功
好句好段 ◈ | Writing Samples

☑ Jim finished his story and then we both carried all our things into a cave and hid the canoe under some trees. We were just in time because then the rains came. It rained for days, and the river got higher and higher. All kinds of things came down the river and one night there was a little wooden house, lying half on its side. We got the canoe out and went to take a look. Through the window we could see a bed, two old chairs and some old clothes. There was something lying in the corner and we thought it looked like a man. Jim went in to see, but he said, "He's dead. Someone shot him in the back. Don't look at his face, Huck. It's terrible!"

吉姆讲完了他的经历，然后，我们俩把我们所有的东西都搬到了一个岩洞里，把独木舟藏在树下。我们刚干完，雨就下起来了。雨接连下了数日，河水越涨越高。各种各样的东西从河上游漂了下来。一天夜里，有一座小木房子斜着浮在水面上。我们把独木舟弄出来，划过去看了看。透过窗户，我们能看到一张床，两把旧椅子，还有一些旧衣服。屋角那儿躺着什么东西，看起来像个人。吉姆进去看了看，可他说，"他死了。有人在他的背后开了枪。别看他的脸，哈克。太可怕了！"

Lesson 45

✦✦（1）✦✦

The world is not hungry, but it is thirsty. It seems strange that nearly 3/4 of the earth is covered with water while we say we are short of water. Why? Because about 97% of water on the earth is sea water. And we can't drink or use it directly. Man can only drink and use the 3% of the water that comes from rivers and lakes. And we can't even use all of that, because some of it has been polluted.

Now we need more water. The problem is: Can we avoid a serious water shortage later on? What can we do?

Firstly, we should all learn how to save water. Secondly, we should find out the ways to reuse it. Scientists are making study in this field. Today, in most large cities, people only use the water once. But we can use it again. Even if every large city reused its water, there still would not be enough. What could people drink next?

The sea seems to have the best answer. There is a lot of water in the sea. All we can do is to get the salt out of the sea water. This is expensive, but it's already in use in many parts of the world. Scientists are trying to find a cheaper way to do it. So you see, if we can find a way out, we'll have more water.

---

1. be covered with sth. 被……覆盖
2. short of sth. 短缺……
3. sea water 海水
4. how to save water 如何节水
5. reuse 再利用
6. in this field 在这个领域

▶根据短文内容，判断下列句子正（**T**）误（**F**）。

1. The world is thirsty because about 97% of water on the earth can't be used directly. ____
2. 97% of the earth is covered with water. ____
3. Man can only drink and use about 25% of water on the earth. ____
4. We must try to find a cheaper way to get the salt out of the sea water in order to have more water. ____
5. The best title of the passage should be "How to Waste Water". ____

133

✦✦ (2) ✦✦

Regina is seventeen years old and she lives in Los Angeles, California. She is in her third year of high school. She's quiet and very nice.

Regina has a sister called Garmen. Every one loves Regina and her sister Garmen. They often compare Regina with Garmen. This makes Regina angry. She does not want to be like her sister, she wants to be herself.

Regina is an active girl. She loves to swim, dance, and ride her bike. She belongs to a bicycle club, and on Saturdays the members go for long rides. Sometimes they ride a hundred miles in a day.

Regina also collects stamps. She has stamps from every country in the world. She buys some and gets others from friends. She has a large collection of stamps from Mexico.

Regina wants to be a Spanish teacher. She was born in California, but Spanish was her first language. She knows Spanish and English well. Some of her friends don't want her to be a teacher. They say the teachers don't make much money. She knows that, but she says that many things in life are more important than money. She wants to help young people learn. Nothing is more important than that.

▶ 阅读上面的短文，从每题所给的四个选项中，选出一个最佳答案。

1. Los Angeles, California is in _____.

    A. England   B. Canada

    C. Mexico   D. Amcrica

2. What makes Regina angry?

    A. Her sister Garmen is very clever.

    B. She wants to be like her sister, but she can't.

    C. She doesn't want people to compare her with her sister.

    D. People only love her sister.

3. What does Regina like to do? She likes to _____.

    A. go hunting

    B. do some sewing

    C. go shopping

    D. dance, swim, and ride her bike

4. Regina's hobby is _____.

    A. watching TV   B. reading novels

    C. gathering stamps   D. taking a long walk

5. Regina thinks that _____ important.

    A. work isn't

    B. metal coins and paper notes aren't

    C. study is

    D. life isn't

英汉翻译◈ Translation Exercises

▶ **翻译下列句子**

1.　整个村子很快知道，有一大笔钱丢失了。

_____

2.　当地的屠户萨姆·本顿在把存款送往邮局的途中把钱包丢了。

_____

3.　萨姆确信那钱包一定是被某个村民捡到了，可是却不见有人来送还给他。

_____

4.　三个月过去了，后来在一天早晨，萨姆在自己的大门外发现了他的钱包。

_____

5.　钱包是用报纸包着的，里面有他丢失的钱的一半。

_____

6.　她很早就到了。

_____

7.　你可不可以给她捎一个信？

_____

8.　他戴上了新手表。

_____

好句好段◈ Writing Samples

☑ So, half an hour later, I, too, left Tarlenheim. I took a shorter way than Sapt and when I reached the moat, I hid my horse in the trees, tied my rope round a strong tree and let myself down into the water. Slowly, I began to swim along under the castle walls. Just after a quarter to one, I came to the pipe and waited quietly in its shadow. Light was coming from Duke Michael's window opposite me across the moat, and I could see into the room. The next window along, which Johann had said was Antoinette's room, was dark.

于是，半小时以后我也离开了塔伦汉姆庄园。比起萨普特来我走了一条近路。到了护城河，我在树林里藏好马，把绳子系在一棵粗壮的树上，然后下到水里。慢慢地，我开始沿着城墙游着，差一刻一点钟的时候，我到了排水管边，在阴影里静静等待。河对岸正对着我的是迈克尔公爵的房间，灯光从窗户里照射出来。我可以看见屋子里面旁边的那扇窗子，照约翰所说，就是安冬纳特的房间了。那间屋子是黑的。

本书所有练习题的参考答案（含阅读理解练习题解析及译文），请登录中国水利水电出版社网站 http://www.waterpub.com.cn/softdown/（下载中心）免费下载。

Lesson 46

Reading Comprehension

✦✦（1）✦✦

It Isn't My Dog

Mrs. Turner is a seventy-two-year old woman. Her husband worked in a post office. One day they went to travel in another city, their bus hit to a rock and began to burn. He broke the window and helped his wife get off but he died in the burning bus. And now the old woman has lived alone for eight years. She often walks near the gardens or sits on a chair quietly. She had a dog and liked it very much. But she lost it one morning. She's sometimes hungry and can't buy another one for herself.

Yesterday afternoon Mrs. Turner was sitting on a chair near the garden while a boy was coming to her with a dog. The old woman saw it docile and asked the boy, "Does your dog bite?"

"No, it doesn't," answered the boy.

Having heard of this, the old woman began to touch its head.

Suddenly it bit her hand and she began to shout at the boy, "Why did you fool me?"

"I've never fooled you, madam," said the boy. "My dog doesn't bite, but it isn't mine."

---

1. docile *adj.* 温顺的
2. bite *v.* 咬（bit 是其过去式）

▶阅读上面的短文，从每题所给的四个选项中，选出一个最佳答案。

1. When Mrs. Turner was _____, her husband died.
   A. fifty   B. sixty-four
   C. sixty-eight   D. seventy-two

2. The old woman often walks and sits near the garden quietly because _____.
   A. she wouldn't stay at home alone   B. she lost her work
   C. She wouldn't work   D. she has enough time

3. The old woman doesn't buy a dog because _____.
   A. she's afraid to lose it again   B. she doesn't like any dogs
   C. she can't bear it   D. she hasn't enough food to give it

4. The old woman touched the dog because _____.
   A. it was very beautiful   B. she knew it very well
   C. she loved docile dogs very much   D. she wasn't afraid it at all

5. The word "fool" in the story means _____.

    A. 傻瓜   B. 诈骗   C. 牺牲   D. 愚弄

✦✦（2）✦✦

Cuckoo

There were two brothers in a family. The elder brother dearly loved his younger brother, and the younger brother loved his elder brother, too. But the stepmother didn't love the elder brother, she didn't want him to stay at home. She thought and thought, and got a bad idea.

One day, the stepmother took out two bags of rice seeds, one of which was cooked by her. In the afternoon, two brothers came home from school. The stepmother threw the cooked rice seeds to the elder brother and gave the other bag of rice seeds to the younger brother. She said, "Listen, boys, I give you some rice seeds. You go to the hill over there, you can see a river by which there are two different ways. The elder brother goes one way, the younger brother goes the opposite way. You cannot stop walking until you see a house in front of you. You are going to grow the rice seeds there. There is food and drinks in the house. When the rice seeds sprout, you can come home; otherwise, never!"

---

1. dearly *adv.* 深深地
2. stepmother *n.* 继母
3. seed *n.* 种子
4. sprout *v.* 发芽
5. otherwise *adv.* 否则

▶阅读上面的短文，根据其内容，回答所提的问题。

1. Why didn't the mother like the elder son?
2. What was the mother going to do?
3. What did the mother do one afternoon?
4. When could the brothers go home?
5. Guess why the mother wanted the two brothers to go to the different ways.

语言基本功
英汉翻译◈ | Translation Exercises

▶翻译下列句子

1. 工人们开始卸下装有服装的一批木箱。

_____

2. 其中有只箱子特别重，可谁也弄不清是怎么回事。

_____

3. 他看到的情景使他大吃一惊。

_____

4.　箱内有一个人正躺在一堆毛织品之上。

_____

5.　此人被责令交付旅费 3,500 英镑。

_____

6.　犯不上跟 6 岁的孩子生气。

_____

7.　换乘十四路公共汽车在哪儿下？

_____

8.　我来接你还是咱们在车站碰头？

_____

语言基本功
好句好段◎ | Writing Samples

☑ Then one year something happened which I can never forget. I was again on the west side of the island and was walking along the shore. Suddenly, I saw something which made me feel ill. There were heads, arms, feet, and other pieces of men's bodies everywhere. For a minute, I couldn't think, and then I understood. Sometimes there were fights between the wild men on the other island. Then they came here to my island with their prisoners, to kill them, cook them, and eat them. Slowly, I went home, but I was very angry. How could men do this?

然而有一年，有些事出现令我永远不能忘记。我又一次在岛的西侧沿着海岸散步。突然，我瞧见令我作呕的东西，那儿到处是人头、手臂、脚和一些人体其他部位的碎块。那一刻，我简直无法思考，随即，我就明白了。以前另一个岛上的野人之间发生了一场战斗，然后他们带着俘虏来到了我的岛上，杀了俘虏，接着烹了吃掉。慢慢地，我走回家中，我愤怒了。人怎么能够做这样的事？

Lesson 47

Reading Comprehension

◆◆（1）◆◆

The Ways to Get Fresh Water from Sea Water

Many places in the world need more fresh water. Every country is trying to find ways to turn salt water into fresh.

Why aren't there many factories like the Symi factory?

In some places, the sun isn't hot enough, or it doesn't shine every day. In these places, other ways of heating sea water can be used. These ways cost more money, but they work faster than the sun. By boiling sea water with high heat, a lot of fresh water can be made quickly.

But heating is not the only way to get fresh water from salt water. Other ways are tried. One way is freeze. The fresh part of salt water freezes first. To get fresh water, the pieces of ice are taken out.

Which way is the best? The one that gives the most water for the least money. It may be a different way for each place.

Symi's way seems very good for small, hot places. It doesn't make very much water at a time. But the factory is easy to build and cost little.

That's why people in many dry places talk about Symi!

1. fresh   *adj.* 淡的，无盐的
2. heat   *v.* 加热，把……加热
3. boil   *v.* 煮沸

▶阅读上面的短文，从每题所给的四个选项中，选出一个最佳答案。

1. From the passage we know that fresh water _____.
   A. is a fresh-water factory
   B. is needed everywhere
   C. can make much fresh water at a time
   D. doesn't need sunshine every day

2. The Symi factory _____.
   A. is a fresh-water factory
   B. may be built everywhere
   C. can make much fresh water at a time
   D. doesn't need sunshine every day

3. Which is the best way for small and hot places to get fresh water?
   A. Boiling or heating the sea water.
   B. The way in sunny places.
   C. The Symi's way.
   D. Freezing the sea water in cold places.

4. The writer is mainly talking about _____.

A. water-making factories in different countries

B. the ways of making fresh water from sea water

C. hot places and dry places

D. how to make good use of the sunlight

5. Which of the following isn't true?

A. New ways are tried to get fresh water.

B. A lot of fresh water can be made quickly by heating.

C. The best way is to get the most fresh water with the least money.

D. The Symi's way doesn't work in dry places.

◆✦ （2） ✦◆

The United States and Great Britain took the war on Iraq in late March, 2003. After over twenty days, American soldiers were in Baghdad, the capital of Iraq. They ended the government of Saddam. Thousands of Iraqi people died in the war.

In some parts of the city there was no light because of the war. Some oil wells were set on fire. Now the Iraqi people need food, water and medicine. Many soldiers and people who were hurt in the war need hospital care. People also need a way to find their family members.

After the war, some Iraqi people broke into Saddam's palace, government buildings, and stores. They stole many things from Iraqi Museums. Others were angry that the US soldiers didn't stop the robbers.

The reason for American soldiers taking the war is that they are looking for weapons of mess destruction. But by June 6, they hadn't found any at all.

▶阅读上面的短文，从每题所给的四个选项中，选出一个最佳答案。

1. The capital of Iraq is _____.

A. Paris   B. Sydney

C. Washington   D. Baghdad

2. The Iraqi people who were hurt in the war need _____.

A. hospital care and medicine   B. the US soldiers

C. the Saddam's government   D. food, water and soldiers

3. After the war, _____ broke into Saddam's palace, government buildings, and stores.

A. the US soldiers   B. Great Britain soldiers

C. some Iraqi people   D. foreign tourists

4. Which of the following is NOT true?

A. Some Iraqi people lost their homes and family members in the war.

B. Many people and soldiers were hurt in the war.

C. Saddam has gone in the war. Several Iraqi people died in the war.

D. The war brought great sufferings and disasters to the people.

140

英汉翻译◈ | Translation Exercises

▶ 翻译下列句子

1. 伊恩·汤普森先生最近才买的一个小酒店现在又要卖出去。

_____

2. 汤普森先生之所以想卖它，是因为那里常闹鬼。

_____

3. 他告诉我有天夜里他怎么也睡不着，因为他听到酒吧里传来一阵奇怪的响声。

_____

4. 虽然汤普森临睡觉时把灯关了，但早晨灯却都亮着。

_____

5. 他还说他发现了 5 只空的威士忌瓶子，肯定是鬼魂昨天晚上喝的。

_____

6. 他把自己关在房子里面。

_____

7. 他被禁止行医。

_____

8. 他在旧金山的一个酒吧喝酒。

_____

好句好段◈ | Writing Samples

☑ People were angry because of that. A man called John Knox came to see me. He was a famous Protestant churchman, but I didn't like him. He was a big, angry man with black clothes. He hated the Catholic church, and wanted all Catholics to leave Scotland. To him, the Protestant church was the only true church of God. He said, "Your Majesty, you're a young woman, like my daughter. Women can't understand difficult things like God or the church. Find a good Protestant husband, girl. Let him rule this country for you."

人们听到这些发怒了。一个名叫约翰·诺克斯的人来见我。他是个有名的新教教士，可我不喜欢他。他个头很大，怒气冲冲，穿着一身黑衣服。他憎恨天主教会，想让所有的天主教教徒都离开苏格兰。对他来说，新教教会才是唯一真正属于上帝的教会。他说道："陛下，你是位年轻女子，就像我的女儿。女人是不会懂得上帝、教会这类难懂的事情的。找一个新教徒的好丈夫吧，女孩，让他来为你统治这个国家。"

本书所有练习题的参考答案（含阅读理解练习题解析及译文），请登录中国水利水电出版社网站 http://www.waterpub.com.cn/softdown/（下载中心）免费下载。

Lesson 48

阅读理解◇ Reading Comprehension

◆◆（1）◆◆

Sign language is very important in communication. Studies show that only 7% of the communication in a daily life is verbal. Westerners expect people to look at each other in the eyes when they talk. If you don't do that while you are talking, it may indicate that you do not like the person, or that you are not interested in what the person says. When shaking hands, Westerners will shake two or three times. Do not shake a Westerner's hand for a long time. When a man shakes hands with a woman, it is preferable for the woman to hold out her hand first. In the West, pointing with a single finger at a person while talking usually means that the person speaking is criticizing the person pointed at. Besides, men in English-speaking countries touch men much less than men touch men in China. But men and women touch each other publicly more frequently than men and women touch each other publicly in China. Boy-friends and girl-friends often hold hands, embrace, or kiss in public. Good friends frequently greet one another with a kiss on the cheek, if they are women or opposite sexes.

---

1. expect *v.* 预料，期待，盼望
2. indicate *v.* 指出，表明，显示。
3. hold out 伸出
4. besides 除此之外，还……（表示所说的包括在内）

▶阅读上面的短文，从每题所给的四个选项中，选出一个最佳答案。

1. The title that best expresses the ideas of this passage is _____?
    A. human language   B. spoke language
    C. body language   D. foreign language

2. If she isn't interested in what you say, she may _____.
    A. look at you carefully
    B. look on you coldly
    C. look off your face
    D. look in your face

3. Boys and girls in Sydney often touch each other publicly more frequently than boys and girls touch each other publicly in _____.
    A. London   B. New Delhi

C. Ottawa   D. Washington

4. What does the word "sex" mean? It means _____.

    A. the age of the women

    B. the race of the women

    C. the character of the women

    D. The difference of the girls, women and boys, men

✦✦（2）✦✦
The Story of Hou Yi Shooting the Nine Suns

Long long ago, there were ten suns in the sky. The weather was very very hot.

Every morning, the ten suns came out in the sky at the same time. It was so hot that all the trees were dying. People had no food to eat, no water to drink. Some old people and small children were dying too.

A man named Hou Yi wanted to shoot the suns. But the suns were very high in the sky, it was not easy to shoot them down. Hou Yi must stand on top of a hill to get near the suns, he might be burnt to death when he shot two suns, three suns, four suns...When there was only one sun in the sky it was not so hot, the weather became fine. Hou Yi said, "Let this sun be in the sky, so that we can have daytime."

So, the sun in the sky today is the sun that Hou Yi left for us.

---

1. so...that... 如此……以致……

2. shoot *v.* 射击，射（shot 是其过去式）

3. be burnt to death 被烧死

▶ 阅读上面的短文，根据其内容，在每个空白处填写一个适当的词，完成句子。

1. The weather was hot _____ there were ten suns in the sky.

2. The nine suns _____ people have no food to eat or water to drink.

3. Hou Yi shot _____ suns and only one was in the sky.

4. If there is no sun in the sky, we can't have _____.

5. From the story we can see Hou Yi _____ a lot for the people.

语言基本功
英汉翻译◈ | Translation Exercises

▶ 翻译下列句子

1. 牙科医生们总是在你无法作出回答的时候向你提出问题。

    _____

2. 我的牙科医生刚刚给我拔掉了一颗牙，叫我休息一会儿。

    _____

3. 他知道我收集火柴盒，于是问我收藏的火柴盒是否在增加。

_____

4. 接着他又问我的兄弟近来如何，问我是否喜欢伦敦的新工作。

_____

5. 我总算能够告诉他，他拔错了牙。

_____

6. 你听见有人在隔壁房间走动吗？

_____

7. 你得找人修修你的电视机。

_____

8. 我觉得有东西在我背上爬。

_____

Writing Samples

☑ Inspector Walsh looked at the things in the front room. There was an old black and white television, and some books on the table. There was a picture of a happy young girl with long brown hair on the table, too. Inspector Walsh looked at the picture for a long time. Who was the girl?

沃尔什探长看着前屋的东西。屋里有一台旧的黑白电视机，桌上还有些书。一个棕色长发、充满快乐的年轻女孩的相片也在桌上，沃尔什探长盯着照片看了好一会。这女孩是谁？

Lesson 49

Reading Comprehension

✦✦ (1) ✦✦

The Dove and an Olive Branch

Why does the dove with an olive branch in the mouth mean peace?

The Great Flood lasted 150 days. Noah's family and all the animals were in the big ship. One day, the rain stopped. Noah flew a crow out of the big ship, but the crow didn't come back. Noah flew a dove, the dove came back after seven days. Noah knew the land was far, far away, the dove didn't find the land. Another seven days passed, Noah flew the dove out of the big ship again. In the evening the dove came back with a green olive branch in the mouth. This time Noah knew that the land was near. He was very pleased. Noah and his family and all the animals got out of the big ship when they reached the land. They built houses and started to farm. Noah had many sons and daughters; the animals and trees all grew up, the land was colourful again.

People think both the dove and the olive branch mean a peaceful land and a peaceful life, so they draw a picture of a dove with an olive branch in the mouth to show their love for peace.

▶阅读上面的短文，根据其内容，回答所提的问题。

1. How long did the Great Flood last?
2. How did Noah know the land was far, far away?
3. How did Noah know the land was near?
4. What did Noah and his family do after the dove with an olive branch in the mouth came back?
5. Why does the dove with an olive branch in the mouth mean peace?

✦✦ (2) ✦✦

A Trick

In 1943, during the Second World War, the body of an English man, William Martin, was discovered off the Spanish coast. The papers he has been carrying were returned to England, where they were carefully examined. They had obviously been changed and that was exactly what the British had hoped would happen, for Martin was a trick designed to fool the Germans.

Martin did not exist. The body was that of a sailor who looked as though he had died when his boat sank, but in fact he had been ill and died. Leaving the boat to go down, his parents allowed the dead body to be put into the sea near Spain. It was hoped that the Germans would find it and read the fake papers he carried.

The papers said that the British would attack the island of Sardinia, when in fact they planned to attack the island of Sicity. The trick was successful. When the British landed on Sicity, most of the heavy German guns had been moved to defend Sardinia.

---

1. design   *v.* 设计
2. fool   *v.* 愚弄，欺骗
3. exist   *v.* 存在
4. sailor   *n.* 海员，水手
5. fake   *adj.* 假的
6. defend   *v.* 防护，防卫

▶ 阅读上面的短文，从每题所给的四个选项中，选出一个最佳答案。

1. Who put the papers on the dead man?
   A. The British.   B. German spies.
   C. Spanish soldiers.   D. William Martin.

2. When the Germans found William Martin they probably thought he _____.
   A. was a British spy with important information about the war
   B. was killed by the British soldiers
   C. died of an illness
   D. had the fake papers of the British Army

3. What did the British conclude when they found out the paper were changed?
   A. Martin did exist.   B. Martin was a Germany spy.
   C. The Germans has read the paper.   D. They should attack Sardinia.

4. The reason why the trick succeeded is that _____.
   A. William Martin pretended to be dead near the sea
   B. the Germans believed what the papers said
   C. the Germans soldiers left Sicily completely
   D. the British planned to defend the Germans

5. According to the passage, which of the order is right?
   a. The Germans found the dead at sea.
   b. The British decided to use the dead body to fool the Germans.
   c. The British planned to attack Sicily.
   d. The papers on Martin was brought to London to be examined.
   e. The Germans found the fake papers on the dead body.
   f. The Germans decided to defend Sardinia.
   g. The Germans believed the papers.
   A. c b d a e g f   B. c a b d g f e
   C. a c b g f e d   D. b c a g e f d

英汉翻译◈ | Translation Exercises

▶ 翻译下列句子

1. 德黑兰的一个年轻人由于对睡地板感到厌倦，于是积蓄多年买了一张真正的床。

   _____

2. 他平生第一次自豪地拥有了一张既有弹簧又带床垫的床。

   _____

3. 由于天气很热，他便把床搬到了他的屋顶上。

   _____

4. 尽管床摔成了碎片，但年轻人却奇迹般地没有受伤。

   _____

5. 这个人伤心地捡起了床垫，把它拿进了屋。

   _____

6. 没有必要查阅每个生词。

   _____

7. 请医生没用，已经太晚了。

   _____

8. 他跳过河去。

   _____

好句好段◈ | Writing Samples

☑ There was a table under a tree outside the house, and the March Hare and the Hatter were having tea. A Dormouse was sitting between them, asleep. The three of them were all sitting together at one corner of the table, but the table was large and there were many other seats. Alice sat down in a big chair at one end.

房子外的树下有一张桌子，三月兔和制帽人正在喝茶。有只睡鼠在他们中间，睡着了。他们三个坐在桌子的一角，可桌子实际上很大，还有很多座位。爱丽丝在一头的一把大椅子上坐下来。

本书所有练习题的参考答案（含阅读理解练习题解析及译文），请登录中国水利水电出版社网站 http://www.waterpub.com.cn/softdown/（下载中心）免费下载。

Lesson 50

Reading Comprehension

♦♦（1）♦♦

Every time when I look at the moon, I wish I could go there. Do you wish you could fly to the moon in a spaceship one day?

For hundreds of years, men have wanted to travel to the moon. When they looked at the moon, they asked many questions. Was the moon hot or cold? Were there any plants or other living things there? They asked many, many other questions. Some people said there were living plants on the moon. Others said nothing could live there because there was no air or water on the moon.

We know much about the moon now. Scientists have studied the moon for many years and have found out many facts. Not long ago spaceships with men in them flew to the moon.

What do we know about the moon? We find that the moon is much smaller than the earth. It is about one quarter size of the earth. It is traveling round the earth all the time.

Days and nights on the moon are very long. One day on the moon is as long as two weeks on the earth. One night is also as long as two weeks on the earth. In the day the moon is very hot. At night it is very cold. The moon is much hotter and much colder than the earth.

There is another surprising thing. On the moon, things are not as heavy as they are on the earth. Isn't that interesting?

Perhaps one day we can all travel to the moon. It must be great fun.

▶阅读上面的短文，从每题所给的三个选项中，选出一个最佳答案。

1. There are not any plants or other living things on the moon because _____.
    A. there is no air there   B. there is no water there   C. both A and B

2. The moon is _____ the earth.
    A. much smaller than   B. much bigger than   C. about as big as

3. One day on the moon is as long as _____ on the earth.
    A. one week   B. two weeks   C. one month

4. The moon is much hotter in the day and _____ at night than the earth.
    A. much hotter   B. much colder   C. as hot as

5. On the moon things are _____ they are on the earth.
    A. heavier than   B. lighter than   C. as heavy as

✦✦ (2) ✦✦

Divers

In the old days divers used to go down into the sea looking for ships that had sunk because they hoped to find gold and jewels. Now divers still search for valuable thing in sunken ships, but they also try to bring to the surface of the ships themselves, or parts of them. The value of different kinds of metals has increased greatly over the last twenty or thirty years and even though a ship has been under the sea for many years, it may be worth a great deal.

One famous sunken ship is the "Titanic" which sank off the southern coast of Ireland in 1915 with a loss of nearly 1,500 lives. It had four very big propellers made of expensive metal. Today each of these propellers is worth $300,000 or more. The ship, lying on the seabed, has been bought by a man called John Light. He paid about $12,000 for the whole ship. He hoped to bring up those propellers and sell them. He also hoped to sell other parts of the ship, for about $600,000 when he brought them to the surface.

---

1. diver   *n.* 潜水者
2. sunken   *adj.* 沉没的，凹陷的
3. a great deal 大量
4. propeller   *n.* （轮船，飞机上的）螺旋推进器
5. seabed   *n.* 海底，海床

▶ 阅读上面的短文，从每题所给的四个选项中，选出一个最佳答案。

1. Different kinds of metals from sunken ships _____.
    A. are more valuable than gold
    B. are worth more and more money
    C. have become better in the sea for many years
    D. are easy to get from the sunken ships
2. When the ship is brought up to the surface, John Light may get at least _____.
    A. $12,000   B. $300,000
    C. $600,000   D. $1,800,000
3. The reason why John Light paid for the ship is that he wanted to _____.
    A. get $ 12, 000 back
    B. sell the propellers and other parts
    C. repair and sell it
    D. keep those valuable propellers
4. Divers used to go down into the sea _____.
    A. to bring up the sunken ships
    B. to find valuable things in the sunken ships
    C. to look for the parts of the sunken ships

D. to put gold and jewels in the sunken ships

5. Which is NOT true according to the passage?

A. Divers hoped to get gold and jewels by going into the sea.

B. In the past twenty or thirty years the value of the metals has decreased.

C. The "Titanic" sank off the southern coast of Ireland.

D. About 1,500 lives were lost in the Titanic Accident.

语言基本功
英汉翻译◈ | Translation Exercises

▶ 翻译下列句子

1. 我喜欢在乡间旅行，但却讨厌迷路。

_____

2. 最近我做了一次短途旅行，但这次旅行所花费的时间比我预计的要长。

_____

3. 我坐在汽车的前部，以便饱览农村风光。

_____

4. 过了一些时候，车停了。

_____

5. 我环视了一下身旁，惊奇地发现车里就只剩我一个乘客了。

_____

6. 你可能被解雇，除非你更加努力工作。

_____

7. 我借给他钱了，条件是下个月得还我。

_____

8. 如果没有山姆，上星期的比赛我们会输的。

_____

语言基本功
好句好段◈ | Writing Samples

☑ It was very quiet in the room after that. It is a little thing, a head—a very little thing. But there was so much blood—blood on her red petticoat, blood on her black dress and her white veil, blood on the executioner's hoes, blood all over the floor. Blood, blood everywhere.

在那之后房间是一片寂静。它只是个小东西，一只头颅——一个非常小的东西。但却有这么多血——鲜血渗到她红色的衬裙上，渗到她黑色的连衣裙和她那白色的纱裙上，鲜血流到了刽子手的鞋上，地板上到处是血，血，到处是血。

Lesson 51

Reading Comprehension

✦✦ （1） ✦✦

Try to Save Mistakes

We can make mistakes at any age. Some mistakes we make are about money. But most mistakes are about people. "When I got that job, did Jim really feel good about it as a friend? Or is he envious of my luck?" "And Paul—why didn't I find that he was friendly just because I had a car?" When we look back, thinking about these can make us feel bad. But when we look back, it's too late.

Why do we get it wrong about our friends—or our enemies? Sometimes what people say hides their real meaning. And if we don't really listen, we miss the feeling behind the words. When someone tells you. "You're a lucky dog." Is he really on your side? If he says, "You are a lucky guy." That is being friendly. But "lucky dog"? There's a little of envy in those words.

How can you tell the real meaning behind someone's words? One way is to take a good look at the person talking. Do his words mean the way he looks? His way of speaking? The look in his eyes? Stop and think. The minute you spend thinking about the real meaning of what people say to you may save mistakes.

---

1. envious   *adj.* 嫉妒的，羡慕的
2. enemy   *n.* 敌人

▶阅读上面的短文，从每题所给的四个选项中，选出一个最佳答案。

1. From the first paragraph we know that the writer _____.

   A. feels happy because his friends are friendly to him

   B. feels he may not have "read" his friends' true feeling right

   C. thinks it was a mistake to make friends with Jim and Paul

   D. feels sad about his friends

2. The writer talks about someone saying "You are a lucky dog." He is saying that _____.

   A. the speaker of this sentence is just being friendly

   B. it means the same as "You're a lucky guy"

   C. people can't use the word "dog" when talking about a person

   D. sometimes the words give a possible answer to the feeling behind the words

3. The writer tells us _____.

A. how we won't make mistakes about money and friends

B. how to get an idea of people

C. how to understand what people tell us without making mistakes

D. to keep people friendly without thinking of what they talk

4. In listening to a person the important thing is _____.

A. not to watch him carefully

B. to listen to his words clearly

C. to look at the "body language" of the person and think about the real meaning

D. not to mind what he says

5. Which of the following is NOT true according to the passage?

A. It's not good to think carefully before we talk.

B. We make more mistakes about people than about money.

C. All those mistakes make us feel unhappy.

D. Sometimes we'd better spend some time thinking about the real meaning of what is said to us.

✦✦ （2） ✦✦

I've Only Sent My Regards to You!

Robert and Steve lived next to each other and they studied in the same school. They went to school and played football together. Robert's father had a shop in the center of the town and brought in a lot of money. But Steve was born in a poor family and often borrowed some money from his friend. The boy never refused.

The two young men went to the different universities after they finished middle school. Now Robert works in a hospital but Steve has become a lawyer. Robert finds it difficult to see his friend though they lived in the same town. He doesn't know the young man is trying to get rich. One day Robert was going to buy a blouse for his wife and met Steve in the store. He asked his friend to help him choose one for her. The next morning he received a bill from Steve and he was told to pay his friend thirty dollars for it. Robert was angry but he had to do so.

A few days later Robert saw Steve in the hospital. He forgot that and said hello to him. But then he hurried to explain. "I have to tell you I've only sent my regards to you!"

---

1. refuse   *v.* 拒绝，谢绝
2. lawyer   *n.* 律师

▶根据短文内容完成下列句子。

1. Robert and Steve went to school and played football together because _____.

2. Steve often borrowed some money from his friend because Robert came from _____.

3. Robert can't often see his friend because _____.

4. After Steve helped Robert _____, he told his friend to pay him thirty dollars.

5. Robert was afraid he would _____, so he hurried to explain the reason to the lawyer.

英汉翻译◈ | Translation Exercises

▶翻译下列句子

1. 我的朋友休一直很胖，但是近来情况变得越发糟糕，以致他决定节食。

_____

2. 他是一星期前开始节食的。

_____

3. 他把我领进屋，慌忙把一个大包藏到了桌子下面。

_____

4. 显然他感到很尴尬。

_____

5. 他解释说，他的饮食控制得太严格了，以致不得不偶尔奖赏自己一下。

_____

6. 别吃太多糖果。

_____

7. 多香的玫瑰花！

_____

8. 冰有助于食品保鲜。

_____

好句好段◈ | Writing Samples

☑ I had a lot to learn, too. I learnt how to make shoes out of brown paper. How to clean the actors' hats with a bit of bread. Then they looked like new again. I ran all over London to buy the best hair for the wigs. I learnt how to make fish, and fruit, and a piece of meat out of wood and coloured paper.

当然我要学的东西很多。我学会了如何用牛皮纸做鞋，学会了用一点面包洗掉演员帽子上的污渍，使帽子焕然一新。我要跑遍伦敦买到最好的头发制成假发，还要懂得如何用木头和彩色纸做成鱼、水果和肉片。

本书所有练习题的参考答案（含阅读理解练习题解析及译文），请登录中国水利水电出版社网站
http://www.waterpub.com.cn/softdown/（下载中心）免费下载。

Lesson 52

Reading Comprehension

✦✦（1）✦✦

Dick was born in a poor family. His father had a small boat and went fishing in the morning and sold the fish in the market in the afternoon. With the money he earned he bought food for his family. When winter came, they were often hungry. One morning the hungry man fell into the river and wasn't found again. Dick's mother married another young man and she left her three-year-old son without saying goodbye. His aunt had to look after him.

Twenty years passed. Dick became a tall strong man. He found work on a farm. He worked hard and wanted to earn more money. He often went to see his aunt with nice presents. The woman was very happy, but one day she was killed in a traffic accident. The young man was in deep sorrow. After he burried her, he decided to buy a beautiful tombstone for her. He went to a shop in town, but all the tombstones were too expensive, and he didn't have enough money. He asked, "Do you sell old tombstones, please?" "Yes, we do, sir." answered the shopkeeper. "Is it as expensive as a new one?" "No, it is much cheaper," said the man. "But the other name is on it." "It doesn't matter," said Dick. "My aunt couldn't read."

▶ 阅读上面的短文，从每题所给的四个选项中，选出一个最佳答案。

1. The family were often hungry in winter because _____.

   A. Dick's father lost his work

   B. Dick's mother left the family

   C. Dick's father couldn't catch any fish and he couldn't get any money

   D. nobody bought fish in winter

2. Dick's aunt had to look after him because _____.

   A. his father died and his mother left him

   B. she loved the boy very much

   C. Dick's mother asked her to do that

   D. she had no child

3. When Dick was _____ years old, he began to work on a farm.

   A. twenty   B. twenty-one

   C. twenty-two   D. twenty-three

4. How did Dick's aunt die?

   A. She fell into a river and couldn't come up again.

B. She couldn't get enough food to eat and died.

C. She died in a traffic accident.

D. She worked too hard and got too tired.

5. Dick decided to buy an old tombstone because _____.

A. his aunt couldn't read

B. he didn't have enough money to buy a new one

C. the old tombstone was as expensive as the new one

D. he didn't want to spend too much on a tombstone

✦✦（2）✦✦

What's your favourite colour? Do you like yellow, orange or red? If you do, you must be a person full of hopeful happy feeling about life. Do you like gray and blue? Then maybe you are quiet, and you would like to go after. And sometimes you feel unhappy.

If you love green, you are strong-minded. You wish to do everything well and want other people to see you are successful. At least this is what psychologists tell us.

They tell us that we don't choose our favourite colour as we grow up. If you happen to love brown, you did so as soon as you opened your eyes, or at least as soon as you could see clearly.

A yellow room makes us feel happier than a dark green one; and a red dress brings warms and gladness to the saddest winter day.

Light and bright colours make people not only happier but more active. It is a fact that factory workers work better, harder, and have few accidents when their machines are painted orange rather than black dark grey.

Remember, then, that if you feel low, you can always brighten your day or your life with a new shirt or a few colourful things.

Remember also that you will know your friends better when you find out what colours they like and dislike. And don't forget that anyone can guess a lot about your character when you choose something in different colours.

▶阅读上面的短文，从每题所给的四个选项中，选出一个最佳答案。

1. From this passage, we know that _____.

A. one can choose his colour liking

B. one is born with his colour liking

C. one's colour liking can be changed

D. one can see bright colours clearly

2. It's important for us to choose colours because _____.

A. colours affect our feeling in many ways

B. sometimes colours will do our feeling good

C. sometimes light and bright colours make us happy

D. colours will help us to do everything well

3. The passage tells us _____.

   A. one's colour liking always shows one's character

   B. we can brighten our life with wonderful colours

   C. psychologists really know everything about colours

   D. one's colour liking had something to do with one's character

语言基本功
英汉翻译◈ | Translation Exercises

▶ 翻译下列句子

1. 我们刚刚搬进一所新房子，我辛辛苦苦地干了整整一个上午。

   _____

2. 我试图把我的新房间收拾整齐。

   _____

3. 更糟糕的是房间还非常小，所以我暂时把书放在了地板上。

   _____

4. 几分钟前，我妹妹帮我把一个旧书橱抬上了楼。

   _____

5. 她走进我的房间，当她看到地板上的那些书时，大吃一惊。

   _____

6. 警察说："任何人都不许进楼。"

   _____

7. 许多吸烟多的人承认吸烟会伤害肺。

   _____

8. 她无论如何都说不出事情是怎样发生的。

   _____

语言基本功
好句好段◈ | Writing Samples

☑ 'I said that our waste products don't make the river water dangerous. We've tested them very carefully for many years, and if they are diluted in water, they are not dangerous at all. There are usually only one and a half parts per million in the river water, that's all. And the seals aren't in the river. They're out at sea. I wrote that in my letter, and I'll say the same thing at the Enquiry next week.'

"我说我们的废料没有对河水造成危害。我们已经谨慎地测试了许多年。如果它们被水稀释，它们根本没有危险。在河水中废料通常仅占一百万分之一点五，仅此而已。而海豹不在河里。他们远在海里。我在信中写了这些，在下周的听证会上我会说同样的话。"

本书所有练习题的参考答案（含阅读理解练习题解析及译文），请登录中国水利水电出版社网站 http://www.waterpub.com.cn/softdown/（下载中心）免费下载。

Lesson 53

Reading Comprehension

++ （1） ++

Fire

Fire can help people in many ways. But it can also be very harmful. Fire can heat water, warm your houses, give light, and cook food. But fire can burn things too. It can burn trees, houses, animals, or people. Sometimes big fires can burn forests.

Nobody knows for sure how people began to use fire. But there are many interesting, old stories about the first time a man or woman started a fire. One story from Australia tells about a man, a very, very long time ago. He went up to the sun by a rope and brought fire down.

Today people know how to make a fire with matches. Children sometimes like to play with them. But matches can be very dangerous. One match can burn a piece of paper, and then it might burn a house. A small fire can become a big fire very fast.

Fires kill many people every year. So you must be careful with matches. You should also learn how to put out fires. Fires need oxygen. Without oxygen they die. There is oxygen in the air. Cover a fire with water, sand, or in an emergency, with your coat or something else. This keeps the air away from a fire and kills it.

Be careful with fire, and it will help you. Be careless with fire, and it will burn you.

▶阅读上面的短文，从每题所给的四个选项中，选出一个最佳答案。

1. Which of the following is true?

    A. We are not sure how people started to use fire.

    B. It is an Australian who started a fire.

    C. We know how people began to use fire.

    D. Nobody knows how to make a fire.

2. Children mustn't play with matches because _____.

    A. matches burn paper

    B. it is not interesting

    C. matches can be dangerous

    D. they don't know how to make a fire with matches

3. If you are going to put out a fire, you _____.

    A. must be careful with matches   B. ought to know it can be harmful

    C. have to cover it with water only   D. should keep air away from it

4. We must be careful with fire, or it _____.

  A. can die   B. warms our houses

  C. might burn us   D. will help us

5. What is the main idea of the passage?

  A. Fire can help people in many ways.

  B. Fire can be both helpful and harmful.

  C. Fire can burn things and people.

  D. We must be careful with matches.

An Accident

Grace Lim, my neighbour's youngest daughter, was returning home from school when a motorbike hit her. She was crossing the road when the motorbike knocked her down. He could not avoid her because he was traveling too fast.

Fortunately, Grace was not badly hurt. There was only a cut on her forehead. A kind gentleman saw what happened and quickly came up to help her. Another woman hurriedly telephoned for the ambulance.

Ten minutes later an ambulance came. The doctor of the General Hospital looked her over carefully and told her to remain in the hospital for a day. He wanted her to take an X-ray of her head. He told her she could go home the next day.

Mrs. Lin, Grace's mother, did not know about the accident until a policeman came to her home and told her about it. The policeman, however, told her not to worry because Grace was not badly hurt. Mrs. Lin immediately rushed to the hospital to see her daughter. She was glad to see Grace and reminded her to be very careful when she crossed the road.

▶ 阅读上面的短文，从每题所给的四个选项中，选出一个最佳答案。

1. The traffic accident happened when _____.

  A. Grace was traveling on a motorbike   B. Grace was going to school

  C. Grace was crossing the street   D. Grace was on the way to school

2. An ambulance came in time and took Grace to _____.

  A. the General Hospital   B. her house

  C. her school   D. see her mother

3. _____ came to help Grace when she was just knocked down.

  A. Doctors   B. Policemen

  C. A kind man and a woman   D. The motorbike

4. When Mrs. Lin saw her daughter in the hospital, she was glad because _____.

  A. her daughter was not badly hurt

  B. the doctors looked her over

  C. her daughter took an X-ray of her head

D. there was only one cut in her daughter's leg

5. What can we learn from this passage?

   A. Look after the patient carefully as a doctor does.

   B. Be careful while crossing the road.

   C. Don't ride a motorbike from now on.

   D. Parents shouldn't worry about their children in hospital.

语言基本功 英汉翻译 ◈ | Translation Exercises

▶ 翻译下列句子

1. 消防队员们终于扑灭了加利福尼亚的一场森林大火。

2. 森林火灾时常由破碎的玻璃或人们随手扔掉的香烟头引起。

3. 他发现了缠绕在 16,000 伏高压线上的一条死蛇。

4. 解释很简单，却异乎寻常。

5. 一只鸟把蛇从地上抓起来，然后把它扔到了电线上。

6. 可能存在技术工人短缺问题。

7. 旅客不得越过此线。

8. 政府必须采取措施抑制交通事故。

语言基本功 好句好段 ◈ | Writing Samples

✔ Only Colin knew how important those crossly spoken, childish words were. All his life he had been afraid to ask about his back, and his terrible fear had made him ill. Now an angry little girl told him his back was straight, and he believed her. He was no longer afraid.

只有柯林明白这些带着怒气说出的孩子气的话有多么重要。他长这么大一直都不敢问起自己的脊背，而他的恐惧总是让他病歪歪的。现在这个愤怒的小姑娘告诉他，说他的脊背是直的，而他相信她。他再也不怕了。

Lesson 54

Reading Comprehension

✦✦ (1) ✦✦

A Trip

I'm going to take my family to have an overseas trip. My wife, our two children and I will all go along. My elder brother is going with us. He has never been overseas and he is even more excited than the children. My father is so old that he'd like to stay at home and takes care of the house.

We're going by train to New York, and then take a ship to Europe. When we arrive in Europe, we're going to several countries for sightseeing. We'll go to places either by train or by bus. We're going to fly home.

It took us a long time to decide where to go, but I think we have planned a very interesting trip. We will go to England, France and Italy. My wife is very interested in going to France because she is a teacher of French. And my brother, who speaks very good Italian, is looking forward to the trip to Italy.

We also talked about how we would go to Europe. At first we wanted to fly because it would be faster and would save more time. But my brother likes to take a boat trip and the children enjoy that, too.

▶阅读上面的短文，从每题所给的四个选项中，选出一个最佳答案。

1. My brother is very excited because _____.
   A. he has many friends in other countries
   B. he has never traveled by plane
   C. he wanted to buy some books in Italy
   D. he has never been overseas

2. We're coming back home by _____.
   A. sea   B. air
   C. bus   D. train

3. In Europe, we will _____.
   A. go sightseeing at the seaside   B. go to different countries by ship
   C. buy a lot of presents   D. go from place to place by train or by bus

4. My wife works in a _____.
   A. hospital   B. factory

C. shop   D. school
5. My brother and my children would like to _____.
   A. do some shopping in Europe   B. study the Italian language in Italy
   C. enjoy a trip by ship   D. learn French in France

✦✦ （2） ✦✦

The Weather in the USA

The United States is a large country. It is so large that on the same day the weather can be very different in different parts of the country. On the same day in the winter, it may be warm in some places and cold in others. In Florida or southern California in the winter, the temperature might be over 80 degrees Fahrenheit, or 27℃. At the same time, in Maine or North Dakota the temperature might be below freezing. In the summer, it may be over 100°F（38℃）in Alabama or Mississippi.

On the same day, the temperature may be 74°F（23℃）in Colorado or Oregon. Part of the country may be having uncomfortable heat wave. Another part of the country may be having pleasant weather. The temperature is not the same in all parts of the United States. The amount of rainfall is also very different throughout the country. In parts of the West there is so little rain that there are deserts, in parts of the South there is so much rain that there are swamps. In most of the States the amount of rainfall is between them.

▶ 阅读上面的短文，从每题所给的四个选项中，选出一个最佳答案。

1. When it is 74°F, it is _____.
   A. 100℃   B. 38℃
   C. 23℃   D. 27℃
2. Florida, California, Maine, North Dakota, Alabama, Mississippi, Colorado and Oregon are the names of _____.
   A. rivers   B. deserts
   C. states   D. countries
3. The writer wrote the article to _____.
   A. give information about the weather in the USA
   B. explain what Fahrenheit is
   C. ask you to live where the best weather is
   D. introduce the US
4. What would happen to the land if there was no rain or very little rain for a long time?
   A. The land would become a swamp.   B. The land would become a desert.
   C. The summer would be cool.   D. The winter would be warm.
5. If there was either too much rain or to little rain, what would happen?
   A. There would be some swamps.   B. That must be in summer or in winter.
   C. There would be swamps or deserts. D. That showed pleasant weather.

▶ 翻译下列句子

1. 早饭后，我送孩子们上学，然后就去了商店。

2. 不一会儿我就忙着调拌起了黄油和面粉，很快我的手上就沾满了黏黏的面糊。

3. 没有什么能比这更烦人了。

4. 我用了 10 分钟的时间才说服她过会儿再来电话。

5. 真是糟糕透了！我的手指上、电话机上以及门的把手上，都沾上了面糊。

6. 服务员收到一大笔小费。

7. 他当然是很英俊的。

8. 你这么说真是太客气了。

语言基本功
好句好段 ◈ Writing Samples

✓ When we rode into London, I began to feel afraid. This was a big, big city, and we were just two unimportant young men from a small town. I'll never forget the noise, and the smells, and the crowds. There were 200,000 people living in the City of London－I never saw so many people before in my life.

我们驱车进入伦敦城时，我开始感到心慌。这是很大、很大的一座城市，而我们只是两个从小镇来的微不足道的小伙子。城市的拥挤、喧嚣掺合着种种气味至今令我记忆犹新。伦敦市内生活着 20 万居民——我以前从未见过这么多的人。

本书所有练习题的参考答案（含阅读理解练习题解析及译文），请登录中国水利水电出版社网站 http://www.waterpub.com.cn/softdown/（下载中心）免费下载。

Lesson **55**

阅读理解◈ | Reading Comprehension
✦✦（1）✦✦

Children like to eat candy. But it's bad for the teeth. Do you know the history of candy?

Once candy was not made for children. In a country, almost 5000 years ago, candy was made only for kings. Then it was made in other countries. Today, children are the candy kings.

Do you ever eat liquorice（甘草）？People in the old times ate liquorice, too. They did not take liquorice as candy at first. They ate liquorice to keep them healthy.

In some countries, people ate liquorice to make them beautiful. Later more people ate it just because it was very delicious.

All candies were made by hand until 1845. In that year, a man made a candy machine. Soon other candy machines were made. At first, not many candies were sold. But after 1904 candies were sold all over the world. Today, candy companies say people eat from 15 to 30 pounds of candies each year. More than 2000 kinds of candy are made.

How many kinds of candy do you eat, candy king?

▶阅读上面的短文，从每题所给的四个选项中，选出一个最佳答案。

1. Almost 5000 years ago, the ＿＿＿ of some countries could eat candy.
   A. children   B. kings
   C. farmers   D. soldiers

2. People in the old times ＿＿＿.
   A. did not eat liquorice at all
   B. took liquorice as candy at first
   C. did not think liquorice could make them beautiful
   D. thought liquorice could keep them healthy

3. Before 1845 ＿＿＿.
   A. all candies were made of hand   B. some candies were made by machine
   C. the first candy machine was made   D. a lot of candies were sold

4. Candies have been sold all over the world for ＿＿＿.
   A. 153 years   B. 50 centuries
   C. more than 90 years   D. more than 2000 years

5. The passage tells us mainly about ＿＿＿.

A. the candy kings   B. liguorice

C. the candy companies   D. the history of candy

✦✦ （2）✦✦

The Problems In Large Cities

Some people think they have an answer to the problem of automobile crowding and pollution in large cities. Their answer is the bicycle, or "bike".

In a great many cities, hundreds of people ride bicycles to work every day. In New York City, some bike riders have even formed a group called "Bike for a Better City". They believe that if more people ride bicycles to work there would be fewer automobiles in the city and therefore less dirty air from car engines.

For several years this group has been trying to get the city government to help bicycle riders. For example, they want the city to paint special lanes—for bicycles only—on some of the main streets, because when bicycle riders must use the same lanes as cars, there may be accidents. "Bike for Better City" feels that if there were special lanes, more people would use bikes.

But no bicycle lanes have been painted yet. Not everyone thinks this is a good idea. Taxi drivers don't like the idea—they say it will slow traffic. Some store owners on the main streets don't like the idea they say that if there is less traffic, they will have less business. And most people live too far from downtown to travel by bike.

▶阅读上面的短文，从每题所给的四个选项中，选出一个最佳答案。

1. In large cities the problem is that _____.

    A. there are too many people   B. there is air pollution

    C. cars are driving too fast   D. there are not enough bikes

2. In a great many cities, people ride bicycle to work in order to _____.

    A. get to their office as soon as possible

    B. be able to do shopping on the way

    C. enjoy the beautiful view of the city

    D. make the air of the city less dirty

3. The group has been trying to get the city government to paint special lanes because they _____.

    A. want to stop cars running in the streets

    B. want to learn riding bicycle in the lanes

    C. must be safe while riding bikes to work

    D. hope their city will be more beautiful

4. No bicycle lanes have been painted because _____.

    A. the city government has not enough money

    B. some people don't agree with bicycle riders

    C. some store owners don't like the idea at all

D. taxi drivers say it will slow traffic

5. From the passage we know that _____.

    A. Americans realize the danger of dirty air

    B. Americans are used to going to work by car

    C. Americans don't all like to drive car

    D. Americans don't agree with the government

语言基本功
英汉翻译◈ Translation Exercises

▶ 翻译下列句子

1. 最近，找到失踪宝藏的梦想差一点儿变成现实。

_____

2. 一种叫"探宝器"的新机器已经被发明出来，并被人们用来探测地下埋藏的金子。

_____

3. 一支用这种新机器装备起来的探宝队进入了这个岩洞，希望找到埋藏着的金子。

_____

4. 但最后找到的是一枚几乎一钱不值的小金币。

_____

5. 队员们接着又把整个洞彻底搜寻了一遍，但除了一只空铁皮箱外什么也没找到。

_____

6. 我珍藏着她给我的书。

_____

7. 我珍惜去巴黎参观的记忆。

_____

8. 宫殿里有各种金银珠宝。

_____

语言基本功
好句好段◈ Writing Samples

☑ When the dogs were dead, the other dogs ate them. The men ate them, too. They were good friends, Bjaaland wrote in his diary. And now they are good food. Two days later, the dogs were fat. Then, in a snowstorm, they began the journey again.

这些狗处死后，活着的狗吃它们的肉，大家也都吃。它们是我们的好朋友，比阿兰德在日记里这样写道，现在又成为好食物。两天之后，群狗都养胖了。随后，他们冒着暴风雪再度跳上旅程。

Lesson 56

阅读理解 ◈ | Reading Comprehension

✦✦ （1） ✦✦

During the last ten years, our cities were full of cars, buses and trucks. Now the streets are completely crowded and it is very difficult to drive a car along them. Drivers must stop at hundreds of traffic lights.

What are our cities going to be like in ten or twenty years? Will many motorways be built across them? With big motorways cutting across them, full of noisy, dirty cars and trucks, our cities are going to be awful places. How can we solve the problem?

There are some good ideas to reduce the use of private cars. In 1971, for example, the authorities in Rome began an interesting experiment: passengers on the city buses did not have to pay for their tickets.

In Stockholm there was another experiment: people paid very little for a season ticket to travel on any bus, trolley bus, train or tram all over the city. In many cities now some streets are closed to vehicles and pedestrians are safe there. In London there is another experiment: part of the street is for buses only, so the buses can travel fast. There are no cars or taxis in front of them.

▶阅读上面的短文，从每题所给的四个选项中，选出一个最佳答案。

1. What does the writer worry about in a big city?

    A. The number of traffic lights.　　　　B. The shortage of buses.

    C. The lack of motorways.　　　　D. The traffic congestion.

2. What city once experimented on a completely free bus service?

    A. London.　　　　B. Stockholm.

    C. Rome.　　　　D. None of the above.

3. What city once experimented on very cheap bus service?

    A. London.　　　　B. Stockholm.

    D. Rome.　　　　D. None of the above.

4. In many cities pedestrians are much safer because _____.

    A. no traffic is allowed in some streets　　　　B. traffic is computer-controlled

    C. cars move very slowly　　　　D. only one-way streets are open to traffic

5. In Chinese "pedestrians" means _____.

    A. 司机　　　　B. 行人

    C. 旅客　　　　D. 动物

Judo and karate（空手道）are sports for self-defence. They started in Japan, but now many Americans enjoy them, too. In fact, schools for teaching them have been opened all over the United States and Canada.

Players in both sports use only their hands, arms, legs and feet. Aside from that, the two sports are quite different. In karate, players hit each other with the open hands and closed fists. They also use the feet. In Judo, then, players touch each other. They also move their arms and legs in large circles. Karate moves, on the other hand, are short and quick. Players stand away from each other. They only touch each other with quick punches and kicks.

Can a karate player win a judo player? It depends on the players. One sport is not better than the other. They are both very good forms of self-defence. Both aims are toward control of the mind and body.

▶阅读上面的短文，从每题所给的四个选项中，选出一个最佳答案。

1. Today judo and karate are practiced in _____.
   A. Japan only
   B. the East only
   C. the USA and Canada only
   D. many countries in the world

2. The underlined phrase "aside from" most probably means _____.
   A. except for
   B. because of
   C. the same as
   D. different from

3. Which of the following is true according to the passage?
   A. In judo, players can't use their feet.
   B. In judo, players don't move so quickly as in karate.
   C. In karate, players mustn't touch each other.
   D. In karate, players can use their head.

4. The writer thinks that _____.
   A. judo is better than karate
   B. karate is better than judo
   C. both the sports are good
   D. neither of the two sports are good

5. The best title for this passage can be _____.
   A. The Start of Karate and Judo
   B. The Americans and Karate
   C. Judy and Karate
   D. The Best Sport-Karate

语言基本功
英汉翻译◎ Translation Exercises

▶翻译下列句子

1. 老爷车比赛每年举行一次。

_____

2. 去年有很多汽车参加了这项比赛。比赛开始之前，人们异常激动。

_____

3. 而最不寻常的一辆则要属只有 3 只轮子的奔驰牌汽车了。

_____

4. 在好一阵喧闹的爆炸声之后，比赛开始了。

_____

5. 这次比赛使每个人都挺开心。

_____

6. 船在水上疾驰。

_____

7. 车驶出城便加速了。

_____

8. 他尽快地飞奔回家。

_____

语言基本功
好句好段 ◈ | # Writing Samples

✔ Time went on and winter came. I went to school most of the time and I was learning to read and write a little. It wasn't too bad, and the widow was pleased with me. Miss Watson had a slave, an old man called Jim, and he and I were good friends. I often sat talking to Jim, but I still didn't like living in a house and sleeping in a bed.

时间流逝，冬天来到了。大部分时间我去学校上学，我学认字，也学着写一点。不太糟，寡妇对我挺满意。沃森小姐有一个奴隶，是个叫吉姆的老头，我和他是好朋友。我经常坐着和他聊天，但我仍然不喜欢住在房子里，睡在床上。

Lesson 57

Reading Comprehension

✦✦（1）✦✦

The Famous Mickey Mouse

People usually hate mice, but one mouse has won the hearts of the people all over the world—the famous Mickey Mouse.

Fifty years ago most movies were silent. A man called Walt Disney made a cartoon mouse that could talk in his movies. He named his mouse Mickey Mouse. People, both young and old, were very excited at the talking mouse. Children loved to see their friend, because he brought joy and laughter to them.

Mickey was a clean mouse right from the beginning. Perhaps this is one reason why people hate real mice and love Mickey Mouse. In his early life Mickey made some mistakes. People were angry. They wrote to Disney and said that they did not want Mickey to do silly things. So Disney made a new animal named Donald Duck. He also made a dog called Pluto. This dog does stupid things and makes mistakes wherever he goes. Now our Mickey Mouse is not only clean but also important; he appears as a beautiful and clever star. He has his friends in almost every country.

▶阅读上面的短文，从每题所给的四个选项中，选出一个最佳答案。

1. Mickey Mouse is a _____ mouse.
   A. dirty   B. cartoon
   C. hateful   D. silent

2. Children loved to see Mickey Mouse because _____.
   A. he brought them joy and laughter   B. he made some mistakes
   C. he brought them cakes   D. he made them angry

3. People hoped that Mickey Mouse _____.
   A. would become a clean mouse   B. would not appear again
   C. would do more silly things   D. would not do silly things

4. Pluto is _____.
   A. a clever dog   B. a real dog
   C. a stupid dog   D. a small dog

5. Mickey Mouse has his friends _____ today.
   A. all over the world   B. in China
   C. in the United Nations   D. in Europe

✦✦ (2) ✦✦

We each have a memory. That's why we can still remember things after a long time. Some people have very good memories and they can easily learn many things by heart, but some people can only remember things when they say or do them again and again. Many of the great men have great memories.

A good memory is a great help in learning a language. Everybody learns his mother language when he is a small child. He hears the sounds, remembers them and then he learns to speak. Some can learn two languages as easily as one because they hear, remember and speak two languages every day. In school it is not so easy to learn a foreign language because the pupils have so little time for it, and they are busy with other subjects, too.

But your memory will become better and better when you do more and more exercise.

---

1. forget (forgot, forgotten)   *v.* 忘记（某事物）；遗忘；忽略；忘记（做某事）。如：
    I've forgotten her name.
    我把她的名字忘了。

2. remember   *v.* 记着或记住（某事物）；回想起。如：
    I remember posting the letters.
    我记得把信都寄出去了。

▶ 阅读上面的短文，从每题所给的四个选项中，选出一个最佳答案。

1. Some people can easily learn many things by heart because _____.
    A. they always sleep very well   B. they often eat good food
    C. they read a lot of books   D. they have very good memories

2. Everybody learns his mother language _____.
    A. at the age of six   B. when he is a small child
    C. after he goes to school   D. when he can read and write

3. Before a child can speak, he must _____.
    A. read and write   B. make sentences
    C. hear and remember the sounds   D. think hard

4. In school the pupils can't learn a foreign language well because _____.
    A. they have no good memories   B. they have no recorders
    C. they have too much time for it   D. they are busy with other subjects

5. Your memory will become better and better _____.
    A. if you have plenty of good food
    B. if you do more and more exercises
    C. if you do morning exercise every day
    D. if you get up early

英汉翻译◈ | Translation Exercises

▶ 翻译下列句子

1. 一位穿着牛仔裤的妇女站在一家高档商店的橱窗前。

_____

2. 这位妇女怒气冲冲地走出了商店，决定第二天教训一下那个售货员。

_____

3. 费了好大劲儿，他爬进橱窗去取那件衣服。

_____

4. 这位妇女对那件衣服只看一眼，就说不喜欢。

_____

5. 她开心地迫使那位售货员把橱窗里几乎所有的东西都拿了出来。

_____

6. 我有点累，你来替我驾驶好吗？

_____

7. 那箱子供我们当桌子用。

_____

8. 有没有人接待你？

_____

好句好段◈ | Writing Samples

☑ They had to leave the caravan in the ditch and walk to the nearest town, five or six miles away. There they asked somebody to take care of the horse, and found somebody who agreed to fetch the broken caravan. Then they caught a train to a station near Toad Hall, took Toad home, went down to the boat, and then at last they sat down to a late supper in rat's comfortable little home by the river.

他们不得不将大篷车先留在沟里，步行到五六英里以外最近的城镇。在那儿，他们叫人照看马，又找了个愿意取回破车的人。然后他们坐火车到蛤蟆宅第附近的车站，把癞蛤蟆送回家后，他们坐上船，最后终于坐在了水鼠舒服的河边小屋吃迟到的晚餐。

Lesson 58

阅读理解◈ | Reading Comprehension

✦✦ (1) ✦✦

Doing Housework

Sometimes David likes to help his mother do some housework. Sometimes he doesn't want to. But sometimes he has to because he has no choice.

One day David is doing his homework at home. His mother asks him to help her. She wants him to move the desk in the bedroom. She says there is no change in the room for a long time. She is tired of them standing in the same place. Now the desk is on the right of the bed. Mother wants the desk to be on the left. There's a very nice lamp on the desk. David picks up the lamp. He must be very careful. He puts it on the round table. He moves the bed to the right. Now he can move the desk. The desk is on the left, and the bed is on the right. Where's the lamp? It's on the round table. David moves the table. Mother says, "Watch out!" The lamp is falling, but David catches it. Now he holds it. Mother is happy because the lamp isn't broken. David isn't happy. He doesn't like to move furniture.

▶ 阅读上面的短文，从每题所给的四个选项中，选出一个最佳答案。

1. David is a _____ in this family.
   A. worker   B. student   C. son   D. helper

2. Mother wants David to move _____.
   A. the table   B. the desk
   C. the lamp   D. the house

3. David picks up the lamp because he wants to _____.
   A. put it on the table   B. move the desk
   C. put it on the bed   D. put it in his room

4. The phrase "watch out" means _____.
   A. be careful   B. be quick
   C. thank you   D. watch carefully

5. Which is NOT right according to the story?
   A. Mother wants David to move the bed to the right.
   B. Mother is happy because David catches the lamp.
   C. David is not glad to help his mother do some housework.
   D. David is happy because he only has to catch the lamp.

ESP

Have you ever suddenly felt that someone you knew was in trouble? Have you ever dreamed something that came true later? Maybe you have ESP.

ESP stands for Extrasensory Perception. It may be called a sixth sense. It seems to let people know about events before they happen, or events that are happening some distance away.

There are thousands of stories on record. Scientists are studying them to find out what's behind these strange mental messages. Here's an example, one of hundreds of dreams that has come true.

A man dreamt he was walking along a road when a horse and carriage came by. The driver said, "There's room for one more." The man felt the driver was Death, so he ran away. The next day, the man was getting on a crowded bus. The bus driver said, "There's room for one more." Then the man saw that driver's face was the same face he had seen in the dream. He would not get on the bus. As the bus drove off, it suddenly crashed and burst into flames. Everyone was killed!

Some people say stories like these are lies of coincidences. Others, including some scientists, say that ESP is real. From studies of ESP, we may someday learn more about the human mind.

▶ 阅读上面的短文，从每题所给的四个选项中，选出一个最佳答案。

1. ESP lets people know about _____.
   A. events before they happen   B. their dreams at night
   C. events after they happen   D. their dates of death

2. The studies of ESP could be an important way to _____.
   A. understand the five senses   B. avoid traffic accidents
   C. understand the human mind   D. predict birth and death

3. The example of the man shows an ability to _____.
   A. avoid traffic accidents
   B. sense a danger that will actually happen later on
   C. know about events that are happening some distance away
   D. judge the good and evil of a person

4. The word "coincidences" probably means _____ in this passage.
   A. things dreamed of only by scientists
   B. things which are only dreams
   C. things which don't happen at all
   D. things which happen by accident without necessary connection

5. The main idea of this passage is _____.
   A. people have the ability to predict the future
   B. sick people will be well
   C. human's mind is strange
   D. people's dreams can come true

英汉翻译◈ | Translation Exercises

▶ 翻译下列句子

1. 据说弗林利这个小村里有一棵"被诅咒的树"。

_____

2. 该树是 50 年前栽在教堂附近的。

_____

3. 据说，谁要是触摸了这棵树，谁就会交上恶运。

_____

4. 很多村民相信此树已经害了不少人。

_____

5. 他指出，这棵树成了一个有用的财源。

_____

6. 服务员给顾客端上茶。

_____

7. 他们待我极坏。

_____

8. 他加快了引擎的速率。

_____

好句好段◈ | Writing Samples

☑ We worked harder than ever at the Rose. Plays were always in the afternoon, because of the daylight. We had rehearsals in the morning, and by lunch-time people were already coming across the river to get their places for the play. And more and more people came. By 1592 London was hearing the name William Shakespeare again and again.

在"玫瑰剧院"，我们比以往更加努力工作。由于需要光线，我们上午预演，下午演戏。到了吃午饭时，人们已经陆续过河来占位子等候看戏，而且每次来的观众有增无减。时至1592 年，威廉·莎士比亚在伦敦已颇具名望。

本书所有练习题的参考答案（含阅读理解练习题解析及译文），请登录中国水利水电出版社网站 http://www.waterpub.com.cn/softdown/（下载中心）免费下载。

Lesson 59

Reading Comprehension

✦✦ (1) ✦✦

Scientists have always wanted to know more about the universe.

Years ago they knew many things about the moon. They knew how big it was and how far away it was from the earth. But they wanted to know more about it. They thought the best way was to send men to the moon.

The moon is about 384,000 kilometers away from the earth. A plane can't fly to the moon because the air reaches only 240 kilometers away from the earth. But something can fly even when there is no air. That is the rocket.

How does a rocket fly? There is gas in the rocket. When the gas is made very hot inside the rocket. It will rush out of the end of the rocket, so it can make the rocket fly up into the sky.

Rockets can fly far out into space. Rockets with men in them have been to the moon. Several rockets without men in them have flown to another planet much farther than the moon. One day, rockets may be able to go to any place in space.

▶ 阅读上面的短文，从每题所给的四个选项中，选出一个最佳答案。

1. Scientists have known _____ the moon is from the earth.

   A. how big   B. how long

   C. how heavy   D. how far away

2. A plane can't fly to the moon because _____.

   A. the plane must be driven by a man

   B. there is no air above 240 kilometers away from the earth

   C. there is no gas in the plane

   D. there is no man in the plane

3. The hot gas in rocket is used for _____.

   A. cooking food

   B. making the rocket fly up

   C. keeping the men in the rocket warm

   D. keeping the men sleeping

4. Several rockets without men in them have flown to _____.

   A. the sun   B. another satellite of the sun

   C. the moon   D. the earth

5.   The earth is about 384,000 kilometers away from the _____.

   A. moon   B. sun

   C. universe   D. star

✦✦ （2） ✦✦

Strange things happen to time when you are traveling because the earth is divided into twenty-four zones, one hour apart. You can with more or fewer than twenty-four hours in a day, and weeks with more or fewer than seven days.

If you make a five-day trip across the Atlantic Ocean, your ship enters a different time zone every day. As you enter each zone, the time changes one hour. Traveling west, you set your clock back, traveling east you set it ahead. Each day of your trip has either twenty-five or twenty-three thours.

If you travel by ship across the Pacific, you cross the international date line. By agreement, this is the point where a new day begins. When you cross the line, you change your calendar one full day, backward or forward.

---

1.   happen   *v.* （偶然或必然地）出现；发生

2.   agreement   *n.* 协定；协议；合约；一致

3.   forward   *adj.* 向前方的；位于前面的，早熟的

4.   backward   *adj.* 向后的；落后的

▶阅读上面的短文，从每题所给的四个选项中，选出一个最佳答案。

1.   Strange things happen to time when you travel because _____.

   A. no day really has twenty-four hours

   B. no one knows where time zones begin

   C. the earth is divided into time zones

   D. how time flies

2.   The difference in time between zones is _____.

   A. one hour   B. more than seven days

   C. seven days   D. one day

3.   If you travel across the Atlantic Ocean, going east, you set your clock _____.

   A. one hour ahead in each time zone

   B. one hour ahead for the whole trip

   C. one full day back for each time zone

   D. neither back nor ahead

4.   From this passage, it seems true that the Atlantic _____.

   A. is in one time zone   B. is divided into twenty-four zones

   C. is divided into five time zones   D. is divided into seven time zones

5.   The international date line is the name for _____.

A. the beginning of any new time zone

B. any point where time changes by one hour

C. the point where a new day begins

D. the point between two different zones

语言基本功
英汉翻译◈ | Translation Exercises

▶ 翻译下列句子

1. 我家的狗雷克斯，过去常坐在大门外面叫。

_____

2. 每当它想到花园里来时，便汪汪叫个不停，直到有人把门打开。

_____

3. 然而上星期我正要出去买东西时，发现它正呆在花园里边靠门的地方。

_____

4. 从那以后，它养成了另外一种坏习惯。

_____

5. 出去之后，它又马上把自己放进来，接着再开始叫。

_____

6. 他们编辑了可供取用的大量统计资料以回答各种咨询。

_____

7. 他把那东西评价得一文不值。

_____

8. 我珍视自己和康斯坦斯的友谊。

_____

语言基本功
好句好段◈ | Writing Samples

☑ She soon reached the wood and was pleased to get out of the hot sun and into the shadows under the trees. 'How nice and cool it is in here, under the … under the … under the what?' she said, surprised that she could not think of the word. She put her hand on a tree. 'What does it call itself? I do believe it's got no name!'

不久她就抵达树林。终于摆脱了烈日烤晒，享受到树荫下的清凉世界，这使她很高兴。"在这儿，在……下，在……下，在什么（？）下，多凉爽啊！"她很奇怪，怎么就是想不起那个词儿。她把手放在树上，问："它怎样称呼自己的？我确信它是无名无姓的。"

本书所有练习题的参考答案（含阅读理解练习题解析及译文），请登录中国水利水电出版社网站 http://www.waterpub.com.cn/softdown/（下载中心）免费下载。

Lesson 60

语言基本功
阅读理解◈ | Reading Comprehension
◆◆ （1） ◆◆

Tears

When you feel sad, tears will roll down your cheeks. When you are happy, especially when you laugh very hard, tears also will roll down your face. But tears have a more important job than showing how you feel.

Tears keep your eyes clean and healthy. They washed away dirt and germs and other things that get in your eyes. Your eyes also need tears to keep them wet. Your eyes must be wet so that they can move smoothly. Your eyes are busy looking here and there all day long. They move quickly from one thing to another. If you didn't have tears, your eyes couldn't move, and soon you would be blind.

But where do these tears come from?

Under each eyelid are tiny sacs called tear glands. That's where tears are made. Every time you blink your eyes, some tears are pushed out of these glands. The tears wash over your eyes and soothe them.

When you're not laughing or crying your tears away, where do they go? They go away through small holes in your lower eyelid. Some of these holes lead into your nose. Many times when you cry, the tears drip down through your nose and it starts to run. The drops that fall from your nose are your tears.

Maybe you don't like tears, but your eyes can't do without them.

▶ 阅读上面的短文，从每题所给的四个选项中，选出一个最佳答案。

1. This story tells us _____.
   A. how and why people have tears
   B. why people cry when they are happy
   C. what makes people sad
   D. why people cry when they are unhappy

2. Tears help you by _____.
   A. filling up your tear glands
   B. washing your cheeks and nose
   C. washing things from your eyes
   D. showing how you feel

3. You probably get extra tears in your eyes when _____.
   A. it is dark and rainy
   B. it is dusty and windy

178

C. it is hot and damp   D. it is cold

4. If your eyes were not wet, your could not _____.

A. look at things quickly   B. see without your glasses

C. show people what you think   D. laugh or cry

5. If your eyes need to be soothed, the first thing that must happen is _____.

A. your nose must start to run

B. your eyes must blink to make tears

C. your tears must go into small holes in your lower eyelid

D. your eyes must open widely

✦✦ （2）✦✦

"All work and no play makes Jack a dull boy" is a populr saying in the USA. It is true that all of us need recreation. We cannot work all the time if we are going to keep good health and enjoy life.

Everyone has his own way of relaxing. Perhaps the most popular way is to take part in sports. There are team sports, such as basketball and football. There are also individual sports, such as swimming and running. Skating and climbing are the most popular recreation for people who like to be outdoors.

Not everyone who enjoys sports events likes to take part in them. Many people like watching TV or listening to them on the radio. So many people like some forms of indoor recreation, such as watching TV, singing and dancing.

It doesn't matter if we like indoor recreation or take part in outdoor sports. It is important for everyone to relax from time to time and enjoy some forms of recreation.

▶ 阅读上面的短文，从每题所给的四个选项中，选出一个最佳答案。

1. If we want to be healthy and enjoy life _____.

A. we must work all the time

B. we should work all the time

C. we cannot work at all

D. we not only work hard but also need recreation

2. Football is a kind of _____.

A. team sport   B. team race

C. group sport   D. individual sport

3. "All work and no play makes Jack a dull boy." Here "dull" means _____.

A. good   B. happy

C. foolish   D. nice

4. "Not everyone who enjoys sporting events likes to take part in them" means _____.

A. many people who like sporting events likes to take part in them

B. they all like sporting events but some of them don't like to take part in them

179

C. many people like sporting events, but only one likes to take part in them

D. only one likes sporting events, but everyone likes to take part in them

5. What is important for everyone to relax from time to time?

A. Outdoor sports.　　　　　　　　　B. Indoor recreation.

C. Both A and B.　　　　　　　　　　D. Neither A nor B.

语言基本功
英汉翻译◈ Translation Exercises

▶ 翻译下列句子

1. 在一个乡村集市上，我决定去拜访一位称做别林斯夫人的算命人。

_____

2. 她将于今天傍晚到达，并准备住上几天。

_____

3. 一位您很熟悉的女人将向您冲来。

_____

4. 她会对您说点什么，然后带您离开这个地方。就是这些。

_____

5. 再有不到一个小时你姐姐就要到这儿了，我们得去车站接她。

_____

6. 他说话总是怒气冲冲地叫喊。

_____

7. 他对我们吼叫着发出一道命令。

_____

8. 那条狗总对那邮递员吠叫。

_____

语言基本功
好句好段◈ Writing Samples

☑ Suddenly, my body shook with a new terror. I sat up in bed and listened hard. Yes, I could hear some low sounds, coming not from the storm outside, but from somewhere inside the house. Quickly, I put on my clothes and started walking up and down the room, trying to shake off my terrible fear.

突然间，我的身体由于新的一波恐惧袭来而打起了寒战。我从床上坐起，努力地谛听着周围的响动。是的，我能听见某种低沉的声音，不是来自外面的暴风雨，而是从宅子内部的什么地方发出来的。我迅速地穿上衣服，开始在房间里来来回回地踱步，希望以此摆脱掉我那不可救药的恐惧。

本书所有练习题的参考答案（含阅读理解练习题解析及译文），请登录中国水利水电出版社网站 http://www.waterpub.com.cn/softdown/（下载中心）免费下载。

Lesson **61**

Reading Comprehension

✦✦（1）✦✦

When the fish rose at last to the top of the water, the old man saw that it was two feet longer than his boat. He had seen many great fish, but this one was the greatest fish he had ever seen. It was also the most beautiful.

On the morning of the third day, the end came. The old man was very tired. He threw his harpoon into the heart of the great fish. It rose high out of the water, showing all its power. The next moment it was dead.

The old man took the fish to the side of the boat. Then he turned back and began to sail towards the shore. He sailed well and he looked often at the huge fish.

Then the first shark came. The old man killed it, but he lost his harpoon and all his rope. Two hours later two more sharks came. He fought them with his knife. Then he used anything he could find. But he knew he was beaten. When he pulled his boat on shore. No fish was left. Only the huge white bone.

The next morning the fishermen in the village all came to the small boat. "What a fish it was!" Someone said, "There has never been such a fish."

▶阅读上面的短文，从每题所给的四个选项中，选出一个最佳答案。

1.　The old man _____.

　　A. had caught a fish of the same size

　　B. had caught only small fish

　　C. had never seen such a great fish

　　D. had seen such a great fish

2.　Just before dying, the fish _____.

　　A. threw away the harpoon　　　　　B. went deeper into the water

　　C. came to the top of the water　　　 D. showed how big it was

3.　The sharks came to _____.

　　A. eat the big fish　　　　　　　　　B. follow the boat

　　C. fight the old man　　　　　　　　D. eat the fish's bone

4.　The old man fought with the great fish for _____.

　　A. one morning　　　　　　　　　　B. three days

　　C. several hours　　　　　　　　　　D. one day

5. The old man was _____.

   A. active

   B. clever

   C. strong

   D. brave

✦✦ （2）✦✦

Something about the Quake

Fifty people died, over 11,000 were injured, and 100,000 houses were heavily damaged or destroyed in an earthquake that struck North China's Hebei Province.

The quake, measuring 6.2 on the Richter scale, hit the area 220 km northwest of Beijing at 11:50AM on January 10,1998.

Scientists made a report of the recent quake. They said that the area of northwestern Beijing, the joint of Shanxi and Hebei provinces and the Inner Mongolia were most easily attacked by earthquakes measuring 6 to a bit over 7 on the Richter scale.

However, scientists did not see the recent earthquake earlier, Clouds covered a large area in the Northern part of North China before the earthquake and experts say that this prevented satellites from correctly watching the temperature at the correct altitude.

Experts say that in the last ten years, about 305 earthquakes have occurred in China with 9 measuring over 7 on the Richter scale, 60 measuring over 6, and 236 measuring over 5. Tens of thousands of people died or were injured. Loss valued over 10 billion yuan.

▶ 阅读上面的短文，从每题所给的四个选项中，选出一个最佳答案。

1. This passage mainly tells us _____.

   A. a heavy damage to people

   B. a number of earthquakes

   C. a quake striking North China

   D. earthquakes measuring on the Richter scale

2. When the earthquake attacked the area, most people there were unlikely to _____.

   A. sleep in bed

   B. work in the fields

   C. walk in the streets

   D. stay at home

3. From the report we know that about nine earthquakes in the past ten years are measured over _____ on the Richter scale.

   A. 7

   B. 5

   C. 9

   D. 6

4. From the report we can infer that the damage caused by the earthquakes could be less heavier if _____.

   A. all the people stayed outside

   B. the earthquake happened at midnight

   C. the people had been warned earlier

   D. the earthquake scale was lower that 6.2 only

5. According to the report, which of the following is NOT true?

    A. We cannot stop earthquakes.

    B. Scientists are working hard at the researches on earthquakes.

    C. We can do our best to have less damages than ever.

    D. Nothing can be done on earthquakes.

语言基本功
英汉翻译◈ Translation Exercises

▶翻译下列句子

1. 哈勃望远镜于 1990 年 4 月 20 日由国家航空航天局发射升空，耗资 10 多亿美元。

_____

2. "奋进"号航天飞机将把宇航员送上哈勃。

_____

3. 当然，哈勃位于地球的大气层之外。

_____

4. 因此，它很快就会给我们传送我们所见到过的、有关行星和远距离星系的最清晰的照片。

_____

5. 哈勃将告诉我们有关宇宙的年龄和大小等许多事情。

_____

6. 关于这个他记不得了。

_____

7. 他忘记了走哪一条路。

_____

8. 我忘记我已经把这事告诉她了。

_____

语言基本功
好句好段◈ Writing Samples

✅ When Lord Henry had left, Dorian uncovered the picture again. He had to choose between a good life and a bad life, he thought. But then he realized that, in fact, he had already chosen. He would stay young for ever, and enjoy wild pleasure that life could give him. The face in the picture would grow old and ugly and unkind, but he would stay beautiful for ever. He covered the picture again, and smiled.

    亨利勋爵走后，多里安又欣开了画像。他想他必须选择过正人君子的生活还是过不道德的生活。但他意识到他实际上已经作出了选择。他将永远年轻，享受生活给予的每一份疯狂的快乐。画像中的脸将变老、变丑、变凶，但是他将永远漂亮。他又盖上画像，露出了笑容。

Lesson 62

✦✦ （1） ✦✦

School education is very important and useful. The students both learn knowledge and get education. Yet, no one can learn everything from school. The scientists, such as Edison, Newton, Galileo and Einstein, didn't learn everything from school. They learned a lot of knowledge outside school or in practice by themselves. A teacher, even he knows a lot, can't teach his students everything.

The teacher's job is to show his students how to learn, how to read and how to think. A good teacher with rich experience in teaching can teach his students the ways of study. Through these ways the students are able to learn and get a lot of things by themselves.

Usually it is very easy for the students to remember some knowledge, but it is very difficult to use it for problems. If a teacher really shows the students the ability of how to use knowledge, it means the teacher has learned lots of knowledge by himself(or herself). The success in learning shows he or she knows how to study.

▶ 阅读上面的短文，从每题所给的四个选项中，选出一个最佳答案。

1. From this passage we know ＿＿＿.

   A. the students are taught everything at school

   B. a teacher can't teach the students everything

   C. school is really not important and useful

   D. Edison learned lots of knowledge at school

2. A teacher's job is ＿＿＿.

   A. to help the students with their lessons

   B. to teach the students everything

   C. to show the students how to study by themselves

   D. to tell them the way to study

3. Which of the following is right?

   A. If we know how to learn, we can get a lot of knowledge.

   B. We can learn everything from our teachers.

   C. It is the only job for the students to learn knowledge.

   D. The writer tells us that practice is more important for the students than learning.

4. Which of the following is that best title ＿＿＿?

A. A Real Job for Teachers

B. Study in and outside School

C. How to Learn Knowledge

D. Practice - the Only Way of Learning

The Stolen Bag

The police received a report that six men had stopped a truck. It was carrying some goods and two bags full of something important. The six men had gone when the police arrived. After searching for three hours the police found the truck near the river. The driver was sitting on a bag in the truck and his hands were tied behind his back. The thieves had tied a handkerchief round his mouth so that he wouldn't shout. The police climbed into the back of the truck and freed the driver. They asked him what had happened.

"I was stopped soon after I left the bank," the driver explained. "Six men stopped me and made me drive to the river. 'If you shout,' one of them said, 'we will kill you.' When I got to the river, they tied me up. Then they threw me into the back of the truck. There were two bags in it and they took one of them."

"How much money did the bag contain?" a police officer asked.

"It didn't contain any money at all," the driver laughed. "It was full of letters. This one contains all the money. I've been sitting on it for three hours!"

▶阅读上面的短文，从每题所给的四个选项中，选出一个最佳答案。

1. The truck was stopped by _____.
   A. the thieves   B. six policemen
   C. an officer   D. a driver

2. The driver told the police that the thieves would _____ if he shouted.
   A. beat him   B. kill him
   C. tie him up   D. free him

3. _____ was taken away by the thieves.
   A. All the money
   B. A lot of money
   C. A little money
   D. No money

4. It took the police _____ hours to find the driver and the truck.
   A. two   B. three
   C. four   D. five

5. What do you think of the driver? He was _____.
   A. lazy（懒惰）   B. lucky
   C. foolish（愚蠢）   D. hard working

英汉翻译◇ | Translation Exercises

▶ 翻译下列句子

1. 消防队员们同那场森林大火搏斗了将近三个星期，最后才把火势控制住。

   _____

2. 冬季即将来临，这些山丘对周围的村庄具有毁灭性的威胁。

   _____

3. 因为大雨不仅会冲走土壤，而且还会引起严重的水灾。

   _____

4. 森林管理当局订购了好几吨一种生长迅速的特殊类型的草籽。

   _____

5. 飞机把这种草籽大量地撒播在地上。

   _____

6. 气球破裂而落到地上。

   _____

7. 地球距离太阳有多远？

   _____

8. 把它埋在地下。

   _____

好句好段◇ | Writing Samples

☑ In the middle of the night Mary woke up. Heavy rain had started falling again, and the wind was blowing violently round the walls of the old house. Suddenly she heard crying again. This time she decided to discover who it was. She left her room, and in the darkness followed the crying sound, round corners and through doors, up and down stairs, to the other side of the big house. At last she found the right room. She pushed the door open and went in.

半夜的时候，玛丽醒了。天又开始下雨了，狂风在房子周围猛烈地刮着。突然，她又听见了哭声，这次她决定要搞清楚那个人是谁。她走出房间，在黑暗中循着哭泣的声音，绕过墙角，穿过一扇扇门，上下楼梯，来到这所大房子的另一侧。终于她找到了那个房间，推开门，走了进去。

Lesson 63

阅读理解 ◎ Reading Comprehension

✦✦ （1） ✦✦

Plants are very important living things. Life could not go on if there were no plants. This is because plants can make food from air, water and sunlight. Animals and men cannot make food from air, water and sunlight. Therefore, animals and men need plants in order to live. This is why we find that there are so many plants around us.

If you look carefully at the plants around you, you will find that there are two kinds of plants: flowering plants and non-flowering plants.

Flowering plants can make seeds. The seeds are protected by the fruits. Some fruits have one seed, some have two, three or four, and some have many seeds. But a few fruits have no seeds at all. An example of a fruit without seeds is the banana fruit.

Most non-flowering plants do not grow from seeds. They grow from spores. Spores are very, very small. Some spores are so small and light that they can float in the air. We may say that spores are quite the same as seeds. When these spores fall on wet and shady places, they usually grow into new plants.

▶ 阅读上面的短文，从每题所给的四个选项中，选出一个最佳答案。

1. The main idea of the first paragraph is that _____.

   A. plants are important for life

   B. plants cannot grow without air

   C. there are many plants around us

   D. we cannot live without water

2. The best title of the passage is _____.

   A. Plants

   B. Living Things

   C. Flowering Plants

   D. Men and Plants

3. Which of the following is NOT true?

   A. Plants have two main kinds: flowering plants and non-flowering plants.

   B. All plants have seeds in them.

   C. Seeds are protected by the fruits.

   D. Some plants grow from spores.

4. The word "non-flowering" in the passage means _____.

   A. 开花的

   B. 有花的

C. 多花的　　　　　　　　　　　D. 无花的

5. In "shady" places there is _____.

    A. a lot of sunshine　　　　　　B. a lot of water

    C. no water　　　　　　　　　　D. little sunshine

◆◆（2）◆◆

Modern life is impossible without traveling. The fastest way of traveling is by plane. With a modern airliner you can travel in one day to places which it took a month or more to get to hundreds of years ago.

Travelling by train is slower than by plane, but it has its advantages. You see the country you are traveling through. Modern trains gave comfortable seats and dining-cars. <u>They</u> make even the longest journey enjoyable.

Some people prefer to travel by sea when possible. There are large liners and river boats. You can visit many other countries and different parts of your country on them. Ships are not so fast as trains or planes, but traveling by sea is a very pleasant way to spend a holiday.

Many people like to travel by car. You can make your own timetable. You can travel three or four hundred miles or only fifty or one hundred miles a day, just as you like. You can stop wherever you wish where there is something interesting to see, a good restaurant where you can enjoy a good meal, or at a hotel to spend the night. That is why traveling by car is popular for pleasure trips, while people usually take a train or plane when they travel on business.

▶阅读上面的短文，从每题所给的四个选项中，选出一个最佳答案。

1. From the passage, we know the fastest way of traveling is _____.

    A. by train　　　　　B. by sea　　　　　C. by plane　　　　　D. by car

2. If we travel by car, we can _____.

    A. make the longest journey enjoyable

    B. travel to a very far place in several minutes

    C. make our own timetable

    D. travel only fifty or one hundred miles a day.

3. The underlined word "They" in the passage refers to（指的是）_____.

    A. modern trains in the country.

    B. comfortable seats and dining-cars

    C. the travelers on the modern trains

    D. the slower ways of traveling

4. When people travel on business, they usually take _____.

    A. a plane or a car　　　　　　B. a car or a boat

    C. a boat or a train　　　　　　D. a train or a plane

5. How many ways of traveling are mentioned in the passage?

    A. Four.　　　　　B. Three.　　　　　C. Two.　　　　　D. Six.

英汉翻译◈ | Translation Exercises

▶ 翻译下列句子

1. 杰里米·汉普登交际甚广，是各种聚会上深受大家欢迎的人。

   _____

2. 最近，杰里米的一个最亲密的朋友请他在一个婚礼上致祝词。

   _____

3. 这正是杰里米喜欢做的事情。

   _____

4. 他认真准备了讲稿，带着珍妮一道去参加了婚礼。

   _____

5. 在回家的路上，他问珍妮是否喜欢他的祝词。

   _____

6. 他不能抑制自己。

   _____

7. 我失去自制力，揍了他。

   _____

8. 请努力抑制你的感情。

   _____

好句好段◈ | Writing Samples

☑ And in the secret garden, where the roses were at their best, and the butterflies were flying from flower to flower in the summer sunshine, they told Colin's father their story. Sometimes he laughed and sometimes he cried, but most of the time he just looked, unbelieving, into the handsome face of the son that he had almost forgotten.

在秘密花园中，玫瑰花盛开着，蝴蝶在夏日的阳光下、在花丛中飞舞，他们向柯林的父亲讲述着他们的故事。他时而开怀大笑，时而落泪，更多的时间只是注视着他儿子那英俊的脸庞，不相信这就是他几乎遗忘的那个孩子。

本书所有练习题的参考答案（含阅读理解练习题解析及译文），请登录中国水利水电出版社网站 http://www.waterpub.com.cn/softdown/（下载中心）免费下载。

Lesson 64

Reading Comprehension

◆◆ （1） ◆◆

Foolish Mr. Evans

Mr. Evans had never managed the farm when his father was alive. He had been interested in nothing but eating and sleeping. Now he had to work on the farm with his wife. With his uncle's help, he grew the corn, watered the plants and had a good harvest. He was sure they would live a happy life again. Winter came. He had no grass to feed his horses. He went to his uncle for advice, but the man was out. "They're useless now," he said to himself. So he drove them to the market. An old man came up to the horses and looked at them carefully and then said, "They're too thin, sir. Nobody would buy them. I can exchange my cow for your horses. It's a young cow. It will be able to supply you with much milk a day and you'll get a lot of money."

The farmer thought it reasonable and agreed. But to his surprise several days passed and the cow had no milk. Mrs. Evans had to send for the vet. The vet looked it over and said, "There's something wrong with the cow. It must take a tablespoon of the medicine twice a day."

"But it has no tablespoon. It always drinks out of a pail."

▶阅读上面的短文，根据其内容，在每个空白处填写一个适当单词（词首字母已给出）。

1. Mr. Evans lived h _____ when his father was alive.
2. Mr. Evans learned l _____ knowledge about farming.
3. After his father d _____, Mr. Evans had to manage the farm himself.
4. Mr. Evan's uncle had to t _____ him how to manage the farm.
5. Mr. Evans wanted his uncle to h _____ him, but the man wasn't in.
6. Mr. Evans didn't think the horses were useful, so he decided to s _____ them in the market.
7. The old man hoped to g _____ Mr. Evans' horses without paying much money.
8. In fact Mr. Evans brought a s _____ cow home.
9. The cow supplied n _____ milk to the Evans.

◆◆ （2） ◆◆

The Cow Brew First

A farmer had a very valuable cow. He took very good care of this cow and one day when she was ill, he was very worried. He telephoned the vet.

"What's the problem?" the vet asked him when he arrived.

"My cow's very sick," the farmer said. "I don't know what's the matter with her. She's lying down and won't stand up. She won't eat, and she's making a strange noise."

The vet looked at the cow.

"She's certainly sick," he said, "and she needs to take some very strong medicine."

He took a bottle out of his case, and put two pills into his hand.

"Give her these," he said. "They should make her better."

"How should I give them to her?" the farmer asked.

The vet gave him a long tube.

"Put this tube in her mouth," he said, "then put the pills in the tube and blow. That'll make her swallow them."

The vet went away.

The next day he came to the farm again. The farmer was sitting outside his house looking very sad.

"How's your cow?" the vet asked.

"No change," the farmer said, "and I'm feeling very strange myself."

"Oh?" the vet said. "Why?"

"I did what you said," the farmer explained. "I put the tube in the cow's mouth and then put two pills down it."

"And?" the vet asked.

"The cow blew first," the farmer said.

▶ 阅读上面的短文，从每题所给的四个选项中，选出一个最佳答案。

1. The farmer was worried about _____.

    A. his cow   B. the vet

    C. the medicine   D. the tube

2. The cow wouldn't _____.

    A. lie down   B. make strange noises

    C. stand up   D. hear the vet

3. The vet _____.

    A. asked the farmer to give the cow some pills

    B. couldn't help the cow

    C. gave the farmer some pills

    D. told the farmer not to worry

4. Why did the farmer put the pills in the tube?

    A. To make the cow swallow them.

    B. To make the cow feel strange.

    C. To throw them away.

    D. To make himself feel strange.

5. What happened to the pills?

    A. The cow swallowed them at last.

    B. The farmer swallowed them.

    C. The tube was broken, so the cow didn't have the pills.

    D. The vet forgot to give the medicine to the farmer.

语言基本功
英汉翻译◈ | Translation Exercises

▶ 翻译下列句子

1. 1858 年，一位法国工程师带着建造一条长 21 英里、穿越英吉利海峡的隧道计划到了英国。

_____

2. 1860 年，一位名叫威廉·洛的英国人提出了一项更好的计划。

_____

3. 42 年以后，隧道实际已经开始建了。

_____

4. 世界不得不再等将近 100 年才看到海峡隧道竣工。

_____

5. 它于 1994 年 3 月 7 日正式开通，将英国与欧洲大陆连到了一起。

_____

6. 有足够根据可以说……

_____

7. 只有出纳员才有权付款。

_____

8. 你现在可以走了，下次不许再迟到了。

_____

Lesson 65

阅读理解◎ | Reading Comprehension

✦✦（1）✦✦

Clean Your Room for a Better Life

Do you love having your own room? Do you love not having to clean it? So do many teens.

But sometimes this means your room becomes so messy, you can't find what you want. You can't even see the floor!

It doesn't get like that because you are lazy. It gets like that because you are not organized.

But don't worry. American mother and daughter authors Julie and Jessie Morgenstern are here to help. They have written Organizing from the Inside Out for Teens to help make your life more organized.

In the book, the authors point out that your room is the only space in the world just for you. If you keep it clean and tidy, you will find things easier and have more success in life!

But, to have success, you must organize all parts of your life. Not just your room! The book gives many tips to help you do this:

1）Always put things back where you found them.

2）Keep anything important in one easy-to-reach drawer.

3）Put labels on your drawers saying what is in them.

4）When you buy a new textbook, put your old ones away.

5）Make a plan for each day. Then you will know what you should be doing at all times.

6）Keep to your plan.

If you follow these tips, you will learn to manage your space and time, and your future will be full of success!

▶阅读上面的短文，根据其内容，回答所提的问题。

1. Do many children keep their rooms clean and tidy?

2. What does a room for a child according to Julie and Jessie Morgenstern?

3. What's the use for making a plan for each day?

4. What will happen to you if you follow the 6 tips?

5. What does Tip (6) mean in Chinese?

✦✦ (2) ✦✦
Our Clever Mother

We walked in so quietly that the nurse at the desk didn't even lift her eyes from the book. Mum pointed at a big chair by the door and I knew she wanted me to sit down. While I watched mouth open in surprise, Mum took off her hat and coat and gave them to me to hold. She walked quietly to the small room by the lift and took out a wet mop. She pushed the mop past the desk and as the nurse looked up, Mum nodded and said, "Very dirty floors."

"Yes. I'm glad they've finally decided to clean them," the nurse answered. She looked at Mum strangely and said, "But aren't you late for work?"

Mum just pushed harder, each swipe of the mop taking her farther and farther down the hall. I watched until she was out of sight and the nurse had turned back to writing in the big book.

After a long time Mum came back. Her eyes were shining. She quickly put the mop back and took my hand. As we turned to go out of the door, Mum bowed politely to the nurse and said, "Thank you."

Outside, Mum told me, "Dagmar is fine. No fever."

"You saw her, Mum?"

"Of course. I told her about the hospital rules, and she will not expect us until tomorrow. Dad will stop worrying as well. It's a fine hospital. But such floors! A mop is no good. They need a brush."

---

1. mop   *n.* 拖把
2. swipe   *n.* 拖一下
3. bow   *v.* 鞠躬

▶阅读上面的短文，从每题所给的四个选项中，选出一个最佳答案。

1. When she took a mop from the small room what Mum really wanted to do was _____.

   A. to clean the floor   B. to please the nurse

   C. to see a patient   D. to surprise the story-teller

2. When the nurse talked to Mum she thought Mum was a _____.

   A. nurse   B. visitor

   C. patient   D. cleaner

3. After reading the story what can we infer about the hospital?

   A. It is a children's hospital.

   B. It has strict rules about visiting hours.

   C. The conditions there aren't very good.

   D. The nurses and doctors there don't work hard.

4. From the text we know that Dagmar is most likely _____.

   A. the story-teller's sister   B. the story-teller's classmate

C. Mum's friend   D. Dad's boss

5. Which of the following words describes Mum best?

    A. Strange.   B. Warm-hearted.

    C. Clever.   D. Hard-working.

语言基本功
英汉翻译◈ | Translation Exercises

▶ 翻译下列句子

1. 去年圣诞节，马戏团老板吉米·盖茨决定送些礼物给儿童医院。

_____

2. 他骑上一头名叫江伯的小象，沿着城里的主要街道出发了。

_____

3. 他本该知道警察绝不会允许这类事情发生。

_____

4. 15个警察不得不用很大的力气把它推离主要街道。

_____

5. 警察虽然吃了苦头，但他们还是感到很有趣。

_____

6. 法院下令他缴付罚款。

_____

7. 情况紧急，非这样做不可。

_____

8. 我们需要额外的帮助。

_____

语言基本功
好句好段◈ | Writing Samples

☑ Roger went across to the window and looked out at the garden. It was a beautiful summer morning. The sky was blue and the garden was green. It was all very quiet. His mother loved this garden. But Tom Briggs wanted the garden. And Roger wanted the garden, too. Roger felt worse and worse.

罗杰走到窗前向外看花园。这是个美丽的夏天清晨，天空蓝蓝的而花园是一片绿色，一切都非常安静。他的妈妈爱这个花园，然而汤姆·布里格斯却打着这个花园的主意，并且罗杰也想要这个花园。罗杰觉得事情越来越糟。

Lesson 66

Reading Comprehension

✦✦（1）✦✦

I've Had My Mouth for Thirty Years

Rechard was born in a shopkeeper's family. His father had a lot of money and he was the richest in the town. He often supported the middle school where his son studied. The young man was overbearing and nobody could displease him. He was often late for school and hardly did his homework. Of course he learned nothing at school except playing. Eleven years ago the young man left school and began to work in an office of his father's shop. He was still overbearing and his workmates were afraid of him.

One day Rechard was asked to dinner. All the people respected him and he drank much that evening. He couldn't stand up himself after that and with his friends' help he got on his car. But before long he decided to get off and go home on foot. The driver had to listen to him and drove away. When the young man walked past a factory, he felt terrible and began to throw up by the gate. The gate keeper who didn't know him called out angrily, "How dare you throw up on the gate?"

"Why did you build it in front of my mouth?"

"But it's been built for fifteen years!"

"I've had my mouth for thirty years!"

▶ 阅读上面的短文，从每题所给的四个选项中，选出一个最佳答案。

1. All the school pleased Rechard because _____.
   A. he was strong enough
   B. he was overbearing
   C. they were afraid his father stopped supporting them
   D. the young man was cleverer than any other student

2. When Rechard was _____, he finished school.
   A. nineteen   B. twenty
   C. twenty-one   D. twenty-two

3. Rechard was respected because _____.
   A. they all worked in his father's shop
   B. they tried their best to make him happy
   C. they hoped to find work in his shop

D. the young man often helped them

4. Rechard decided to get off because _____.

    A. he felt terrible   B. he wanted to throw up

    C. he hoped to have sport   D. he had drunk too much

5. Which of the following is true?

    A. The factory was built in front of Rechard mouth.

    B. The gate-keeper made Rechard say sorry to him.

    C. Rechard thought he did wrong.

    D. Rechard was utterly unreasonable（蛮不讲理）.

✦✦ （2） ✦✦

Life in the Future Is Different

Life in the twenty-first century will be very different from life today. Between then and now many changes will take place, but what will the changes be?

The population is growing fast. There will be many people in the world and most of them will live longer than people live now.

Computers will be much smaller and more useful and there will be at least one in every home. And computer studies will be one of the important subjects in schools.

People will work fewer hours than they do now and they will have more free time for sports, watching TV and travelling. Travelling will be much easier and cheaper. And many more people will go to other countries for holidays.

There will be changes in our food, too. Maybe no one will eat meat every day, instead they eat more fruit and vegetables. Maybe people will be healthier.

Work in the future will be different, too. Dangerous and hard work can be done by robots. Because of this, many people will not have enough work to do. This will be a problem.

▶阅读上面的短文，从每题所给的四个选项中，选出一个最佳答案。

1. There will be _____ in the future.

    A. small population   B. few changes

    C. more people   D. fewer people

2. In the future the computer will be _____.

    A. much bigger and few people will use it

    B. much smaller and more useful

    C. smaller and not many people will use it

    D. bigger and a lot of people will use it

3. In the future more people _____.

    A. will go to the other countries for holidays

    B. will study at school

    C. will go earlier

D. will work for many hours

4. People will prefer _____ to _____ in the future.
   A. fruit and vegetables, meat   B. meat, fruit and vegetables
   C. fruit and meat, vegetables   D. meat and vegetables, fruit

5. The robots will _____ in the future.
   A. do the dangerous work   B. do all the work
   C. do only housework   D. do the easy work for people

语言基本功
英汉翻译◈ | Translation Exercises

▶翻译下列句子

1. 于是，到了 1989 年，飞机失事 26 年后，在对小岛的一次航空勘查中那架飞机被意外地发现了。

    _____

2. 到了那个时候，状况良好的兰开斯特轰炸机实属罕见，值得抢救。

    _____

3. 法国政府让人把飞机包装起来，一部分一部分地搬回法国。

    _____

4. 一群热心人计划修复这架飞机。

    _____

5. 一群蜜蜂把发动机当做了蜂房，发动机在蜂蜡中被完整地保存了下来。

    _____

6. 他们一生中追求的皆为享乐。

    _____

7. 你到这里是来工作还是来玩？

    _____

8. 这抽屉关不上。

    _____

Lesson 67

阅读理解◇ | Reading Comprehension

✦✦（1）✦✦

On Computer

Mr. And Mrs. Stokes were sitting in the garden of their London home when I arrived to interview them and their fourteen-year-old son Carl. But Carl was working upstairs. "He doesn't often leave his room," his mother explained.

At the moment Carl is working on a program for a new computer game. Computers have become his whole life. In the past Carl has made over 25, 000 from writing programs. "When did he buy the computer?" I asked. "We bought it for him eighteen months ago for his birthday," said Mrs. Stokes. "We didn't know what we were doing. Our son has changed. Eighteen months ago, he didn't see a computer. Now he doesn't talk about anything else. And we don't understand a thing about computer." "And do you think it's good for him?" was my question. "No, we don't. We worry about him," said Mrs. Stokes. "He doesn't have any other interests now. And he hasn't done any work for his school exams."

Carl's parents don't understand computers, but Carl certainly does. "I love computers," he said, "I soon got tired of playing games. I like writing programs much better. I've got three computers now. I bought two more. I didn't make much money at first, but now I do. My parents make me put most of it in the bank."

▶阅读上面的短文，从每题所给的四个选项中，选出一个最佳答案。

1. The Stokes bought their son the computer _____.
   A. to make him study better   B. as a present
   C. to make him interested in it   D. to make some money for him

2. From the text we know that the Stokes _____.
   A. helped Carl with his lessons
   B. regretted having bought Carl a computer
   C. were good at computers
   D. made much money by writing programs themselves

3. Carl used to _____.
   A. spend much time playing computer games
   B. help his parents do housework
   C. show little interest in his homework

D. write programs day and night

4. Carl is probably _____.

A. Chinese   B. French   C. American   D. British

5. Carl spends most of his time working with the computer because _____.

A. he doesn't like to talk much

B. he can make a lot of money for his family

C. he is interested in the computer

D. he wants to make enough money to buy better computers

✦✦ （2） ✦✦

The Driver's Answer

Once, Einstein travelled to many places in America to give lectures. He travelled in a car, and soon made friends with his driver.

Each time, Einstein gave the lecture; his driver always sat in the front row and listened to him very carefully. The same lecture was given so many times that the driver learned it well enough to give it himself.

One day, when Einstein was told about it, he asked the driver to give the lecture for him in a small town.

That evening, both Einstein and the driver went into the lecture room. Nobody there had seen Einstein before. When the driver took his place, everybody applauded. Then he began the lecture. When it was over, the people warmly applauded. The driver turned to look at Einstein. Einstein nodded with a smile on his face.

When they began to leave the lecture room, a man stopped them and asked the driver a very difficult question. The driver listened carefully, then he smiled and said the question was interesting but really quite easy. "To show how easy it is, I'll ask my driver to answer it." Said the driver.

▶阅读上面的短文，从每题所给的四个选项中，选出一个最佳答案。

1. Why did Einstein travel to many places in America? Because he _____.

A. wanted to visit his friends

B. wanted to know something about America

C. went for some important meetings

D. went to give lectures in different places

2. What did the driver usually do when Einstein was giving his lecture?

A. He sat in the front row and read something.

B. He slept in his car.

C. He listened to the lecture carefully.

D. He talked with other people.

3. Who gave the lecture in a small town one day?

A. Einstein himself.   B. The driver.

C. Another scientist.   D. A man in the small town.

4. When the lecture was over, _____.

     A. everyone laughed   B. Einstein got angry

     C. Einstein was very pleased   D. everyone didn't understand what he said

5. The driver did not answer the question because _____.

     A. it was really too easy for him

     B. he was too busy to answer it

     C. he would ask another driver to answer it instead

     D. he knew nothing about it

语言基本功
英汉翻译◈ | Translation Exercises

▶翻译下列句子

1. 波兰科学家哈罗恩·塔捷耶夫花了毕生的精力来研究世界各地的活火山和深洞。

_____

2. 1948 年他去了刚果的基伍湖，对一座后来被他命名为基图罗的新火山进行观察。

_____

3. 尽管他设法拍了一些十分精彩的照片，但他却不能在火山附近停留太长的时间。

_____

4. 他等到火山平静下来，两天以后又返回去。

_____

5. 塔捷耶夫经常冒这样的生命危险。他能告诉我们的有关活火山的情况比任何在世的人都要多。

_____

6. 中国人民正努力工作，以把中国建成一个具有现代农业、现代工业、现代国防和现代科学技术的强大国家。

_____

7. 他在上海逗留期间，拜访了几个老朋友，参观了两所大学。

_____

8. 我们将采纳他的建议，尽快改组领导班子。

_____

本书所有练习题的参考答案（含阅读理解练习题解析及译文），请登录中国水利水电出版社网站 http://www.waterpub.com.cn/softdown/（下载中心）免费下载。

Lesson 68

Reading Comprehension

✦✦（1）✦✦

A Brave Man

A rich man owned a large house with an outdoor swimming pool. He also owned a crocodile, which he kept in the pool. One day, he invited his friends and neighbors to a party.

"How about a swim?" he asked. The pool looked very inviting, but no one dared to go in for a swim. They were afraid of the crocodile.

The rich man challenged them. "If anyone dares to swim across the pool," he said, "I'll give him five thousand dollars." But nobody moved, five thousand dollars was a lot of money, but there was a BIG crocodile.

Suddenly there was a loud splash. A young man began swimming at great speed across the pool. He reached the other side and climbed very quickly out of the pool.

Everyone applauded the young man and praised him for his courage. But the young man seemed nervous... and quite angry.

"What's the matter?" said the rich man. "Aren't you happy to receive five thousand dollars?" "Well ... perhaps," said the young man looking at people on the other side of the pool, "but first I want to know just one thing—WHO PUSHED ME IN!"

▶阅读上面的短文，从每题所给的四个选项中，选出一个最佳答案。

1. People didn't dare to swim in the pool because ＿＿＿.

    A. The rich man didn't let them

    B. They were afraid of the big crocodile

    C. They were having a party

    D. It was very cold

2. The rich man promised to give ＿＿＿ dollars to the person swimming in the pool.

    A. one thousand   B. two thousand

    C. five hundred   D. five thousand

3. The young man was really a brave man, wasn't he?

    A. Yes, he was.   B. No, he was.

    C. Yes, he wasn't.   D. No, he wasn't.

4. The young man looked ＿＿＿.

    A. happy and excited   B. angry

C. nervous   D. both B and C

5.   Which of the following is wrong?

A. The young man would receive five thousand dollars.

B. The young man jumped into the pool bravely.

C. Someone pushed the young man into the pool.

D. The crocodile in the pool didn't hurt the young man.

Fast Food in the USA

The favorite food in the United States is the hamburger. The favorite place to buy a hamburger is a fast food restaurant. At fast food restaurants, people order their food, wait a few minutes, and carry it to their tables themselves. People also take their food out of the restaurant and eat it in their cars or in their homes. At some fast food restaurants, people can order their food, pay for it and pick it up without leaving their cars.

There are many kinds of fast food restaurants in the United States. The greatest in number sell hamburgers, French fries and so on. They are popular among Americans. Besides, fast food restaurants that serve Chinese food, Mexican food, Italian food, Chicken, seafood and ice-cream are very many. The idea of a fast food restaurant is so popular that nearly every kind of food can be found in one.

Fast food restaurants are popular because they reflect American life style. Customers can wear any type of dress when they go to a fast food place. Second, they are fast. People who are busy do not want to spend time preparing their own food or waiting while someone prepares it. In fast food restaurants, the food is usually ready before the customers order it. Finally, most food in a fast food restaurant is not expensive. Therefore, people often buy and eat at a fast food restaurant, while they may not be able to go to a more expensive restaurant very often.

▶阅读上面的短文，从每题所给的四个选项中，选出一个最佳答案。

1.   _____ is the favorite food in the United States.

A. Chicken   B. Meat

C. Hamburger   D. Fish

2.   Americans like to go to fast food restaurants because _____.

A. people can find fast food restaurants very easily

B. people like to eat hamburgers

C. there are all kinds of food in them

D. they are fast, informal and inexpensive

3.   Is the food in fast food restaurants always ready before the customers order it?

A. Yes, it is.   B. No, it is seldom ready.

C. Yes, it is always ready.   D. No, not always, but usually.

4.   Are seafood and ice-cream served at all fast food restaurants?

A. Certainly.   B. Yes, they are.

C. No, they aren't.   D. No, only at a few of them.

5. Is Chinese food served in all fast food restaurants?

A. Yes, it is.   B. Yes, they are.

C. No, it isn't.   D. No, only a few of them.

语言基本功
英汉翻译◈ | Translation Exercises

▶ 翻译下列句子

1. 我穿过马路以便避开他，但他看到我并朝我跑过来。

2. 若再装做没看见他已是没有用了，我只好向他招手。

3. 我就怕遇到奈杰尔·戴克斯。

4. 他从来都是无事可做。

5. 我得想办法不让他整个上午缠着我。

6. 他的病是由于不良食物所致。

7. 这个结果是出人意料的。

8. 他们的争论终于造成战争。

语言基本功
好句好段◈ | Writing Samples

✔ The room was large and long, with high narrow windows, which let in only a little light. Shadows lay in all the corners of the room and around the dark pieces of furniture. There were many books and a few guitars, but there was no life, no happiness in the room. Deep gloom filled the air.

房间又大又长，窗户又高又窄，只能容许一点点天光射入，屋子的所有角落以及一件件深色的家具四周都是阴影。屋里摆放着好多书籍和几把吉他，但是毫无生气，毫无快乐可言。空气中满是浓重的阴悒氛围。

Lesson 69

语言基本功
阅读理解◈ Reading Comprehension

✦✦ （1） ✦✦

Samson

When Samson was born, God said to his mother, "The child will be a man of great might. You cannot cut his hair. He will be an officer of Israel." Samson grew up, he was so strong that he had the greatest strength. One time he killed a lion with his hands. Another time, he alone killed thirty thousand enemies; the third time, many enemies caught him and closed him in a big house. Samson took apart the house. What was the secret of Samson's great strength? The secret was his hair. Samson's parents never cut his hair. He himself never cut his hair, the enemies knew it. One day, when Samson was in bed, the enemies came. They cut his hair and caught him. Without the hair, Samson had no strength. The enemies cut Samson's eyes and asked him to work very hard. One evening, when the enemies had a big supper, they wanted Samson to wait on them. Seeing so many enemies, Samson said to himself, "God, give me strength for the last time, let me kill my enemies and myself at the same time." He used all his strength. "Bang!" the big house fell down, Samson succeeded.

---

1. might   *n.* 力量
2. Israel   *n.* 以色列
3. strength   *n.* 力气
4. enemy   *n.* 敌人
5. succeed   *v.* 成功

▶阅读上面的短文，根据其内容，回答所提的问题。

1. What did God say to Samson's mother?
2. What was Samson's secret?
3. Say something Samson did.
4. How did the enemies cut Samson's hair?
5. Samson succeeded in killing enemies, do you like this way?

✦✦ （2） ✦✦

The cost of medical care in the United States is very high. One reason is that the medical education will cost a lot of time and money.

A visit to a doctor's office costs from fifteen to fifty dollars. It is almost impossible for people to pay for the medical care they need. Many people in the United States think that doctors are overpaid. Most doctors, however, disagree. They say that they were required to study medicine for a long time. Tuition for many years of medical education costs a lot of money. Doctors say that it is necessary for most medical students to borrow money from bank to pay their tuition. Because their money must be repaid to the bank, young doctors need to receive a lot of money for their work. So, they charge people high prices for medical care.

Therefore, it is possible that the high cost of medical care in America is unnecessary, because high tuition is one cause of high costs. One way to lower costs would be to make medical schools free or have low tuition.

▶阅读上面的短文，从每题所给的四个选项中，选出一个最佳答案。

1. The word "tuition" in the passage probably refers to _____.

   A. tuition in medical school is high

   B. studying the courses

   C. payment for education

   D. living at school

2. The reason for the high medical cost told in the passage is that _____.

   A. tuition in medical school is high

   B. the price of medicine is high

   C. doctors are overpaid

   D. doctors must pay money to the banks

3. One way to lower the cost of medical care would be _____.

   A. not to see a doctor

   B. to pay doctors less money

   C. to let medical students have free or partly free medical education

   D. to forbid doctors to ask their patients for too much money

4. The main idea of the article is that _____.

   A. a visit to a doctor's office may cost as much as $ 15 to $ 50 in the USA

   B. the cost of medical care is the main reason for the high costs in the USA

   C. medical care in the USA costs a lot of money because doctors want to be rich

   D. the high cost of tuition in medical schools is one reason for the high cost of medical care in America

5. The cost of medical care in the United States is very high. What does the writer think about it?

   A. He agrees that doctors are overpaid.

   B. He thinks it is a big problem and suggests a way to settle it.

   C. He doesn't think the medical students should borrow money from banks.

   D. He doesn't think it necessary for the medical students to study for a long time.

英汉翻译◈ | Translation Exercises

▶ 翻译下列句子

1. 我第三次接受驾驶执照考试。

_____

2. 确信我已通过考试，所以我几乎开始喜欢起这次考试。

_____

3. 让我们假设一个小孩子突然在你前面穿过马路。

_____

4. 我突然用力踩紧刹车踏板，结果我俩的身体都向前冲去。

_____

5. 主考人伤心地看着我。

_____

6. 小李会说一点英语。

_____

7. 最后一个晚上她终于能吃到一顿丰盛的晚餐。

_____

8. 他认为这两个人不可能是骗子。

_____

好句好段◈ | Writing Samples

☑ There was no hope for Spitz now. Buck got ready for his final attack, while the circle of sixty dogs watched, and crowded nearer and nearer, waiting for the end. At last Buck jumped, in and out, and Spitz went down in the snow. A second later the waiting pack was on top of him, and Spitz had disappeared. Buck stood and watched. The wild animal had made its kill.

现在斯皮兹已回天乏术。巴克业已做好最后一击的准备。而另外 60 条狗围成一圈观望着，躁动着越来越近，等着战斗的尾声。最后巴克跳起来，一进一退之时，斯皮兹已倒在雪地上，不过一秒钟光景他就葬身在狗群之下，斯皮兹从此渺无踪影。巴克站在那里冷眼旁观。这野性的动物终于完成了他的捕杀。

Lesson 70

Reading Comprehension

◆◆ (1) ◆◆

Tea is a popular drink around the world. But tea does not mean the same thing to everyone. In different countries people have very different ideas about drinking tea.

In China, for example, tea is always served when people get together. The Chinese drink it at any time of the day at home or in teahouse. They prefer their tea plain, with nothing else in it.

Tea is also important in Japan. The Japanese have a special way of serving tea called a tea ceremony. It is very old and full of meaning. Everything must be done in a special way in the ceremony. There is even a special room for it in Japan.

Another tea-drinking country is England. In England, the late afternoon is "teatime". Almost everyone has a cup of tea then. The English people usually make tea in a teapot and drink it with milk and sugar. They also eat cakes, cookies and little sandwiches at teatime.

In the Untied States people have a tea mostly for breakfast or after meals. Americans usually use tea-bags to make their tea. Tea-bags are faster and easier than making tea in teapots. In summer, many Americans drink cold tea—"iced tea". Sometimes they drink iced tea from cans, like soda.

▶阅读上面的短文，从每题所给的四个选项中，选出一个最佳答案。

1. The passage is about _____.
   A. why tea is important B. the teatime in England
   C. different ways of drinking tea D. Chinese tea

2. Tea is popular _____.
   A. all around the world B. only in the USA
   C. only in English-speaking countries D. in Asian countries

3. The Chinese often have a tea _____.
   A. for breakfast B. when they get together
   C. only in teahouses D. in a special ceremony

4. The English like to _____.
   A. drink their tea in a special room
   B. have tea with dinner
   C. eat cakes and cookies with their tea
   D. drink their tea plain

5. Iced tea is popular _____.

    A. in winter   B. in England

    C. for breakfast   D. in the USA

✦✦ （2） ✦✦

The Earth Is Our Home

The world itself is becoming much smaller by using modern traffic and modern communication means. Life today is much easier than it was hundreds of years ago, but it has brought new problems. One of the biggest is pollution. To pollute means to make things dirty. Pollution comes in many ways. We see it, smell it, drink it and even hear it.

Man has been polluting the earth. The more people, the more pollution. Many years ago, the problem was not so serious because there were not so many people. When the land was used up or the river was dirty in a place, men moved to another place. But this is no longer true. Man is now slowly polluting the whole world.

Air pollution is still the most serious. It's bad to all living things in the world, but it is not only one kind of pollution. Water pollution kills our fish and pollutes our drinking water. Noise pollution makes us become angry more easily.

Many countries are making rules to fight pollution. They stop the people from burning coal in houses and factories in the city, and from blowing dirty smoke into the air.

The pollution of SO_2 is now the most dangerous problem of air pollution. It is caused by heavy traffic. It is certain that if there are fewer people driving, there will be less air pollution.

The earth is our home. We must take care of it. That means keeping the land, water and air clean. And we must keep careful of the rise in population at the same time.

▶阅读上面的短文，从每题所给的四个选项中，选出一个最佳答案。

1. Our world is becoming much smaller _____.

    A. because the earth is being polluted day and night

    B. because science is developing

    C. because of the rise in population

    D. because the earth is blown away by the wind every year

2. Thousands of years ago, life was _____ it is today.

    A. much easier than   B. as easy as

    C. as hard as   D. much harder than

3. Pollution comes in many ways, We can even hear it. Here "it" means _____.

    A. water pollution   B. air pollution

    C. noise pollution   D. rubbish

4. Air pollution is the most serious kind of pollution because _____.

    A. it's bad to all living things in the world

    B. it makes much noise

C. it has made our rivers and lakes dirty

D. it makes us become angry more easily

5. Which of the following is NOT true?

A. Many countries are making rules to fight pollution.

B. The pollution of the earth grows as fast as the world's population does.

C. From now on, maybe people try to go to work by bus or by bike instead of by car or by motorbike. It is helpful to fight against the problem of SO2.

D. The problem of pollution is not so serious because there are not so many people.

语言基本功
英汉翻译◈ | Translation Exercises

▶翻译下列句子

1. 在一次斗牛时，一个醉汉突然溜达到斗牛场中间。

_____

2. 对挑衅显然非常敏感的公牛完全撇开斗牛士，直奔醉汉而来。

_____

3. 观众突然静了下来。

_____

4. 可这醉汉像是很有把握似的。

_____

5. 当公牛逼近他时，他踉跄地往旁边一闪，牛扑空了。

_____

6. 每个人都意识到真诚的重要性。

_____

7. 最近金价上涨了。

_____

8. 他以低于其价值的价格买下了这座房子。

_____

Lesson **71**

Reading Comprehension

✦✦（1）✦✦

Bamboo

The bamboo is a kind of useful plant. Its stems are strong and they are divided by solid rings into sections. Between these rings are hollow stems.

In Guangzhou bamboos are widely used. Some are used as props in house building. Some are cut, and made into baskets, chairs and tables, etc. Some are split into strips. These strips are fastened together to make curtains for windows and doors to keep out flies and the light of the sun. We can eat the young shoots of bamboo, too. It is quite tasty.

In Hangzhou, along the hill-side we can find many bamboo trees. Some are green and some are yellow in color. Their stems are long and their leaves are small and pointed. The bamboo trees don't need much water for them to grow.

Four thousand years ago, there was a wise king in China, named Shun. He had two wives. When Shun died, his two wives were very sad. They cried day and night. Their tears fell on the stems of bamboo, so the stems of bamboo had many dots here and there. And these dots couldn't be washed out. This kind of bamboo which has so many spots on it named "Mottled Bamboo" and grows in Hunan.

▶阅读上面的短文，从每题所给的四个选项中，选出一个最佳答案。

1. ＿＿＿＿ are hollow.

   A. The stems of bamboo

   B. The "Mottled Bamboo" trees

   C. The solid rings between the sections

   D. The sections between the solid rings

2. Bamboo are used as props in building houses in ＿＿＿＿.

   A. Hangzhou   B. Hunan

   C. China   D. Guangzhou

3. The story about the death of Shun and his two wives happened ＿＿＿＿.

   A. few thousand years ago   B. two thousand years ago

   C. in 2000 B. C.   D. in 1900 B. C.

4. The spots on a kind of bamboo are made by ＿＿＿＿ and it can't be washed ＿＿＿＿.

   A. one of the Shun's two wives; of

B. one of the Shun's two wives; out

C. the two wives of Shun; off

D. two of Shun's wives; out

5. The "Mottled Bamboo" grows in _____.

    A. Guangzhou　　　　　　　　　　B. Hangzhou

    C. China　　　　　　　　　　　　　D. Hunan

✦✦ （2） ✦✦

Modern Zoos

Modern zoos are different from those built fifty years ago. Those zoos were places where people could go to see animals from many parts of the world. The animals lived in cages with iron bars. Although the zoo keepers took good care of them, many of the animals did not feel comfortable, and they often fell ill.

In modern zoos, people can see animals in more natural conditions. The animals are given more freedom in large places so that they can live more comfortable as they would in nature. Even the appearance of zoos has changed. Trees and grass grow in cages, and water flows through the places the animals live in. There are few bars; instead, there is often a deep ditch, filled with water, which surrounds a space where several sorts of animals live together as they would naturally. In an American zoo, the visitors can walk through a huge special cage that is filled with trees, some small animals and many birds. It is large enough for the birds to live naturally. In a zoo in New York, with the use of special night light, people can observe certain animals that are active only at night, when most zoos are closed. Some zoos have special places for visitors to watch animals that live in the desert or under water.

Modern zoos not only show animals to visitors, but also keep and save rare animals. For this reason, fifty years from now, the grandchildren of today's visitors will still be able to enjoy watching these animals.

▶阅读上面的短文，从每题所给的四个选项中，选出一个最佳答案。

1. It seems that _____ is something most important for animals.

    A. eating good food　　　　　　　　B. living in cages

    C. living with other animals　　　　　D. living in natural conditions

2. In modern zoos _____.

    A. different kinds of animals are kept separately

    B. animals are no longer taken good care of

    C. animals have more freedom

    D. visitors can walk wherever they like

3. In a modern zoo _____ feel comfortable.

    A. the animals, not the visitors　　　　B. the visitors, not the animals

    C. neither visitors nor animals　　　　D. both visitors and animals

4. In some zoos people can _____.

    A. walk through huge special cages to watch all sorts of animals

    B. see animals which live in special conditions

    C. during the day observe animals that are active at night

    D. watch all the rare animals that may not be seen in the future

5. The main idea of the passage is that _____.

    A. zoos are now places where animals can live naturally

    B. zoos are places where people can see animals from all over the world

    C. there should be old and modern zoos alike

    D. rare animals may soon die out

语言基本功
英汉翻译◈ | Translation Exercises

▶ 翻译下列句子

1. 当你游览伦敦时，首先看到的东西之一就是"大本"钟，即那座从英国广播公司的广播中全世界都可以听到它的声音的著名大钟。

    _____

2. 如果不是国会大厦在 1834 年被焚毁的话，这座大钟永远也不会建造。

    _____

3. "大本"钟得名于本杰明·霍尔爵士，因为当建造新的国会大厦时，他负责建造大钟。

    _____

4. 当大钟打点的时候，你可以从英国广播公司的广播中听到，因为钟塔上接了麦克风。

    _____

5. "大本"钟很少出差错。

    _____

6. 那幢房子过去属于我祖父。

    _____

7. 我想我是不会成功的，但还是试一下吧。

    _____

8. 过境时请出示护照。

    _____

Lesson 72

✦✦ （1） ✦✦

The Best Way to Know English New Words

When you are reading something in English, you may often meet with a new word. What's the best way to know it?

You may look it up in an English-Chinese dictionary. It will tell you a lot about the word: the pronunciation, the part of speech, the Chinese meaning and also how to use the word. But how can you know where the word is in thousands of English words? How to find it in thousands of English words? How to find it in the dictionary both quickly and correctly?

First, all the English words are arranged in the alphabetical order in a dictionary. In the dictionary you can first see the words beginning with the letter A, B, C, D... That means, if there are two words "general" and "monitor", "general" will be certainly before "monitor". Then if there are two words both beginning with the same letter, you may look at the second letter. Then the third, the fourth... For example, "before" is before "begin", "foreigner" is before "forest", etc.

The dictionary will be your good friend. I hope you'll use it as often as possible in your English learning.

▶ 阅读上面的短文，从每题所给的四个选项中，选出一个最佳答案。

1. According to the passage, if we don't know a word, we'd better _____.
   A. think hard   B. write it again and again
   C. ask our teacher or classmate   D. look it up in a dictionary

2. When you look up a word in the English-Chinese dictionary, you should understand not only its Chinese meaning, but also _____.
   A. its pronunciation   B. its part of speech
   C. the use of it   D. A, B and C

3. In the English-Chinese dictionary, the first part is _____.
   A. the words beginning with the letter A
   B. the words beginning with the letter E
   C. the simple words
   D. the very short words

4. Here are four words: (1) regular (2) relative (3) reject (4) religion. The right order in the English-Chinese dictionary is _____.

A. (1), (2), (3), (4)   B. (1), (3), (2), (4)

C. (2), (3), (4), (1)   D. (3), (1), (4), (2)

5. The English-Chinese dictionary is _____.

A. useful in our Chinese learning

B. our good friend in learning Chinese

C. a good friend in our English learning

D. not useful in learning English

✦✦（2）✦✦

Man has always wanted to fly. Some of the greatest men in history have thought about the problem. One of these, for example, was the great Italian artist, Lenorado Da Vinci. In the sixteenth century he made designs for machines that would fly. But they were never built.

Throughout history, other less famous men have wanted to fly. An example was a man in England 800 years ago. He made a pair of wings from chicken feathers. Then he fixed them to his body and jumped into the air from a tall building. He did not fly very far. Instead, he fell to the ground and broke every bone in his body.

The first real step took place in France, in 1783. Two brothers, the Montgolfiers, made a very large "hot air balloon". They knew that hot air rises. Why not fill a balloon with it? The balloon was made of cloth and paper. In September of that year, the King and Queen of France came to see the balloon. They watched it carrying the very first air passengers into the sky. The passengers were a sheep and a chicken. We do not know how they felt about the trip. But we do know that the trip lasted eight minutes and that the animals landed safely. Two months later, two men did the same thing. On 21 November, two Frenchmen rose above Paris in a balloon of the same kind. Their trip lasted twenty-five minutes and they traveled about eight kilometers.

▶阅读上面的短文，从每题所给的四个选项中，选出一个最佳答案。

1. Who made the first air trip in history?

A. The Montgolfiers.   B. Two Frenchmen.

C. A man in England.   D. Leonardo Da Vinci.

2. Leonardo Da Vinci _____.

A. drew many beautiful pictures of birds

B. said that man would fly in the sky one day

C. built a kind of machine which never flew

D. made designs for flying machine

3. Eight hundred years ago an Englishman _____.

A. made a kind of flying machine

B. tried to fly with wings made of chicken feathers

C. wanted to build a kind of balloon

D. tried to fly with a large bird

4. _____ trip lasted twenty-five minutes.

    A. The two Frenchmen's   B. The English man's

    C. The sheep and the chicken's   D. Leonardo's

5. The very first air passengers in the story were _____.

    A. nobody   B. some animals

    C. the King and Queen   D. the two Frenchmen

语言基本功
英汉翻译◈ | Translation Exercises

▶ 翻译下列句子

1. 杰出的赛车选手马尔科姆·坎贝尔爵士是第一个以每小时超过 300 英里的速度驾车的人。

_____

2. 他驾驶的"蓝鸟"牌汽车是专门为他制造的。

_____

3. 但他很难把汽车控制住，因为在开始的行程中爆了一只轮胎。

_____

4. 他的平均时速实际是 301 英里。

_____

5. 从那时以来，赛车选手已达到每小时 600 英里的速度。

_____

6. 今年夏天雨下得很多。

_____

7. 我重质不重量。

_____

8. 数学是研究纯量之科学。

_____

Reading Comprehension

✦✦（1）✦✦

Just a Little Help

Mark was walking home from school one day when he saw the boy in front of him fall over and drop all of the books he was carrying, along with two sweaters, a basketball and a walkman. Mark stopped and helped the boy pick up these things. Since they were going the same way, he helped to carry some of his things. As they walked, Mark knew that the boy's name was Bill, that he loved computer games, basketball and history. He was having lots of troubles with his other subjects and had just broken up with his girlfriend.

They arrived at Bill's home first and Mark was invited in for a Coke and to watch some television. The afternoon passed happily with a few laughs and some small talk, then Mark went home. They often saw each other at school, had lunch together once or twice, and then they both finished middle school. They ended up in the same high school where they sometimes saw and talked with each other over the years. At last just three weeks before they finished high school, Bill asked Mark if they could talk.

Bill asked Mark if he still remembered the day years ago when they had first met. "Did you ever think why I was carrying so many things home that day?" asked Bill. "You see, I cleaned out my locker because I didn't want to leave anything for anyone else. I had put away some of my mother's sleeping pills and I was going home to kill myself. But after we spent some time together talking and laughing, I began to understand that if I killed myself, I would have missed that time and so many others that might follow. So you see, Mark, when you picked up those books that day, you did a lot more. You saved my life."

▶阅读上面的短文，从每题所给的四个选项中，选出一个最佳答案。

1. When Mark met Bill the first time, Bill was going _____.

   A. to have a basketball game　　　　B. to his classroom

   C. to see Mark　　　　　　　　　　D. back home

2. From what Bill was carrying, we can know that he _____.

   A. was a good student　　　　　　B. liked sports and music

   C. liked all the subjects in school　　D. was a good friend

3. Mark and Bill _____.

   A. were in the same middle school and high school

217

B. were in the same middle school but not in the same high school

C. often had lunch together at school

D. had known each other before they began to study in middle school

4. In this passage, the phrase "break up" means "_____".

    A. 相处很好   B. 和好如初

    C. 关系破裂   D. 保持联系

5. When Mark helped Bill to pick up some of his things, he _____.

    A. knew he could save Bill's life

    B. knew who Bill was and wanted to help him

    C. didn't know why he was going to help him

    D. didn't know what he was doing was very important to Bill

Nose

The human nose has given to the language of the world many interesting expressions. Of course, this is not surprising. Without the nose, we could not breathe or smell. It is the part of the face that gives a person special character. Cyrano de Bergerac said that a large nose showed a great man — courageous, manly and wise.

A famous woman poet wished that she had two noses to smell a rose! Blaise Pascal made an interesting remark about Cleopatra's nose. If it had been shorter, he said, it would have changed the whole face of the world!

Man's nose has had an important role in his imagination. Man has referred to the nose in many ways to express his emotions. Expressions dealing with the nose refer to human weakness, anger, pride, jealousy and revenge.

In English there are a number of phrases about the nose. For example, to hold up one's nose expresses a basic human feeling—pride. People can hold up their noses at people, things, and places.

The phrase to be led around by the nose, shows man's weakness. A person who is led around by the nose lets other people control him. On the other hand, a person who follows his nose lets his instinct guide him.

There are a number of others. However, it should be as plain as the nose on your face that the nose is more than an organ for breathing and smelling.

▶阅读上面的短文，从每题所给的四个选项中，选出一个最佳答案。

1. The passage is about _____.

    A. an organ, with which people can breathe and smell

    B. the nose, which gives different and useful expressions

    C. the nose giving a person special character

    D. interesting remarks about the nose made by some people

2. From the passage we know _____.

   A. "Cleopatra's nose" changed the whole face of the world indeed

   B. Cleopatra had a strong will to change the whole look of the world

   C. Cleopatra's nose was not short

   D. Cleopatra hoped would change the whole face of the world

3. The nose expresses _____.

   A. some human weakness or other   B. people's shortcomings

   C. people's different emotions   D. human feelings in bad sense

4. A person who follows his nose _____.

   A. won't take others' advice   B. is easily controlled by others

   C. is weak-minded   D. has will of his own

5. How many expressions about the nose are mentioned in the passage?

   A. Two.   B. Three.

   C. Four.   D. Five.

语言基本功

英汉翻译◈ Translation Exercises

▶ 翻译下列句子

1. 逃学的孩子们都缺乏想象力。

   _____

2. 他们通常能够做到的，至多也就是安静地钓上一天鱼，或在电影院里坐上 8 个小时，一遍遍地看同一部电影。

   _____

3. 他搭便车到了多佛，天快黑时钻进了一条船，想找个地方睡觉。

   _____

4. 司机给了他几块饼干和一杯咖啡，就把他丢在了城外。

   _____

5. 他在那儿被一个警察抓住了，之后被当局送回了英国。

   _____

6. 别忘了夸奖那个男孩。

   _____

7. 人们都羡慕他的学问。

   _____

8. 游客们赞美登塔远眺的景色。

   _____

Lesson 74

◆◆（1）◆◆

Many teenagers feel that the most important people in their lives are their friends. They believe that their family members, and in particular their parents, don't know them as well as their friends do. In large families, it is quite often for brothers and sisters to fight with each other and then they can only go to their friends for advice.

It is very important for teenagers to have one good friend or a circle of friends. Even when they are not with their friends, they usually spend a lot of time talking among themselves on the phone. This communication is very important in children's growing up, because friends can discuss something difficult to say to their family members.

However, parents often try to choose their children's friends for them. Some parents may even stop their children from meeting their good friends. The question of "choice" is an interesting one. Have you ever thought of the following questions?

Who chooses your friends?

Do you choose your friends or your friends choose you?

Have you got a good friend your parents don't like?

Your answers are welcome.

▶ 阅读上面的短文，从每题所给的四个选项中，选出一个最佳答案。

1. Many teenagers think their _____ know them better than their parents do.

   A. friends   B. parents

   C. brothers and sisters   D. family members

2. When teenagers stay alone, the usual way of communication is _____.

   A. to go to their friends

   B. to talk with their parents

   C. to have a discussion with their family by phone

   D. to talk with their friends on the phone

3. Which of the following is different in meaning from the sentence "Some parents may even stop their children from meeting their good friends"?

   A. Some parents may even not allow their children to meet their good friends.

   B. Some parents may even ask their children to stay away from their good friends.

   C. Some parents may even not let their children meet their good friends.

D. Some parents may want their children to meet their good friends.

4. Which of the following sentences is right according to the passage?

   A. Parents should like everything their children enjoy.

   B. In all families children can choose everything they like.

   C. Parents should try their best to understand their children better.

   D. Teenagers can only go to their friends for help.

5. The sentence "Your answers are welcome" means "_____".

   A. You are welcome to have a discussion with us

   B. We've got no idea, so your answers are welcome

   C. Your answers are always correct

   D. You can give us all the right answers

6. Which is the best title of the passage?

   A. Only Parents Can Decide.   B. Parents And Children.

   C. Teenagers Need Friends.   D. A Strange Question.

Friends Are Treasures

Jim was feeling very sorry for himself. His birthday was in two weeks, and he didn't have any friends that he could invite to his birthday party.

During the summer, Jim and his mother had moved to the city from another city. In that city, Jim didn't have many friends, either. But he thought that, once he was in a new school and living in a new city, he could make friends easily. But he hadn't.

"It'll be some birthday party," Jim thought. "I'll be the only guest."

He went into his bedroom. He threw himself down on his bed. His mother hadn't come home from her job at the bank. Jim had time to think.

"What's wrong with me?" Jim asked himself. "Why don't I make friends? It must have something to do with my personality. I guess maybe I just don't have any personality."

Jim got up off the bed and went into the kitchen. He ate a piece of cake, some potato chips and drank a bottle of cola. He turned on the TV to his favourite channel. They played the MTV that he liked. Watching the program made him feel better.

He began to feel less sorry for himself.

▶ 阅读上面的短文，从每题所给的四个选项中，选出一个最佳答案。

1. How would you explain the title "Friends are Treasures" in a simple language?

   A. Friends are more important than anything else in the world.

   B. Friends can help you get rich more quickly.

   C. Friends can help you a lot when you need them.

   D. Friends can give you some expensive things.

2. Why was Jim feeling sorry for himself? Because _____.

A. he missed some classes

B. all the people thought he was a bad boy

C. he had no friends to come to his party

D. all his friends didn't like him

3. How many friends would come to his party?

A. Only one.   B. No one else but he himself.

C. His mother and he himself.   D. A few friends.

4. What kind of reason did Jim find out for his lack of friends?

A. He had few chances to make friends.

B. He was too poor.

C. His mother didn't let him.

D. He wasn't good.

5. What is the explanation for the phrase "to throw somebody down on one's bed"?

A. To lie slowly onto his bed.

B. To beat somebody and put him down on the bed.

C. To fall down on the bed.

D. To move the bed by himself.

语言基本功
英汉翻译◈ | Translation Exercises

▶ 翻译下列句子

1. 一辆古旧的汽车停在一条干涸的河床边，一群著名男女演员下了车。

_____

2. 他们戴着墨镜，穿着旧衣裳，特别小心以防别人认出他们。

_____

3. 但他们很快就发觉，化装的效果有时过分完美了。

_____

4. 没有记者，没有影迷！我们为什么不经常来这里呢？

_____

5. 此时，另外两位演员，罗克沃尔·斯林格和默林·格里夫斯，已经把两个大食品篮子提到了一片树荫下。

_____

6. 他们作了最坏的准备。

_____

7. 他转过身来准备上楼。

_____

8. 他住在车站的旁边。

_____

Lesson 75

阅读理解◇ | Reading Comprehension

♦♦（1）♦♦

How Much Are School Bags?

Are you carrying too much on your back at school? I'm sure lots of children of your age will say "Yes". Not only the students in China have this problem, but children in the United States also have heavy school bags.

Doctors are starting to worry that increasingly younger students are having back and neck problems as a result of school bags being too heavy for them.

"It's hard for me to go upstairs with my bag because it's so heavy," said Rick Hammond, an 11-year-old student in the US.

Rick is among students who have common school bags with two straps to carry them, but many other students choose rolling bags.

But even with rolling bags, getting upstairs and buses is still a problem for children. Many of them have hurt their backs and necks because of the heavy school bags.

But how much is too much? Doctors say students should carry no more than 10% to 15% of their own body weight.

Scott Bautch, a back doctor, said children under Grade 4 should stay within 10%. But it is also important that older children don't stay with over 15%, because their bodies are still growing. "Children are losing their balance and falling down with their school bags," he said.

Parents and teachers are starting to tell children to only take home library books they will be reading that night. Some teachers are using pieces of paper or thin workbooks for students to take home.

One of the best answers is, as some children said, to have no homework at all!

▶ 阅读上面的短文，从每题所给的四个选项中，选出一个最佳答案。

1. From the passage we can know that _____.
   A. only children in China carry too heavy school bags
   B. children in other countries don't carry too heavy bags
   C. both children in China and the US carry too heavy school bags
   D. only children in the US carry too heavy school bags

2. Children feel it hard for them to go upstairs because _____.
   A. they are too young   B. their school bags are too heavy

223

C. they don't know how to go upstairs

D. their parents don't always go upstairs with them together

3. If a child carries a heavy school bag, _____.

    A. his back and neck will be hurt   B. his head and arms will be hurt

    C. his hands will be hurt   D. his feet will be hurt

4. According to the doctor, Scott Bautch, if a child in Grade 5 weighs about 30 kilos, the school bag he carries should not be over _____.

    A. 5 kilos   B. 3 kilos

    C. 5.5 kilos   D. 4.5 kilos

5. Some students think the best answer to his problems is that _____.

    A. they should have a little homework to do after they get home

    B. their teachers had better not ask them to do any homework

    C. they should only take home library books they will read that night

    D. they should use thin workbooks instead of thick ones

✦✦ (2) ✦✦

Pet Monkeys

Most people have dogs or cats as pets. But some have other animals as pets, such as monkeys. Monkey though clever, are not easy to control. They are mischievous.

There is an old story about a monkey and an old man. The monkey belonged to the old man. The monkey was very clever.

When birds came to the garden, he chased them away. He also helped the old man in many other ways.

The old man often fell asleep during the day in his chair.

Then the monkey sat at the old man's side and chased the flies away from the old man's face.

One hot afternoon in the summer the old man was asleep in his chair. A fly came and sat on the old man's nose. The monkey chased it away. Soon the fly returned and sat on the old man's nose again. The monkey chased it away again and again. This went on for five or six times.

The monkey at last became very angry. He jumped up, ran to the garden, and picked up a large stone. When the fly came and sat on the old man's nose again, the monkey hit it hard with the stone. He killed the fly, but unfortunately he also broke the old man's nose.

There is also a modern story about a monkey. This monkey is a pet of a woman. The interesting fact about this monkey is that he can wash dishes. He will spend hour after hour washing dishes. He never breaks a dish. He washes dishes for the woman every day. But sometimes he washes the same dishes over and over. If the woman tries to stop him, he then gets angry. He begins to throw the dishes in all directions. But this does not happen very often.

The woman's husband is most happy, because he does not have to help his wife wash dishes. The monkey does all the work.

▶阅读上面的短文，从每题所给的四个选项中，选出一个最佳答案。

1. The writer thinks monkeys are _____.

   A. foolish
   B. clever

   C. mischievous
   D. clever, but mischievous

2. One hot afternoon _____.

   A. a bird came and sat on the old man's nose

   B. a fly came and sat on the old man's ear

   C. the monkey killed a fly and broke the old man's nose with a stone

   D. the old man was reading in the garden

3. The second monkey in the story can _____.

   A. chase flies away for the old man
   B. chase birds away for the old man

   C. throw dishes in all directions
   D. wash dishes very well

4. Which of the following is NOT true?

   A. Many people have monkeys as pets.

   B. The woman's husband like the monkey.

   C. Sometimes the monkey will wash the same dishes again and again.

   D. The monkey often throws dishes in all directions.

5. Which of the following is wrong?

   A. The monkey was very helpful to the old man.

   B. One hot afternoon the old man was sleeping in his garden.

   C. The woman's monkey is good at washing dishes.

   D. The monkey broke the old man's nose.

语言基本功
英汉翻译◈ Translation Exercises

▶翻译下列句子

1. 机上仅有的乘客，一位年轻的妇女和她的两个女婴却平安无事。

   _____

2. 此时正值隆冬季节。

   _____

3. 夜里，天冷得厉害。

   _____

4. 她在雪地上踩出了"SOS"这三个字母。

   _____

5. 不久，一架直升飞机飞抵失事现场，来搭救这几名幸存者。

   _____

Lesson 76

Reading Comprehension

✦✦（1）✦✦

Stone Walls in New England

In some parts of the United States, farming is easy. But farming has always been difficult in the northeastern corner of the country, which is called New England.

New England has many trees and thin, rocky soil. Anyone who has wanted to start a new farm has had to work very hard. The first job has been cutting down trees. The next job has been digging the stumps of the trees out of the soil. Then the farmer has the most difficult job of removing stones from his land.

The work of removing stones never really ends, because every winter more stones appear. They come up through the thin soil from the rocks below. Farmers have to keep removing stones from the fields. Even today, farms which have been worked on for 200 years keep producing more stones.

That is why stone walls are used instead of fences around New England fields. The stone walls are not high, a man can easily climb over them. But they keep the farmer's cows from joining his neighbour's cows.

▶阅读上面的短文，从每题所给的四个选项中，选出一个最佳答案。

1. New England lies in _____.
   A. England
   B. the United States
   C. the northeastern of England
   D. California

2. In what order a farmer in New England do the following things to start a new farm?
   a. Digging out the stumps of the trees.　b. Cutting down the trees.
   c. Removing the stones from the land.　d. Building a stone wall.
   A. a b c d
   B. c b a d
   C. b a c d
   D. b c d a

3. The word "remove" means _____.
   A. carry out
   B. move again
   C. bring out
   D. take out

4. Stone walls are used instead of fences around New England fields _____.
   A. because the walls are not high
   B. because there aren't enough trees

C. because stones keep coming up from under the farms

D. because they can stop the farmer's cows from joining his neighbour's cows

5. What is the most difficult thing for a farmer in New England?

   A. There are too many trees there.

   B. The soil is rocky and thin.

   C. Stones keep coming up from under the ground every year.

   D. The weather is too bad.

The Bully

Tony Wheedle was the meanest kid at school. He was big, ugly, and huge—like a tree! Tony likes to trouble the other students, especially the smart ones. After school, he chased his classmates and took their backpacks. Then, he put the backpacks (and sometimes his classmates) in a tree.

Tony never studied, so he got very bad grades. In his third year at junior high school, he had a problem. He was falling two classes. He had to pass them both to graduate.

"Hey, Frank," Tony said to a very smart student. "Come here."

"Please don't hurt me," Frank said as he shook with fear.

"Don't worry, you big baby. Look, I need to pass math and science, or I won't graduate. So, congratulations. You're my new tutor."

Tony went to Frank's house after class each day. Tony had a hard time with math. In fact he found science interesting. They did simple experiments with Frank's chemistry set.

Tony started passing his tests, and his grades slowly got better. He passed both his classes and graduated from junior high school.

"Thanks for your help," Tony said to Frank. "You know, I want a chemistry set. Where can I buy one?"

"A store near my house sells them. Come on, I'll show you where <u>it</u> is."

Frank and Tony became good friends. Tony stopped acting like a bully, and he even thought about becoming a scientist.

▶ 阅读上面的短文，从每题所给的四个选项中，选出一个最佳答案。

1. How did Tony treat his classmates?

   A. Very badly.   B. Kindly.

   C. He ignored them.   D. He was nice to everybody.

2. Tony did badly in school because _____.

   A. he was stupid   B. he never went to class

   C. he didn't study   D. all of his friends were smart

3. What happened after Frank started tutoring Tony?

   A. Tony hated school even more.   B. Tony started to like math.

C. Tony did better in school.　　　　　　D. Tony enjoyed science.

4. What does the underlined word "it" mean?

   A. Frank's house.　　　　　　　　　　B. A store.

   C. The school.　　　　　　　　　　　D. Tony's house.

5. After Tony graduated from junior high school, _____.

   A. he remained friends with Frank　　　B. he stopped talking to Frank

   C. he put Frank's books in a tree　　　　D. he became a scientist

语言基本功
英汉翻译◈ | Translation Exercises

▶ 翻译下列句子

1. 通心粉在这个地区已经种植了 600 多年了。

_____

2. 这里您可以看到两个工人，他们协力割下了三车金黄色的通心粉秸。

_____

3. 全村的人都日夜奋战，要赶在 9 月的雨季之前把今年的庄稼收获上来，打完场。

_____

4. 目前的冠军弗拉特里先生，自 1991 年以来，年年获胜。

_____

5. 现在我们回到电视演播室。

_____

6. 我们最后作出决定，派王先生到总部去作详细的汇报。

_____

7. 关于这一点，你同意他的意见吗？

_____

8. 他赞同我们尽早动身。

_____

Lesson 77

阅读理解◈ | Reading Comprehension

◆◆（1）◆◆

Johnny Smith was a good maths student at a high school. He showed great interest in his computer. He came home early every day. Then he worked with it till midnight. But Johnny was not a good English student, not good a bit. He got an F in his English class. One day after school, Johnny joined his computer to the computer in his high school office. The school office computer had the grades of all the students, the maths grades, the science grades, the grades in arts and music, and the grades in English. He found his English grade. Ah F! Johnny changed his English grade form F to A. Johnny's parents looked at his report card. They were very happy and really satisfied with the result.

"An A in English!" said Johnny's Dad. "It has turned out that my son is a very clever boy."

Johnny is a hacker. Hackers know how to take information from other computers and put new information in them. Using a modem, they join their computers to other computers secretly. School headmasters and teachers are worried about hackers. So are the police, for some people even take money from bank computer accounts（账户）and put it into their own ones. And they never have to leave home to do it! They are called hackers.

▶阅读上面的短文，从每题所给的四个选项中，选出一个最佳答案。

1.　Johnny changed his English grade with the computer just in _____.

　　A. the classroom　　　　　　　　　B. the school office

　　C. a bank near his house　　　　　　D. his own house

2.　When Johnny's parents saw the report, they were happy because _____.

　　A. Johnny was good at maths

　　B. Johnny loved computers

　　C. Johnny could join one computer to another

　　D. they thought Johnny was not poor in English any longer

3.　Who are worried about hackers in the story?

　　A. Johnny's parents.

　　B. School headmasters, techers and the police.

　　C. The police.

　　D. School headmasters and teachers.

4.　What should the hackers know well, do you think, after you read this story?

A. Information.   B. Bank computer accounts.

C. Computers.   D. Grades.

5. The last paragraph is about _____.

A. Johnny   B. computers

C. hackers   D. modem

✦✦ （2）✦✦

Out of School

There are many things we need to know that we do not learn at school. For example, if we want to use our money wisely, we need to shop carefully. We need to know how to compare the prices of things in different shops. We need to be able to compare the quality of different brands. We need to know how to make best choices when we shop.

Knowing how to make such choices is a "life skill", and we need these skills if we are to lead useful and happy lives.

Some of these choices are small. For example, will I take an apple for lunch or a pear? Will I get the bus to school today or will I walk? Will I wear the red T-shirt or the blue one to the movies? Other choices are more important. For example, will I eat healthy food for lunch or will I eat junk food because it is tastier? Will I work hard in all my classes or will I only work hard in the classes I enjoy? We make decisions like this every day.

Making the wrong choices can result in unhappiness. We have to realize that the choices we make can affect the rest of our lives. Just as importantly, our choices can also affect other people. The next time you decide to waste time in class, play a joke on someone or talk loudly at the movies, consider this: Who else does your choice affect?

▶阅读上面的短文，从每题所给的四个选项中，选出一个最佳答案。

1. What's the main idea of this passage?

A. We learn everything we need to know at school.

B. It's important to know how to compare prices.

C. It's important to know how to shop well.

D. It's important to make the right choices.

2. Why do we need "life skills"?

A. To know how to shop well.

B. To lead useful and happy lives.

C. To compare brands and prices.

D. To learn things at school.

3. Which of these choices is most important?

A. Which fruit to take for lunch.

B. How to get to school.

C. Which T-shirt to wear to the movies.

D. Which subjects to work hard in.

4. Why is it important to make the right choices?

A. Because they can affect the rest of our lives.

B. Because they can make us waste time.

C. Because they keep us from being happy.

D. Because we make choices most days.

5. What does "junk food" mean in this story?

A. 好吃的食品。   B. 垃圾食品。

C. 外表花哨的食品。   D. 难吃的食品。

语言基本功
英汉翻译◈ | Translation Exercises

▶ 翻译下列句子

1. 死于公元前 800 年的一位埃及妇女的木乃伊刚刚接受了一次手术。

_____

2. 唯一办法就是手术。

_____

3. 医生们至今还未确定这位妇女的死因。

_____

4. 他们曾担心在把木乃伊切开后，它会散成碎片，但幸运得很，这种情况并未发生。

_____

5. 这具木乃伊成功地经受了这次手术。

_____

6. 最后他得到四千英镑的赔偿金。

_____

7. 大火对财产造成了重大损失。

_____

8. 他提起诉讼要求赔偿损失。

_____

本书所有练习题的参考答案（含阅读理解练习题解析及译文），请登录中国水利水电出版社网站 http://www.waterpub.com.cn/softdown/（下载中心）免费下载。

Lesson 78

✦✦ (1) ✦✦

A Christmas Present

Jessie lived on the side of a valley. One summer a lot of houses below Jessie's were washed away by a big flood. Jessie's house was high enough to escape the flood, so when the water had disappeared and the other houses were standing there with no roofs or walls and all covered with mud, her house was still quite all right.

Jessie's house was quite small, her husband was dead and she had six children. But Jessie took one of the families that lost everything in the flood and she shared her home with them until it is possible for them to rebuild their houses.

One of Jessie's friends was very puzzled when she saw Jessie do this. She could not understand why Jessie wanted to give herself so much work and trouble when she already had so many children to support.

"Well," Jessie explained to her friend, "At the end of the First World War, a woman in the town where I then lived in Germany found herself very poor, because her husband had been killed in the war and she had a lot of children, as I have now."

"The day before Christmas, this woman said to her children, 'We won't be able to have much for all of us. Now I'll go and get it. She came back with a little girl who had no mother and father. 'Here's our present,' she said to the children."

"The children were very excited and happy to get such a present. They welcomed the little girl, and she grew up as their sisters. I was that Christmas present."

▶阅读上面的短文，从每题所给的四个选项中，选出一个最佳答案。

1. One summer _____.

   A. Jessie's house was washed away by a big flood

   B. a lot of houses below Jessie's were washed away by a big flood

   C. Jessie's husband died

   D. Jessie's husband was killed in a war

2. Jessie had six children, _____.

   A. so she couldn't help others

   B. but she tried to help other people

   C. but she adopted one little girl

D. so she had to move to Germany

3. On the Christmas Day the children got _____.

    A. some new coats   B. a lovely dog

    C. a nice radio   D. another sister

4. Jessie lived _____ as a child.

    A. in England   B. in Germany

    C. in Australia   D. on the side of a valley

5. Which of the following is wrong?

    A. The big flood didn't wash away Jessie's house.

    B. Jessie lost her parents as a child.

    C. Jessie's friend didn't understand her until she told her story.

    D. Jessie's husband was killed in the first world war.

✦✦（2）✦✦

Old Gremona Violins

Most musicians agree that the best violins were first made in Gremona, Italy, about 200 years ago. These violins sound better than any others. They even sound better than violins made today. Violin makers and scientists try to make instruments like the Italian violins. But they aren't the same. Musicians still prefer the old ones.

Some people think it is the age of the violins. But not all old violins sound wonderful. Only the old violins from Gremona are special. So age cannot be the answer.

Other people think the secret to those violins is the wood. The wood must be from certain kinds of trees.

But the kind of wood may not be so important. It may be more important to cut the wood in special way. Wood for a violin must be cut very carefully. It has to be the right size and shape. The smallest difference will change the sound of the violin. Musicians sometimes think that this was the secret of the Italians. Maybe they understood more than we do about how to cut the wood.

Size and shape may not be the answer either. Scientists can make new ones that are exactly the same size and shape. But the new violins still do not sound as good as the old ones. Some scientists think the secret may be the varnish. Varnish is what covers the wood of the violin. It makes the wood look shiny. It also helps the sound of the instrument. But no one knows what the Italian violin makers used in their varnish.

▶阅读上面的短文，从每题所给的四个选项中，选出一个最佳答案。

1. The passage is about _____.

    A. making violins   B. musical instruments

    C. scientific ideas   D. the old Italian violins

2. Some people think that modern violins _____.

    A. will sound better in the future   B. will sound worse in the future

C. sound wonderful   D. sound poor

3. Other people think the Italian violin makers _____.

    A. did not know much about violins   B. were lucky

    C. used many kinds of wood   D. knew something special

4. Violins made today _____.

    A. have the same size and shape as the old ones

    B. sound the same as the old ones

    C. are better than the old ones

    D. have the same varnish as the old ones

5. Some scientists believe that the secret of the old violins was _____.

    A. their sound   B. their colour

    C. their varnish   D. the music

语言基本功
英汉翻译◇ | Translation Exercises

▶ 翻译下列句子

1. 我聚精会神而又愉快地吸着这支烟。因为我确信这是我最后一支烟了。

    _____

2. 我具备了戒烟者通常表现出来的所有症状：脾气暴躁和食欲旺盛。

    _____

3. 我周围的每个人都在吸烟，我感到非常不自在。

    _____

4. 当我的老朋友布莱恩极力劝我接受一支香烟时，我再也忍不住了。

    _____

5. 一切又都恢复了正常，为此我妻子十分高兴。

    _____

6. 我想不出他现在在干什么。

    _____

7. 我猜想不出那人究竟是谁。

    _____

8. 我料想夏天我们会放假。

    _____

Reading Comprehension

♦♦（1）♦♦

Across the Desert

Richard Gray was a famous explorer. He was also a millionaire. He had visited every country in the world. He had crossed Antarctica, flown across the Atlantic by balloon, and climbed Mount Everest. Last year he decided to walk across Death Valley, the hottest place on earth. He walked for days over the hot desert sand. One night he found the camp where he had been the night before. Gray had walked in a circle. He was lost.

Two days later he had drunk all his water. He couldn't walk. He crawled to the top of a sand dune, and there he saw a man. The man was wearing smart, clean trousers, a white shirt and a tie. Gray crawled over to him.

"Water...water..." he said.

"I'm terribly sorry, old boy," replied the man, "but I haven't got any water with me."

"Help me!" shouted Gray, "I'm a rich man... a millionaire... I'll give you anything."

"That's very nice of you, old boy," said the man. "Look, I can't give you any water, but would you like to buy my tie?"

"A tie? Of course not!" screamed Gray, and crawled away. He crawled slowly up the next sand dune. His mouth was full of sand. His lips were cracked and dry. He couldn't breathe. He reached the top of the dune and there he saw a huge good hotel. Girls were swimming in the large swimming pool. Beautiful mountains were all around the hotel.

"Is it a mirage?" he thought. "Am I dying?" He stood up and staggered down the dune.

A waiter in a shining white uniform came out of the door.

"Water...water... A bath! Food!" screamed Gray.

"I'm sorry, you can't come into this hotel," said the water.

"Why not? I've got plenty of money... I'm a millionaire."

"Ah", replied the waiter, "but you aren't wearing a tie!"

▶阅读上面的短文，从每题所给的选项中，选出一个最佳答案。

1. The famous explorer _____.

   A. had crossed Antarctica and the Atlantic by balloon   B. had traveled all over the world

   C. had walked across Death Valley   D. had ever been a millionaire

2. Death Valley is _____.

A. a valley where people may die from loss of water

B. a dead place where people dare not go

C. a terribly hot valley where people may die of heat

D. a place's name

3. Two days later Richard Gray _____ .

    A. was lost in a circle

    B. was drunk

    C. began to search for water in the desert

    D. crawled to the top of a sand dune to see a man

4. The man offered to sell his tie to Gray because _____ .

    A. he wished to get some money from Gray

    B. Gray was a rich man

    C. he didn't have any water with him

    D. he thought a millionaire needed to wear a tie

5. At last Richard Gray _____ .

    A. got some water to drink   B. was not permitted to enter the hotel

    C. was very sorry for the waiter   D. was dying

✦✦ (2) ✦✦

Marconi Discovered Wireless Machines

Young Marconi loved books, especially those on science. "Sounds can be made to travel, "he thought," if they are given a push by electricity. If I can push a piece of wood across the waves on water, I can also send sounds through the air waves by electric power."

One day he called his mother and father up to his workroom for a surprise. He touched a little machine, and two floors below there was the sound a buzz. "How did you do it?" they asked. "Your machine is so far from the sound."

"That's right," he said joyfully. "I have just found a way to carry sounds without wires—a wireless way."

Later he made a wireless machine and took it to England, where the public was ready to hear new ideas. "What will those machines do?" they asked. "I can send messages through the air," he replied.

"Show us!" they said. And he did. On March 27, 1899, Marconi pressed the key on his wireless at a small village on the coast of France. After a few minutes of dead silence, a sound returned from England: "Your message was received. Very good." Still this was not enough for a scientist. He wanted to send his messages across the Atlantic Ocean, and he would not rest until this was done.

On the night of December 12, 1901, a thin, sick man climbed to the top of a hill on the Newfoundland coast. He waited there to receive the message from England.

The time came. "Now they are saying things to me," he said. A half-hour passed. No sound.

Another half-hour and then—a faint sound—One, two, three times! "This must be it!" he cried. But he told no one. Instead, he waited for other messages sent during the next three days. All came through to him.

On December 15, 1901, Marconi told the world that he had heard messages by wireless from across the Atlantic Ocean. His great discovery led to many more wonderful things, like radios, which we enjoy today.

▶根据短文内容回答下列问题。

1. What kind of books did young Marconi love?
2. Why did Marconi call his parents to his room?
3. What did Marconi do at a small village on the coast of France?
4. Was his first success enough for him?
5. What can wireless machine do?

语言基本功
英汉翻译◈ | Translation Exercises

▶翻译下列句子

1. 我在幼年的时候，曾多次乘飞机旅行。

2. 我的父母曾经住在南美洲，所以假期里我常从欧洲乘飞机到他们那里。

3. 一位空中乘务员告诉我们要保持镇静，待飞机一着陆，就马上不声不响地离开飞机。

4. 飞机上的人都很着急，大家都急于想知道究竟出了什么事。

5. 有人报告警察，说飞机上被安放了一枚炸弹。

6. 一名敌军军官被活捉了。

7. 他是世界上最快乐的人。

8. 四十多人被活活烧死。

本书所有练习题的参考答案（含阅读理解练习题解析及译文），请登录中国水利水电出版社网站 http://www.waterpub.com.cn/softdown/（下载中心）免费下载。

Lesson 80

阅读理解◇ | Reading Comprehension

✦✦ （1）✦✦

In 1826, a Frenchman named Niepce needed pictures for his business. But he was not a good artist. So he invented a very simple camera soon. He put it in a window of his house and took a picture of his garden. That was the first photo.

The next important date in the history of photography was in 1837. That year, Daguerre, another Frenchman, took a picture of his reading room. He used a new kind of camera in a different way. In his pictures you could see everything very clearly, even the smallest thing. This new way of taking photos was called a Daguerre type.

Soon other people began to use Daguerre's way. Travellers brought back wonderful photos from all around the world, people took pictures of famous buildings, cities and mountains. In about 1840, photography was developed. Then photographers could take pictures of people and moving things. That was not simple. The photographers had to carry a lot of films and other machines. But this did not stop them.

Mathew Brady was a famous American photographer. He took many pictures of great people. The pictures were unusual because they were very lifelike.

Photography also became one kind of art by the end of the 19th century. Some photos were not just copies of the real world. They showed feelings, like other kinds of art.

▶ 阅读上面的短文，从每题所给的四个选项中，选出一个最佳答案。

1. The first photo taken by Niepce was a picture of _____.

   A. his business   B. his house
   C. his garden   D. his window

2. The Daguerre type was _____.

   A. a Frenchman   B. a kind of way
   C. a kind of camera   D. a photographer

3. If a photographer wanted to take pictures of moving things in the year of 1840, he had to _____.

   A. watch lots of films

   B. buy an expensive camera

   C. stop in most cities

   D. take many films and something else with him

4. Mathew Brady was good at taking photos of _____.

    A. moving people   B. animals

    C. great people   D. mountains

5. This passage tells us _____.

    A. how photography was developed

    B. how to show your ideas and feelings in pictures

    C. how to take pictures in the world

    D. how to use different cameras

 (2)

Hans, the Butterman

When New York City was not very big, there was a market on the East River. On market day all the farmers came there to sell their vegetables, butter, eggs, and fruit. They laughed and talk together, so no one could hear the river that ran beside them.

But Hans, the butterman sat without a smile. He sold pounds of butter from a table beside him.

Once the weighmaster came walking down the road. He was looking for people who did not sell the full weight. Someone told him, "Watch Hans, the butterman." Many people said that his butter wasn't the right weight. They said that his rolls of butter didn't weigh as much as a pound.

Hans had good eyes. He saw the weighmaster and quickly put a heavy piece of gold into the first roll of butter, between the butter and its cover.

A captain was standing beside Hans's table, and he had seen Hans put the piece of gold into the roll. He stood at Hans's side when the weighmaster came up to him.

"Good morning," said the weighmaster.

"Good morning," said Hans. "I think that you are looking for farmers who trick the people of our town."

"I am," said the weighmaster. "Someone told me that your rolls of butter don't weigh a full pound."

"Oh, yes, they do. Here, Weighmaster. Here is a roll of butter. Weigh it yourself," said Hans.

Hans took the first roll of butter and gave it to the weighmaster. The roll weighed more than a pound.

"I've made a mistake," said the weighmaster. "You are an honest man. There is enough butter in this roll."

Then the captain stood in front of Hans's table. "You are an honest man, so I want to buy some of your butter," he said. Before Hans could speak, the captain picked up the roll of butter with the piece of gold in it. "I'll take this one."

Hans's heart began beating more quickly. "No, not that one. I've sold that one to a friend of mine. Take another one."

"No, I want this one," said the captain.

"I won't sell it this one to you. I told you that I've sold it to a friend," said Hans.

"Don't make me angry. The weighmaster weighed this roll. Give your friend another one."

"But I want to give him this one," said Hans, who was now very uncomfortable.

"I ask you, good weighmaster," said the captain angrily, "don't I have the right to choose the piece of butter that I want? I will pay good money for it."

"Of course you have the right, Captain," said the weighmaster. "What are you afraid of, Hans? Aren't all the rolls of butter alike? Perhaps I have to weigh all of them."

What could Hans say? What could he do? He had to smile and sell the butter to the captain. The captain gave Hans three cents for the butter.

The captain and the weighmaster walked away together.

"You punished the thief," said the weighmaster.

"No, he punished himself," said the captain, smiling.

▶ 阅读上面的短文，从每题所给的四个选项中，选出一个最佳答案。

1. _____ sold vegetables on the market on the East River.
   A. Hans   B. The captain
   C. The weighmaster   D. All the farmers

2. Hans put _____ in the first roll of butter.
   A. a coin   B. an egg
   C. a piece of gold   D. an apple

3. Hans didn't want to sell the first roll of butter to the captain because _____.
   A. he didn't like the captain   B. it was more than one pound
   C. he had sold it to a friend   D. he had put a piece of gold into it

4. _____ was a thief.
   A. Hans   B. The captain
   C. The weighmaster   D. The captain and the weighmaster

5. Hans had to sell the first roll of butter to the captain because _____.
   A. the captain paid enough money
   B. he was afraid of the weighmaster
   C. he didn't want to sell it to his friend any more
   D. the first roll of butter was much more delicious

Lesson 81

✦✦（1）✦✦

Babies love chocolate and sometimes they also eat the paper wrapping it. My cat enjoys a meal of good, thick paper, old letters, for example. But she doesn't like newspaper very much.

Of course, the best paper comes from wood. Wood comes from trees, and trees are plants, vegetables and fruit are plants too, and we eat a lot of them. So can we also eat wood and paper?

Scientists say, "All food comes in some way from plants." Well, is that true? Animals eat grass and grow fat. Then we eat their meat. Little fish eat little sea-plants; then bigger fish swim along and eat the smaller fish... chickens eat bits of grass and give as chicken. Think for two minutes. What food does not come from plants in some way?

Scientists can do nice things with plants. They can make food just like meat and cakes. And they make it without the help of animals. It's very good food, too. Now they have begun to say, "We make our people from wood. We can also make food from wood. The next thing is not very difficult."

What is the next thing? Perhaps it is food from paper. Scientists say, "We can turn paper into food. It will be good, cheap food too; cheaper than meat or fish or eggs."

So please keep your old books and letters. (Don't feed them to your cat.) One day, soon, they will be on you plate. There is nothing like a good story for breakfast.

▶阅读上面的短文，从每题所给的四个选项中，选出一个最佳答案。

1. When they eat chocolate, children _____.
    A. have some meat, too   B. have a little bread then
    C. maybe eat some paper at the same time   D. like to drink a cup of tea

2. From the text, we know that _____.
    A. a man sometimes eats some paper instead of bread
    B. a cat sometimes eats some paper
    C. a man often feeds some waste paper to a cat.
    D. all people in the world like to eat chocolate

3. A lot of facts show that _____.
    A. a man can live for ever
    B. all food comes in some way from plants
    C. a cat have a lot of paper at a time

D. vegetables and fruit can be made into chocolate

4. Scientists think that they can make _____.

　A. wood into the food in some way

　B. meat into the best food in the world

　C. wood kept well for ever

　D. chickens eat less food grow up fast

5. Scientists tell us that _____.

　A. they call make some cheaper food than meat, fish or eggs

　B. they can make any things into all kinds of food

　C. a person won't need to eat food any longer in the future

　D. everybody in the world can live to one hundred years in the future

Protect the Rainforests

More than 50,000,000 people live in the rainforests of the world and most of them do not hurt the forest they live in. They eat the fruits that grow on the forest trees, but they do not cut them down. They kill some animals to eat, but they do not destroy them.

When we cut down the rainforests, we destroy these forest people, too. In 1900, there were 1,000,000 forest people in the Amazon forest. In 1980, there were only 200,000.

The Yanomami live along the rivers of the rainforest in the north of Brazil. They have lived in the rainforest for about 10,000 years and they use more than 2, 000 different plants for food and for medicine. But in 1988, someone found gold in their forest, and suddenly 45,000 people came to the forest and began looking for gold. They cut down the forest to make roads. They made more than one hundred airports. The Yanomami people lost land and food. Many died because new diseases came to the forest with the strangers.

The Yanomami people tried to save their forest, because it was their home. But the people who wanted gold were stronger.

Many forest people try to save their forests. Chico Mendes was famous in Brazil because he wanted to keep the forest for his people. "I want the Amazon forest to help all of us—forest people, Brazil, and all the Earth," he said. A few months later, in December 1988, people who wanted to cut down the forest killed Chico Mendes.

In Borneo, people were cutting down the forest of the Penan and to sell the wood. The Penan people tried to save their rainforest. They made blockades across the roads into the forest. In 1987, they blocked fifteen roads for eight months. No one cut down any trees during that time.

In Panama, the Kuna people saved their forest. They made a forest park which tourists pay to visit.

The Gavioes people of Brazil use the forest, but they protect it as well. They find and sell the nuts which grow on the forest trees.

▶ 阅读上面的短文，从每题所给的四个选项中，选出一个最佳答案。

1. The number of the people living in the Amazon forest in 1980 was _____ of that in 1900.

   A. half   B. one-third

   C. two-fifths   D. one-fifth

2. The people who _____ have destroyed the rainforest of the Yanomami.

   A. pick fruits and kill animals to eat

   B. use plants for food and medicine

   C. have lived there for about ten thousand years

   D. made the roads and the airports

3. Those people built roads and airports in order to _____.

   A. carry away the gold conveniently   B. make people there live a better life

   C. stop spreading the new diseases   D. develop the tourism there

4. Which of the following is wrong?

   A. The Penan people closed 15 roads with blockades to save their forests.

   B. The Penan people were cutting down the trees to sell the wood.

   C. The Penan people didn't want other people to destroy their forest.

   D. Those who wanted to cut down the trees were stopped at the road blockades.

5. From the passage, we learn that _____.

   A. we need wood to build houses, so we have to cut down trees

   B. the rainforest people have done something to protect their home

   C. to humans, gold is more important than trees

   D. we mustn't cut down any trees or kill any animals

语言基本功
英汉翻译◈ Translation Exercises

▶ 翻译下列句子

1. 那个战俘杀死卫兵以后，迅速地把尸体拖进了灌木丛。

   _____

2. 正在此时，一辆黑色大轿车在军营门口停了下来。里面坐了四个军官。

   _____

3. 这人显然是想聊天。

   _____

4. 他上了年纪，有着灰白的头发和明亮的蓝眼睛。

   _____

5. 当这个人走近时，战俘一拳把他打倒在地。

   _____

6. 煤气管在漏气。

   _____

Lesson 82

✦✦（1）✦✦

Perhaps you have heard a lot about the Internet, but what is it, do you know? The Internet is a network. It uses the telephone to join millions of computers together around the world.

Maybe that doesn't sound very interesting. But when you're joined to the Internet, there are lots of things you can do. You can send E-mails to your friends, and they can get them in a few seconds. You can also do with all kinds of information on the World Wide Web (WWW). There are many different kinds of computers now. They all can be joined to the Internet. Most of them are small machines sitting on people's desks at home, but there are still many others in schools, offices or large companies. These computers are owned by people and companies, but no one really owns the Internet itself.

There are lots of places for you to go into the Internet. For example, your school may have the Internet. You can use it during lessons or free time. Libraries often have computers joined to the Internet. You are welcome to use them at any time.

Thanks to the Internet, the world is becoming smaller and smaller. It is possible for you to work at home with a computer in front, getting and sending the information you need. You can buy or sell whatever you want by the Internet. But do you know 98% of the information of the Internet is in English? So what will English be like tomorrow?

▶阅读上面的短文，从每题所给的四个选项中，选出一个最佳答案。

1. What is the passage mainly about?
   A. Internet.   B. Information.
   C. Computer.   D. E-mail.

2. Which is the quickest and cheapest way to send messages to your friends?
   A. By post.   B. By E-mail.
   C. By telephone.   D. By satellite.

3. Which may be the most possible place for people to work in tomorrow?
   A. In the office.   B. At school.
   C. At home.   D. In the company.

4. Who's the owner of the Internet?
   A. The headmaster.   B. The officer.
   C. The user.   D. No one.

5. What does the writer try to tell us with the last two sentences of the passage?

    A. English is important in using the Internet.

    B. The Internet is more and more popular.

    C. Most of the information is in English.

    D. Every computer must have the Internet.

 （2）

Two students started quarreling at school. One student shouted dirty words at the other, and a fight began.

What can be done to stop fights like this at school? In some schools, the disputants sit down with peer mediators. Peer mediators are student with special training in this kind of problems.

Peer mediators help the disputants to talk in a friendly way. Here are some of the ways they use:

1. Put what you think clearly but don't say anything to hurt the other. Begin with "I feel ..." instead of "You always..."

2. Listen carefully to what the other person is saying. Don't stop the other person's words.

3. Keep looking at the other person's eyes when he or she talks.

4. Try to see the other person's side of the problem.

5. Never put anyone down. Saying things like "You are foolish" makes the talk difficult.

6. Try to find a result that makes both people happy.

Peer mediators never decide the result or the winner. They don't decide who is right and who is wrong. Instead, they help the two students to find their own "win-win" result. A "win-win" result can make everyone feel good.

Peer mediators' work is often successful just because it gets people to talk to each other. And getting people to talk to each other is the first step in finding a "win-win" result.

▶阅读上面的短文，从每题所给的四个选项中，选出一个最佳答案。

1. What can be done when there is a fight at school?

    A. The peer mediators and the disputants talk together.

    B. The peer mediators decide the winner.

    C. The students themselves decide who is the winner.

    D. The two students sit down and listen to the peer mediators.

2. Peer mediators' work is _____.

    A. to give lessons to disputants

    B. to help find a way to make both sides happy

    C. to find out who starts a quarrel

    D. to give students some special training

3. What should you do when the other person is speaking?

    A. Try to tell him or her what you think.

B. Think who is right and who is wrong.

C. Listen carefully and look at his or her eyes all the time.

D. Ask the peer mediators as many questions as possible.

4. During the talk, if you say "You are lazy" or "I feel angry", _____.

A. the other person will know he or she is wrong

B. the other person will understand you better

C. it's easy for you to decide who is right

D. it's hard for you to get a "win-win" result

语言基本功
英汉翻译◈ | Translation Exercises

▶ 翻译下列句子

1. 渔夫和水手们有时声称自己看到过海里的妖怪。

_____

2. 一条小渔船被一条咬住钩的强壮的大鱼拖到了几英里以外的海面上。

_____

3. 那位渔民意识到这根本不是一条普通的鱼，于是千方百计不让它受到丝毫伤害。

_____

4. 它长着一个像马一样的头，有着大的蓝眼睛和闪闪发光的银色皮肤，还有一条鲜红色的尾巴。

_____

5. 此鱼叫桨鱼，被送进了博物馆，现正接受一位科学家的检查。

_____

6. 那婴儿的蓝眼睛清澈明亮。

_____

7. 这病人只能吃流食。

_____

8. 这辆油槽汽车装载着液态氮。

_____

本书所有练习题的参考答案（含阅读理解练习题解析及译文），请登录中国水利水电出版社网站 http://www.waterpub.com.cn/softdown/（下载中心）免费下载。

Lesson 83

阅读理解◈ | Reading Comprehension

✦✦ （1）✦✦

For millions of people the American dream of owning a home seemed to be slipping out of reach.

"Maybe young couples can no longer afford to buy a ready made house as their parents did," says 40-year-old building instructor Par Hennin. "But they can still have a home. Like their pioneer ancestors, they can build it themselves—and less than half the cost of a ready-made house."

The owner-builders come from every occupational group, although surprisingly few are professional building workers. Many take the plunge with little or no experience. "I learned how to build my house from reading books," says John Brown, who built a six-room home for $25,000 in High Falls, New Jersey. "If you have patience and the carpentry skill to make a bookcase, you can build a house."

An astonishing 50 percent of these owner-builders hammer every nail, lay every pipe, and wire every switch with their own hands. The rest contract for some parts of the task. But even those who just act as contractors and finish the inside of their homes can save from 30 percent to 45 percent of what a ready-made home would cost. One survey showed that 60 percent of owner-builders also design their homes. Many other buy commercial house plans for less than $100, or use plans available from the U.S. Department of Agriculture.

▶阅读上面的短文，从每题所给的四个选项中，选出一个最佳答案。

1. What is the main subject of the passage?

　　A. The cost of having a house built.

　　B. The American dream of owning a house.

　　C. A description of owner - builders in America.

　　D. A comparison between young couples and their parents.

2. It can be inferred from the passage that many Americans find it difficult to _____.

　　A. build a house　　　　　　　　　B. find a ready-made house

　　C. have a good job　　　　　　　　D. buy a house

3. "Take the plunge" in the third paragraph most probably means "_____".

　　A. decide to build a house　　　　　B. decide to pull down a house

　　C. decide to buy a house　　　　　　D. decide to rent a house

4. According to the passage, owner-builders are those who _____.
   A. are professional house builders   B. build houses of their own
   C. are contract house builders   D. sell or rent houses

✦✦ （2） ✦✦

The Roadrunner and the Coyote

One afternoon a coyote surprised a roadrunner when it was half asleep and leaning against a wall.

"Ah! Ah!" the coyote shouted, "I've got you! There was no escape!"

"Don't touch me! If I move, this wall will fall down on both of us!" cried the bird. "I'll tell you what we should do. You hold up the wall for me for a while. I'll go and find some food for both of us."

The coyote agreed and leaned closely against the wall, while the roadrunner—the bird he had intended to have for dinner—ran away.

A few weeks later, the bird was taking her nap under a shady branch. She had hung a bag on a branch. On the bag was a string that went all the way to the ground.

Suddenly, the coyote jumped out. "Ah! I've got you again. I remember very well that you told me a big lie last time we met."

"Now, wait a minute," answered the roadrunner. "I've got a big bag full of chickens up there. You can always get me, but how often can you eat fat chickens?"

"Well then, I'll have the chickens."

"Do you want them one by one or all at once?"

"All at once, of course!" said the greedy coyote.

The roadrunner pulled the string, and a whole bag of rocks fell upon the coyote.

Many months passed before they met again. This time, it was in the middle of night. The roadrunner was drinking by the side of a lake.

The moon was so bright that the coyote was able to see the bird from the top of a nearby hill. He ran down and easily cornered the bird.

"Before you open your mouth again to tell another lie," the coyote warned, "let me tell you that I won't believe a word you say."

The moon was shining round and yellow upon the water of the lake. The roadrunner said, "You can see for yourself that I am not telling a lie this time. Look at the big yellow cheese floating on the water, just a few yards away from us. It would be so easy for you to go and get it. You're hungry. I know. But think how much better a nice juicy piece of cheese would taste than I would. I'm all skin and bones!"

The coyote had to agree. He could see the cheese already.

"All right," said the bird. "Tie the rope I've got here to your neck, and if cheese is too hard to pull, then I'll be able to help you."

With the rope around his neck, the coyote started to swim toward the moon. At the end of the rope, there was a big stone. The coyote, the rope and the stone slowly began sinking in the mud at the bottom of the lake.

▶ 阅读上面的短文，从每题所给的四个选项中，选出一个最佳答案。

1. When the coyote met the roadrunner one afternoon, _____.
   A. the bird was half asleep
   B. he caught the bird easily
   C. a wall was falling down
   D. the bird was going out to look for some food

2. A few weeks later, the coyote saw the roadrunner _____.
   A. near a lake
   B. in a tree
   C. on a bag
   D. under a tree

3. In fact, _____ in the bag.
   A. there was nothing
   B. there were many rocks
   C. there were many chickens
   D. there was a roadrunner

4. The coyote mistook _____ for a big yellow cheese.
   A. the roadrunner
   B. himself
   C. the moon in the sky
   D. the moon on the lake

5. Which of the following is NOT true?
   A. In the end, the coyote would probably die.
   B. The roadrunner was cleverer than the coyote.
   C. The roadrunner was good at telling lies.
   D. The coyote didn't know the roadrunner would tell lies.

语言基本功
英汉翻译◆ | Translation Exercises

▶ 翻译下列句子

1. 前首相温特沃兹·莱恩先生在最近的大选中被击败。
   _____

2. 我的朋友帕特里克一直是莱恩先生所在的激进党的强烈反对者。
   _____

3. 大选结束后，帕特里克来到了前首相的住处。
   _____

4. 当他询问莱恩先生是否住在那里时，值班的警察告诉他这位前首相落选后出国去了。
   _____

5. 他已经退出了政界去国外了！
   _____

6. 敌人突袭我们的左翼。
   _____

Lesson 84

Reading Comprehension

♦♦（1）♦♦

An Advertisement

A man once said how useless it was to put advertisements in the newspaper. "Last week," said he, "my umbrella was stolen from a London church. As it was a present, I spent twice its worth in advertising, but didn't get it back."

"How did you write your advertisement?" asked one of the listeners, a businessman.

"Here it is," said the man, taking out of his pocket a slip cut from a newspaper. The businessman took it and read, "Lost from the City Church last Sunday evening, a black silk umbrella. The gentleman who finds it will receive ten shillings on leaving it at No. 10 Broad Street."

"Now," said the businessman, "I often advertise, and find that it pays me well. But the way in which an advertisement is expressed is of extreme importance. Let us try for your umbrella again, and if it fails, I'll buy you a new one."

The businessman then took a slip of paper out of his pocket and wrote: "If the man who was seen to take an umbrella from the City Church last Sunday evening doesn't wish to get into trouble, he will return the umbrella to No. 10 Broad Street. He is well known."

This appeared in the paper, and on the following morning, the man astonished when he opened the front door. In the doorway lay at least twelve umbrellas of all sizes and colours that had been thrown in, and his own was among the number. Many of them had notes fastened to them saying that they had been taken by mistake, and begging the loser not to say anything about the matter.

▶阅读上面的短文，从每题所给的四个选项中，选出一个最佳答案。

1. What is an advertisement?

    A. A news item.   B. A public announcement in the press, on TV, etc.

    C. One way to voice one's view.   D. Public opinions.

2. The result of the first advertisement was that _____.

    A. the man got his umbrella back

    B. the man wasted some money advertising

    C. nobody found the missing umbrella

    D. the umbrella was found somewhere near the church

3. The merchant suggested that the man should _____.

   A. buy a new umbrella

   B. go on looking for his umbrella

   C. write another and better advertisement

   D. report to the police

4. "If it fails, I'll buy a new one." suggested that _____.

   A. he was quite sure of success

   B. he was not sure

   C. he was rich enough to afford a new umbrella

   D. he did not know what to do

5. This is a story about _____.

   A. a useless advertisement

   B. how to make an effective advertisement

   C. how the man lost and found his umbrella

   D. what the merchant did for the umbrella owner

✦✦ （2）✦✦

Sociologist, working in western countries, have found that a large number of women wished they had been born men. The number is said to be as high as 60% in Germany.

"Women often wish they have the same chances as men have and think it is still a man's world," said Dr. James Hellen, one of the sociologists who did the study.

Many men say that they have more duties than women. A man has to make money to support his family and to make the important decision, so it's right for men to be paid more. Some are even against their wives working at all. When wives go out to work, they say, the home and children cannot be taken good care of. If women take full-time jobs, they won't be able to do what they are best at doing: making a nice home and bringing up the children.

Some women disagree. They say they want to get out of their homes and to have freedom to choose between work and home life. Women have the rights of equal pay and equal opportunities.

Anne Harper has a very good job. She also believes in "Women's Liberation". "I don't wish I were a man." She says, "and I don't think many women do. But I do wish people would stop treating us like second class people. At work, for example, we usually do the work that men do but get less paid. There are still a lot of jobs only for men to do—usually they are the best ones. If you are a man, you have a much better chance of living a wonderful life. How many women are scientists or engineers?"

▶阅读上面的短文，从每题所给的四个选项中，选出一个最佳答案。

1. Many men think _____.

   A. women can't do what men can

   B. men have to work much harder than women

C. men can make money more easily than women

D. women's duty is mainly to do housework at home

2. Some women have different ideas. They say that _____.

A. women need chances to go out of the home more often

B. women want more freedom in deciding the kind of life they want

C. if women are given equal pay, they can do everything instead of men

D. women are no longer interested in taking care of their homes and children

3. Anne Harper didn't wish to be a man _____.

A. because she believed in "Women's Liberation"

B. but she wished to get the same job as men

C. because she had got a good job

D. but she wished to be treated the same as a man

4. Anne Harper thought that _____.

A. women should live a better life than men

B. women should be really liberated

C. women should be given better jobs than men

D. women should live a more wonderful life than men

5. Which of the following is NOT true according to the passage?

A. There are more men scientists, engineers than women ones.

B. Women are second class people, so they couldn't live a better life.

C. Women do the same job as men, but get paid less than men.

D. There are some of the best jobs that women have few chances to take.

语言基本功
英汉翻译◈ | Translation Exercises

▶ 翻译下列句子

1. 公共汽车司机决定下星期罢工。

_____

2. 谁也不知道会持续多久。

_____

3. 司机们声称此次罢工将一直持续到就工资和工作条件问题达成全面协议为止。

_____

4. 多数人认为此次罢工至少会持续一个星期。

_____

5. 所有的学生都是开车的能手。

_____

6. 能再吃一片吗？

_____

Lesson 85

Reading Comprehension

✦✦ （1） ✦✦

When she looked ahead, Florence Chadwick saw nothing but a wall of fog. Her body was numb. She had been swimming for nearly sixteen hours.

Already she was the first woman to swim the English Channel. Now, at the age of 34, she wanted to become the first woman to swim from Catalina Island to the California coast.

On the morning of July the fourth is 1952, the seawater was not very cold and the fog was so thick she could hardly see anything. Sharks swam around her, only to be driven away by rifle shots. Against the cold of the sea, she never stopped swimming— hour after hour—while millions watched on national television.

Alongside Florence in one of the boats, her mother and her trainer encouraged her. They told her it wasn't much farther. But all she could see was fog. They asked her not to give up. She never had... until then. With only a half mile to go, she asked to be pulled out.

Several hours later, she told a reporter, "Look, I'm not excusing myself, but if I could have seen land I might have made it." It was not fatigue or even the cold water that defeated her. It was the fog. She was unable to see her goal.

Two months later, she tried again. This time, no matter how thick the fog was, she swam with her goal clearly pictured in her mind. She knew that somewhere behind that fog was land and this time she made it! Florence Chadwick became the first woman to swim the Catalina Channel!

▶ 根据短文内容回答下列问题。

1. Was Florence Chadwick the first woman to swim the English Channel?

   _____

2. When did Florence Chadwick swim the Catalina Channel first?

   _____

3. How many hours did Florence Chadwick need to swim the Catalina Channel first?

   _____

4. What made Florence Chadwick fail to swim the Catalina Channel first?

   _____

5. Why could she make it last?

   _____

✦✦ (2) ✦✦

The Thief and the President

A thief entered the bedroom of the 30th President of the United States, who met him and helped him flee.

The event happened in the early morning in one of the first days when Calvin Coolidge came into power. He and his family were living in the same third floor suite at the Willard Hotel in Washington that they had moved in several years before. The former President's wife was still living in the White House.

Coolidge awoke to see a stranger go through his clothes, removed a wallet and a watch chain.

Coolidge spoke, "I wish you won't take that."

The thief, gaining his voice, said, "Why?"

"I don't mean the watch and chain, only the chain. Take it near the window and read what is on its back," the President said.

The thief read, "Presented to Calvin Coolidge."

"Are you President Coolidge?" he asked.

The President answered, "Yes, and the House of Representatives gave me that watch chain. I'm fond of it. It would do you no good. You want money. Let's talk this over."

Holding up the wallet, the young man said in a low voice, "I'll take this and leave everything else."

Coolidge, knowing there was $80 in it, persuaded the young man to sit down and talk. He told the President he and his college classmate had overspent during their holiday and did not have enough money to pay their hotel bill.

Coolidge added up the roommate and two rail tickets back to the college. Then he counted out $32 and said it was a loan.

He then told the young man. "There is a guard in the corridor." The young man nodded and left through the same window as he had entered.

▶阅读上面的短文，从每题所给的四个选项中，选出一个最佳答案。

1. What cause the thief to meet the President?

    A. He knew the President had lots of money.

    B. He knew the President lived in the suite.

    C. He wanted to be a rich businessman.

    D. He wanted to steal some money.

2. Why did Calvin Coolidge live at the Willard Hotel in those days?

    A. Because the former President was still living in the White House.

    B. Because the First Lady hadn't left the White House.

    C. Because the First Lady liked to live there.

D. Because he liked to live there.

3. Coolidge counted out $32 _____.

A. in order not to be killed by the thief

B. in order to get rid of danger

C. so as to help the young man overcome his difficulty

D. because he had no more money

4. The young man's roommate went back to the college _____.

A. by air   B. by water

C. by bus   D. by train

5. Which of the following might happen afterwards?

A. The young student repaid the $32.

B. The thief was put into prison.

C. The President told many reporters the thief's name.

D. The President ordered the young man to repay the money.

语言基本功
英汉翻译◈ | Translation Exercises

▶翻译下列句子

1. 很多老同学都准备参加下星期四为他举行的告别宴会。

_____

2. 佩奇先生退休的前一天正好是他执教满 40 年的日子，这真是奇妙的巧合。

_____

3. 他退休后，将致力于园艺。

_____

4. 对于他来说，这将是一种全新的爱好。

_____

5. 我把大衣寄放牌丢了。

_____

6. 两份文本完全一样。

_____

7. 服务员给他拿来了账单。

_____

Lesson 86

语言基本功
阅读理解◇ | Reading Comprehension

✦✦（1）✦✦

A Way of Life for Students

The Internet is a way of life for US college students, with research showing them to be one of the most connected groups.

A recent study by Harris Interactive and 360 Youth found that 93 percent of American college students visit the Internet, and this market is expected to grow from 15.2 million in 2003 to 16.4 million in 2007.

That is slow but it could be the result of the already high number of college Internet users.

About 88 percent of American college students own a computer, and more than half have broadband connections. Besides, 67 percent own cell phones and 36 percent use their mobile devices to visit the Internet.

Study findings are that 42 percent go online mainly to communicate socially, and 72 percent of college students check e-mails at least once a day, with 66 percent using at least two e-mail addresses.

The most popular online social activity is forwarding messages to friends of families, with 37 percent of college students saying they do so.

The study also looked beyond the Internet surfing habits and into the buying habits of this group, and found them responsible for more than $210 billion in sales last year alone.

College students have learned how to spend their money, with 93 percent saying low prices were important when shopping.

The study also showed that 65 percent make loan payments, 41 percent of freshmen have a credit card, and 79 percent of seniors have a credit card.

A large number of <u>changes</u> on those credit cards are likely to be for entertainment and leisure expenses.

▶阅读上面的短文，从每题所给的选项中，选出一个最佳答案。

1. College students in American, we can know _____.

   A. don't have to learn their lessons in their classrooms

   B. spend too much time visiting the Internet

   C. live an exciting life by using the Internet

   D. waste much time visiting the Internet

2. To communicate with friends, nearly half of the college students use _____.

    A. telephones   B. e-mails

    C. fax   D. telegraphs

3. From the fourth paragraph we can find that in the US _____.

    A. most college students are from rich families

    B. college students can have a computer from their college

    C. cell phones will take the place of computers in colleges

    D. mobile phones make Internet life easy for college students

4. By using the Internet, college students in the US can do the following except _____.

    A. looking through news   B. chatting with friends

    C. buying goods   D. going fishing

5. The underlined word "changes" in the last paragraph means "_____".

    A. cost for goods or services   B. work given as a duty

    C. money in small pockets   D. control at high speed

✦✦（2）✦✦

A Brave Lady

One bright summer day, a number of little boys and girls were out walking with their teacher. They walked in groups of two, and were very happy.

In their walk they came to a bridge over the river, and they turned to go across it. They had just reached the middle, when there arose a great shout behind them. The teacher told them to stop, and turned and listened. When she heard the cry "Mad Dog!" She knew what was happening. Before she could do anything, she saw the dog running to the bridge.

"Children," said the teacher, "keep close to the wall of the bridge. Don't move or cry." Then she went and stood before the boys and girls, so that the dog would meet her first.

The animal came, his mouth wide open. He ran up quickly, and seemed to be going by; but when he had just passed the teacher, he made a snap at one of the little girls. At this moment, the teacher saw a man running up with a gun to shoot the dog. The children must be kept safe until the man could come up.

So she ran to the dog, and thrust her right hand into the animal's mouth. It bit her, but she kept her hand there until the man came near, and shot the animal dead.

The dog had bit her so seriously that the brave lady died soon after the doctors came. She had given up her own life to save the lives of the children. When people heard of it, they loved her for her brave deed. They said, "The deed of this brave lady should never be forgotten."

▶ 阅读上面的短文，从每题所给的四个选项中，选出一个最佳答案。

1. As soon as the teacher and her pupils reached the middle of the bridge, they heard _____.

    A. people running   B. the cry "Mad Dog"

    C. a great shout   D. the running of the water

2. The teacher told her pupils to _____ when the dog turned to run across the bridge.

    A. run away as fast as possible   B. jump into the river

    C. keep close to the wall of the bridge   D. stand still

3. The teacher went and stood before her pupils to _____.

    A. protect them from the dog   B. shoot the dog

    C. see what was happening   D. hit the dog

4. She kept her right hand in the dog's mouth _____.

    A. because the dog was dead

    B. until the man came and shot the dog dead

    C. when she saw people were coming to save her

    D. because the dog was hungry

5. People loved the teacher because she _____.

    A. saved the lives of her pupils   B. was brave in her daily life

    C. died in her fight against a dog   D. could fight the dog

语言基本功
英汉翻译◈ | Translation Exercises

▶ 翻译下列句子

1. 当那人试图让快艇转弯时，方向盘脱手了。

_____

2. 快艇撞上了一个浮标，但它仍在水面上快速行驶着。

_____

3. 它现在正以惊人的速度直冲他们驶来。

_____

4. 汽油几乎已经用光。

_____

5. 没过多久，噪音便彻底消失，快艇开始在水面上慢悠悠地漂流。

_____

6. 阑尾已穿孔。

_____

7. 花蕾正在绽开。

_____

8. 城里到处是游客。

_____

Lesson 87

阅读理解◈ Reading Comprehension

✦✦ （1） ✦✦

Busy Weekends

Most American businesses are open five days a week. American school children go to school five days a week, too.

American families usually have a two-day weekend. The weekend includes Saturday and Sunday. People spend their weekends in many different ways. Many families enjoy weekends together. They may go shopping or go to visit friends. They may also invite friends to have a party at home. Many American families have sports during the weekends. Running, bicycling, playing volleyball and swimming are popular in summer. Skiing and skating are the favourite winter sports.

Weekends are also a time for American families to work on something in their yards or their houses. Many families plant flowers and they usually have vegetable gardens. Some families use weekends to paint or repair their houses. So, most Americans are very busy on weekends.

In American colleges and high schools, students often have dances at their schools on weekends. Students usually do the dances and do a lot of work for them. They do this in committee.

There was a dance last Friday night at Peter and Mary's school. Mary was on the decorating committee and Peter was on the cleanup committee. The dance was in the school gymnasium. Every student paid two dollars for the dance. They spent some of the money on decoration and they hired a band to play music. They also bought some food and drinks. The dance began at 7 o'clock. Over 500 people came. Most of them were students of Peter and Mary's school. Some students brought friends from other schools. Everyone danced and had a good time there.

▶阅读上面的短文，判断下列各句正（T）误（F）。

1. American families usually have a three-day weekend.　　　____
2. There are dances in all the American schools on weekends.　　　____
3. There were two dances in Peter's school last Sunday.　　　____
4. The dance began at half past six.　　　____
5. More than 500 people came to the dance.　　　____

✦✦ (2) ✦✦

The Largest Island In The World

Do you know Australia? Australia is the largest island in the world. It is a little smaller than China. It is in the south of the earth. Australia is big, but its population is not large. The population of Australia is nearly as large as that of Shanghai.

In Australia there are enough laws to fight pollution. The cities in Australia have got little air or water pollution. The sky is blue and the water is clean. You can clearly see fish swimming in the rivers. Plants grow very well.

Last month we visited Perth, the biggest city in Western Australia, and went to a wild flowers show. There we saw a large number of wild flowers we had never seen before. We had a wonderful time. Perth is famous for its beautiful wild flowers. In spring every year Perth has the wild flowers show. After visiting Perth, we spent the day in the countryside. We sat down and had a rest near a path at the foot of a hill. It was quiet and we enjoyed ourselves. Suddenly we heard bells ringing at the top of the hill. What we saw made us pick up all our things and run back to the car as quickly as we could. There were about three hundred sheep coming towards us down the path.

Australia is famous for its sheep and kangaroos. After a short drive from any town, you will find yourself in the middle of white sheep. Sheep, everywhere are sheep.

▶ 阅读上面的短文，从每题所给的四个选项中，选出一个最佳答案。

1. Australia is _____.
    A. the largest country in the world   B. as large as Shanghai
    C. not as large as China   D. the largest island in the north of the earth

2. There are _____ in Australia.
    A. too enough laws to fight pollution
    B. so many laws that they can hardly fight pollution
    C. enough laws that they can hardly fight pollution
    D. enough laws because the pollution is very serious

3. Which of he following is NOT true?
    A. Perth is famous for its beautiful wild flowers.
    B. Perth is bigger than any other city in Western Australia.
    C. Perth lies in the west of Australia.
    D. No other city is larger than Perth in Australia.

4. In Perth you may visit a wild flowers show in _____.
    A. October   B. January
    C. May   D. July

5. Which of the following is TRUE?
    A. Australia is famous for its sheep, kangaroos and wild flowers.

B. We ran back to the car because we were in the middle of white sheep.

C. Three hundred sheep came towards us because they saw us.

D. If you go to the countryside in Australia, you will see a large number of white sheep.

▶ 翻译下列句子

1. "在凶杀发生的时候，我正坐在 8 点钟开往伦敦的火车上。"那人说。

_____

2. 我认为可以，但我从来不乘晚一点儿的车。

_____

3. 您乘的不是 8 点钟的火车，而是 8 点 25 分的，这次车同样能使您按时上班。

_____

4. 您看，在凶杀发生的那天早晨，8 点钟的那次车根本没有发。

_____

5. 它在芬格林车站出了故障而被取消了。

_____

6. 她哭得泪眼朦胧。

_____

7. 泪水盖住了她的眼睛。

_____

8. 他们把这个镜头拍了三次。

_____

语言基本功
好句好段◈ Writing Samples

☑ Soon the days grew shorter, and the cold weather kept the animals inside their comfortable houses. The Rat slept a lot in the winter, going to bed early and getting up late. During his short day, he wrote songs and did small jobs in the house. And, of course, there were always animals calling in for a comfortable talk round the fire, telling stories and remembering the good times and the adventures of the past summer.

不久，白天越来越短，寒冷的天气使得动物们都呆在自己舒适的家里。水鼠在冬季也是早睡迟起，瞌睡很多。在短短的白天里，他在家里写些歌，干些小活。当然，总是有些动物来串门，围坐在火炉边舒舒服服地闲聊，说说故事，回忆逝去的夏日里的美好时光和冒险经历。

本书所有练习题的参考答案（含阅读理解练习题解析及译文），请登录中国水利水电出版社网站 http://www.waterpub.com.cn/softdown/（下载中心）免费下载。

Lesson 88

| Reading Comprehension

◆◆（1）◆◆

Reading newspapers has become an important part of everyday life. Some people read newspapers as the first thing to do in the morning; others read newspapers as soon as they have free time during the day so that they can learn what is happening in the world.

Sometimes, we do not have enough time to read all the news carefully, so we just take a quick look at the front page. At other times, we may be in such a hurry that we only have a few minutes to look at the names of the passages.

Newspapers can be found everywhere in the world. We can get many different kinds of newspapers in big cities, but in some mountain villages we can see few newspapers.

Some newspapers are published once a week, but most of the papers are published once a day with many pages, some even published twice a day! You know different people enjoy reading different newspapers. Some like world news, and others prefer short stories. They just choose what they are interested in.

Today newspapers in English have the largest number of readers in the world. The English language is so popular that many Chinese students are reading English newspapers such as China Daily and 21st Century. They bring us more and more messages together with the Internet.

▶ 阅读上面的短文，判断下列各句正（T）误（F）。

1. Reading newspapers is the most important part of life for everybody. ＿＿＿＿

2. Usually we do not read all the passages in newspapers. ＿＿＿＿

3. People in some mountain villages can see many kinds of newspapers. ＿＿＿＿

4. Different people like to read different newspapers. ＿＿＿＿

5. We can get more and more messages in English newspapers together with the Internet. ＿＿＿＿

◆◆（2）◆◆

I Saw U!

Ellen is a young woman who was attracted to a man in her neighborhood. She often saw him at the bus stop or at the supermarket. He was tall and dark and had a beautiful smile. Ellen never spoke to him because she was very shy. She didn't know what to say to him.

Ellen is lucky because she lives in Seattle. In a Seattle newspaper called The Stranger, there is a special section called "I Saw U." It is similar to a personal ads page, where people write in looking for love. But the "I Saw U" section is unique to Seattle. Many people in their 20s and 30s read it. Anyone who finds his or her name in this section feels very excited and tells everyone, "Someone saw me! I've been seen!"

The Stranger has about 40 "I Saw U" advertisements every week. The section is so popular that people have to wait for months to get their advertisements in the paper. People usually write when they see someone they want to meet in a coffee shop or on the street. People write things like "Who are you?" and "Would you like to meet?" Sometimes the messages are sad. They say "I wish I knew your name" or "Where are you now?"

Finding love is difficult for many people. Ellen, who is 26, is a teacher. She doesn't meet many single men. She thought about the mysterious man for many months. Finally she decided to put and advertisement in the "I Saw U" section. She waited nervously. Then it happened the young man called her. He said his name was Richard, and he was a computer programmer. He wanted to meet her.

Ellen and Richard met in a coffee shop. They talked for a long time, they liked each other very much. They dated for several months, and now they are engaged. They both say that the "I Saw U" column helped them meet, Ellen says. "I never talk to strangers. I'm so happy I wrote to the 'I Saw U' column. I found Richard."

---

1. Seattle   *n.* 西雅图
2. section   *n.* 栏目
3. ads = advertisement   *n.* 广告
4. unique   *adj.* 独特的
5. mysterious   *adj.* 神秘的
6. computer programmer   程序师
7. engage   *v.* 订婚

▶阅读上面的短文，从每题所给的四个选项中，选出一个最佳答案。

1. From the passage we learn that _____.
   A. Ellen was young, tall and beautiful
   B. Richard loved Ellen, but she didn't know it
   C. Ellen loved Richard, but he didn't know it
   D. "I Saw U" was a Seattle newspaper
2. The story happened in the country of _____.
   A. Japan   B. UK
   C. USA   D. Germany
3. "I Saw U" was _____.
   A. a newspaper   B. an English sentence
   C. a company   D. a special column
4. Ellen got to know Richard with the help of _____.

A. a friend B. a stranger
C. a magazine D. "I Saw U"

5. Which of the following is wrong?
   A. The other newspapers didn't have "I Saw U".
   B. Young people liked "I Saw U".
   C. In the end, Ellen and Richard would get married.
   D. Richard, who was 26, was a computer programmer.

语言基本功
英汉翻译 ◈ | Translation Exercises

▶ 翻译下列句子

1. 6个人被困在矿井里已有17个小时了。

   _____

2. 如果不把他们尽快救到地面上来，他们就有可能丧生。

   _____

3. 然而，事实证明营救工作非常困难。

   _____

4. 他们一直被告知营救工作进行得非常顺利。

   _____

5. 如果他们知道了钻透那坚硬的岩石有多么困难，他们会丧失信心的。

   _____

6. 我们在湖边扎营。

   _____

7. 你说的话近乎于傲慢。

   _____

8. 七月平均雨量是多少？

   _____

Lesson 89

语言基本功
阅读理解◈ | Reading Comprehension

✦✦ （1） ✦✦

Have you ever heard the saying "If you want a friend, be one." ?

Here is how a new teacher made friends with the girls and boys in her class on the first day of school. As the bell rang, the teacher smiled at each girl and boy. Then she said in a quiet voice, "Good morning. How nice it is to have all of you in my class this year. I'd like to know each of you. I am sure we will enjoy working together." Everyone felt pleased because of her sweet voice and her friendly look.

She told the girls and boys her name and wrote it on the blackboard. Then she told them some of the things she liked to do and she was hoping to do with them during the year.

Then she said to the class, "Now you know my name and the things I like, and I want to know your names and the things you like. Then I will feel that I know you."

Could you make friends by doing the same as this teacher did?

One way of getting to know girls and boys in your class is to find out more about them. It is easy to be friends with those people who have the same hobbies with you. You can play the same games and go on journeys together.

You may find that some new comers in your class miss their old friends and feel strange and lonely. You can invite them to take a walk or to ride bikes with you. You will find many things in common to talk about. It is a good way to make friends by talking together in a friendly manner.

▶阅读上面的短文，从每题所给的四个选项中，选出一个最佳答案。

1. How do you understand the saying "If you want a friend, be one." ?

    A. If you want to have a friend, try to make one by your friend.

    B. You can make friends by doing what a friend should do.

    C. You may have a friend by doing everything for him.

    D. When you need a friend, you have to be a friend of yourself.

2. The teacher's sweet voice and her friendly look _____.

    A. showed that she would like to be a friend of the girls and boys

    B. made every girl and boy happy

    C. told the girls and boys everything about herself

    D. meant she wanted to tell the boys and girls something interesting

3.　A new comer will be your friend if _____.

A. he always thinks of his old friend

B. you ask him to do something

C. he knows you very well

D. you talk with him in a friendly way

✦✦ (2) ✦✦

George Frederich Handel, a small boy of six, lived in Germany. He loved music most. But his father didn't let him play any music.

Then one day he waited until he was alone at home. Quickly he ran to his hiding place, and he and a friend carried a small piano into the house. He decided to put it in his hiding place. There no one could see it.

That night, when everyone else was asleep, he went to his hiding place. The moon was shining through a broken window.

He sat on a box and began to play the piano. At that moment he knew that he could only be happy by playing music.

He played on and on, and he filled his house with his music.

"George!" cried his father. "What are you doing? Stop that playing now!"

The music stopped. George cried. Then he turned to his father and said, "Father, you must understand. I love music. It is my whole life."

"Now listen to me, my dear son," said Mr. Handel. "I want you to be a rich man. I want you to live a happy life. I don't want you to be a poor man all your life. You must leave music and become a doctor. Don't let me see you at the piano again."

But George didn't do as his father said. He still loved music very much.

Later a good teacher taught him well and helped him write his own music. George became famous when he was eleven years old. Now his music is played all over the world.

▶阅读上面的短文，从每题所给的四个选项中，选出一个最佳答案。

1.　George Frederich Handel _____ very much.

　　A. wanted a piano　　　　　　　　B. loved music

　　C. wanted to be a doctor　　　　　D. loved his father

2.　George's father told George _____ when he found George in the hiding place.

　　A. not to play the piano at night　　B. to learn from a good teacher

　　C. not to make a noise　　　　　　D. to stop playing the piano

3.　Why didn't George's father let George play any music? _____

　　A. Because he didn't love music.

　　B. Because he was too poor to buy a piano.

　　C. Because he thought playing music would make his son a poor man.

　　D. Because he wanted his son to be a doctor like himself.

4. Which of the following is true? _____

    A. Both George and his father loved music.

    B. George's teacher wrote some music for George.

    C. Many people knew George though he was very young.

    D. George left music since his father asked him to.

英汉翻译◈ | Translation Exercises

▶翻译下列句子

1. 人们总要想尽办法看不花钱的演出——哪怕是拙劣的演出。

    _____

2. 不幸的是，这次演出是我们看过的最乏味的演出了。

    _____

3. 那天晚上唯一有趣的事情是节目开始时那个报幕员的开场白。

    _____

4. 他显然非常紧张，局促不安地在麦克风前站了好几分钟。

    _____

5. 他刚一开口说话，人们便哄堂大笑起来。

    _____

6. 今天的汤浓，昨天的汤稀。

    _____

7. 这玻璃厚度不够。

    _____

8. 避免和像他那样的人接近。

    _____

Lesson 90

◆◆ （1）◆◆

Sweet Talk

Valentine's Day is on February 14. It's the day when people talked about love. How do you tell someone you love them? You can send chocolates or flowers. You can write a love letter or buy a Valentine card. Or you can send a sweet message on a candy heart with words such as "Kiss me" and "Be mine".

People started to give candy hearts in 1902. The Necco Company in Cambridge, Massachusetts, makes them. It sells 8 billion hearts every year, mostly for Valentine's Day. There are 125 different messages on the hearts. The messages say things such as "Hello" and "Hug me." People have bought the same messages for many years. But now there are some new messages. They say things such as "Page me" and "Fax me".

Who writes the messages on the hearts? Walter J. Marshall. He works for the Necco Company that makes the candy hearts. He is 62 years old, and he started to work at the Necco Company 40 years ago, the same year he got married. On the Valentine's Day, he gives his wife flowers and candy hearts. His favorite message on a candy heart is "Sweet talk".

Marshall decides what to put on the hearts. "I decide on the message," he says. "But I get ideas from everyone." Last year, he heard his grandchild say "That's awesome!" a lot, so he decided to put "Awesome" on a candy heart.

Marshall also decides when to take old messages off the hearts, and some people are not happy about this. They like the old messages, and they don't like the modern ones on the hearts. "Don't change any messages on the hearts!" one woman said. "I sent the same messages when I was a little girl!" But other people really like the new messages. People who use computers like the messages that say things such as "E-mail me." "I think it's a cute idea," one man said.

▶阅读上面的短文，从每题所给的四个选项中，选出一个最佳答案。

1. What time is Valentine's Day celebrated?
   A. On June 1.   B. On December 25.
   C. On April 1.   D. On February 14.
2. You can't tell someone you love them on Valentine's Day by _____.
   A. sending flowers   B. sending chocolates
   C. sending apples   D. sending a candy heart

3.　The Necco Company is in _____.

    A. Japan   B. Canada

    C. UK   D. USA

4.　Which of the following is true?

    A. candy heart can be a chocolate.

    B. The Necco Company sells 9 million candy hearts every year.

    C. Marshall was 40 years old when he started to work at the Necco Company.

    D. Marshall got married at the age of 22.

5.　Which of the following is wrong?

    A. Marshall decides not only what to put on the hearts, but also when to take the old messages off the hearts.

    B. No one likes the old messages because they are too old.

    C. Not Everyone likes the modern messages on the hearts.

    D. Most candy hearts are sold on Valentine's Day.

✦✦ （2） ✦✦

One day, I happened to talk to a stranger on the bus. When he found out that I was from Chicago, he told me that one of his good friends lived there and he wondered if I happened to know him. At first I wanted to say that it was foolish to think like that, for out of all the millions of people in Chicago, I could not possibly know his friend. But, instead, I just smiled and said that Chicago was a very big city. He was silent for a few minutes, and then he began to tell me all about his friend.

He told me that his friend was an excellent tennis player and that he even had his own tennis court. He added that he knew a lot of people with swimming pools, but that he only knew two people in the country that had their own tennis courts. And his friend in Chicago was one of them. I told him that I knew several people like that, for example, my brother and my next-door neighbour. I told him that my brother was a doctor and he lived in California. Then he asked where my brother lived in California. When I said Sacramento, he said that last year his friend spent the summer in Sacramento and lived next door to a doctor. The doctor had a tennis court. I said that my next-door neighbour went to Sacramento last summer and lived in the house next to my brother's. For a moment, we looked at each other, but we did not say anything.

"Would your friend's name happen to be Roland Kirk-Wood?" I asked finally. He laughed and said, "Would your brother's name happen to be Dr. Ray Hunter?" It was my turn to laugh.

▶阅读上面的短文，从每题所给的四个选项中，选出一个最佳答案。

1.　How many persons does the story involve?

    A. Four.   B. Five.

    C. Six.   D. Seven.

2.　Which of the following is the title of the story?

A. ON A BUS   B. TWO TENNIS PLAYERS

C. ONE`IN A MILLION   D. CHICAGO IS A LARGE CITY

3. The writer said that Chicago was a very big city. That means _____.

A. it was possible for him to happen to know the stranger's friend

B. he didn't want to look for the stranger's friend

C. it was impossible to find the stranger's friend

D. he didn't possibly know the stranger's friend

4. When the stranger told the writer that only two people in the country had their own tennis courts, he meant that _____.

A. his friend was a famous person

B. his friend was an excellent player

C. the writer could find his friend

D. the writer would happen to know his friend

5. Which of the following is true?

A. The story happened in Chicago.

B. The writer's brother lived in Sacramento.

C. Both the writer and the stranger lived in Chicago.

D. Both the writer and his brother lived in California.

语言基本功 英汉翻译◈ | Translation Exercises

▶ 翻译下列句子

1. 油煎鱼加炸土豆片一直是英国人喜爱的一道菜。

2. 因此，听说北海石油钻井平台上的潜水员受到巨型鱼类的恐吓，确实很让人吃惊。

3. 现在他们有了特制的笼子，用来保护他们免受大鱼的侵袭。

4. 这些鱼能长得这么大是由三个因素造成的。

5. 结果是，这些鱼就在可爱的温暖的水流中吃呀吃，长呀长。究竟谁吃谁呢？

6. 那家公司经营两家工厂。

7. 医生说他也许不得不动手术。

8. 那电梯是用电操作的。

Lesson 91

Reading Comprehension

✦✦（1）✦✦

The sun is our most important star. It can be dangerous to man both here on earth and in outer space. We need to find out something about its dangers.

Many stars are larger than our sun. However, the sun is about 250,000 times closer to the earth than any other star. Most of our energy comes from the sun's rays. We can trace electricity, wind, water power, and even the energy in our bodies back to the sun.

Not all kinds of solar rays reach the earth. The earth is wrapped in a blanket of air which keeps out rays that might harm us. Now man is exploring space. He is going outside his blanket of air. He has become interested in the dangerous solar rays.

Sometimes there are storms in the sun's hot gases. These storms are called solar flares. During solar flares, the sun puts out heavy rays that move at faster speeds than usual. These rays can make space-craft engines break down. They might cause men in space to become ill or die.

There is no way to tell when a solar flare will take place. Before it is safe for men to go on long trips through space, we need to know more about solar flares. We must find better ways to protect men from the sun's dangerous rays.

▶ 阅读上面的短文，从每题所给的四个选项中，选出一个最佳答案。

1. The storms caused by the sun's hot gases are called _____.

   A. heavy rays   B. blankets of air

   C. solar flares   D. dust storms

2. The text says that _____.

   A. the sun's rays are not important to us

   B. dangerous solar rays do not reach the earth

   C. solar flares are caused by electricity

   D. solar flares are caused by wind

3. The earth is wrapped in _____.

   A. a blanket of air   B. solar rays

   C. dangerous solar flares   D. electricity

4. Why is man going outside his blanket of air?

   A. He is tired of the earth.

   B. He wants to reach the sun.

C. He wants to explore outer space.

D. He wants to help spacecraft engines move faster.

5. This article is mainly about _____.

    A. spacecraft going to the sun   B. the sun's rays

    C. electricity, wind and water power   D. men in space

✦✦ （2） ✦✦

We've talked about snails（蜗牛）and their slow move. But much of the time snails don't move at all. They're in their shells—sleeping.

Hot sun will dry out a snail's body. So at the least sign of hot sun, a snail draws its body into its shell and closes the opening with a thin cover. Then it goes to sleep. A snail will die in a heavy rain. So whenever it rains, it goes inside its shell house—and goes to sleep. A snail can sleep for as long as it needs to. It can take a short sleep. Or it can sleep for days at a time. And it spends all the winter months in its shell, asleep.

In the spring the snail wakes up. Its body, about three inches long, comes out from the shell. When hungry, the snail looks for food. It can't see very well. Its eyes, at the end of the top feelers, are very weak. But its sense of smell is very strong. It helps the snail to the new greens. Then the snail's little mouth goes to work.

A snail's mouth is no bigger than the point of a pin. Yet it has 25, 600 teeth! The teeth are so small that you can't see them. But they do their work. If you put a snail in a hard paper box, it will eat its way out! And if a snail wears out its teeth, it will grow new ones.

Mostly, a snail looks for food at night. But on cloudy days it eats in the daytime. It eats all day long. A snail can go on eating for hours and never feel full.

▶ 阅读上面的短文，从每题所给的四个选项中，选出一个最佳答案。

1. A snail _____.

    A. moves more slowly in day-time   B. has thousands of feet

    C. doesn't move at all   D. sleeps much of the time

2. In the sentence "A snail draws its body into its shell", the word "draw" means _____.

    A. to make with a pen   B. to keep away from

    C. to pull   D. to move to the end

3. From the story we know _____.

    A. the snail's shell is very thin

    B. a snail can't see well

    C. the snail's body changes in different seasons

    D. the snail's nose is quite short

4. A snail goes to sleep when _____.

    A. it feels hungry   B. it is put into a paper box

    C. spring is coming   D. it rains heavily

5. Which of the followings is NOT true?

   A. A snail doesn't like living under the sun.

   B. In winter the snail doesn't eat or move.

   C. The snail's teeth can't be worn out.

   D. The snail's strong sense of smell helps to find food "far away".

语言基本功
英汉翻译◈ | Translation Exercises

▶ 翻译下列句子

1. 一个飞行员发现了一只气球，它像是正飞往附近的一个皇家空军基地。

2. 他马上把情况报告给该基地，但那里的人没有一个能解释这到底是怎么回事。

3. 飞行员设法绕着气球飞了一阵。

4. 当气球飞临基地上空时，飞行员看见有一个人在拍照。

5. 不久，气球开始降落，在一个停机坪附近着了陆。

6. 她极想出国。

7. 炭在烧着。

8. 房子被烧成灰烬。

语言基本功
好句好段◈ | Writing Samples

✔ At that moment two things happened. A man ran out of the factory, shouting angrily. And the wind suddenly became stronger. It caught the sail and sent it quickly from one side of the boat to the other. The back of the sail hit Christine hard on the back of the head. She fell into the water, like a bag of potatoes. Then the wind caught the sail again and threw it back across the boat. This time the boat fell over on its side and lay with its sail under the water.

在那一时刻发生了两件事情。一个人跑出工厂愤怒地叫喊。风突然刮得更猛。风扯倒了帆，迅速把它从船的一边刮到另一边。帆的尾部沉重地打在克里斯汀头的后部，她像一袋土豆一样栽入水中。然后风又把帆掀起抛到船的另一边。这次船侧翻与帆一同沉入水底。

Lesson 92

阅读理解◈ | Reading Comprehension

✦✦（1）✦✦

The compass is very necessary for guiding ships and planes. Hikers often need a compass, too. A compass will always make it possible for you to know where is the north.

The compass is a special magnet. The Chinese were the first people to use the magnet as a compass. They first used compasses to guide their ships between the years 100 BC and AD 100. Their compasses were simple and inconvenient.

To make their compass, these early Chinese placed the magnet needle on a cork and then put the needle-cork system in a bowl of water. The floating magnet turned easily, and made itself with the directions, north and south.

Later the Chinese invention was put together with a Babylonian invention the degree. A compass points out directions according to degrees. There are sixteen main points on a compass. Each main point is the same as a certain number of degrees. North on the compass, for example, is 0℃, east is 90℃, and so on.

Compasses worked well on wooden ships. But when metal ships appeared in the 1880s, the simple magnetic compass was not correct any more. The gyrocompass and the radio compass began to be used for navigation.

▶ 阅读上面的短文，从每题所给的四个选项中，选出一个最佳答案。

1. The "compass" most probably is _____.
   A. 雷达   B. 磁针
   C. 温度计   D. 指南针
2. What is the most important part of a compass?
   A. The poles.   B. The magnet.
   C. Degrees.   D. The sixteen points.
3. The Chinese started to use a compass _____.
   A. over 1, 900 years ago   B. about 1, 000 years ago
   C. before 100 BC   D. in the 1800s
4. Modern ships never use the magnetic compass because _____.
   A. it is simple and inconvenient
   B. the gyrocompass and the radio compass are better than it
   C. the sixteen points on a compass are few for the use of seamen

D. the metal in the ship may attract the magnet

5.　Which of the following is true? _____

　　A. The Babylonian first used the compass.

　　B. In all compasses, each main point is the same as certain number of degrees.

　　C. Compass worked well on all ships.

　　D. In a metal ship, the gyrocompass is more useful than the radio compass.

✦✦（2）✦✦

A Special School

In the country of Burma in Asia there are many little one-room schoolhouses. They hold one pupil at a time.

On the first day of school a wrinkled old teacher stands at the gates waiting for the pupil to arrive.

The pupil is only five years old. He is brought to school by teenage boys. But he doesn't go in at once. He is not sure he wants an education. The teacher helps him make up his mind by pushing him into the schoolhouse from behind. Then the boys close the gate.

Now the pupil is sure he doesn't want an education! He starts to howl.

The boys gather around. Giving him bananas and sweets. The pupil is very fond of eating, so he stops howling now and then to take a banana. Finally, after many bananas, he decided that school isn't so bad. Perhaps he will stay.

What kind of school is this?

It is a school for little elephants. The wrinkled, old teacher is a wrinkled old elephant about 50 years old called koonkie.

The boys or men who help to the little elephant are elephant riders. They are called oozies.

One oozie will become the little elephant's own driver and will stay with all his life if he can.

What does the little elephant learn at school?

After pounds of pounds bananas, he learns to let the oozie sit on his head. He learns the meaning of a few words, such as "Sit down!" and "Stand up!" But mostly he learns touch signals. If the oozie touches him on the ear or leans forward or backward. The elephant knows he is to go faster or slower or to stop or to kneel.

If the elephant is trained with kindness and patience, he will learn quickly. When he is older, he will work for men and become very useful.

▶ 阅读上面的短文，从每题所给的四个选项中，选出一个最佳答案。

1.　The story happens in the country of _____.

　　A. China　　　　　　　　　　　　B. India

　　C. Burma　　　　　　　　　　　　D. Thailand

2.　The special school is for _____.

　　A. children　　　　　　　　　　　B. little elephants

C. old elephants   D. elephant riders

3. The pupil comes to decide that school isn't so bad because _____.

    A. the old teacher is kind to him

    B. there are many pupils in the school

    C. the boys gives him many bananas to eat

    D. the old teacher is his parent

4. The oozie are _____.

    A. little elephants   B. elephant riders

    C. old teachers   D. elephant schoolhouses

5. Which of the following is wrong?

    A. There is only one little elephant in each special school.

    B. An wrinkled, old elephant will help to train the little elephant.

    C. In the school the pupil mostly learns to say a few words.

    D. In the school the pupil is treated kindly.

语言基本功
英汉翻译◈ | Translation Exercises

▶ 翻译下列句子

1. 我回到家时，肯定已是凌晨两点左右了。

    _____

2. 我按响了门铃，试图唤醒我的妻子，但她睡得很熟。

    _____

3. 我向下面看去。当我看清是一个警察时，差一点儿从梯子上掉下去。

    _____

4. 我回答了他的话，但马上又后悔那样说，我是这样说的："我喜欢在夜里擦窗子。"

    _____

5. 当一个人在忙着干活时，我是不愿意去打断他的，但请您跟我到警察局去一趟好吗？

    _____

6. 暗礁对船只是一种危险。

    _____

7. 这对中东和平是一种威胁。

    _____

8. 那就是危险所在。

    _____

本书所有练习题的参考答案（含阅读理解练习题解析及译文），请登录中国水利水电出版社网站 http://www.waterpub.com.cn/softdown/（下载中心）免费下载。

Lesson 93

阅读理解◈ | Reading Comprehension

✦✦ (1) ✦✦

Out of Petrol

It was already late when we set out for the next town, which according to the map was about fifteen miles away on the other side of the hills. There we felt sure we would find a bed for the night. Darkness fell soon after we left the village, but luckily we met no one as we drove swiftly along the narrow winding road that led to the hills. As we climbed higher, it became colder and rain began to fall, making it difficult at times to see the road. I asked John, my companion, to drive more slowly.

After we had traveled for about twenty miles, there was still no sign of the town which was marked on the map. We began to get worried. Then without warning, the car stopped. A quick examination showed that we had run out of petrol. Although we had little food with us, only a few biscuits and some chocolates, we decided to spend the night in the car.

Our meal was soon over. I tried to go to sleep at once, but John, who was a poor sleeper, got out of the car after a few minutes and went for a walk up the hill. Soon he came running back. From the valley below, the lights of the town we were looking for. We at once unloaded all our luggage and, with a great effort, managed to push the car to the top of the hill.

Then we went back for the luggage, loaded the car again and set off down the hill. In less than a quarter of an hour we were in the town, where we found a hotel quite easily.

▶阅读上面的短文，从每题所给的四个选项中，选出一个最佳答案。

1. The next town was _____ miles away from the village.

   A. fifty   B. twenty

   C. fifteen   D. thirty

2. The car stopped because _____.

   A. there was something wrong with it   B. it was raining

   C. John, the driver, could not find the road   D. there was no petrol

3. They had _____ for supper.

   A. some rice and fish   B. some bread and chicken

   C. some take-away food   D. a few biscuits and some chocolates

4. In the end, they spent the night _____.

   A. in the car   B. in a hotel

C. in the open air   D. on the top of the hill

5. Which of the following is wrong?

    A. In the end, we got to the town.

    B. We had to push the car up to the top of the hill.

    C. The driver saw the lights of the town they were looking for.

    D. They didn't bring map with them.

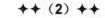

A Dangerous Plant

At the side of the water, a beautiful, blue butterfly is moving around. It flies over the flowers and grasses, and then sees an interesting plant with strange leaves. The butterfly hovers above the plant and looks more closely, then it lands on the leaves. It is a big mistake. SNAP! The leaves close together and catch the butterfly. The sides of the leaves are like a comb, and they lock together very tightly. The butterfly can't move. Soon it will be dead.

It grows in North and South Carolina in the USA. And it is one example of carnivorous plant—in other words a plant that eats meat. These meat-eating plants are quite unusual, and are a very interesting group to study.

There are about 250,000 different kinds of plants in the world, but only a small number of these are carnivorous, but why did plants start eating meat? Many animals are carnivorous...surely plants only eat meat in horror movies!

Carnivorous plants grow in wet areas, where the ground is very soft. The ground in these places is not very good for plants to grow. There aren't enough minerals in the ground to provide food for the plants. So the plants get extra minerals from insects—and they have learnt how to catch them and eat them to live. They have learnt how to be hunters.

It is possible for these carnivorous plants to live without eating insects, but the extra minerals help them to grow better and stronger.

When you read about a plant like eating an insect, it all looks very simple. But it is not very easy for a plant to catch an insect. The Venus flytrap can't move around. And it has no eyes to see the flies above or beside it. It can't hear the noise of insects coming near. So how does it catch something in its leaves—especially something that can move very fast, like a fly?

The plant doesn't have to move, it just waits for the meal to come to it. Like all traps, the Venus flytrap uses a special bait. This means it has something that will attract or invite the insects to come near. The Venus flytrap has a very sweet, sugary liquid on its leaves. The insects can smell this, and they think it is delicious—this is the bait. The sweet liquid smells like a tasty meal, so the insects fly nearer and land on the leaves. Of course, they are right—it is a tasty meal, but the delicious meal is self! Themselves!

The plant has to work very fast to catch the insect, so when the insect lands on the leaves, the trap starts to work immediately. There are three very small hairs on each leaf, and these are like tiny triggers. As soon as the insect touches these hairs the trap closes, like the teeth in a mouth.

And this happens very quickly. In less than a second, the sides of the leaves close, and the insect can't get out. This is enough to trap a large insect like the butterfly. Now the Venus flytrap has caught its dinner—but it takes a long time to eat it.

The leaves slowly move closer and closer together, and about half an hour, they are shut tight. Now the leaves are like a cup, and it fills with a special liquid. In fact it is more like a stomach, and over the next week or two the body of the insect becomes liquid inside this "stomach". Now the plant has a cup of "insect soup"! The Venus flytrap can drink this liquid soup through its leaves, and in this way it takes in extra vitamins to help it grow.

▶阅读上面的短文，从每题所给的四个选项中，选出一个最佳答案。

1. The name of the dangerous plant is _____.
   A. Butterfly   B. Fly
   C. The Venus flytrap   D. Comb
2. The word "carnivorous" means _____.
   A. grass-eating   B. meat-eating
   C. insect-eating   D. animal-eating
3. The word "bait" means "_____" in Chinese.
   A. 植物   B. 装置
   C. 诱饵   D. 液体
4. Which of the following is wrong?
   A. The Venus flytrap grows in wet place.
   B. The Venus flytrap can't live without eating insects.
   C. It takes a long time for the plant to eat the butterfly.
   D. The Venus flytrap can catch an insect very quickly.
5. Which of the following is true?
   A. People don't know why the Venus flytrap needs to eat insects.
   B. The Venus flytrap can eat the insect in a day or two.
   C. The Venus flytrap has a special bait to attract the insect to come near.
   D. The Venus flytrap can move from one place to another to catch insects.

Lesson 94

✦✦（1）✦✦

Claude and Louise are "giraffies"（长颈鹿）. So are police officers Hankins and Pearson. These men and women don't look like giraffes; they look like you and me. Then, why do people call them "giraffes"?

A giraffe, they say, is an animal that sticks its neck out, can see places far away and has a large heart. It lives a quiet life and moves about in an easy and beautiful way. In the same way, a "giraffe" can be a person who likes to "stick his or her neck out" for other people, always watches for future happenings, has a warm heart for people around, and at the same time lives a quiet and beautiful life himself or herself.

"The Giraffe Project" is a 10-year-old group which finds and honors "giraffes" in the US and in the world. The group wants to teach people to do something to build a better world. The group members believe that a person shouldn't draw his or her head back; instead, they tell people to "stick their neck out" and help others. Claude and Louise, Hankins and Pearson are only a few of the nearly 1,000 "giraffes" that the group had honored.

Claude and Louise were getting old and they left their work with some money that they saved for future use. One day, however, they saw a homeless man looking for a place to keep warm and they decided that they should "stick their neck out" and give him some help. Today, they live in Friends' House, where they invite twelve homeless people to stay every night.

Police officers Hankins and Pearson work in large city. They see crimes every day and their work is sometimes dangerous. They work hard for their money. However, these two men put their savings together and even borrowed money to start an educational center to teach young people in a poor part of the city. Hankins and Pearson are certainly "giraffes".

▶阅读上面的短文，从每题所给的四个选项中，选出一个最佳答案。

1. Which of the following is true?

   A. Some of the people around us look like giraffes.

   B. Giraffes are the most beautiful animal in the world.

   C. "Giraffe" is a beautiful name for those who are ready to help other people.

   D. A "giraffe" is someone who can stick his neck out and see the future.

2. "The Giraffe Project" is a group _____.

   A. of police officers   B. which appeared ten years ago

C. of ten-year-old children   D. which takes care of children

3. People call Claude and Hankins "giraffes" because they _____.

    A. do what is needed for good world

    B. are not afraid of dangerous work

    C. found a home for some homeless people

    D. made money only for other people

4. What does "The Giraffe Project" do?

    A. It tells people how to live a quiet life.

    B. It helps the homeless and teaches young people.

    C. It tries to find 1,000 warm-hearted people in the US.

    D. It shows people what their duty is for a better world.

✦✦ （2）✦✦

Thirty years ago, Lake Ponkapog in Hartwell, New Jersey, was full of life. Many birds and animals lived beside the water, which was full of fish. Now there are few birds, animals and fish. The lake water is polluted. It is in a colour of dirty brown, and it is filled with strange plants.

How did this happen? First, we must think about how water gets into Lake Ponkapog. When it rains, water comes into the lake from all around. In the past, there were forests all around Lake Ponkapog, so the rainwater was clean.

Now there are many dwelling districts around the lake. People often use chemicals in their gardens. They use other chemicals inside their houses for cleaning or killing insects. There are also many factories. Factories use chemicals in their machines. Other chemicals fall onto the ground from cars or trucks. When it rains, the rainwater picks up all the chemicals from houses and factories and then carries them into the lake. They pollute the water and make the animals ill.

Boats on the lake are also a problem. Lake Ponkapog is a popular place for motorboats. But oil and gas from motor boats often get into the lake. So more bad chemicals go into the water this way.

People in Hartwell are worried. They love their lake and want to save it. Will it be possible? A clean lake must have clean rainwater going into it. Clean rainwater is possible only if people are more careful about chemicals at home and at work.

They must also be more careful about gas and oil and other chemicals on the ground, and they mustn't use motorboats any more on the lake. All these may change people's lives. Only then can Lake Ponkapog be a beautiful, clean lake again.

▶ 阅读上面的短文，从每题所给的四个选项中，选出一个最佳答案。

1. In the past, the water in Lake Ponkapog was made clean through _____.

    A. forest   B. rain

    C. birds   D. fish

2. Chemicals from houses and factories _____.

    A. are always clean   B. can help the animals

    C. are good for the lake   D. get into the rainwater

3. Cleaner rainwater means _____.

    A. more boats on the lake   B. more dirty things in the lake

    C. a cleaner lake   D. a dirtier lake

4. To save Lake Ponkapog, people need to _____.

    A. be more careful about chemicals   B. use less water

    C. grow fewer plants in the gardens   D. use more motorboats on the lake

5. The passage is about _____.

    A. boats on Lake Ponkapog

    B. the reasons why the lake becomes dirty and the reform ways

    C. clean rainwater

    D. pollution from chemicals

语言基本功
英汉翻译 ◈ Translation Exercises

▶ 翻译下列句子

1. 实验证明，儿童在很小的时候就可以开始学习游泳。

_____

2. 孩子们甚至在还没有学会走路时就已经能熟练地在水下屏住呼吸了。

_____

3. 两个月的婴儿并未显得不愿意入水。

_____

4. 有些孩子能够游完游泳池的全长而不用露出水面换气。

_____

5. 他们将来是否能成为奥运会的冠军，这只能由时间来作出回答。

_____

6. 你获利多少？

_____

7. 你那样做一点好处都没有。

_____

8. 获得的利润用来购买更多的设备。

_____

本书所有练习题的参考答案（含阅读理解练习题解析及译文），请登录中国水利水电出版社网站 http://www.waterpub.com.cn/softdown/（下载中心）免费下载。

Lesson 95

✦✦（1）✦✦

What Makes a Good Newspaper Story?

Hundreds of years ago, news was carried from place to place by people on foot or by horse. It took days, weeks and sometimes months for people to receive news. Now it is possible to send words and pictures around the world in seconds. Billions of people learn about news stories of their own country and all over the world every day, either by watching TV or reading newspapers.

Newspapers have been an important part of everyday life since the 18th century. Many countries have hundreds of different newspapers. How do newspaper editors decide which news stories to print? Why do they print some stories and not others? What makes a good newspaper story?

Firstly, it is important to report news stories. TV stations can report news much faster than newspapers. Yet, newspapers give more about the same story. They may also look at the story in another way, or they may print completely different stories to those on TV.

Secondly, a news story has to be interesting and unusual. People don't want to read stories about everyday life. As a result, many stories are about some kind of danger and seem to be "bad" news. For example, newspapers never print stories about planes landing safely, instead they print stories about plane accidents.

Another factor is also very important in many news stores. Many people are interested in news in foreign countries, but more prefer to read stories about people, places and events in their own country. So the stories on the front page in Chinese newspapers are usually very different from the ones in British, French and American newspapers.

▶阅读上面的短文，从每题所给的四个选项中，选出一个最佳答案。

1. According to the passage, how do people learn about news stories in the world now?

   A. They carry news stories and tell others from place to place on foot or by horse.

   B. They tell each other what they have seen with their eyes.

   C. They watch TV or read newspapers. D. They listen to the radio every day.

2. The difference between newspaper stories and TV news reports is that_____.

   A. people can learn more about the same news story from a newspaper

   B. people can read the news story more quickly in a newspaper

C. people can read news stories in other countries

D. people can read news stories about their own country

3. To make a good newspaper story, how many factors does the passage talk about?

    A. Two.   B. Three.

    C. Five.   D. Six.

4. According to the passage, which of the following can you most possibly watch on TV?

    A. You often play football with your friends after school.

    B. Your teacher has got a cold.

    C. A tiger in the city zoo has run out and hasn't been caught.

    D. The bike in the front of your house is lost.

5. Which of the following is NOT true of this passage?

    A. News stories on the front page of every country are always the same.

    B. People like to read interesting and unusual news.

    C. Not only TV but also newspapers can help people to learn what is happening around the world.

    D. Newspapers have been an important part of everyday life for more than three hundred years.

✦✦ （2） ✦✦

In the 13th century, the famous Italian traveller, Marco Polo, traveled a long way to China. During his stay in China, he saw many wonderful things. One of the things he discovered was that the Chinese used paper money. In western countries, people did not use paper money until the 15th century. However, people in China began to use paper money in the 7th century.

A Chinese man called Cai Lun invented paper almost 2,000 years ago. He made it from wood. He took the wood from trees and made it into paper. He then put these pieces of paper together and made them into a book.

Now paper still comes from trees. We use a lot of paper every day. If we keep on wasting so much paper, there will not be any trees left on the earth. If there are no trees, there will be no paper. Every day, people throw away about 2,800 tons of paper in our city. It takes 17 trees to make one ton of paper. This means that we are cutting nearly 48,000 trees every day. Since it takes more than 10 years for a tree to grow, we must start using less paper now. If we don't, we will not have enough time to grow more trees to take the place of those we use for paper.

So how can we save paper? We can use both sides of every piece of paper, especially when we are making notes. We can choose drinks in bottles instead of those in paper packets. We can also use cotton handkerchiefs and not paper ones. When we go shopping, we can use fewer paper bags. If the shop assistant does give us a paper bag, we can save it and reuse it later.

Everyone can help to save paper. If we all think carefully, we can help protect trees. But we should do it now, before it is too late.

1. When he was in China, Marco Polo _____.
   - A. discovered Cai Lun invented paper
   - B. learned to make paper
   - C. saw many wonderful things
   - D. read a lot of books

2. People in western countries first used paper money in the _____ century.
   - A. 17th
   - B. 15th
   - C. 13th
   - D. 7th

3. About _____ tons of paper are thrown away every day in our city.
   - A. 1,700
   - B. 2,000
   - C. 2,800
   - D. 48,000

4. Which of the following is NOT the way of saving paper?
   - A. To use both sides of every piece of paper.
   - B. To use the paper bags from shops more than once.
   - C. To use cotton handkerchiefs instead of paper ones.
   - D. To grow more trees.

5. Which of the following is NOT true?
   - A. If we keep on wasting paper, we will have no paper to use.
   - B. The Chinese used paper money much earlier than the people in western countries.
   - C. About 48,000 trees can be used to make 2,800 tons of paper
   - D. It is never too late to plant trees for paper.

语言基本功
英汉翻译◈ Translation Exercises

▶翻译下列句子

1. 当艾斯卡罗比亚国的大使回到家吃午饭时，把他的夫人吓了一跳。

   _____

2. 他面色苍白，衣服也搞得不成样子。

   _____

3. 今天上午大学生们放火点着了大使馆。

   _____

4. 我一定要把那个家伙打发走。

   _____

5. 有人向我办公室窗户开了一枪。

   _____

6. 把那一行数字加起来。

   _____

7. 让我看看你腿伤的地方。

   _____

8. 把你的舌头给医生看看。

   _____

Lesson 96

Reading Comprehension

✦✦ (1) ✦✦

When the world was very young, people lived only in hot countries. They did not live in cold countries because they could not keep warm. Then they learnt how to make clothes. When an animal was killed, its skin was cut off. They wrapped the skin around their bodies. The skins kept them warm. Skins which had fur on them were the best. Even today some people wear the furs of animals to keep them warm.

At first men did not know how to make fire. Sometimes a forest was hit by lightning. Then a fire was started. The people took some of this fire to start a fire near their homes. A fire was very important for three reasons. It kept them warm. Wild animals were frightened by it. They did not attack when they saw a fire. Then another thing was discovered. When food was cooked, it tasted much better! But men still did not know how to make fire. When they had a fire, they did not let it stop burning. If it went out, they could not start it again. They had to wait for lightning to start another fire! Sometimes they had to wait for years!

Later, they discovered how to make fire. If you rub two pieces of wood together, they become hot and burn. You have to rub very fast! One way of doing it is to make a little hole in a piece of wood. Little pieces of wood or dry leaves are put into the hole. Then the end of a stick is put into the hole. The stick is rubbed between the hands.

This makes it burn very quickly. The end of the stick becomes very hot. The small pieces of wood and dry leaves begin to burn. Another way of making fire is to knock two pieces of stone together. A spark is made. This can be used to start a fire.

Nowadays we have matches. We can carry them in our pockets and make a fire when we want to. Many people use heaters to keep warm. Oil heaters burn oil. Gas heaters burn gas. Electric heaters use electricity. Gas, oil and electricity can also be used for cooking.

▶阅读上面的短文，从每题所给的四个选项中，选出一个最佳答案。

1. When the world was very young, people only lived in _____.
   A. cold countries   B. their homes
   C. hot places   D. the forests

2. In the old days people wore _____ to keep themselves warm.
   A. animal skins   B. heavy clothing
   C. light clothing   D. silk clothes

3. Fire was very important to _____.

    A. the animals

    C. the living things

    B. the people

    D. everything in the world

4. If you rub _____, they become hot and then start a fire.

    A. two pieces of stone

    C. two pieces of iron sticks

    B. three pieces of wood

    D. two pieces of wood

5. In the old days people learnt _____.

    A. to use four ways of making a fire

    C. to use two ways of making a fire

    B. to use three ways of making a fire

    D. to use one way of making a fire

✦✦ （2）✦✦

Traveling can be a good way to get life experiences, especially during Spring Break—a weeklong school vacation in the United States. But what if you're a student and don't have enough money for a trip? Don't worry. Here are some useful trips.

Save: This probably is the most important preparation for traveling. Cut expenses to fatten your wallet so you'll have more choices about where to go and how to get there.

Plan ahead: Don't wait until the last minute to plan your trip. Tickets may cost more when bought suddenly. Giving yourself several months to get ready can mean security and savings.

Do your homework: No matter where you go, research the places you will visit. Decide what to see and where to have dinner. Travel books will offer information on the cheapest hotels and restaurants.

Plan reasonably: Write down what you expect to spend for food and hotels. Stick to your plan, or you may not have enough money to cover everything.

Travel in groups: Find someone who is interested in visiting the same places. By traveling with others you can share costs and experiences.

Work as you go: need more money to support your trip? Look for work in the places you visit.

Go to a lesser-known place: Tourist cities may be expensive. You may want to rethink your trip and go to a lesser-known place. Smaller towns can have many interesting activities and sights.

Pack necessary things: The most important things to take are not always clothes. Remember medicine in case you get sick and snacks in case you cannot find a cheap restaurant.

Use the Internet: The Net can help to save money. Some useful websites include www.Travelocity. com, www. Bargains-lowestfare. com and www. Economytravel. com.

By planning reasonably, students can enjoy traveling. You will remember your travel experiences all your life.

▶阅读上面的短文，从每题所给的四个选项中，选出一个最佳答案。

1. Before your trip, the most important thing you should do is to _____.

    A. make a plan of the route

    B. get information on the Internet

C. save money by spending less   D. buy tickets in advance

2. The writer advises you _____.

A. not to share costs with other people   B. not to go to well-known places

C. not to visit dangerous places   D. to buy anything you want to buy

3. During your trip, _____.

A. you need more medicine than clothes

B. you should look for work all the way

C. you should remember to do your homework

D. you can get useful life experiences

4. The main idea of the passage is _____.

A. where to spend your holidays   B. how to save the money for your trip

C. when to prepare your trip   D. how to spend your trip

语言基本功
英汉翻译◈ Translation Exercises

▶翻译下列句子

1. 日本每年过一次"亡灵节"。

_____

2. 特制的灯笼挂在各家的门外，为的是帮助亡灵看清道路。

_____

3. 整个夜晚人们载歌载舞。

_____

4. 一大早，人们便把为死者摆放的食品扔进河中或海里。

_____

5. 这是一个感人的场面。

_____

6. 他发出一阵狂笑。

_____

7. 汽车轰响着驶去。

_____

8. 群众高喊表示同意。

_____

本书所有练习题的参考答案（含阅读理解练习题解析及译文），请登录中国水利水电出版社网站
http://www.waterpub.com.cn/softdown/（下载中心）免费下载。

288